Samuel Miller

The Life of Samuel Miller, D. D., LL. D.

Second Professor in the Theological Seminary of the Presbyterian Church

Samuel Miller

The Life of Samuel Miller, D. D., LL. D.
Second Professor in the Theological Seminary of the Presbyterian Church

ISBN/EAN: 9783337168551

Printed in Europe, USA, Canada, Australia, Japan

Cover: Foto ©Raphael Reischuk / pixelio.de

More available books at **www.hansebooks.com**

THE LIFE

OF

SAMUEL MILLER, D.D., LL.D.,

SECOND PROFESSOR

IN THE

THEOLOGICAL SEMINARY OF THE PRESBYTERIAN CHURCH,

AT PRINCETON, NEW JERSEY.

BY

SAMUEL MILLER.

PHILADELPHIA:

CLAXTON, REMSEN AND HAFFELFINGER,

Nos. 819 and 821 Market Street.

1869.

JAS. B. RODGERS CO., Printers,
52 & 54 North Sixth St.

PREFACE.

1. Biography.

"To delineate a character faithfully in its leading features, whether great and honorable, or otherwise, is the duty of every good biographer."[1]

" There are two extremes into which biographers are apt to fall. The one is adopting a continued strain of eulogy, and endeavoring either wholly to keep out of view, or ingeniously to varnish over, the errors and weaknesses of those whose lives they record. To this fault in biographical writing Mr. Hayley discovers, perhaps, too strong a tendency. If I do not greatly mistake, his *Life* of Milton and his *Life* of Cowper may both be justly impeached on this ground. The other, and a more mischievous, extreme is, recording against departed worth, with studied amplitude, and disgusting minuteness, the momentary mistakes of forgetfulness, the occasional vagaries of levity, and the false opinions, expressed not as the result of sober reflection. but thrown out either in a mirthful hour, or in the heat of disputation. Of the latter fault Mr. Boswell's *Life* of Johnson furnishes perhaps the most singular example. The proper course is between these extremes ; and of this course it is to be lamented that we have so few models."[2]

Excellencies may be imitated, and defects avoided, most successfully, when we know their origin and the manner of their production. Hence, besides

[1] Dr. Miller's Retrospect, II. Vol., 152.   [2] Id., 153, note.

showing what a person was, and what he did, it is very important to explain how he became what he was, and how he accomplished what he did. Here God's providence will often come profitably into view; and no unimportant part of the biographer's aim, nay, his grand, constant object, should be to illustrate and confirm divine truth. In attempting this, he may always have the encouragement offered by the fact, that he is employing one of the Bible's favorite methods of impressing and enforcing its own doctrines and precepts. To bring Jehovah to view, as he ever works in or by, over or in spite of, individual men, in manifold relations to our race, whether as lost or saved, is the most salutary lesson which our fallen world can either give or receive.

2. Lapse of Time.

More than nineteen years have passed away since Dr. Miller died, and delay in the preparation of a biography has doubtless occasioned the loss of some precious materials for the work. "But," he himself being the judge, "even with regard to this loss, there are counterbalancing considerations. Time has been left for the first fervour of feeling on the departure of an eminent man to subside. His character is now viewed with the calmness and impartiality of a long and leisurely retrospect. The statement and portrait about to be presented are not drawn under the painful impression of a recent bereavement. There has been time to consult the award of faithful public suffrage. Perhaps the most candid and impartial, if not the most feeling and racy biographical sketches, are those which have been formed many years after their subjects have passed from the stage of action."[1]

[1] Dr. Miller's *Memoir of Dr. Nisbet*, who died in 1801, published in 1840.

TABLE OF CONTENTS.

PART FIRST: DELAWARE.

1710–1793.

CHAPTER FIRST.

1710–1769.

ANCESTORS.—1. *John Miller, the Grandfather.*—Immigration—Marriage to Mary Bass—John Alden—Samuel Bass—Education, business, church and family—13–15.—2. *Rev. John Miller, the Father.*—Birth—Education—Profession—Licensure—Call to Dover and Duck Creek—Settlement—Residence—Marriage—Family—Labours—The Revolution—Character—John Dickinson—New England Friends—Congregation—Old and New Sides—Church Standards—General Assembly—Dr. Matthew Wilson—Health—Habits—14–25.—3. *Mrs. Margaret Miller, the Mother.*—Influence—Son's account—Benevolence—Conversion—26, 27.—   13–27.

CHAPTER SECOND.

1769–1789.

BIRTH, YOUTH AND EDUCATION.—1. *Birth and Early Youth.*—Birth—Death of Joseph—Death of Benjamin—Declaration of Independence—John, the Army Surgeon—His death—Marriage of Elizabeth and Mary—Philadelphia—Constitutional Convention—Dr. Edward Miller—Joseph—28–33.—2. *Preparation for College.*—*Profession of Religion.*—First eighteen years—Father's letter—33, 34.—3. *The College Student.*—The University—Letters from mother and father—Dr. Ashbel Green—Synod and General Assembly—Letters from father—Graduation—Commencement—A classmate—Improvement—34–42.—   28–42.

CHAPTER THIRD.

1789–1792.

THE THEOLOGICAL STUDENT.—1. *Home Theology.*—Return home—Diary—Letter to Dr. Green—Reply—Letter from father—Diary—Death of mother—Letters from father—Letter to Richard Renshaw—Letters from father—Diary—Letter from father—Theological studies—Diary: Trials for license: Death of father—Family circumstances—43-54.—2. *Licensure.*—Diary: Licensure—Exceptions to the Confession: Letter to Dr. Halsey—Presbyterial authority—Letter from Col. McLane—54-56. —3. *Dr. Nisbet.*—Principal of Dickinson College—A winter in Carlisle —Mr. Miller's account—57-60.—   43-60.

CHAPTER FOURTH.

1792.

THE LICENTIATE.—1. *Seeking a Settlement.*—Visit to New York—Dr. John H. Livingston—Return—Second Visit to New York—Letter from Dr. Green to Mr. Morse—Journeying in New England—Relatives—61-63.—2. *Calls to New York and Dover.*—Call to New York—Candidates —Letter to Mr. Morse—Labors in Delaware—Call to Dover and Duck Creek—Diary—Minute of Presbytery—Testimonial—Diary—63-66.—3. *Farewell to Delaware*—Valedictory—Characteristics—John Dickinson— Letter to Hon. G. C. Verplanck—Departure—Style of preaching— 66-70.—   61-70.

CHAPTER FIFTH.

1749-1792.

DELAWARE LIFE.—1. *A Pilgrimage.*—Attachment to Delaware—Visits —Biographer's Visit—Dover—Presbyterian church—Church-yard— Family graves—Reparation—Jail and pillory—Wilhelmina Ridgely— Health of Delaware—Letter from John Fisher—Old State Road—The Turf—Fox hunting—Mrs. Loockerman's residence—Parson's farm and dwelling—Decay—Burial plot—Tin Head Court—Duck Creek Cross Roads—71-76.—2. *Old Papers.*—Testamentary accounts—Personal estate —Diplomas—Education of Children—A. M.—76-79.—   71-79.

PART SECOND: NEW YORK CITY.

1793-1813.

CHAPTER SIXTH.

1793.

NEW YORK CITY.—1. *The City and its Churches.*—Population, etc.— Columbia College—Clergy—Presbyterian Church in U. S.—First Presb. church of New York—History—Collegiate pastors—80-82.—2. *Colleagues.*—Dr. Rodgers—Extracts from Memoirs—Influence on Colleague —Dr. McKnight—82-86.—   80-86.

CHAPTER SEVENTH.

1793-1798.

The "Boy Minister."—1. *Ordination and Settlement.*—Diary—Ordination and Installation—Session—Routine of service—Commencement of pastorate—"Boy Ministers"—Chancellor Kent—87-89.—2. *Published Discourses—Slavery and the French Revolution.*—Fourth of July Sermon—Extracts—Sermon of 1797—Slavery—Extracts—French Revolution—Dr. Nisbet's Opinion—Retraction—89-96.—3. *Devotion and Affliction.*—Diary—Letter to Dr. Green: Magazine—Death of James—Letter from him—Mrs. Patten—Diary—96-98.—4. *Published Discourses—Masonry.*—Sermon before the Grand Lodge—Royal Arch Mason—Objections to Masonry—Fourth of July Sermon—98-100.—5. *Valetudinarianism.*—Burdens—Ill health—Letter to Dr. Green—Diary: Journey on horseback—100-102.—6. *Doctor Edward Miller in New York.*—Extract from Biographical Sketch: Removal: Success—Beneficial results—Ill health—Diary—102, 103.—7. *Missions.* History of American Missions—Letter to Dr. Green—The New York Society—Its operations—Monthly Concert—Quarterly Concert—104-106.—8. *Despondent Activity.—Literary Projects and Pastime.—Politics.*—Diary—Visit to Connecticut—Rutgers-street church—Diary—Correspondence, foreign and domestic—Letter to Dr. Morse—History of New York—Act of Legislature—Dr. Samuel L. Mitchill—De Witt Clinton—Foreign correspondence—The Friendly Club—Fast day sermon—Extract—Diary—106-112.— 87-112.

CHAPTER EIGHTH.

1798.

The Yellow Fever.—Residences—Epidemic Yellow Fever—Doctor Edward Miller's theory—Death of Joseph—Charles Brockden Brown's account—Death of Italian—Death of Dr. E. H. Smith—Mr. Miller's account—Thanksgiving sermon—Extract—Mortality—Diary—Mr. Brown—Monthly Magazine—Letters to Dr. Morse—Call to Market street church, Philadelphia—Letter to Dr. Green—Rev. John Blair Linn and Dr. James P. Wilson.— 113-121.

CHAPTER NINTH.

1799-1801.

Politics and Projects.—1. *Death of Washington.*—Absence from New York—Sermon on Washington—His religious character—Correspondence with Governor Jay: Political parties—122-127.—2. *City life—Social, Literary and Political.—Thomas Jefferson.*—Diary—Influence of city life—Clerical politicians—Federalists and Republicans—Extracts from sermons—Correspondence with Mr. Gemmil—More mature opinions—Character of Mr. Jefferson—127-133.—3. *Politics and the Clergy.*—Before, during, and after the Revolutionary War—Natural rights and natural duties of citizenship—134, 135.—4. *Projects and Correspondence.*—Letters to Republicans—*Cacoëthes Scribendi*—Extract from note-book—Foreign Correspondents—136-138.— 122-138.

CHAPTER TENTH.

1801.

MARRIAGE.—Death of Major and Mrs. Patten—General Assembly—
"Plan of Union"—Opinion in 1847—Rev. Archibald Alexander—Another plan of union—Sarah Sergeant—Introduction—Engagement—
Letters—Marriage—Wedding tour—Letter to Mr. Dickinson.—139–144.

CHAPTER ELEVENTH.

1778–1803.

MRS. MILLER.—1. *Ancestors—Birth.*—Jonathan Dickinson Sergeant—
Ancestors—Birth—Graduation—At the Bar—In Congress—Wife, Margaret Spencer—Revolutionary Scenes and Adventures—145–148.—2.
Youth—Memoirs.—Occasion of Writing—Early years—Religious education and impressions—Family changes—Boarding schools—Yellow Fever
—Father—French immigrants—Father's devotion to sick—Religious
Impressions—Father's death—Infidelity—The Bible—Fashionable dissipation—Card-playing—Reading—Princeton—Long Branch—Broken
resolution—Bible and prayer—Darkness and Distress—Decision—Usefulness—Temptation—Marriage—Causes and preventives of suffering—
Father's plain habits—Boarding-school at Bethlehem—148–167.—3.
Married Life.—Residence—Missionary sermon—Diary: First child—Anniversary of marriage—Anniversary observances—Diary-keeping—Mrs.
Miller's profession—Vacation—167–172.—   145–172.

CHAPTER TWELFTH.

1804, 1805.

"RETROSPECT OF THE EIGHTEENTH CENTURY."—1. *Preparation of the
Work.*—Authorship—Extracts from preface—Doctor E. Miller's Assistance—173–176.—2. *Reception of the Work*—John Dickinson—Contents—
Completion prevented—Doctor of Divinity—Dr. Adam Clarke—Anecdote—Lindley Murray—London edition—Letter from publisher—
Aikin's Review—176–181.—   173–181.

CHAPTER THIRTEENTH.

1804–1806.

CORRESPONDENCE.—1. *Miscellaneous Topics.*—Opening Century—Letter to Mr. Griffin—Abolition convention—Hamilton and Burr: Letter
to Mr. Nott—Burr's plausibility—Letter to Mr. Griffin: Cowper—Letters to Dr. Green: Candidates: Independent in Philadelphia—Dr. Nisbet's works—182–186.—2. *Sermons on Suicide.*—Extracts—Correspondence with intended suicide—186–190.—3. *Episcopacy.—Theological Education.*—Letters to Mr. Griffin—to Dr. Green—to Dr. Nott—to Dr. Morse
—Diary: Wife's conversion—Letters to Mr. Griffin—to Dr. Green—Dr.
Green's overture—Suggestion of a Seminary—Dr. Miller's activity—
Address to the Church—Theol. Sem. of Associate Ref. Church—190–197.
—4. *Valetudinarianism.—Miscellaneous Topics.*—Ill health: Letters to

Mr. Nisbet and Mr. Griffin—Retreat to Mr. Griffin's—Horse-back rides
—Call of Dr. Milledoler—Grammar school—Doctorate for Mr. Griffin—
Ill health—New house—197–200.—5. *Theological Education.*—Moderator
of the General Assembly—Lack of candidates for ministry—Means of
theological training—'Princeton establishment'—200–203.—6. *Miscellaneous Topics.*—Letter to Dr. Nott—to Dr. Griffin: from New York to
Albany—Ill health—Rambles—Sermon before General Assembly—
200–205.—   182–205.

CHAPTER FOURTEENTH.

1807.

EPISCOPAL CONTROVERSY.—1. *History of the Controversy.*—Previous
writings—Spirit of Episcopacy—Presbyterian opponents—Harmony in
New York—Dr. Miller's account—High church "insolence"—206–210.
—2. *The Rev. John Henry Hobart.*—Call to New York—"Companion
for the Altar"—"Companion for Festivals and Fasts"—Extracts—
211–213.—3. *High Churchism.*—Denial of Invisible Church—Romanism
—High church principles—Reformation doctrine—213–216.—4. *Dr.
Miller's Letters.*—Controversy—Dr. Hobart's views—Christian's Magazine—Letters on the Christian Ministry—Account of its preparation—
216–219.—5. *Opinions of Friends.*—Dr. Wm. Linn—Judge Livingston—
Noah Webster—Chancellor Kent—Rev. Evan Johns—Ebenezer Hazard
—James K. Paulding—Rev. Conrad Speece—219–223.—6. *Reception by
Opponents.*—Number of answers—Dr. Miller's account—223–227.—
                                                          206–227.

CHAPTER FIFTEENTH.

1807, 1808.

CORRESPONDENCE.—1. *Miscellaneous Topics.*—Trustee of Columbia
College—of College of New Jersey—Letter to Mr. Griffin—to Dr. Green:
Memoir of Dr. Nisbet—to Mr. Griffin—228, 229.—2. *Andover and Boston.*—Letter to Mr. Griffin: Theological Seminary: Church in Boston—
Panoplist: Letter to Dr. Morse—to Mr. Griffin—Mrs. Miller to Mrs.
McLane—Cedar street church—229-235.—3. *President Jefferson.*—Correspondence about day of religious observance—Dr. Miller's comments—
235-237.—4. *Andover.*—Letters to Mr. Griffin—Theological Seminary at
Andover—237-239.—5. *Woman's Rights.*—Charity Sermon—Extracts—
239-240.—6. *Presbyterian Theological Seminary.*—Letters to Dr. Green—
240-244.—7. *Call to Dickinson College.*—Letter from Dr. Rush—Reply—
Election by Trustees—Letter from Dr. Rush—from Dr. Miller to James
Armstrong—Final Answer—244-250.—   228-250.

CHAPTER SIXTEENTH.

1801–1808.

MRS. MILLER'S MEMOIRS.—Notes of Sermons—Religious books—Wilberforce's Practical view—Instruction of children—Loneliness—Ignorance—Melancholy and unbelief—Increasing light and conviction—Ex-

tremity—Helps—Family prayer—Moving—Light breaking—Struggles
—Darkness—Dr. Nott's sermon—Taste for the Word—Warfare—Conclusion.—   251-264.

CHAPTER SEVENTEENTH.

1809.

DISSOLUTION OF THE PASTORAL RELATION.—1. *History of the Dissolution.*—Evils of collegiate relation—Opposition to dissolution—Dr. Miller's opinion and efforts—Dissolution—265-268.—2. *Troubles.*—Difficulties in the way of separation—Remedies proposed—Letters to Mr.
Speece and Dr. Griffin—Dr. McKnight's dissatisfaction—Charges against
Dr. Miller—Arbitrators—Decision—Reconciliation—Renewed trouble—
Issue—268-272.—   265-272.

CHAPTER EIGHTEENTH.

1809, 1810.

LABORS AND CORRESPONDENCE.—1. *Ordination of Ruling Elders.*—
Laying on hands—273, 274.—2. *Miscellaneous Topics.*—Review of Dr.
Dwight's sermon—Letters to Dr. Griffin: Farewell—Chaplain of State
Artillery—New York Bible Society—New York Historical Society—
Letter to Dr. Green: President Atwater—to Dr. Griffin—to Dr. Green:
felicitations—274-278.—3. *Episcopal Controversy.*—Continuation of Let-
ters on the Ministry—Dr. Bowden's reply—278-280.—4. *Theological
Seminary.*—Letters to Dr. Green—Three plans—Letter to Dr. Griffin in
Boston—Decision of Assembly in favor of a Seminary—Committee to
form Plan—Pastoral Letter—Bloomingdale—Letter to Dr. Green—280-
287.—5. *New Wall Street Church.*—287, 288.—6. *Settlement of the Rev.
Gardiner Spring.*—Ordination and installation services—Dr. Miller's
charge—Extracts—Hopkinsianism—Dr. Spring's reminiscence—288-
291.—7. *Exchanges with Unitarians.*—Unitarian controversy—Dr. Miller's letter to Mr. Codman—to Dr. Sprague—The Old South—Diary—
Letter to Dr. Griffin—291-296.—   273-296.

CHAPTER NINETEENTH.

1811.

MISCELLANEOUS MATTERS.—1. *Hopkinsianism.*—Dr. Milledoler's reminiscences—Hopkinsian controversy in New York—Original New England Theology—President Edwards—Drs. Hopkins and Emmons—Disinterested Benevolence—New Theology—Dr. Miller's opinion of Hopkins
and Emmons—Letter from Dr. Hopkins—Spread of Hopkinsianism—
Dr. Edwards—Dr. Dwight—Moderate Hopkinsianism in the Presbyterian Church—297-304.—2. *Correspondence*—Letter to Dr. Griffin—Correspondence with Dr. Adam Clarke—Correspondence with Ex-President
Adams—Letter to Dr. Green—Theological Seminary—304-308.—3.
Memoirs of Dr. Rodgers.—Decline and death of Dr. Rodgers—Funeral—
Sermon—Memoirs—Extracts—Dr. Miller's affection for his colleague—

Letter to Dr. Green—Letters from Dr. Livingston, Dr. Rush and Rev. George Burder—Historical contributions—308-313.—4. *Theological Seminary.*—Location at Princeton—Plan—Subscriptions—Wealth of the Presbyterian Church—College Lottery—313-315.—5. *Temperance.*—Committee of General Assembly—Dr. Rush's " Inquiry "—Narrative of Religion—Report—315-316.—6. *Dr. Griffin's Installation.*—Letter of excuse to Dr. Griffin—Letter after installation—Mrs. Miller's Diary—316-320.—   297-320.

CHAPTER TWENTIETH.

1812.

AFFLICTIONS.—1. *Burning of the Richmond Theatre.*—Sermon—Extracts—Dr. Alexander's sermon—321, 322.—2. *Death of Edward Millington Miller.*—Letters to Drs. Griffin and Green—322, 323.—3. *Death of Doctor Edward Miller.*—Brotherly affection—Mutual influence for evil and good—Edward Miller's general character—Domestic relations—His death—Diary—Letters from Dr. Rush—Notice by William Dunlap—Biographical Sketch—Complimentary addresses—"To John Warren, M. D."—323-331.—   321-331.

CHAPTER TWENTY-FIRST.

1812, 1813.

LAST YEARS OF THE PASTORATE IN NEW YORK.—1. *The Theological Seminary and Dr. Alexander.*—Letter from John Sergeant to Mrs. Miller—Establishment of the Seminary—Choice of Dr. Alexander—Subscriptions—Inauguration of Dr. Alexander—Dr. Miller's sermon—Inaugural discourse—332-335.—2. *Calls to Colleges.*—Doctorate from the University of North Carolina—Call to the presidency declined—Call to Hamilton College—Reply, declining call—335, 336.—3. *Dr. Green and the College of New Jersey.*—Dr. Green's account of his election to the presidency—Part taken by Dr. Miller—Letters to Dr. Green—Selection of Vice-President—Plan of inauguration—Courtesy to Dr. Smith—Letters to Dr. Green—Inauguration omitted—336-343.—4. *Correspondence.*—Sermon at Wilmington, etc.—Letter to Miss Ann Patten—to Dr. Green—343-346.—   332-346.

CHAPTER TWENTY-SECOND.

1813.

CALL TO THE THEOLOGICAL SEMINARY AT PRINCETON.—1. *Election to the Second Professorship.*—General Assembly—Historian of the Presbyterian Church—Materials—Election of Dr. Miller—347, 348.—2. *Doubts and Fears.—Acceptance.*—Letters to Dr. Green—Desecration of the Bible in College Hall—348-351.—3. *Farewell to New York.*—Letter to officers of Wall street church—Sensitiveness—Welcome from Dr. Livingston—Dissolution of pastoral relation—Diary—351-356.—4. *Inauguration as Professor.*—Diary—Form of inauguration—Subscription—Inaugural discourse—Diary—Illness—356-359.—   347-359.

CHAPTER TWENTY-THIRD.

1793–1813.

NEW YORK LIFE.—1. *Matters Ecclesiastical.*—Dividing Line—Success in the pastorate—Infant baptisms—Qualifications of parents—Dismission to Baptists—Catechizing—Lord's Supper—Elders and Deacons—Collections for poor—360–363.—2. *The Stipend*—Salary—Fees—Domestic management—363, 364.—3. *In the pulpit.*—Vestments—Bishop Southgate's charges—Dr. Sprague's estimate—Dr. Halsey's—First Sabbath in New York—Dr. Magie—Dr. Spring—Grant Thorburn—Manner of preaching—Public prayer—Memoriter preaching—Memory—364–371. —4. *Miscellaneous Topics.*—Comparative morality—Mrs. Miller's account —Her prayer—Activity in church judicatories—Friends in New York.— James and Abel T. Anderson, Esquires—Honorary Memberships—371– 373. 360–873.

LIFE

OF

SAMUEL MILLER, D.D.

PART FIRST.

DELAWARE.

1710–1793.

CHAPTER FIRST.

ANCESTORS.

1710–1769.

1. JOHN MILLER, THE GRANDFATHER.

DR. MILLER, a memorial of whom is here attempted, alluding, at the age of forty-four, to some inquiries which he had been called to make, wrote in his diary, 'How much I regret not having gained a more full account of my ancestors, when it was in my power to obtain it. * * I have nothing to claim that is adapted to gratify pride; but some of them had the best of all nobility—that which takes hold of God and heaven—unfeigned piety. In this I rejoice—yea, and will rejoice!'

In the year 1710, his grandfather, John Miller, emigrated from Scotland, and settled in Boston, Massachusetts. He married Mary, daughter of Joseph Bass, who was originally of Braintree, now Quincy, near Boston where he resided during the latter part of his life. Joseph was a grandson of Samuel Bass and of John Alden, by the intermarriage of their children, John Bass and Ruth Alden.

John Alden was one of the original pilgrims, not, however. from Delft Haven, but from Southampton, where he was taken on board the Speedwell, for the sake of his services as a cooper, and with the understanding, although a "hopful yong man" and "much desired," that he was to return, if so minded. Transferred afterwards to the May Flower, he soon resolved to cast in his lot with the pilgrims, and he signed, with the rest, the compact of civil government, before they landed on Plymouth Rock. One tradition mentions him as the first who leaped upon the rock; but another, almost universally received, accords that honor to Mary Chilton. His attempted courtship of Priscilla Mullins, on behalf of his friend, Captain Miles Standish, and the romantic result, are celebrated in New England history and poetry. The naive question, "Prithee, John, why do you not speak for yourself?" drew out the disinterested friend as a blushing lover. He was in the Court of Assistants from 1633 to 1675, being Senior Assistant after 1666; in the General Court[1] from 1641 to 1649; and in the Council of War after 1653; and he survived all the other male signers of the civil compact. 'He settled in Duxbury, a town near Plymouth, on a farm which is, at this day, the best in that town, and has been always in possession of one of his descendants.'[2] "He was distinguished for a holy life and conversation; a man of great integrity and worth; and held in great honor by the men of his time, as he has been by all succeeding generations. He was blessed with a competence, and with a goodly number of children, all of whom delighted in the ordinances of God."[3] John Alden died, at a patriarchal age, in 1687.

Samuel Bass immigrated to New England, with his wife Anne, and, probably, one or two young children, about the year 1630. Settling at Roxbury, in the Massachusetts colony, he and Mrs. Bass were the first, or among the first, members of the church there formed as early as 1632; and, in 1634, he was admitted freeman. In 1640, he removed

<hr>

[1] These courts were legislative.
[2] Letter of Ex-President John Adams to Dr. Samuel Miller, 12th April, 1811.
[3] Vinton Memorial.

to Braintree, to the First Church of which he was dismissed and recommended; and, in the same year, he was chosen the first deacon, or one of the first two deacons of that church. Until his death, fifty-four years afterward, he served in this office, declining, as it would seem, in 1653, that of ruling elder, to which he was elected. He was of vigorous mind, and a leading man in the community. From 1641, onward for twelve years, he represented his town in the General Court. The town records declare, that before he died, aged ninety-four, he "was the father, and grandfather, and great-grandfather of a hundred and sixty-two children, the youngest whereof was Benjamin Bass, the son of Joseph Bass, and Mary his wife, born eleven days before his death."[1] His family, with some others at Braintree, are truly enough said to "have multiplied at a great rate."[2]

Of John Miller's origin, or of his life before he immigrated to America, little is known. After a somewhat liberal education, extending, at least, to a good knowledge of the Latin language, he had been trained to the business of sugar baking or refining. He was counted a remarkably grave, shrewd, discreet man, and carried on, with great success, a sugar-refinery and a distillery. He had been bred a Presbyterian, but united in Boston with the Old South (Congregational) Church, of which the Rev. Dr. Pemberton[3] was then pastor. His wife, "a very pious woman," "died about the year 1740." He survived her until 1749. They had three children. John, the eldest, died an infant. The next was also named John. The third, Joseph, went to sea, and, after a number of voyages, among the rest one to discover the long-sought "Northwest Passage," sailed from Philadelphia in command of a vessel bound, it was supposed, to the South Seas, though, probably first or last, to Great Britain also, and was never heard of afterwards. A very doubtful tradition mentions his marriage, about 1749, to a Miss Mallet of Charlestown, by whom he had two children.

---

[1] Thayer's Family Memorial, 53.
[2] Hancock's Century Sermon (1739), 26.
[3] See 1 Sprague's Annals, 250.

2. The Reverend John Miller, the Father.

The second son, John Miller, was born in Boston in 1722. He had not the advantage of a college education, but attended, in his native city, a public classical school of very high repute, under the tuition of Mr. John Lovell, the honored preceptor of many, in New England, who afterwards enjoyed great eminence. He studied diligently, and made himself a very accurate Latin and Greek scholar. Toward the latter part of his attendance at this school, he became, under the ministry of the Rev. Dr. Sewall, then pastor of the Old South, a decided Christian, and afterwards joined that church.

On the 27th of March, 1830, his son Samuel wrote to Dr. Wisner, of Boston,

'I hope, in your contemplated memorial of your church, you will do ample justice to the character of Dr. Sewall. I have a real affection, as well as veneration, for the memory of that man. My father was born in the bosom of the Old South Church; was baptized by Dr. Sewall; was much and affectionately noticed by him; was savingly brought to the knowledge and love of the truth, as he believed, by means of the sermons preached by Dr. Sewall from John xvi. 8, etc., and afterwards published in a little volume. I think my father has told me, that there was a revival of religion in the church about the time those sermons were delivered.'

Soon determining to devote himself to the gospel ministry, Mr. Miller, studied divinity under the direction of the Rev. John Webb, becoming a proficient, for that day, in Hebrew. Licensed, in May, 1748, by the association with which the Old South Church was connected, he visited Delaware and Maryland; and having received, in the former colony, a unanimous call from the united Presbyterian Churches of Dover and Duck Creek Cross Roads, now Smyrna, a village twelve miles north of Dover, was ordained in the Old South in April, 1749, by a council, of which Dr. Sewall and other eminent ministers of Boston were members.[1]

[1] The certificate of ordination may not be uninteresting, and will supply some dates and facts.

'BOSTON IN NEW ENGLAND, April 26, 1749.

'To the united Presbyterian Congregations in Dover and Duck Creek—

'Grace, Mercy & Peace from God the Father and from our Lord Jesus Christ be multiplied unto you.

About four miles from Dover, upon what is called the Old State Road, Mr. Miller fixed his dwelling, between the two churches; and in their service spent the whole of his retired and exemplary ministerial life—more than forty-two years. He resided upon a farm of one hundred and four acres, which, although it passed away from the family long ago, has remained undivided and unchanged in boundary till a very recent date.[6] His son, Samuel, in giving reminiscences of this Delaware home, has stated that it was purchased by his father soon after his settlement. The deed, of the 10th of May, 1750, from William Killen, mentions thirty pounds currency—say eighty dollars—as the consideration money. A tradition upon the spot is, that Chancellor Killen was so much pleased with the young licentiate, as to be particularly desirous that he should accept the call, and strongly urged his doing so. How am I to live? was the very natural question. The Chancellor, it is said, at once presented him with this farm; and when the requisites of travel over so wide a circuit came into consideration, added a horse, saddled and bridled. A variation of the story implicates other members also of the congregation in these generous gifts. If each of the statements is partially true, and the congregation, headed by Chancellor Killen, materially assisted Mr. Miller in purchasing, all of them are satisfactorily accounted for, and the facts assume a type so common as to be exceedingly probable. Whether a house already stood upon the land,

‘Christian Brethren,
        ‘We have received yours of the 29th of March last, signifying the Call that You had given to Mr. John Miller to be your Pastor, and your Desire that We would ordain Him to said Office among you. By these We certifie You, that having taken this Matter into our serious Consideration, We have granted your Request, and accordingly have this Day, in a publick Manner, solemnly separated Him to the Work of the Ministry, and the Pastoral Office over You, with Prayer and the laying on of the hands of the Presbytery. And now We recommend Him and You to the Grace of God, with our repeated earnest Prayers, that He may come to You in the Fulness of the Blessing of the Gospel of Christ; and desiring your prayers for Us, We are
            ‘Your Brethren in the Bonds of the Gospel,
                            ‘JOSEPH SEWALL,[1]
                            ‘THOMAS PRINCE,[2]   Associate
                            ‘JOHN WEBB,[3]   Pastors
                            ‘MATHER BYLES,[4]   in Boston.’
                            ‘ELLIS GRAY.[5]

    [1] See 1 Sprague's Annals, 278.   [2] Id. 304.   [3] Id. 267, note.   [4] Id. 376.   [5] Id. 373, note.
    [6] 1861.

or was afterwards erected, cannot now be determined.
The whole property was sold, in 1805, for one thousand
dollars, and recently[1] was said to be worth about three
thousand.

In 1751, Mr. Miller was married to Margaret, eldest
daughter of Allumby and Elizabeth Millington. Her
father was an Englishman, who, for many years, had com-
manded a merchant ship, trading regularly to London from
Wye River, then had settled down as a planter upon a
moderate estate in Talbot County, Maryland, seven or
eight miles north-east from Easton. Her mother's maiden
name was Harris. She was the daughter of an Englishman, who married a lady from Ireland. Nine children[2]
were the issue of Mr. Miller's marriage.

Doubtless Mr. Miller made his farm a source of recrea-
tion after pastoral toils, and of some little addition to his
revenue. This addition, however, must evidently have
been very small, for his temporal circumstances were never
affluent, and often were uncomfortably straitened. His
salary was utterly inadequate to the support of such a
household, and but poorly paid.[3] The farm, it is probable,
was not very productive: he can hardly have had either
much time or skill to apply to the development of its
resources; and neither the day nor region in which he
lived was noted for successful agriculture. But no doubt
his retired estate and quiet country life, almost without
any stirring incidents, were peculiarly favorable to the
happy nurture, and faithful home education, which his

[1] 1864.

[2] I. JOHN MILLER.—B. 24 Sep., 1722.—M. 23 Nov., 1751 (O. S.)—D. 22
July, 1791 (N. S.) II. MARGARET MILLINGTON.—B. 21 Sep., 1730 (O. S.)—
D. 22 Nov., 1789 (N. S.)—1. *John.*—B. 1752.—D. 28 Feb., 1777.—2. *Eliza-
beth.*—B. 16 Apr., 1755 (N. S.)—M. Col. Samuel McLane, 25 Nov., 1779.—D.
29 Oct., 1817.—3. *Joseph.*—B. 26 Feb., 1758.—D. 4 Oct., 1759.—4. *Edward.*—
B. 9 May, 1760.—D. 17 Mch., 1812.—5. *Mary.*—B. 26 July, 1762.—M. (1)
Vincent Loockerman (D. 5 Apr., 1790), 14 Nov., 1787.—(2) Major John Patten, Jan., 1795.—D. 13 Mch., 1801.—6. *Joseph.*—B. 8 Mch., 1765.—M. Elizabeth Loockerman, 1798.—D. 4 Sep., 1798.—7. *Benjamin.*—B. 10 Nov., 1767.—
D. 18 Nov., 1772.—8. **Samuel.**—B. 31 Oct., 1769.—M. Sarah Sergeant,
24 Oct., 1801.—D. 7 Jan., 1850.—9. *James.*—B. 17 July, 1772.—D. 15 Apr.,
1795.

[3] A presbyterial investigation, in 1766, showed that two years previously
Mr. Miller had agreed to remit all other arrearages, which were very great,
provided those at that time holding seats would pay their balances due,
and, thereafter, the congregation of Dover a salary of £50 ($133.33), and that
of Duck Creek, £40 ($106.66). But now, of this newly stipulated salary over

children enjoyed. His own studies were untiring. He somehow gathered round him a much larger library than almost any of his brethren in the ministry possessed, and was ever ready to advocate the cause of education, or, opportunity offering, to strive for the advancement of Christian learning. In 1763, he received the degree of Master of Arts from the Academy and College, afterwards University, of Pennsylvania. With many temptations, in his secluded residence and straitened circumstances, to slight the literary culture of his children, or content himself with a "business training" for his sons, he nevertheless made out to give every one of them, that lived beyond childhood, an education counted liberal in those times. The five sons he himself, assisted with the younger by the older, instructed, with great care, in the Latin and Greek languages, and sent them, afterwards, four to the University of Pennsylvania, where they were regularly graduated bachelors of art, and one—Edward—to a seminary of almost collegiate reputation. Regarding his own sacred profession as the noblest to which any mortal could aspire, he was determined that nothing on his part should be wanting to prepare his sons for it, if so be any of them might be called thereto by God's sovereign grace.

Through all the troublous times of our revolutionary war, Mr. Miller seems to have lived without any serious disturbance of his pastoral work. This was due, doubtless, to his quiet life, and the retired scene of his labors. Nevertheless, true to both his national and church allegiance, he was a zealous, uncompromising Whig. Though naturally of a nervous and timid habit, he was animated with the greatest zeal in maintaining the cause of his country. He preached the Revolution, and prayed for its success. A few days before the Declaration of Independence, he so far anticipated that measure, as to address the people of his pastoral charge from the decisive language of the revolting

£50 were behind at Dover, and over £25 at Duck Creek. For more than a year the Presbytery dealt pretty sharply with the two churches,—which professed attachment to their pastor, and entire satisfaction as to his pastoral fidelity,—putting them in mind 'not only of their injustice to Mr. Miller, but also of their disregard of the Gospel, and their want of generosity and public spirit, which were a manifest disgrace.' Finally, they entered into bonds for his security, 'and, on Mr. Miller's professing his willingness to stay with them, and confidence in their obligation, the Presbytery dismissed the affair.' —*MS. Minutes of Presbytery of Lewes*, 32, 33, 34, 48.

tribes in the days of Rehoboam: "We have no part in David, nor any inheritance in the son of Jesse: to your tents, O Israel!"[1]   At another time, a member of his congregation, returning from public worship, being asked whether he had been to hear Parson Miller, answered in the affirmative. 'Then I have no doubt you have heard treason enough,' was the rejoinder. This interest in public affairs, and this zeal for civil and religious freedom, he maintained until his dying day, and transmitted to his children, as an important part of their inheritance.

Letters which remain prove that Mr. Miller was greatly respected for his learning and ability; that he was regarded, generally, as a wise counsellor, high deference being paid to his opinions; and that he was influential in the State as well as in the Church. Among his brethren, he seems to have been looked up to for the exertion of influence with the civil government, and for managing the courtesies of intercourse, then more frequent perhaps than now, between the presbytery and the magistracy.[2]

[1] 1 Kings xii. 16.

[2] The following letters of John Dickinson are worthy of preservation. Born in Talbot county, Maryland, in 1732, he received his literary education in Delaware; read law in Philadelphia and London; then practised with success in the former city. In the Legislature of Pennsylvania, and in the old Congress, colonial, revolutionary and national, he won high distinction as an orator and statesman. His "Letters of a Pennsylvania Farmer," State papers, and other political writings, were among the most polished, eloquent, and effective of the times. He was President of Pennsylvania and Delaware successively. He died at Wilmington in 1808.

An extract from the Minutes of Presbytery, in 1781, will explain the first letter, and illustrate also, in some respects, the culture and character of Mr. Miller.

'The Presbytery considering the noble and pious efforts of his Excellency, John Dickinson, Esquire, for discountenancing vice and immorality in the Delaware State, resolved to send him an affectionate address, of which the Moderator [the Rev. John Miller] having drawn a copy, the same being reviewed, was ordered to be presented by the Moderator and Clerk in the name of the Presbytery; a copy of which follows, viz.:

'Sir,—The Presbytery of Lewes being here providentially convened for the purpose of promoting the important ends of the Christian institution, are happy in embracing this first opportunity, since your accession to the President's chair, of congratulating you as a warm and distinguished friend, not only to the civil, but religious interest of the State.

'Convinced that the practice of piety and virtue is the best support and noblest ornament of every community, it gave us no little pleasure to find you so early, and so publicly, exerting your influence to promote it; nor can we think, so far as our observation has extended, that it has been without good effects, particularly with regard to some instances of the gross profanation of the Christian Sabbath, which gave great disgust to all serious persons among us.

'But, Sir, you will not think it strange, considering the general prevalence

With his old pastor in Boston, Dr. Sewall, until his death, Mr. Miller kept up a correspondence, which, no doubt, often cheered him amid his many toils and priva-

of vice and immorality, that we most earnestly wish you to continue your benevolent exertions for advancing a reformation of manners so ardently desired by the good people under your government.

'Your very respectable character, your great abilities and active spirit, induce us to believe that no endeavors of yours will be wanting, to persuade the legislature of the State to revise the laws respecting the suppression of profaneness and vice, and make effectual provisions for preventing those public diversions, which, as they are conducted, are not only inconsistent with a laudable frugality and industry, but also productive of many vices most pernicious to society.

'That all good men may unite in supporting your wise and virtuous administration, and the Supreme Ruler crown it with his blessing, is the prayer of your obliged, humble servants.

'Signed by order. * * '

'My dear Sir,
          'I intend very shortly to publish a Proclamation in this State for the Discouragement of Immorality, etc.; and as it has been usual to publish addresses, I should be exceedingly glad, if that with which I was honored by the Presbytery of Lewes, could appear in the same newspaper, as it will be a testimony of some good effects having attended my efforts in the Delaware State.

'In truth, I want every support against the madness or wickedness of my opponents, in the course I am determined to hold in my public life, the first point of which will be the constant expression of the highest veneration for Religion.

'If you will, therefore, be pleased to let that publication come out in the manner I have mentioned, and inclose it to Mr. Thomas Bradford or myself immediately by a safe hand, you will much oblige,
          'Dear Sir,
                    'Your very sincere Friend,
                              'John Dickinson.
                    'Philadelphia, Nov. 14th, 1782.

'Reverend Mr. John Miller.'

'Dear Sir,
          'I am very much obliged to you for your friendly letter of the 29th past, which did not come to my hands till the beginning of this week; and I return you my unfeigned thanks for the affectionate expressions of your regard.

'I perceive the difficulties you mention; and am too sensible of my own defects, to promise myself any great success in encountering them. But duty engages me in the attempt.

'I am perfectly convinced that the happiness of men in this life, as well as in the next, depends on the prevalence of piety and virtue among them. How great and indispensable an obligation, then, is laid upon persons in public offices, both as Christians and Magistrates, to promote, by all means in their power, practices of so extensive, so durable, so momentous consequence!

'How far it is possible to reclaim people from folly, madness, and vice, I know not; but this I am unalterably resolved upon—to take the opportunity offered by my present unsolicited and earnestly-avoided station, as it will not now look like affectation, of bearing my testimony at least, if I can do no more, to those sacred truths which I revere, and wish others to revere.

'There is no solid glory, but what has reference to God, and points at eternity. The rest is a bubble. Happy shall I think myself, if it can be said of my administration at its conclusion, that it made the people better.

tions. He corresponded also with some of his New England relatives—chiefly with Benjamin Henshaw, of Middletown, and Joseph Henshaw, of Leicester, Connecticut, and Dr. Edward (afterwards Bishop) Bass,[1] of Newburyport, Massachusetts. His people seem to have been affectionate, for the most part, and united; yet, occasionally, trouble arose in this quarter. In 1763, he had a complaint lodged against him in Presbytery 'for introducing and singing *Dr. Watts's version of David's Psalms* in the congregation of Duck Creek.' At a subsequent session, the complainants being absent, the presbytery, 'considering that Mr. Miller fully owned the charge in all its parts,' proceeded to deliberate upon it, and unanimously decided against the complainants; one of whom was immediately cited to answer for an abusive insult offered to presbytery, during the progress of this affair, 'which they suspected proceeded from drunkenness.'[2] As late as 1770,—how much longer we cannot tell,—it appears that Rouse's version was still used in the Church at Dover.[3]

Mr. Miller was a thorough and zealous Calvinist of the old school; and, though bred a Congregationalist, and, therefore, not so warmly zealous as some others for Presbyterian Church order, he yet cordially fell in with it, as the pastor of a Presbyterian congregation. At the time of his settlement the Presbyterian Church was rent asunder. Two parties, called the *Old* and the *New Side*, after long disagreement, had separated in 1741, and ever since formed two independent communions, the former represented by the Synod of Philadelphia, the latter by the Synod of New York. A lover of peace, and drawn both ways by kindly associations and amiable feelings, he joined neither side at once. The very year of his removal to Delaware, the Synod of New York made overtures for a reunion, which was not consummated, however, for about

'I beg that I may be favored with your prayers, and those of other good men, for divine assistance

'With perfect sincerity, I am,
'Dear Sir,
'Your obliged friend,
'and most obedient humble servant,
'John Dickinson.

'Rev'd Mr. Miller.'   'Dover, January 19th, 1792.'

[1] 5 Sprague's Annals, 142.
[2] MS. Minutes of Presbytery of Lewes, 16.   [3] Id., 85.

nine years. In 1758, the two synods met together, and became one—the Synod of New York and Philadelphia. Only about a year before, and then probably in prospect of an approaching reconciliation of the two sides, Mr. Miller had joined the Old Side Presbytery of New Castle.[1] He was a regular attendant thereafter upon church judicatories, and was twice[2] elected moderator of the highest of them—at that time the Synod last mentioned—an honor which, in its repetition, seems to have been conferred in only one other case.[3]

Upon the evidence remaining, it has been generally concluded that the Presbyterian Church in this country had no formally received standards before the year 1729; yet that it was as thoroughly Presbyterian then as now; the Westminster formularies exhibiting practically, though not by express adoption, its rule of agreement, organization, and action. With the Church of Scotland it sustained intimate and most amicable intercourse. In the year mentioned, the general Synod, by a formal "Adopting Act," made the Westminster Confession and Catechisms its own, with only some slight exceptions, relating to the power of the civil magistrate in matters of religion. At the same time, the Directory for worship, discipline, and government, commonly annexed to the Confession and Catechisms, was earnestly recommended, as "agreeable in substance to the Word of God, and founded thereon."

In 1786, in anticipation of subdividing the Synod, and establishing a General Assembly, a committee was appointed for the revision of "the Book of Discipline and Government." In 1787, their draught was approved; another committee revised the Directory for Worship; the Synod altered the Confession as to the single point before indicated—the power of civil magistrates; and the whole was printed for general examination. The next year these

---

[1] Each Side had a Presbytery of New Castle. About a year after the reunion of the Synods, the two were consolidated. In May, 1758, the Presbytery of Lewes was formed, and to that Mr. Miller was attached.

[2] In 1765 and 1780.

[3] Elihu Spencer (afterwards D.D.), in 1760 and 1766. But five of the moderators of Synod were subsequently moderators of the General Assembly—John Rodgers, D.D., (S. 1763) in 1789; Robert Smith, D.D., (S. 1774) in 1790; John Woodhull, D.D., (S. 1788) in 1791; James Latta, D.D., (S. 1782) in 1793; and Alexander McWhorter, D.D., (S. 1770) in 1794. No one has been twice moderator of the General Assembly.

revised standards, after striking out four words from the Larger Catechism, to make it agree with the altered Confession, were finally ratified.[1]

To these measures, which secured a near approach to unanimity in Synod, Mr. Miller made at least no public opposition, of which any account remains. His intimate and beloved friend and co-presbyter, the Rev. Matthew Wilson,[2] of Lewes, Delaware, held peculiar views upon the subject of church government, and was very active and earnest in maintaining them before Synod and elsewhere; and wrote so freely to Mr. Miller in regard to them, and with such evident assurance that the latter concurred with him, as to some important points at least, that we must presume a general coincidence in their opinions on these points. Dr. Samuel Miller's recollection was, that his father had seconded Mr. Wilson's efforts.[3] The latter regarded every congregation, with its proper officers, as independent, and synods or councils, under which names he included all judicatories above the church-session, as not for government, but for concord and advice; and for 'acting in concert to promote a general reformation and advancement of religion.' The session, which he often called a presbytery, though not always expressing himself consistently, he considered supreme and of final jurisdiction, in every matter of government. This was Congregationalism, modified by a representative ruling eldership in each church. In one letter, Mr. Wilson speaks of the Presbytery of Lewes, a very small one, as agreeing with him in the condemnation, as unscriptural, of appeals to higher judicatories.[4]

[1] Baird's Digest. Book I.   [2] D.D. from 1786.   See 3 Sprague's Annals, 178. [3] Memoirs of Dr. Rodgers (1813), 259, 260.

[4] The account above given of Mr. Wilson's opinions is taken directly from his letters to Mr. Miller. A fuller statement may be found in the second volume of Dr. Hodge's Constitutional History, pages 502, 503. The letters referred to illustrate Mr. Wilson's character, the friendship between him and Mr. Miller, and also some of the ecclesiastical controversies of the times. As a member of the Committee upon the Book of Discipline and Government, he labored strenuously to prevent the 'Scots' Hierarchy,' as he called it, from being fastened on the Church; and earnestly sought Mr. Miller's aid in the effort. 'Considering,' he wrote, 'your age, and experience, and character among them, I cannot but think that such a motion from you would be probably successful, especially if you use some previous influence out of doors.' But the advocates of strict Presbyterianism prevailed, and Dr. Wilson poured into his friend's ear bitter complaints.

In August, 1788, he wrote,

Mr. Miller was never robust in health, yet, by uniform and strict temperance, and vigilant self-denial, was enabled to perform the duties of his station with little interruption, and with general comfort. In an uncommon degree, he succeeded in fulfilling the various obligations of a husband and father, a citizen, a Christian, and a minister of the Gospel. His character, circumstances, and life will be further illustrated by the letters which will appear in the sequel. He did not attend Synod after the Spring of 1786, and never attended the General Assembly as a Commissioner, if at all; but this was probably owing, as will hereafter appear, to age and enfeebled health, soon resulting in his demise.

Mr. Miller, though himself addicted, according to the prevailing custom in his neighborhood, to the use of tobacco, which he both smoked and chewed, decidedly, and not without effect, discouraged the use of it by his sons.

'With regard to Synod, I learn they gave my remonstrance a reading, as also some others from the Eastward, and Dr. Rodgers pleaded that they should be considered, but in vain; the two *Scots' Doctors* and the poor wrangling wiseacres of our mountains carried all. There was none to plead the cause of truth. But had *Cicero* or *Demosthenes* pleaded there, they had in vain opposed the torrent. The *Scots' unscriptural Hierarchy* was determined beforehand to be adopted. Our Presbytery is arbitrarily annexed to a Philadelphia Presbytery, and subjected with appeals to a General Assembly. I think from the remonstrance we sent, we are not bound. At least I am not. Nor do I mean ever to meet the Synod any more, though I should live, which is also uncertain.'

Again, in April, 1789, he says:

'The Hierarchy is crammed down our throats. If the Presbytery should agree to it, I think we ought to send them a presbyterial remonstrance, declaring that we cannot, in conscience, be subject to any unscriptural government, as we esteem theirs to be, * * as to the subordination of presbyteries to synods, and these to the Assembly, etc. But if they will allow us, as we are agreed with them in doctrine and discipline (though not in government), we will, as a presbytery, send *messengers* to the great Council, to consult the advancement of Christ's kingdom, but not to wrangle, or exercise the discipline which only belongs to a presbytery. Whether the Presbytery agree to this or not, I purpose never to *submit to* or *attend on* one of their *unscriptural Synods.* This, I presume, is agreeable also to your sentiments. Now, as you have a dear child in the city, I think it probable you would wish to attend Council at their meeting, and let them know this our determination; when you may make any use of this letter among them you please.

Dr. Wilson, however, was the Commissioner from the Presbytery of Lewes to the first General Assembly, Mr. Miller being his alternate, and actually attended its sessions; yet only to carry out himself what he had urged upon his friend. He "threw in a case of conscience by the Committee of Overtures," which is given at length in the Minutes of Presbytery, and, in substance, in those of the Assembly. *MS. Min. Presb. of Lewes*, 134, 5. *Min. of G. Assemb.*, 11.

3. MRS. MARGARET MILLER, THE MOTHER.

A mother's influence, in moulding the character of her children, and the record of it, in elucidating divine truth, especially God's precious promises to faithful parents for their offspring, are particularly important. Of his mother, Dr. Miller, in after life, in all the fervency of the strongest filial affection, wrote,

'I have heard the Rev. Dr. Rodgers, of New York, say, that he had very often seen my mother, soon after her marriage, and that he thought her decidedly one of the most beautiful women that he ever saw in his life. But her moral and spiritual beauty were still more remarkable. * * She was bred a rigid Episcopalian, but, soon after her connexion with my father, joined in communion with the church of which he was pastor, and continued a member of it while she lived. She was one of the most pious women that I ever knew. Courteous and benevolent in a very uncommon degree, she endeared herself to all who knew her. To the poor, she was assiduously and tenderly beneficent; and in her every domestic relation a pattern to her acquaintances. I never think of her character, taken all together, without a mixture of veneration, wonder and gratitude. The fidelity with which she instructed me; the fervor and tenderness with which she prayed with me; and the unceasing care with which she watched over all my interests, especially those of a moral and religious nature, have been, as I should think, seldom equalled. I have reason to be deeply humbled that I did not profit more by them; and yet I am persuaded I do not live a day without deriving some benefit from them.'

Dr. Miller never talked of his mother, excepting in terms like these of strong, and as some might say, extravagant eulogy. But the tenderness with which he cherished such recollections showed, conclusively, that she had at least succeeded in deeply and lastingly influencing her son's mind. We may safely conclude, therefore, that she possessed all those qualities which were necessary thus to endear her to her children; and we cannot doubt that the character of this son was, in various most important respects, moulded and permanently established by her example, her instructions, and her devoted maternal watchfulness and care. Her letters, of which several have been preserved, while they give evidence of no high literary cultivation, yet conclusively reveal excellence of another kind: true warmth of heart, tenderness of affection, and fervent piety breathe through them all without exception. The brief extracts from these letters, which will appear in a subsequent chapter, will help to illustrate the influences under which her son Samuel passed his early years, and received his preparatory training. The first, highest wish of both parents, for all their children, seemed to be their everlasting salvation.

Mrs. Miller's benevolence to the poor, and to her own servants, is particularly mentioned in co-temporaneous notices of her death. These servants appear to have been all slaves. Mr. Miller was, certainly, a slave owner, though his circumstances must have kept this part of his household small in number. Her kindness toward such dependants seems greatly to have exceeded that which is commemorated so indiscriminately upon the tomb-stones of slave-holders, under certain stereotype forms—'A kind Master'—'A humane Mistress.' But "the institution," at that earlier day, was doubtless commonly more "patriarchal" than at a later date. In the Delaware pastor's house, at any rate, the servants were evidently considered and treated as a part of the family, falling just below the children as objects of Christian regard and attention.

Mrs. Miller always dated her conversion to Christ as having occurred after her marriage.

CHAPTER SECOND.

BIRTH, YOUTH, AND EDUCATION.

1769–1789.

1. BIRTH AND EARLY YOUTH.

SAMUEL MILLER, the eighth child and sixth son of the Rev. John and Margaret Miller, was born at the family residence on the 31st of October, 1769.

More than ten years before his birth, his parents had been called to mourn, for the first time, the loss of a child —their infant son Joseph. Of the death of the latter, a father's fondness made the following record:—

'October 5th, 1759. Last night my son Joseph, a promising child, aged nineteen months and eight days, departed this life, after a short but violent illness in the lungs. My heart was far too much bound up in the child. His little, pretty ways insensibly stole my affections from objects infinitely superior to all earthly comforts: the parting stroke has given me a much more affecting view of this than I had before. Oh that I may see the rod and him that has appointed it—see that God has a controversy to plead with me and my house.'

Samuel had but just completed his third year, when a second family bereavement occurred, in the death of his brother Benjamin, at the age of a little over five. He was only turned of six years, when the Declaration of Independence was made; but his father's active interest in national affairs kept all the family awake to passing political occurrences, and even the boy of six had his own notions of the great events of the day, which were so frequently discussed in his hearing. In after life, he could recollect, that his earliest idea of the Declaration was, that of a large body of men forming a ring, and throwing up their hats with loud hurrahs. But soon afterwards, to the boy of

28

eight, the Revolution presented itself in a very different
aspect, bringing upon the retired household a deeper sorrow than any by which it had before been clouded.   And
doubtless this bereavement produced some lasting impression
upon the heart of one exercised as he had been, assiduously,
in the knowledge and natural experience of divine truth.
John was the eldest child.   Graduated at the University
of Pennsylvania, he had studied Medicine, and entered
upon the practice of that profession in the neighborhood of
his father's residence.   Though of a slender and delicate
constitution, he seems to have been buoyant in spirit, and
active in effort.   Possessed of excellent talents, a liberal
education, and many endearing qualities, his professional
prospects were peculiarly bright.   But he was thoroughly
imbued with that patriotism which distinguished his father;
and in 1776 or '77, he joined the American army, as a
volunteer surgeon, and devoted himself to the cause of his
country.   Two letters of his yet remain, the earlier of
which, without date, but endorsed 1777, says,
' Honored Parents,

 'I am just ready to set off for Camp.   My present feelings cannot be described by any language I am master of.
Notwithstanding the necessity of my going, and the justice of
this cause, the reflection that I may never return to the dearest, the best, of parents, fills me with distress that I never before experienced.   But he who condescends to make even the
chief of sinners the object of his compassion, will, I trust, guard
me in the hour of danger, and support me in all my afflictions.
I beg that you may not be too unhappy on my account, as
nothing so much increases my uneasiness as your inquietude.'

The reference in this letter to the Saviour of sinners affords the only remaining evidence of what may have been
the young patriot's resort upon the dying bed, on which
he was so soon to lie down.

If the indorsement mentioned be correct, the young surgeon could not have been in camp more than six or seven
weeks, the earliest of 1777.   But they were very momentous weeks for the American cause.   On the 2d of January
occurred the battle (it really deserved that name) of the
Assunpink, at Trenton; on the 3d, the battle of Princeton;
and the operations of the next sixty days in New Jersey
were very stirring, and ended with the almost entire ex-

pulsion of the British and Hessian troops, so long a terror to the State, from its limits. With surprising resolution and energy, young Dr. Miller endured the fatigues and hardships of camp and hospital life. "His calmness and intrepidity upon the field of danger were conspicuous. He was peculiarly attentive to the wounded soldiery;" manifesting in his practice a rare and "happy combination of compassionate tenderness and manly firmness." Probably his exposure and unremitted service for several months had produced symptoms warning him of danger to life; for he was on his way home from the American camp in New Jersey, when he was seized, at Darby, seven miles from Philadelphia, with peripneumony, which all attributed to the hardships of his military service. On the 21st of February, 1777, he wrote to his parents, encouraging the hope that he would see them in two or three days. But subsequently his disease assumed a more serious aspect, and rapid and agonizing in its progress, soon terminated his life. "When he felt the approach of" dissolution, "so keen and so lively a sense had he formed of that affecting scene which usually attends a dying bed, surrounded by a circle of weeping friends, that upon being pressed to apprise his distant relatives of his dangerous situation, he strenuously" resisted "the proposal, adding, that he wished the conflict might be over, before the heavy tidings of his malady should have reached their ears, lest they should be witnesses to the painful combat." He died on the 28th of February, 1777, and was interred at Dover.[1]

Other events, of a different character, now and then agitated the current, for the most part so quiet and uniform, of home life. In 1779, Samuel's sister Elizabeth was married to Colonel Samuel McLane; and in 1787, his younger sister, Mary, married Vincent Loockerman, who belonged to a Delaware family, and resided in the immediate neighborhood of her parents. Col. McLane lived in Philadelphia, and his residence there gave to his wife's family in Delaware a place of occasional sojourn, of which her

[1] The quotations, and indeed the whole estimate of the young surgeon's character, are from a notice of his death, dated March 4, 1777, in "The Pennsylvania Packet," contributed by Dr. John Warren, of Boston, a fellow-surgeon in the army, who was with him when he died. Dr. Warren was afterwards Professor of Anatomy—the first in New England—at Harvard University. His older brother, Gen. Joseph Warren, fell at Bunker's Hill.

brother Samuel seems to have availed himself, to some extent, even before he joined the University. Of course, this city—the largest in the Union[1]—was a great attraction to the people of the surrounding country; the more so, because, at that time, the seat of our National government. Here in May, 1787, assembled the memorable convention which formed the present Constitution of the United States. Dr. Miller often spoke, in after years, of the pleasure he had in his youth experienced, standing within the great hall of entrance, at the State House, to observe the members of this convention, as they went to and from the chamber, where they sat with closed doors. Thus repeatedly passed before him, in review, some of the greatest men of their day; men whose names he had previously learned to pronounce with a respect akin to reverence. There he saw the Father of his country, chosen to preside over the convention, whose career in arms had ended, and his career of statesmanship begun. There, Alexander Hamilton, the accomplished scholar, soldier, jurist, financier and politician; the confidential friend, and afterwards the Cabinet Secretary, of Washington; gifted with genius that won universal admiration; yet capable of sin and folly, which sunk him down to an untimely and dishonored grave. There, Benjamin Franklin, who, as through all the years of his high and well-deserved worldly renown, the admired companion of philosophers and statesmen, of courtiers and kings, still carried with him the simple manners and practical good sense of his humblest days. He was now not far from the end of his career, and was so infirm, that he had to be borne, in a sedan-chair, by two strong men, daily, to the place of assembly. There he saw Roger Sherman, the Morrises, his father's well-known friend John Dickinson, James Madison, the Pinckneys, and others of as much, or scarcely less note. No doubt, he had the opportunity of seeing nearly all the leading public men of the day, those of them who were not in the constitutional convention being often, doubtless, at the seat of government. His pleasurable recurrence, even late in life, to these scenes, proved that they had strongly impressed him; and unquestionably they exerted an im-

---

[1] As late as 1800, New York was below Philadelphia, in population, by nearly 10,000; and it was above the latter, in 1810, by only 86.

portant influence in moulding his character, quickening his patriotism, fostering a deep permanent interest in public affairs, and strengthening that disposition to revere the truly great and good, which made him even too ready to admit a claim of excellence, and marked many an unaffected effort to cast back honor upon those, who had thought only of honoring him.

Samuel's oldest brother Edward, the only son that came to years of manhood without a college training, had been, however, assiduously and liberally educated, first by his father, then, from the age of fourteen, at a classical seminary of very high reputation, in the village of Newark, Delaware. Here, under the tuition of Francis Alison, D. D.,[1] succeeded by the Rev. Alexander McDowell,[2] he had devoted four years to the diligent study of Latin and Greek, and gone through the usual course of the arts and sciences. For the languages, especially, he seems to have had a decided taste; and it is probable that his proficiency in these was much greater than common. Afterwards, he studied medicine with Dr. Charles Ridgely, an eminent practitioner of Dover, with whom he appears to have been an especial favorite; then, in 1780, he accepted an appointment as surgeon's mate in the Revolutionary army. About a twelve-month later, he set out on a cruise of nearly a year, in an armed ship bound to France; whence he returned, in 1782, with a good knowledge of the French language, improved professional culture, and much general information. In 1784, having, meanwhile, attended two full courses of medical lectures in the University of Pennsylvania, he commenced practice at Frederica, a village seventeen miles south of his father's house. Soon, however, he removed to Somerset county, Maryland, and in 1786, on the death of Doctor Ridgely, to Dover. Here he continued in practice until his removal to New York in 1796.

His brother Joseph, graduated at the University of Pennsylvania in 1787, seems to have been settled also at Dover, as a practising lawyer, within two years, at latest, after his college graduation. Tradition says, 'that he once brought an action for damages accruing from the practice of witch-

<hr>

[1] 3 Sprague's Annals, 73.   [2] Id. 178, note.

craft, and quoted copiously from the Bible to enforce the claims of his client. The adverse counsel, being more familiar with books of law than with the Book of God, was considerably perplexed at this mode of conducting the case. The Biblical lawyer lost his cause nevertheless.'

2. Preparation for College.—Profession of Religion.

Dr. Miller left among his papers the following brief account of his earlier years:

'The first eighteen years of my life were spent under my parental roof. I was never placed in any school, or public seminary, of any kind, prior to my entrance into the University of Pennsylvania in 1788, when I was eighteen years and eight months old. From the age of about twelve, I had been studying the Latin and Greek classics, at home, under the direction of my father, (who was an excellent Latin, Greek, and Hebrew scholar * *), and of two elder brothers, who had preceded me in acquiring a knowledge of classic literature under parental instruction. But I pursued this object with many interruptions and with little zeal, owing to an expectation and desire of relinquishing the study of the learned languages, and entering a counting-house, with a future view to merchandise as a profession. Hence I studied little, and that little to small purpose. But about my eighteenth year, it pleased God, in a remarkable manner, to direct my views otherwise, (for which I desire here to record my sincere thanks), and to excite in me a desire for the acquisition of knowledge; though without any settled purpose as to a future profession. After this change of feeling and of purpose respecting a classical education, I was, for some months, under great perplexity and embarrassment, how to pursue and complete my education in a better manner than I could possibly do under the tuition of an aged and infirm parent. During this anxiety, I was brought under very serious impressions of religion, which I hope soon after issued in a cordial acceptance of the Saviour as my hope and life. Early in the Spring of 1788, I made a profession of religion in the church of Dover, under my father's pastoral care. I have often looked back on that step, with its preceding and attending exercises, with much solicitude as to the question, whether it was founded on a saving acquaintance with Christ or not. I can only say, that I had a hope in Christ, which, though afterwards and often painfully interrupted, was then steady and comfortable; and that my excellent mother, an intelligent and faithful counsellor in such matters, concurred in the measure of uniting myself with the church.'

A letter from the father, written at this time to Col. Mc-Lane, will explain, in part at least, the perplexity and embarrassment mentioned in the foregoing extract.

'My dear Son,   'Near Dover, July 17, 1788.

'Prest on all hands by my friends, (not considering my having no income adequate to the support of my family, as they live, and the very probable want and distress, to which they may be reduced soon after my removal), I have at length consented to Sammy's going to Philadelphia, to spend some short time at the University, which I should not have done, had I not a very great dependence on your and Betsey's attention to him, and giving him such advices and counsels, as, with the blessing of heaven, may effectually tend to form him, should he be spared, to important usefulness in the world.

'You well know what my desire is respecting him; viz., that he may be a well-informed, sincere, prudent and humble follower of Christ. Unless his education is sanctified, by divine grace, for this purpose, I think he had better be without it. Were he, from right principles, disposed and prepared for the gospel ministry, it would be inexpressibly pleasing to me, and I doubt not to you, notwithstanding the temporal discouragements, which, at present, may lie in the way of it.

'The other professions of Physic and Law, as they are now conducted by the generality, appear to me unfriendly to a life of real piety, especially the last. And as to the first, I dread Sammy's spending so much time in Dover, as would be necessary to qualify him for it. Such a number of idle young fellows you could scarcely find in so small a place. Should he be found qualified for the Senior Class, he will want to continue there until the next Commencement; otherwise his stay will be much shorter. On the whole, I must warmly solicit you, to direct him into such a path of prudence, and urge him to such a veneration for a pious and virtuous life, as may give us all, by the will of God, much comfort concerning him.

'Your mamma is in her usual state. The rest of your friends well so far as I know. May the best of heaven's blessings rest and abide with you forever!   Yours affectionately,
                                          'John Miller.'

3. THE COLLEGE STUDENT.

With, or just after, his father's letter of the 17th of July, Samuel Miller went to Philadelphia and took up his abode with Colonel and Mrs. McLane. His diary very briefly notices his admission to College:

'July 21st, 1788. Entered this day the University of Pennsylvania. Was admitted at once into the Senior Class. I am now eighteen years and eight months old.'

The following letters and extracts from letters, written during his college course, give a little insight into the events of this year at the University, and illustrate the home influences, especially of a religious kind, which had been, and were yet, thrown over him:

Mrs. Margaret Miller to Col. McLane.

July the 19th, [1788].

'My very dear Son,

'By this time I hope your brother Sammy has arrived safe in Philadelphia, and though, I was so much hurried getting him ready to set off, I did not send you a line, I cannot omit it now. Oh, my dear Sir, it is with gratitude I recollect your kind invitation to him, which no length of time will efface from my mind. And I rely very much on your care of him. Please to exercise the most unlimited control of his conduct, and I think he will love you the better for it. Sammy is at a very trying time of life. I hope, my dear Child,[1] you will have a watchful eye over him at all times. Oh, may that eye which never slumbereth nor sleepeth direct him in all his way—is the prayer of your afflicted mother; and I ask for him and myself also an interest in your prayers.'

Rev. John Miller to Col. McLane.

Near Dover, August 26, 1788.

'My dear Son,

'I am just now crawling out again, after a spell of the bilious fever. With great difficulty I went last Sabbath and preached a sermon at Dover, and seem still to be recruiting. * * I hope Sammy is doing well, and have no fear at present of his industry and application to business; but may he and all of us remember that one thing is needful. Eternity, my dear Son, is infinitely important.'

Rev. John Miller to Mrs. McLane.

Near Dover, Sept. 15, 1788.

' * * I am now, through divine goodness, in the way of recovery, have preached twice, but, by fevers continuing, am still

---

[1] Mrs. McLane.

in a feeble state. Your mamma likewise has intermitting fevers; but keeps chiefly about house; and both of us by such growing infirmities as commonly attend our advanced period of life, are admonished of the approaching day, when we shall leave you all in a world of sin and sorrows, from the snares of which nothing less than God's special grace in Christ Jesus can secure you. May we be found waiting for the coming of our Lord, living by faith and attempered for the heavenly blessedness!

' * * I am sorry to hear of Sammy's purpose of going to Princeton, as I am sure he has neither money nor time to spend on any such jaunt. Did he know that almost every resource for the support of the family has lately failed; that the chief of our people pay me nothing; that perquisites are reduced to a trifle, and that I have not received twenty shillings since he left us, I think he would be more prudent. He is disposed, I fully believe, to be diligent; but considering my present straitened situation, he must also make a point of being very frugal; otherwise he will be under the necessity of returning home, without answering his chief purpose.

'My earnest wish is, that he may be serious, and with deep solicitude pursue an early and experimental acquaintance with vital religion, without which every other accomplishment will avail him nothing.'

Rev. John Miller to Col. McLane.

Near Dover, December 26, 1788.

'My dear Son,

'Mr. Loockerman came down late on Sabbath evening (a very improper time to travel), extremely pinched with the cold. He since has been sick with an inflammatory fever; but being bled largely, he is better, and sitting up again. By him we received your letters, with a gown for your mamma, and a pair of breeches for myself, for which I am greatly obliged to you, though they happen to be much too big for me, as I am sure they must be for yourself. * * Your mamma is as well as usual, busy about her family affairs, but, I believe, very intent on the one thing needful. * * We live, on the whole, comfortably, but chiefly on the produce of our little farm. Your mammy has a good turkey in keeping for you, as we expect a visit from you this season, and wish it may be convenient for you to gratify us with your company. Poor Sam is indeed poor, beggarly poor, as he himself suggests; but let him know, if he loves and fears God, he won't want anything that will be best for him. I here enclose a guinea, received last week, for him. I earnestly wish, my dear daughter, with yourself, much of God's gracious, sanctifying and comforting presence.'

Mrs. Margaret Miller to Mrs. McLane.

March the 19th, 1789.

'My very dear Betsey,

'*   *   *   *   *   *   *

Your brother informs me that you, for some reasons, advise him to decline going to the singing school. I have no doubt but your reasons are good; therefore I desire you and Mr. McLane to give him your advice as you would a child of your own; and though I have a great desire he should go, yet if it would interfere with his other learning I must give it up. * * Oh, my dear Betsey, of what infinite importance it is that we be prepared for eternity.'

Poor 'Sammy' never recovered from the effects of this disappointment as to the singing school. He could not, his life long, turn a single tune. Perhaps Colonel McLane thought the case, even then, utterly hopeless.

Rev. John Miller to Col. McLane.

'Near Dover, March 27, 1789.

' * * I hope such trials will be blessed by heaven, to convince you of the transitory nature of all worldly enjoyment, and lead you to place your happiness in the possession of such objects as no earthly occurrence can deprive you of. Oh may we be more and more sensible, that unless God in Christ is our friend and portion, we can neither truly enjoy the comforts of this life, nor obtain the blessedness of that to come!

' * * The infirmities of an advanced period of life I find increasing upon me. The severity of the winter has confined me almost altogether at home, together with a frequently disordered stomach, attended with fever, by which I have been much reduced. For some days past I have been considerably better; but through the winter have been prevented several Sabbaths from going abroad.

'I am anxious to hear of Sammy's indisposition—whether he is likely to get well of his cough. If he is not more careful than, I fear, he has been, it will be difficult to remove.'

Rev. John Miller to Col. McLane.

'Near Dover, May 12, 1789.

' * * The letters brought us the agreeable news of your being all well, Sammy excepted, who, we understand, is in a fair

way of recovery. Very ardently do we wish, that his spared
life may be devoted to the service of Christ! * * As to cloth
for a coat and breeches for myself * * a black, or deep blue,
or clergyman's grey, would very well suit me.'

To Mrs. McLane, upon the same sheet.

' * * But you will, I hope, be much more solicitous for your
own and our spiritual welfare, than for any of our temporal
concerns. Eternity, with all its most solemn and important
scenes, will very soon be opened to our view : we are living on
the borders of it, and need to be continually realizing it, that
we may live above the present world, and have our hearts
chiefly placed on God and heaven. Under these lively impressions, we wish you frequently to take opportunities of conversing with your brother Sammy, and giving him such advice and
counsels, as may tend to a proper improvement of the affliction
God has been pleased to visit him with, and the mercy that has
been shown him, in his being so far restored to health. You
will endeavor to direct his views, should his life be spared, to
such studies and pursuits, as will, by the divine blessing, render
him most useful in the world, and the greatest comfort to his
connexions. You will endeavor to guard him against the dangerous snare of vain and trifling company; against imbibing the
spirit, and following the maxims and habits of a degenerate
world; against all those things, which, in your devoutest hours,
you will judge are inconsistent with a spiritual and holy life.

'Your mamma and I have been in a poor state of health a
great part of the past winter; but at this time enjoy as much
health as our time of life and growing infirmities give us reason
to expect. May the Lord prepare us for our great change, and
afford us the comfort of seeing our dear children engaged in the
ardent pursuit of heavenly wisdom before we leave them! * *

'From your loving father,

'J. M.

'P. S.—Dr. Wilson, I expect, will attend what is called your
General Assembly.'

It was during his year at the University, perhaps during
the illness referred to in several of the foregoing letters,
that our young student first became acquainted with the
Rev. Dr. Ashbel Green,[1] with whom he enjoyed, particularly after entering the ministry, a very profitable intimacy.
Late in life, he thus recurred to the circumstances of his
earliest introduction to Dr. Green, who was a little more
than seven years his senior.   .

[1] 3 Sprague's Annals, 179.

"My acquaintance with that great and good man began about sixty years ago, when he was the beloved and highly popular co-pastor of the Second Presbyterian Church in the city of Philadelphia, and when I was a youthful student in the University of Pennsylvania. In the course of my connection with the University, I was a boarder in the family of a beloved sister, who was a worshipper in the church in which he preached, and in which, for that circumstance, as well as from choice, I was a constant hearer.

"In a few months after I entered the University, I was seized with a severe inflammatory fever, which brought me very low, and confined me to the house for a number of weeks. In the course of this illness, Dr. Green, though I had no other claim upon him than being the son of a brother minister, and a boarder in the house of one of his flock, kindly and affectionately called, more than once, to see me, and conversed and prayed with me with a fidelity and tenderness which I shall never forget, and which marked, at that early period of his pastoral life, a sacred regard to his official duties, and a happy talent in the fulfilment of them."[1]

Doubtless his father's zeal for the Presbyterian Church had given already to our young collegian a rising interest in ecclesiastical affairs. Philadelphia was, ordinarily, the place of meeting of the Synod of New York and Philadelphia, and of its successor, as the supreme judicatory of the Church, the General Assembly. Here were convened the last Synod, in May, 1788, and the first Assembly, in May, 1789. The latter, of course, was in session while Samuel Miller attended the University. Over this Assembly presided as Moderator, Dr. John Rodgers, a friend and former neighbor of his father's in Delaware, and afterwards his own senior colleague in New York; and the body was particularly interesting, not only as the first of its kind, but also for the large proportion of distinguished men which it contained, and for its influence in this formative period of the Presbyterian Church in the United States. It numbered thirty-five members, of whom twenty-four were ministers; and of these just two-thirds have been thought worthy of commemoration in Dr. Sprague's Annals, besides three, or more, briefly mentioned in the notes to that work. Among them were Dr. Alexander McWhorter, Dr. John

____
[1] Life of Dr. Green by Dr. Jones, p. 524.

Witherspoon, Dr. Samuel S. Smith, Dr. George Duffield, Dr. John Ewing, Dr. Robert Smith, Dr. Matthew Wilson, Dr. Patrick Alison, with others of scarcely less note. What interest the college student actually took in the deliberations of this Assembly is unknown; but, having so lately made a profession of religion, and, doubtless, having seriously entertained, already, the question of entering the gospel ministry, he could not well have slighted such an opportunity of witnessing the proceedings of so important a Presbyterian church court, or have witnessed them without an impression influencing, in some degree, his religious character, his ecclesiastical attachments, and his professional aims. It was one of the happy results of his long living, that he was intimately connected with the church of his affections through so many of its vicissitudes, and until it had grown in numbers and strength so vastly beyond its condition, when he was first growing up into acquaintance with it.

Rev. John Miller to Mrs. McLane.

Near Dover, July 12, 1789.

'Had you been present with me, when I called upon Joseph at the tavern, after he took his degree and received, with his class, a solemn charge from the Provost, you would have been shocked—several intoxicated, all in disorder and, seemingly, without the fear of God. I wish you would use your utmost influence with Sammy to dissuade his class from making any such an entertainment. Robert Clark lately assured me, that when his class commenced, they resolutely refused to have any dinner at all. 'Tis a scandalous custom, which the professors, did they discharge their duty, would by no means countenance.

'Did you know my feeble state and growing infirmities, you would fully excuse my not attempting a journey to Philadelphia. Only riding to the Cross Roads, or Dover, I find very fatiguing to me, and commonly, in this warm weather, it makes me very unwell.'

Rev. John Miller to Col. McLane.

'Near Dover, July 20, 1789.

' * * Sammy we expect will leave you the last of this week. A shallop from Duck Creek, belonging to Mr. Henery, will be up about the middle of the week, and 'tis thought will return about Friday morning; which opportunity we hope Sammy will embrace, if he desires soon to see his friends here. Another so convenient may not, at this season, soon offer; though possibly Mr. Williamson may contrive a way for him to come down with his brother, who proposes, I hear, to visit Kent immediately after Commencement.

'As Sammy is now about leaving your family, where he has been so affectionately treated, you will be pleased to let me know the amount of his board, and I shall acknowledge the receipt of it on the bond in my possession. Could you and Betsey, by your utmost influence, prevent Sammy, with his class, from going into a scene of folly and riot, immediate'y after a solemn charge from the Provost, you would much oblige me. Once I was a passing witness of such a Bachanalian carouse, when Joseph commenced; but wish ardently that none of my family may be concerned in another. Your Mamma and I still continue in our usual health; but can scarcely expect it long at this season. It becomes us to be waiting for our great change. And, Oh that we and our dear children may, through the riches of divine grace, be collected together, when we leave this world, in the society above, to be forever with the Lord! Let us not neglect to prepare for it. You know 'tis of all the most important concern.'

Mr. Miller received the "first honor" in his class; in token of which, according to the practice of the day, the Latin Salutatory Oration was awarded to him. From a contemporaneous account of the commencement exercises, it appears that they occupied two days—the 30th and 31st of July, and were held in the Rev. Dr. Weiberg's church—German Reformed—in Race street; whither a stately procession, composed of the lower schools, the University students, the faculty and trustees, and various public men who honored the occasion, moved each morning from the Hall of the University on State House square. After prayer by the Provost, came immediately the "Salutatory Oration in Latin—digression before the close in English, remonstrating against the neglect of female education—by Mr. Samuel Miller." On the second day, there was a "Dialogue in verse on the Federal Government, between Mr. George M. Baynton, of Philadelphia and Mr. Samuel Miller." At this Commencement, the "Degree of Doctor of Physic was conferred on Mr. Edward Miller."

Of a particular classmate Mr. Miller subsequently wrote,

'—One of the handsomest and one of the most profligate

young men I ever saw. He afterwards had a short, very licentious course, and died miserably.'

Of Samuel's college life little account can be given. From the new impulse to study which he had received, his recent profession of religion, several closely written volumes, which remain, of notes upon the different branches of study, and his standing at the close of his course, as well as occasional remarks in his father's letters, it may be inferred that he improved his collegiate opportunities with a good degree of diligence and zest; and that he was already forming those habits of patient, methodical industry which marked his whole life, especially his labors as a writer. He always retained a lively recollection of the advantages which he had enjoyed during this year at the University. His reminiscences, too, of Philadelphia, at this, an eventful time in both our national affairs and the affairs of the Presbyterian Church, were often vividly set before his family and friends. Among his instructors, the Rev. Dr. Ewing, the Provost, made the deepest impression on his mind and heart; and he has left on record[1] an exalted opinion of the patriotism, talents, learning, dignity, influence—the varied and solid accomplishments—of this distinguished man, who became subsequently a connection of his by marriage. Mrs. McLane, possibly thinking that her brother had been quite plainly enough brought up, was disposed rather to insist on his going a good deal into company, during his college course: perhaps too she saw that close confinement to study threatened his health. But it is not probable that the forced application to his books of this single year at the University allowed much time for general society.

[1] 3 Sprague's Annals, 216.

CHAPTER THIRD.

THE THEOLOGICAL STUDENT.

1789–1792.

---

1. HOME THEOLOGY.

Nothing remains to inform us, whether Mr. Miller returned home, from Philadelphia, laden with his commencement honors, by shallop to Duck Creek, the nearest navigable waters to his father's residence, or by some other equally primitive mode of travel. We soon find him at home however, and anxiously asking, without much loss of time, the important question, "Lord, what wilt thou have me to do?" Of this his diary affords the following evidence:—

'August 20th, 1789. Set apart a day of fasting and prayer for the divine direction in my choice of a profession. Before the day was closed, after much serious deliberation, and, I hope, some humble looking for divine guidance, I felt so strongly inclined to devote myself to the work of the ministry, that I resolved, in the Lord's name, on this choice. How solemn the undertaking. May the Lord help me to make a suitable estimate of its character, and to enter upon it with the deepest humility, and at the same time with confidence in the riches of his gracious aid.

'O my Father's and my Mother's God, I yield myself to thee! Yet, what an office for a poor, polluted, weak creature, who is helpless in himself, to aspire unto! Lord, help me to realize my own weakness and unworthiness; to lie in the dust of abasement, and habitually to look for strength to him who can "make me strong in the power of his might." Lord, I, this day, devote myself to thy most worthy service. I am thine by creation and preservation; I ought to be thine by a holy regeneration and a gracious adoption; and I would humbly devote myself to the promotion of thy glory to my latest breath.

'Samuel Miller.

43

'After this I immediately set about the regular study of Theology, under the direction of my Father.'

The earliest letter from Mr. Miller's pen remaining, was written two days later to Dr. Green.

'Dover, August 22, 1789.

'Rev'd Sir,

'Convinced of your readiness to lend your advice and assistance to a student, I hope you will excuse the intrusion of the present address.

'Since my leaving Philadelphia, the result of my deliberations, on a future profession in life, is a fixed resolve to study Divinity. In this pursuit, especially, I expect many difficulties will occur, and such as cannot be surmounted, without the advice and directions of those who have passed through it under distinguished advantages. To this subject, therefore, I have presumed, Sir, to solicit your attention.

'It is so long since my father first studied and formed his system, that it is no way strange he should be in a great degree unacquainted with the improvements in method which may have since taken place, and with the latest and most approved writers on Divinity. And on these points, it is of great importance to me, that I should collect minute information.

'If there are any authors which should be attended to by a student, not immediately connected with his business, previously to his entering on this study, I should be extremely obliged, Sir, by receiving from you an enumeration of them.

'My present plan is, to remain at home with my father for one year, and here, if possible, to collect so much knowledge on the subject as will enable me to hear, with the greatest improvement, Dr. Nesbit's Lectures to his class of *Theologists;* from whom I think I might derive very considerable advantages, if it were for no other reason than studying in that associated manner.

'I am, Sir, with the most perfect ·
'respect and esteem,
'your obedient, humble servant,
'Samuel Miller.

'The Rev. Mr. Green.'

Dr. Green's answer to this letter has not been preserved, but long afterwards Dr. Miller referred to it in the following terms:—

"Soon after I had completed my course in the University, this benevolent and devoted man, ever on the watch to do good, having heard that I had resolved to engage in the study of theology with a view to the gospel ministry, wrote me a long, affectionate, and most instructive letter, filled with those large views of ministerial furniture and duty for which he was always remarkable, and written with that wisdom, piety, learning and kindness, which were adapted at once to give light, and a happy impulse, to an inexperienced, youthful student. I felt myself much his debtor for this act of friendship, and shall never cease to regard it with fervent gratitude."[1]

Mr. Miller's father, a few days after the date of the foregoing letter, wrote to Mrs. McLane as follows:—

'Dover, August 27, 1789.

' * * Your brother Sammy seems to have improved considerably, not only as to his progress in learning, but on other accounts, which we ascribe very much to your and Mr. McLane's attention to him, for which we feel ourselves under great obligations to you and him. He is very attentive to his books, and seems much more serious and thoughtful than I expected to find him, and probably will study divinity, which I shall encourage, if I have reason to think his views and motives are suitable to that important undertaking.'

The following entry is from the son's diary:—

'October 8th, 1789. This day I set apart for solemn fasting, humiliation and prayer, in view of attending on the Sacrament of the Lord's Supper on the ensuing Sabbath, and also to implore the blessing of God upon my theological studies. A pleasant day on the whole, yet compassed about with many anxious fears concerning my state, motives, etc.'

About six weeks later, death again invaded the household. Now the devoted wife, the tender mother was called away, leaving a void never to be filled. Her son Samuel thus noticed the bereavement:—

' On Sunday morning, a little before one o'clock, November 22d, 1789, my dear, honored, tender, faithful, affectionate and pious mother departed this life, and went to a heavenly and better world. She had been more than a week ill of inflammatory fever. Her death was probably one of the most joyful and triumphant ever known. A very short time before she expired, she repeated with a hallowed and most animating confidence, the latter verses of Dr. Watts's version of the 17th Psalm, beginning with the 3d verse: "What sinners value I resign——." Heaven grant that I may always keep in remembrance her tenderness and faithfulness as a parent; her universal benevo-

[1] Life of Dr. Green, pp. 524, 5.

lence and charity as a neighbor; her sincere and almost unexampled piety and holiness as a Christian. And may I be enabled, through divine grace, to walk in all her steps, that my latter end may be like hers, composed, serene, joyful and triumphant; and thus may her death be my spiritual and eternal life.'

To Colonel McLane Mr. Miller afterwards wrote as follows:—

'My dear Son,   Near Dover, Dec. 10, 1789.

'Your very affectionate letter was most acceptable to us. The heavy loss we have sustained affords just reason for mourning, but none for distress with respect to the dear departed. She appeared to walk with God, in an habitual course, for many years past. Her humility shone with an amiable lustre. Never did I hear an elated word drop from her lips respecting herself, though she had the most extensive charity for others. She often complained to me of her ignorance, and earnestly desired to know more of the sin of her nature, and have a deeper sense of her utter unworthiness. The older she grew, the more she seemed pleased with the gospel plan of salvation, and a life of strict holiness. And though she was early and late attentive to her domestic affairs, studying always to redeem her time; yet I have reason to believe, that she retired three or four times a day, in a constant course; at which time, she read her Bible on her knees, and poured out her heart in fervent supplications at the throne of grace, frequently observing days of secret fasting, humiliation, and extraordinary prayer; in all which, I believe, she had much communion with her heavenly Father. In my absence, or inability by sickness, she statedly kept up family prayer, in which she appeared remarkably solemn and engaged. She also loved the public worship and ordinances of the gospel, and was always grieved when unfavorable weather, or bodily indisposition, prevented her attendance on them. Her children were very dear to her, and perhaps indulged to an extreme; but her counsels and admonitions were not wanting, and her heart was deeply engaged for their salvation. Her servants, too, were treated with great humanity and kindness, and were frequently instructed by her in their most important concerns. Her benevolence to all was very evident, and her neighbors, I believe, are losers by her death, and will long lament it. Indeed she was of a disposition remarkably obliging to all who came in her way. Her friends knew it, and deplore their loss: strangers, providentially at her house, who partook of her hospitality, experienced the same.

'In all these amiable qualities she shone more and more, as she advanced in years and experience. She seemed to ripen fast for heaven. Her friendship and benevolence were probably the occasion of her last illness. In visiting sick neighbors and attending one of their funerals, she too much exposed her feeble frame. The day after, having had the influenza before, but mildly, she was seized with an inflammatory fever, which, notwithstanding the best medical assistance here, put a period to her life in seven days. In her sickness, though deranged a little at times, her piety and benevolence were very conspicuous. Many texts of Scripture she repeated with peculiar force, relish and application; as also those lines in the 17th Psalm—

> What sinners value I resign ;
> Lord, 'tis enough that thou art mine, etc.

The blood of Christ was then her refuge and hope, as her dying lips signified a few minutes before her departure. She finished her course with great composure and serenity. Mr. Read preacht at her funeral, and many attended her remains to the grave. I think she was universally beloved and lamented.

'And now, my dear son, shall such a life, and such a death, of one so nearly connected with us, pass by unimproved? For you all I am deeply concerned that you should follow her excellent example, as she followed Christ. For my part, I blush with shame; my heart condemns me, that I have been so far her inferior in every moral and spiritual excellence. May the Lord make her death a mean of my being quickened to every good word and work! May the Lord prepare us for, and give us, a happy meeting at last with our dear departed! And now, I can assure you, that the best way for my children to support and comfort me, is for them to follow the faith, the piety and holiness of their dear mother.

'I hope to do without any white housekeeper. Such an one would not answer my purpose, as well as those I have, provided they behave as they lately have done. My dear Polly[1] is very attentive, though very infirm. I hope she will derive great benefit from her affliction. You will remember me in your prayers, and visit us when you can conveniently.

'Your distressed, but affectionate father,
'J. Miller.'

To Mrs. McLane Mr. Miller wrote,

'Be it so, that the desire of our eyes is removed from us, and the friend of our bosom taken away, if God has made an everlasting covenant with us, through a glorious Redeemer, ordered well and sure, containing all our salvation, and all that can

---

[1] His daughter, Mrs. Loockerman.

reasonably be our desire, we may well rejoice, and look forward to that glorious day, when, through the riches of divine grace, all our tears shall be wiped away, and we shall see no more sorrow. In the mean time, let us be daily looking forward to that glorious world and preparing for it, where we have reason to believe our dear departed is gone, and where we know our blessed Lord is ready to receive all his humble followers, as soon as they leave the body and the world.'

' * * The negro women have behaved, hitherto, better than I expected, especially Hannah and Lid; the latter exceedingly well, always studying, in every particular, to oblige me. Poor creatures, they loved their mistress, and I love them for it. May the Lord reward them! Notwithstanding this, the house seems a dreary habitation, the sweetest, the dearest creature in it, the best part of myself, having left us. May the Lord be the staff of my age, and the portion of my soul! On him, who has hitherto taken a fatherly care of me, I desire to cast my burdens, and rely for support and comfort, in the remaining part of my pilgrimage. If my dear children set their faces heavenward, and love the Lord Jesus, I think it will give me more comfort, than all the world could give without it. Be you, my dear child, an affectionate and faithful counsellor to them; spare none of them; but exercise the same solicitude for them that your dear mother has long done. Oh, that her counsels, and prayers, and tears, may not be in vain! They must be remembered sooner or later. Wishing you every support and comfort from him, who, I hope, is your heavenly Father, I am

'Your loving and afflicted parent,

'J. Miller.'

After Mr. Miller's graduation, he kept up for some time a correspondence with one of his classmates, Mr. Richard Renshaw, of which the following letter is a specimen :—

Dover, May 15th, 1790.

' My dear Friend,

'By Cæsar Rodney I received your very acceptable and friendly letter about three weeks ago; and nothing but the expectation and most ardent wish of paying a visit to Philadelphia, about this time, should have induced me to defer answering it until now. It appears, however, that in this I cannot be gratified at present, but must submit to the pain of having my social feelings wounded by an absence from you of longer duration than I am willing to admit.

'You will receive this tribute of esteem by my father, who attends the General Assembly of Clergy this year. By his return you will be furnished with such an excellent opportunity of writing me a line, that I flatter myself you will not suffer him to leave Philadelphia without furnishing him with a long letter to me.

'Your scheme of preserving the most cordial intimacy and closest connection between the members of our *memorable class*, is highly becoming and laudable, and I only regret that from present appearances I am not likely to make one of the number at the time you propose. I am truly sorry for this; but "Voluisse sat est"—that it would afford me inexpressible happiness you cannot doubt.

'Cæsar Rodney, I believe, is well. Miss Lavinia is also in good health, as you may tell your sister, Miss Nancy, to whom you will be pleased to make my most respectful compliments.

'Yours sincerely and affectionately,

'Sam'l Miller.'

To Col. McLane the father writes,

'Near Dover, August 16, 1790.

'* * The heat, with the fatigue of riding to the Cross Roads yesterday, and preaching, was rather severe; but I am not sensibly the worse of it now. But here I must stop, having an express come for me to go immediately to Dover, to lay the corner brick of the new church (as you call it) erecting there. May that glorious being, who dwelleth not in temples made with hands, give his blessing to the undertaking!'

In a letter to Mrs. McLane, dated the 6th of October, in the same year, after referring to his severe bodily disorders, and repeated illnesses, her father writes,

'The last Sabbath I went, in my feeble state, to Dover, and preached a very short sermon; but have since been the worse for it. When I shall be restored to my usual health, God only knows. I desire with patience and resignation to wait his time, praying that his grace may be sufficient for me, and made perfect in all my weakness. The period cannot be far off, when I shall be removed from my present state of existence: may the Lord grant me his sanctifying and composing presence, and conduct me safely to a better world, when my worthless services are over here!

'I should be glad to see you and Mr. McLane here, if any way consistent with your circumstances at home, and wish I could accommodate myself to the plan you propose. But, my dear child, I am in too weak a state to be left entirely without a white person with me in the house, which must be the case should Sammy go up. And as to our horse and carriage, they are now scarcely fit to go to Dover; the horse nearly blind,

5

and the carriage ready to fall to pieces. Your sister, indeed, has both, but no one about her that could be trusted with them. At present, poor child, she is bad with the ague and fever, and on many accounts so embarrassed in her situation that, if you knew all, you would greatly pity her. * *

'After receiving your last, Dr. Magaw's notes and Mr. Bend's sermon came to hand. I wish some things had been left out in the former, and more of the gospel found in the latter.'

Other letters from Mr. Miller, earlier and later in this year, contain references to frequent attacks of illness, which often interfered with preaching. and other pastoral duty. Indeed, it was quite evident that he must ere long succumb to these repeated assaults upon his health; and he himself was evidently prepared soon to put off the clay tabernacle.

Samuel Miller's diary presents just here the following entry:—

'October 31, 1790. This day I attained the *age* of *twenty-one* years. Bless the Lord, O my soul! and forget not all his benefits, in thus preserving my life and crowning me with his loving kindness and tender mercy. What reason have I more than ever to be humbled before God, that I have hitherto been so useless in the world—have so little glorified his name, or served my fellow creatures! Lord prepare me for extensive usefulness. Give me wisdom, understanding and strength to walk in all the ways of thy commandments blameless; and such activity and diligence, as to be a means of doing some good in the world.'

November 23, 1790, Mr. Miller writes to Col. McLane,

'My complicated disorders still continue obstinate, and keep me in a very languishing state. * * Polly is not fully recovered, but is much better. * * Sammy, amidst her perplexed affairs, gives her all the assistance in his power, and thereby loses much of his time, that otherwise would be employed in his studies. But it is his duty, and he seems very ready in attending on it.'

Mr. John Miller's letters are written in a small, close, neat, and easily legible hand, with unusual accuracy as to punctuation and all grammatical rules. Only those to Col. and Mrs. McLane, from 1787 to the time of his death —indeed probably not all these—have been preserved.

It was amidst the circumstances of family trial and affliction which the foregoing letters disclose, that Samuel pursued at home, for more than two years, his theological studies. Probably he was the only white person with his father, until the death of the latter, during most of the time—about a twelve month—after his brother James went to the University. What with his father's infirmities, Mrs. Loockerman's troubles, and the assistance he may naturally have been called upon to render, as to the business of both farm and congregation, it is likely that his scholastic pursuits were often interrupted. Yet the habits of diligence brought with him from college doubtless fitted him to struggle with many difficulties. In the school which the Master had chosen for him, and in circumstances to which he was providentially shut up, he was studying divinity, practical as well as theoretical. No doubt he learned much from the duties and trials of such a home, which he could not well have learned so profitably elsewhere. Great as the advantages are of a public seminary, all will admit that in a pastor's domicil some branches of theology may best be studied. And in the house of an aged father, struggling with poverty, infirmity and multiplied afflictions added to his pastoral burdens, a son especially might receive lessons, otherwise hardly to be obtained, of submissive patience and self-denial, of elevated, unearthly, Christian hope, of perseverance to the end, of all which that father's experience could make known, or his condition, example and practical instructions suggest.

In the son's diary are found the following records:—

'April 12, 1791. Supremely great and infinitely glorious Jehovah! who art worthy to receive worship, and honor, and glory from all thine intelligent creatures on earth and in heaven; unto thee I desire to present myself, at this time, with reverence and holy fear, knowing that thou searchest the thoughts and intents of the heart.

'I confess and bewail, O Lord, the aggravation of my apostacy, the pollution of my original, and the exceeding vileness of my nature. My heart is corrupt, hard and rebellious: it is deceitful above all things and desperately wicked. My life has been contrary to thy will; I have transgressed thy holy and reasonable commandments times and ways without number; and deserved, long ago, to be cut off from every hope, and banished from thy presence and glory forever.

'But blessed be thy name, that thou hast contrived a way for our recovery from this fallen state. Blessed be thy name, that those who come unto thee, through Jesus Christ, thou wilt in no wise cast out; but will take them into covenant with thee, and wilt be their God and Father, and make them thy happy children.

'I desire, with an affecting sense of this thine infinite condescension, to renew my own covenant engagements to thee, and to consecrate myself and all my active powers to thy service. I beseech thee, O Lord, to accept of me in this transaction, and to ratify in heaven what I now wish to perform, with humility and love, upon earth.

'I trust I desire with sincerity, this day, to renounce all other lords who have had dominion over me; to renounce the corrupt affections and deceitful lusts which have hitherto led me astray from thee; and to renounce, with a holy indignation and disdain, all those vain pursuits which are inconsistent with godliness, and oppose the progress of the divine life in my soul.

'I desire solemnly and sincerely to yield myself a living sacrifice, holy and acceptable unto thee, which is my most reasonable service. May I be, henceforward, entirely thine; may I live unto thy honor and glory, while my life is mercifully spared; and employ, with diligence, all my active powers in promoting the great end for which I was sent into the world. Fill me, O my God! with an ardent desire, and an humble resolution, to continue thine through all the endless ages of eternity. To thy direction and righteous disposal I wish to resign myself and all I possess. Do with me as seemeth good in thy sight; and conduct me henceforth in such a manner as to make me most subservient to the great purposes of thy glory.

'But, Lord, without thee I can do nothing: the best resolutions are of no avail without the assistance and the sanctifying influences of thy Spirit. Leave me not, nor forsake me, thou God of my salvation! Grant me thy special grace at all times. Keep me from falling by the right hand of thy power. Guide me by thy counsel, I entreat thee. Preserve me from all sin. Save me from grieving the Holy Spirit. Grant me the light of thy countenance and the joy of thy salvation, in life, at death, and through eternity. May I be steadfast, immovable, always abounding in the work of the Lord.

'And, O thou God, in whose hands are the spirits of all flesh, may I never be weary in well-doing, knowing that in due season I shall reap if I faint not. And finally, may an abundant entrance be administered to me into the everlasting kingdom of my Lord and Saviour, in whose name I now address thee; and to whom, with thee, O Father, and the Holy Spirit, be everlasting praises.   Amen.'

"April 19th, 1791.   This day, agreeably to a design formed some time since, I presented myself to the Presbytery of Lewes, met at Wicomico, in Somerset county, Maryland.   After an examination respecting my experimental acquaintance with religion, and my views in seeking the holy ministry, the Presbytery declared themselves fully satisfied, and agreed unanimously to receive me on trials.   After this I was examined on the Latin and Greek languages, and preached a homily to the Presbytery on 1 Corinthians 15, 22; of all which performances they were pleased to express their approbation.

The minutes of Presbytery mention the place of meeting as *Rockawakin*, dating the commencement of its session on the 19th, and Mr. Miller's reception on the 20th of April. His father was not able to attend this or, apparently, any subsequent, meeting.

'June 21, 1791.   This day I presented myself a second time to the Presbytery of Lewes, which met at Fishing Creek, near Cambridge, in Maryland, and proceeded on my trials.   Agreeably to their appointment I read two exercises, one a lecture on Luke 10, 30–38; the other an exegesis on this question—"*An Jesus post mortem ejus in infernum descendit?*"   Both were by the Presbytery approved.   I was also examined on Rhetoric and Logic, and this part of my trials was entered on the record "approved." '

'O my God, whose I am and whom I am bound to serve, I entreat thee, as I advance in this pursuit, and whilst I am endeavoring to prepare myself to serve thee in the ministry of reconciliation, be pleased to add thy blessing to the whole.   Oh grant me that "preparation of the heart," and that "answer of the tongue," which thou alone art able to give.   O Lord, suffer me not to undertake to dispense the bread of life to others, in Christ's name, without being fed and nourished by it myself; without knowing, experimentally, "what I say and whereof I affirm." '

'July 22d, 1791.   This morning, [Friday,] about 1 o'clock, my dear, honored and venerable father departed this life in the sixty-ninth year of his age, after an illness of about eleven days.

'He had been in a weak, infirm state of health for more than a year before, and had been, for a month or two previously, indisposed with a large and painful *anthrax* on his back, but which was nearly well when he was seized with the dysentery, a complaint very prevalent and considerably mortal in the neighborhood at that time. The power of the disease was so great as to deprive him of his speech entirely for twenty-four hours, at least, before he expired, and to induce such a lethargy as could by no means be overcome. This prevented our receiving his dying counsels and testimonies, which we earnestly desired; yet we have unspeakable reason to be thankful, that his long, exemplary and uniform life of piety and evangelical labor left no one in the least doubt of his happy change. It was on our own account, and not his, that we desired to receive those counsels and testimonies.

'May all his relatives, and especially we his children, be suitably impressed with this melancholy event, and be enabled to make a suitable improvement of it. May we imitate the bright example which was set before us, in the various departments of duty, by this our pious and excellent parent. May we all endeavor to follow him as he followed Christ. May we never sully his unblemished reputation by irreligious or dishonorable conduct. But may we all prove worthy of such a father.'

At the father's death, Mrs. McLane was living in Philadelphia, and Mrs. Loockerman where she had lived with her husband; Joseph was practising Law, and Edward Medicine, at Dover, but possibly lodging at the homestead, where Samuel certainly was; and where, two months later, he was joined by James, just graduated at the University. As yet the brothers were all of them struggling with fortune; but closely united as they were with one another, as also with their sisters, in the warmest and most disinterested affection, each seemed to feel that his brother's success was his own; and they were constantly interchanging offices of the tenderest kindness. This happy result of a Christian training secured the completion of the father's plans for the liberal education of his sons, and the more ready and successful progress of all in their several pursuits. Especially the younger were assisted by the older; and the ties of family affection were thus drawn constantly closer, to be relaxed only by the hand of death.

Samuel, in a devotional spirit, was now assiduously pursuing his theological studies.

2. LICENSURE.

'September 22, 1791. This day I set apart for fasting and extraordinary prayer, to renew my solicitations at the throne of grace for the blessing and assistance of heaven in pursuing my theological studies; in going on to prepare myself for the various important duties of a minister of the gospel and an ambassador of Christ; and, especially, to implore the Giver of all grace, to grant me his presence and blessing at the approaching session of Presbytery; when, with his permission, I expect to undergo a third examination, and possibly may be *licensed.*   *   *'

'October 13th, 1791. The Presbytery of Lewes met in Dover yesterday. I then delivered the popular sermon which I had been directed to prepare from Romans 8, 14. After undergoing a long and strict examination on college studies and especially on Theology, I was this day licensed to preach the Gospel.

'Oh, the solemnity of this transaction! To be a public teacher of the way of salvation! Who is sufficient for these things? O thou, with whom is the Spirit, vouchsafe to grant me thine enlightening, sanctifying and strengthening grace. Deliver me from vain glory and self-dependence. Help me to walk humbly with God, and daily to grow in conformity with thine image, and in preparation for thy service.'

The Rev. Luther Halsey, D.D., in a communication to the New York Observer, in 1836, said, "We differ from other Presbyterian churches in so adopting these formulas" —the Confession and Catechisms—"that ONLY THE ESSENTIAL OR FUNDAMENTAL DOCTRINES shall be the test of ministerial and Christian fellowship." To support this assertion, he alleged, among other things, that "The Rev. Dr. Miller of Princeton was admitted notwithstanding his objections to the Confession, Chap. xxiv."

Replying, in a letter dated Princeton, March 16, 1836, to this allegation, Dr. Miller made the statement which follows.

"When I was licensed by the Presbytery of Lewes, between forty and fifty years ago, just before standing up to make the profession and engagement required of candidates for license, I informed the Presbytery, that the only article in the Confession of Faith concerning which I had the smallest doubt, was a short clause in the fourth section of the 24th chapter, which treats of "Marriage and Divorce." The clause was this: "The man may not marry any of his [deceased] wife's kindred nearer in blood than he may of his own, etc." I had happened, a few weeks before, to listen to a discussion of the question, whether a man might lawfully marry the sister of his deceased wife;

and my mind was brought into a state of doubt on the subject. Of this I thought it my duty candidly to inform the Presbytery, assuring them, that I could heartily adopt every other article of the Confession. They *unanimously* concluded that this doubt was no valid obstacle to my subscribing in the usual form, which I accordingly did, and was forthwith licensed.

"Soon afterwards my doubts were removed, and I became satisfied that the Confession of Faith, in relation to the matter in question, took the wisest, safest, and most Scriptural ground. For a number of years before I ceased to be a pastor, I thought it my duty to decline sanctioning any matrimonial connexion condemned by the clause referred to, and to set my face in every proper way against it.

"It has given me, I confess, some pain to be held up to view as objecting to a *whole chapter* of the Confession of Faith, without discrimination ; and to have the impression probably made and left on the readers of Dr. Halsey's letter, that I still adhered to objections, or rather doubts, which I entirely dismissed many years ago. Besides, if I do not altogether mistake, that respected Brother was distinctly informed, seven or eight years since, when it was proposed to expunge the clause in question from the Confession of Faith, that I objected to the proposal, and was earnestly desirous that the clause should be retained."

The idea of presbyterial authority and control which prevailed at that time in the Presbyterian Church is well illustrated by the action of the Presbytery of Lewes, from time to time, in regard to Mr. Miller as their licentiate.

'Mr. Miller was appointed to supply at Dover the 4th Sabbath of October, and the next Sabbath day at Duck Creek Cross Roads; the 1st Sabbath of November at Dover, and the next Sabbath at Duck Creek; and the remainder of his time at discretion until our Spring meeting of Presbytery. * *

'Mr. Samuel Miller, having asked leave of absence for some time from the bounds of the Presbytery, before our next session, obtained his request.'[1]

In a letter of the 9th of November to Edward Miller, Col. McLane writes,

'Brother Samuel appeared in Market street meeting last Sunday afternoon, and gave pleasing sensations to his friends. I believe he is allowed by most to offer well. I hope the dear youth may have the needful graces for the sacred office plentifully given him by his Master.'

[1] Min. of Presb. of Lewes, 150.

3. Dr. Nisbet.

The permission obtained from Presbytery prepared the way for Mr. Miller's enjoying, for a few months, the instructions of a distinguished scholar and theologian, whom he held, ever afterwards, in grateful and admiring remembrance, and whose biography, almost fifty years later, he wrote under the impulse of a sort of filial affection. This was Charles Nisbet, D. D., first Principal of Dickinson College—a Scotch clergyman, whose early fame for talent, power of utterance in both public and private, wit and erudition, had crossed the Atlantic, and induced the founders of the college mentioned to call him unanimously to the head of that infant institution. An ardent friend of the American colonies in their struggle against oppression, and a warm admirer of the republican government established in this country upon the ruins of kingly power, he had accepted the call, and, coming to the United States, had settled himself at Carlisle in 1785.

Mr. Miller, after fulfilling his presbyterial appointments to preach at Dover and Duck Creek, on the first and second Sabbaths, the 6th and 13th, of November, seems to have hastened at once to put himself, in his theological studies, under Dr. Nisbet's direction. The following account he has himself given, in the Life of his revered preceptor, of the winter spent thus at Carlisle.

"It was in the Autumn of the year 1791, that the acquaintance of the author of this memoir with the venerable subject of it commenced. The author had, anterior to this, pursued his theological studies under the direction of a beloved and venerated parent, near Dover, in Delaware, his native place. On the decease of that parent, who had been the pastor of the Presbyterian church in Dover for nearly half a century, and after having received license to preach the Gospel, he determined to avail himself, for at least a few months, of the conversation and guidance of the distinguished man, whose learning, and whose course of theological lectures, had received so large a share of public approbation. For this purpose, in the month of November of the year above mentioned, he repaired to Carlisle, and found Dr. Nisbet in good health and spirits, and busily engaged in his labours as the head of Dickinson College, the winter session of which had, a few weeks before, commenced.

" He had never until then seen the eminent man whose instructions he sought. He expected· to find so much learning connected with reserved and formal, if not repulsive, manners; but was agreeably surprised to find Dr. Nisbet as affable, as easy of access, as simple and unostentatious in his manners, and as attractive in all the intercourse of social life, as any man he had ever seen. He received the inexperienced young licentiate with all the condescension and kindness of a parent; and, after the first hour, placed him as much at his ease, as if he had been hanging on the lips of that parent according to the flesh, whose loss he had recently been called to mourn.

"Such were the habits and manners of this venerable man, and also of his amiable family, that the writer, from the first day of his arrival in Carlisle, felt himself at home in his presence. His practice, in ordinary cases, was regularly, every evening, to sit with him in his domestic circle two or three hours. And on whatever subject he might desire information, whether in Theology or Literature, ancient or modern, he had but to propose the topic, and suggest queries, to draw forth everything that he wished. Nor were Dr. Nisbet's instructive communications of that declaiming or preaching kind which some learned men are fond of exhibiting, but which can scarcely with propriety be called "conversation," since they are all on one side. They presented a constant flow of rich amusement and information, and yet so entirely free from ostentation, dogmatism, or pedantry, that every listener was at once instructed, entertained and gratified. Probably no man on this side of the Atlantic ever brought into the social circle such diversified and ample stores of erudition;—such an extraordinary knowledge of men, and books, and opinions; such an amazing fund of rare and racy anecdotes; and all poured out with so much unstudied simplicity, with such constant flashes of wit and humour, and with such a peculiar mixture of satire and good nature, as kept every company, whether young or old, hanging upon his lips, and doing constant homage to his wonderful acquirements.

"Sometimes, when in the midst of these delightful effusions, a new visitor would step in, and introduce a new topic of discourse, it was wonderful with what facility he could change the train of conversation; strike upon a new and rich vein of thought; and excite new and endless surprise by his intellectual resources. And if any member of the circle attempted to enter the lists with him as a competitor in either wit or learning, as was sometimes the case with those who did not "know their man," he soon manifested, with perfect good humour, with what entire ease he could distance every one on either track. Of scenes of this kind, the writer of this memoir has been so often a witness, that he cannot call them to mind at the present hour without mixed feelings of surprise and admiration.

"He was led, too, in consequence of the strong impressions then made by the instructions of the living teacher, to doubt whether the popular estimate of the means of knowledge anterior to the discovery of the art of printing, is not, in some measure, both inadequate and incorrect. * * It is certain that the writer of this memoir, when he left Carlisle, in the spring of 1792, carried with him a deeper impression than he ever had before, of the immense advantage to be derived from coming into contact daily with an acute, active and richly furnished mind, from which as much might be learned in one hour, (especially on subjects concerning which books rare and difficult of access are the only sources of instruction from reading,) as from the private study of a week. He left it also with no small regret that he had not derived from the enjoyment of this privilege more ample benefit; and a conviction, that if he had been more aware of its value at the time, and more awake to its importance, it might have been far more productive of fruit than it was. Alas! it was with him, as with most others, that the most precious advantages are seldom adequately appreciated until the possession of them is withdrawn."

"The compiler of this volume has never seen a man so well adapted to benefit those around him, in these respects, as Dr. Nisbet. The rapidity and force of his mind in conversation; the preëminent richness of his mental furniture; his vivacity; his wit; his inexhaustible store of striking anecdotes and of happy classical allusions, rendered him at all times a most instructive and entertaining companion; and served more indelibly to impress upon the mind what came from his lips than from those of almost any other man.

"The writer was not so happy as to enjoy the privilege of hearing any part of Dr. Nisbet's course of theological lectures. Their delivery had been completed ten months before he took up his temporary abode in Carlisle; and they were never repeated to a second class. A number of individual students, indeed, from time to time, resorted to him for direction in their studies; but the regular formation of a theological class was never again accomplished. The reasons for this reflected little credit on the youthful candidates for the ministry at that time. Some were discouraged by the prospect of a course of study, which was to extend to between two and three years! This seemed a long time to those who imagined that an adequate course of theological instruction might be brought within a much shorter compass and whose parents, still more impatient, could not be persuaded that such a long, and, as they thought, tedious training could be necessary to prepare candidates for the ministry for their work. They saw some other denominations, with none of these advantages, and indeed with scarcely any study, sending forth scores of popular men; and hastily supposed that so much protracted labor in preparing for the ministry could not be needful.

"It was understood, too, that the requisition of the learned and venerable lecturer, that every member of his theological class should commit to writing the whole of each lecture, as it fell from his lips, was regarded with aversion, and seemed a drudgery too severe to be pursued through several years. This requisition would never have been made in other circumstances. But the lecturer well knew that books were extremely scarce, especially in the western parts of our country; and that, therefore, the possession of a complete system of theology, prepared with great care, would be a treasure of permanent and peculiar value. Even this, however, was not properly appreciated by short-sighted young men, and still more short-sighted parents. On these accounts, a second class was never formed; and, although the lectures in question were copied by several theological students, who had not the privilege of hearing them delivered, and were read in manuscript by a number of the neighboring divines, they were never again repeated in public."[1]

With Dr. Nisbet Mr. Miller thus formed an intimacy, "which was a source of great pleasure, not only to himself, but to those to whom he imparted his cherished recollections, as long as he lived."[2] He often talked, with evident zest, of his venerable teacher, representing him as a man of prodigious literary and theological acquirements, most ready wit, with some oddity, and unusual powers of thought and verbal expression as an extemporaneous preacher. No doubt the honored preceptor left more than one visible mark upon the mind and habits of his fondly appreciative pupil.

[1] Pp. 210–216.   [2] 3 Sprague's Annals, 600.

CHAPTER FOURTH.

THE LICENTIATE.

1792.

1. SEEKING A SETTLEMENT.

MR. MILLER remained in Carlisle until the beginning of
March, when he set out to visit a vacant church on Long
Island, to which he had been invited as a candidate. In
New York City, however, calling on Dr. Rodgers, his
father's former friend, previously settled at St. George's,
Delaware, he was prevailed upon to tarry two weeks and
preach repeatedly.

Here he first met the venerable John H. Livingston, D.
D., of whom long afterwards he wrote,

"My acquaintance with Dr. Livingston began when he was
far advanced in life, and when I was, I had almost said, in my
clerical boyhood. On my first visit to New York, in 1792, my
friend, and my father's friend, and soon afterwards my colleague, the Rev. Dr. Rodgers, (whose name I can never mention, without associating with it some epithet of honor, and
some emotion of filial affection,) introduced me to him as one
whose acquaintance and friendship he deemed particularly
worth cultivating. At my first interview with him, I was
struck with his venerable and commanding figure; his truly
gentlemanly deportment; his condescending kindness to the
young and inexperienced; his instructive conversation; his unusual familiarity with everything relating to biblical and theological inquiries; his deep spirituality; and his evident disposition to encourage youthful candidates for the sacred office."[1]

Returning to Delaware, Mr. Miller there remained,
preaching at Dover and Duck Creek until the beginning of
June. Meanwhile, the impression he had made in New

[1] Gunn's Memoirs of Dr. Livingston, 512.

York had induced an effort there to secure from him another visit.[1] The Presbytery of Lewes met at Broad Creek, now Laurel, April 17th, and was opened with a sermon, from John vi. 35, by Mr. Miller, who reported his fulfilment of the Presbyterial appointments of the previous fall. The minutes of this session contain the following entries :—

'A call was delivered in to Presbytery from the congregation of Dover for Mr. Samuel Miller, to take the pastoral charge of said congregation, which call was put into the hands of Mr. Miller for consideration.

'Mr. Miller was appointed to supply at Dover and Duck Creek alternately until the 1st of June next; from which time, until our Fall meeting, he was allowed, at his discretion to visit the United Presbyterian Congregations in New York, at their earnest request by them signified to us.'[2]

These appointments for Delaware were to the letter fulfilled. Doubtless, Mr. Miller had signified his acceptance of the flattering invitation from New York, and early in June he went thither, proposing to spend a little time there, and afterwards journey onwards into New England, where he intended to visit numerous relations, known, hitherto, only, or chiefly, through the correspondence which had been kept up with the Delaware family. Reaching New York about the 10th of June, he remained in that city a month, preaching again every Sabbath and with continued acceptance. While thus engaged, he procured from his friend,

[1] At a meeting of the Trustees, the Elders, and Deacons of the First Presbyterian Church, on Wednesday the 28th day of March, 1792.

'Whereas Mr. Samuel Miller, a licentiate from Dover in the State of Delaware, has lately preached sundry Sermons to the United Presbyterian Congregations in this city : and whereas it appears to us that his performances have met with such a degree of approbation, by the hearers at large, that they are generally desirous to receive another visit from him :

'Thereupon *Resolved* unanimously, that the said Mr. Samuel Miller be requested to make another visit to the United Presbyterian Congregations aforesaid, as soon as he is discharged from all previous engagements after the first of June next; and the Trustees do hereby engage to make him a reasonable compensation for the services he may render the Church aforesaid in his ministerial capacity :

'Ordered that Doctor Rodgers and Doctor McKnight be requested to take the earliest opportunity to communicate to Mr. Samuel Miller the aforesaid resolution and request.

'By order of the meeting,
'New York, March 28th, 1792.   Jno. Broom, Chairman.
'Test. David Cation, Clerk.'

[2] Min. of Presb. of Lewes, 151, 2.

Dr. Green, then colleague of Dr. Sproat in the Second Church of Philadelphia, the following letter of introduction to the Rev. Jedediah Morse, [1] of Charlestown, Massachusetts.

'Philadelphia, June 19, 1792.

'Rev. & dear Sir,

'The bearer of this letter is a young clergyman, who visits your country, for the purpose of improvement and to see his friends. I can unreservedly recommend him to your notice and friendly attention. He will probably please both you and your people as a preacher, and in his personal qualities you will find him modest, amiable and, I trust, truly pious. He is a young gentleman for whom I have a sincere affection, and any attentions you may show him, I shall accept as done to myself. He has not long been licensed; but he preaches memoriter and has a handsome address in the pulpit.'

Leaving New York about the 10th of July, Mr. Miller proceeded on his way to New England, embarking, with his horse and sulky, on board a packet bound to Newport, Rhode Island. Thence, in the sulky, he set out on a leisurely tour through the Eastern States, which occupied his time until the end of September. What places and persons he visited, besides Charlestown and Mr. Morse, cannot now be determined. Old memoranda, prepared, perhaps, for this very tour, mention families of the name of Bass at Boston, Newburyport and Portsmouth; of Phillips at Boston; and of Henshaw at Shrewsbury and Leicester, Massachusetts, New Hartford and Middletown, Connecticut. But at such "a great rate" had the descendants of John Alden and Samuel Bass increased, that these were probably but a small part of the relatives, with whom Mr. Miller became acquainted, in the course of his New England pilgrimage.

2. CALLS TO NEW YORK AND DOVER.

While the young licentiate was rambling over the Eastern States, the United Congregations in New York were making arrangements to secure, permanently, his ministerial services. On the 29th of August they ordered a formal call to be made out, as appears from the following extract from their session-book.

[1] D.D. from 1795. See 2 Sprague's Annals, 247.

'Agreeably to a resolve of the Session, at their last meeting, and notice given accordingly to the congregation, a very numerous and respectable meeting of the congregation was had in the New Church on Wednesday evening last; when it was unanimously agreed that a call should be prepared for Mr. Samuel Miller, to be signed by the Session, Trustees and Deacons, on the behalf of the Congregation; and that the sum of three hundred pounds be proposed as his present yearly salary, to be augmented as circumstances may require, at the discretion of the congregation. Dr. Rodgers presided in the conducting the business, and Dr. McKnight officiated as clerk.'

It seems not to have been the custom, at this early date, to distract a church with a dozen, or even half a dozen, candidates on trial all together, as a preliminary to the delicate business of uniting them upon a single one. It was, doubtless, thought wiser to decide, formally or informally, upon the merits of each after he had been thoroughly tried; and, if Mr. Miller had not the honor of being selected from a long list of aspirants, he was, at least, spared the pain of finding a minority opposed to him, and the trouble of reconciling parties in a divided church. "He has been heard to remark, that he had never, at that time, aspired to anything beyond an ordinary country charge; and that nothing could have surprised him more than that he should have been thought of for such a public and important sphere of labour."[1]

Early in October Mr. Miller returned to Delaware, whence he addressed the following letter to his new acquaintance, Mr. Morse:—

'Dover, October 4, 1792.

' Rev. & dear Sir,

' I reached home on Tuesday last [2d] after a leisurely and highly agreeable journey, from Boston to Dover, of four weeks. I was much entertained and pleased with the inhabitants of the country, as I passed through Massachusetts and Connecticut. Upon the whole, I felicitate myself exceedingly on having taken such a ride at this time of life.

' I embrace the first opportunity of sending the Constitution of Delaware, which was lately formed. I fear it will arrive too late; but it was impossible for me to send it sooner. You will see that, like all other human productions, it has some faults.

' Be pleased to make my best compliments to Mrs. Morse, and to all others in Boston who may inquire for me; especially

[1] 3 Sprague's Annals, 600.

to the clergy who honored me with their acquaintance and attention.

'With sentiments of the highest respect and esteem,
'I am, Sir, your obedient and humble servant,
'Samuel Miller.'

After his return, Mr. Miller seems to have resumed his labors in the churches of Dover and Duck Creek for a few weeks. If the call to New York was a strong testimony to the promise of his early preaching; that from the congregations which his father had so long served, and in the midst of which he had been brought up, was a testimony still stronger to his irreproachable life. His diary at this time discloses the state of his mind in regard to these conflicting calls.

'November 15, 1792. I have set apart this day for fasting and special prayer—among other important purposes, to ask divine direction in the following affair.

'The Presbytery of Lewes I expect will meet next week, when there is a probability that a call from the United Presbyterian Congregations of New York will be put into my hands. There is a call already before me from the church in Dover * * unanimous and very affectionate in its character; but which of them I ought to accept is the question—the solemn question—which requires serious and prayerful deliberation. For direction in the case, I would this day solemnly address the throne of grace.

'I confess myself to be rather inclined to favor the application from New York; and I hope for reasons which will stand the test of Christian examination. But my deceitful heart may lead me astray. O my God enlighten and guide me! If I know my own heart, I desire to go where I may, most effectually, by thy grace, promote the glory of God and the good of my fellow-men.

The following extracts from the Minutes of Lewes Presbytery carry forward the history of this affair.

'Broad Creek, Nov. 20, 1792.
'A *pro re nata* presbytery having been regularly called by the moderator, for the purpose of furnishing an opportunity to the United Presbyterian Congregations of New York of offering a call to Mr. Samuel Miller, our licentiate, to be their pastor, met, etc. * *.

'The Presbytery put said call into the hands of Mr. Miller for his consideration. * * The moderator asked Mr. Miller, "Do you accept the call from the United Congregations of New York or not?" Mr. Miller answered, "I do accept the call from New York, and consequently give up the call which I have in my possession from Dover."

'Mr. Miller then asked a dismission from the Presbytery of Lewes, that he might join the Presbytery of New York; upon which Presbytery did dismiss Mr. Miller, and he is hereby dismissed, with the following recommendation.

'The Presbytery of Lewes received Mr. Samuel Miller with a fair character and the best recommendations. He has preached in our bounds and under our direction to the general acceptance of those who heard him. It affords us pleasure to testify that his moral and religious conversation has been unexceptionable. We dismiss him with regret, believing him to be of promising talents, and likely to be of use in the churches of Christ with us. We commit him to the holy keeping of God, and pray that he, the Presbytery, and the Congregations in which he may labor, may have mutual comfort and advantage.'[1]

Upon the same day Mr. Miller wrote in his diary,

'O Lord, may it please thee to add thy blessing to the decision which I have made this day! I have endeavored, as I hope, to decide in thy fear. May the step which I have taken be made to promote thy glory, and the good of that great cause which I hope I love!'

3. FAREWELL TO DELAWARE.

Soon after this, at the close of a Sabbath morning service in the church at Dover, Mr. Miller delivered the following valedictory address. The new house of worship to which it refers, a tradition upon the spot declares to have been erected to secure his settlement, which is not impossible. His father, indeed, as we have seen, laid the 'corner brick,'[2] but not before his son had commenced his studies for the ministry.

'As I have accepted a call to settle in the City of New York, and design, with the permission of Providence, to set out for that place to-morrow, it is not probable I shall preach here again for a considerable time. * *

'In taking leave of the County, I feel all that painful regret which departure from my native place, added to many other

1 Pp. 154, 5.

2 See p. 49.

considerations, is calculated to inspire. To bid adieu to a place in which my earliest and strongest attachments are fixed, and to which I am bound by numberless and endearing ties, is indeed a melancholy task, which I undertake with peculiar reluctance.

'But there is an aditional source of regret, which occupies and affects my mind. The particular regard which I feel for this congregation, and my anxious concern for its various interests, give rise to many painful emotions, in reflecting on the distant removal that is before me. When you call to mind that my dear and ever honored father sustained the pastoral relation to this church for more than forty years; and that its welfare was an object of his constant pursuit and unwearied labor ; you may easily conclude that his sons's heart is deeply engaged, and his highest solicitude excited, for its prosperity and happiness. The tender recollection also, that near these walls lie the remains of both my beloved parents, and three brothers, attaches me to this little spot in a manner which I cannot express, and renders the prospect of a separation from it truly distressing.

'But these, my friends, however interesting, are not the only considerations which bind me to this society. Gratitude demands, that I should make farther acknowledgments, and call to mind some of the numerous favors which I have received at your hands. Disposed to overlook my youthful imperfections, you have received my public ministrations with kindness and candor, and have attended on my feeble labors with a degree of indulgence which I had little reason to claim. The unanimous and affectionate manner in which you invited me to take the pastoral charge of your church, the uniform friendship and attention which I have experienced from you ; and the many testimonies of regard and attachment with which I have been favored ;—all these form a weight of obligation on me, which I not only sensibly feel, but also wish for an opportunity of expressing in a suitable manner. For thus affectionately taking a youth by the hand, on his first entrance into the world, may God reward you ! I beg you to accept of my grateful acknowledgments, and to be assured that I shall always feel a deep and lively impression of these favors.

'From a society to which I am thus tenderly attached, and under such high obligations, it is unnecessary to say again, that I depart with peculiar reluctance and sorrow. Nothing but the fullest conviction that duty, and the voice of Providence, call me to another quarter of the Christian vineyard, would induce me to violate so many of my tenderest feelings, and surmount so many difficulties as oppose the decision I have made. In doing this, I engage indeed in an arduous task, and enter on a situation rather too responsible for my youth and inexperience. But I rely for assistance and direction on the same great Hand, by whose beneficence I have been hitherto preserved.

'In bidding you adieu, I indulge the most flattering hopes of your prosperity and welfare. Your active and exemplary zeal in erecting a church; your diligent exertions to establish the worship of God regularly among you; and your care to revive the congregation and watch over its various interests, have amply deserved, and have doubtless received, the applause of every friend of religion. I feel the highest confidence that these exertions will continue and increase; and that, through the blessing of the great Head of the Church, you will grow in respectability and flourish more than ever. I trust that a merciful and gracious God will not suffer such favorable prospects to prove abortive; but that he will make you the objects of his peculiar care, and refresh you with the liberal effusions of his Holy Spirit! I fervently pray, that he may speedily give you a pastor after his own heart, in connection with whom you may enjoy the highest advantage, and the most uninterrupted comfort. I pray that all your interests may be precious in his sight, and that by his continual blessing you may speedily become a holy and a happy church!

'Should my life be spared, it will afford me great pleasure to return frequently, and in person to witness and partake of your happiness. But, however this may be, I shall always retain an affectionate and grateful remembrance of you; and preserve unalterable that attachment which has so long influenced my mind. And though we be scattered over the world, by that God who knows what is best for us, yet I hope that through the merit of the only Saviour, we shall at last meet in heaven, and be happy forever more.

'Under the influence of these comforting sentiments, my beloved friends, I bid you farewell! May grace, mercy and peace be multiplied unto you! May the blessing of God Almighty, the Father, the Son, and the Holy Spirit, be and remain with you all, both now and forever. Amen!'

The foregoing address, whatever defects may be discovered in it, and considerately attributed to the immaturity of twenty-three, presents, in a remarkable degree, some of the most prominent characteristics of Mr. Miller's mind and manners in even his riper years. It seems to prove, that, for the more striking results of literary and social culture, he was indebted almost wholly to the influences exerted upon him before he left Delaware; not to those of his after residence in New York. As there appears to have been nothing remarkable in his distinguished preceptor, Dr. Nisbet, as to external polish or elegance, it must have been in his parents, or one of them, or in some other person with whom he had frequent intercourse, during his home, or collegiate studies, that he found the model of courtesy, refinement, and Christian regard to the feelings of others, which he seemed to keep ever afterwards before him. With the biographer it has been a conviction, growing constantly as his work has advanced, and perhaps already participated in by the reader, who has shared in most of the evidence on which it rests, that it was in that retired, rural, Delaware home, that Mr. Miller laid the foundation of every accomplishment, which particularly characterized his subsequent life; and, if so, the fact is but one proof among many of the power of early home influences. To John Dickinson, his father's intimate friend, allusion has already been made. His example may have exerted no small influence upon the family at the parsonage, which he doubtless not unfrequently visited. Of him Dr. Samuel Miller wrote to the Hon. Gulian C. Verplanck, on the 31st of August, 1814,

'I have often heard * * that Mr. Dickinson's first appearance at the bar was attractive and interesting in the highest degree; and that, as long as he continued to practice his profession, he was pre-eminently popular * *

'[He] was *the most polished man I ever saw.* His face was remarkably indicative of refinement and cultivation. His whole person was peculiarly elegant. He had more the appearance of a man of rank—a nobleman, (if you please,) than almost any other man that it has fallen to my lot to know. His voice was singularly sweet. His manners were unusually graceful. His animal spirits were always excellent; and his conversation more rich, various, delicate, entertaining and full of vivacity, than that of one man in a million. In the drawing-room, and especially in female company, he was pre-eminently splendid and captivating.

'Mr. Edmund Burke, in the course of a debate on American affairs, at the commencement of the Revolutionary War, having occasion to mention him, said, "I have the pleasure of knowing Mr. Dickinson, and he is one of the most elegant and accomplished men I ever saw."

'Mr. Dickinson was bred a Quaker. During his public life he pretty much threw off the dress and language which distinguish that sect. But after his retirement to private life in Wilmington, (which took place about the year 1788,) he returned again to the habits of Friends; and, though he never lost his elegance of manners, he was ever after, as far as such a man could be, a plain Quaker.

'Mr. Dickinson was, undoubtedly, a man of great talents of a particular kind; as, I think, his writings testify. He was also very industrious, a great reader, and of an active mind. All that my female friend says, in her eulogium, of his *religious* character, of his *benevolence*, of his uniform *exemplariness and dignity*, of his remarkably rigid *temperance*, etc., may be considered as entirely correct.

'Mr. Dickinson was probably the most opulent individual residing in the State of Delaware. I take for granted his property could not have been less than $300,000 or $400,000. He was, on great occasions, munificent to a degree worthy of himself. He was the principal benefactor of Dickinson College, in Carlisle, Pennsylvania, on which account that Seminary bears his name. He was also a large contributor to other public institutions.

'Mr. Dickinson was a *timid* politician. I have understood that, on the Day of the Declaration of Independence, in 1776, he was not in his seat in Congress. Dr. Ramsay, I think, gives some account of his conduct on that occasion. On Governor McKean's announcing the event to him, he said, "I wish I had your nerve." "I wish, my Friend," replied the Governor, "you had even half of it."'

When, exactly, Mr. Miller left Delaware, is uncertain, but he did not reach New York until early in January. It is probable that he spent some little time upon the way thither—most of it, doubtless, with his friends in Philadelphia. What he was, at this time, in personal appearance, manners, literary and theological culture and pulpit power—must be gathered, mainly, from the foregoing narrative. Says a friend, 'I have heard the late Judge Fisher, of Dover, speak of the great change in Dr. Miller's style of preaching, after he' left 'the Presbyterian church of Dover; and deplore his transition from the vehement and fervid, to the deliberate, mode of speaking.'

CHAPTER FIFTH.

1749–1792.

1. A PILGRIMAGE.

There is often a strange inconsistency between, not only our conscientious convictions, but even our heart feelings, and our practice. Dr. Miller evidently cherished, to the last, a strong attachment to his native state, his native county, his old church home in Dover, and his rustic family home. From his frequent and marked expression of this attachment, all his children imbibed a real affection for the scenes of his boyhood. Yet he seldom visited Delaware, and had, even in middle life, apparently, given up all idea of refreshing his recollections by occasional returns thither; while several of his children knew nothing, before his death, of that early home, or its surroundings, excepting what they had heard from his lips. This was no doubt due, in part, to mere *vis inertiæ;* but also, in part, to the speedy breaking up, and almost total disappearance of the Delaware family—its entire disappearance, in fact, from Kent County, and all the scenes with which it had once been associated. Dr. Miller survived the last of his brothers and sisters full thirty-two years; and his sister Mary, who remained longest in the State, died in 1801. Besides, as he often remarked, the old families, with which he had been familiar in his youth, and on the heads of which he had regarded the honor of his native State as resting, had either also disappeared, or had become so changed,—so entirely new and unknown to him,—that they seemed, most of them, no longer like the families he had left behind, with such unaffected regret, when he had re-moved to another sphere of activity. Nay, some of the changes which had taken place were painful to his feelings. Scenes and interests, which his own recollections made almost sacred, had suffered from ruthless strangers. He would not exchange, if he could help it, hallowed reminiscences for new impressions of things spoiled by a profane contact. He preferred looking back to a sort of heroic age, created and embellished by his youthful fancy, to a chastened and maturer vision of present realities. The ideas of Delaware which his children received and treasured up were, of course, ideas, chiefly, of that heroic age; and were none the less cherished for the vagueness which left so much to the imagination.

But the biographer has gone on a pilgrimage,[1] which mere filial feelings never prompted him to make, although certainly giving a far higher zest now to all his peregrinations and inquiries. Since the day, seventy-five years ago, when the young graduate of the University of Pennsylvania returned home, possibly by a shallop to Duck Creek, modes of travel have undergone wonderful revolutions. Now the voyage to Smyrna, and the drive thence to the old pastor's farm, would cost much more, in money as well as time, than the comfortable rail-road trip of three or four hours from Philadelphia. Here we are at the Dover Station, just out of the village on the north west.

Dover, county town, at once, and State capital, has, at present, about five thousand inhabitants. Upon a central, open square, bisected by the Old State Road, are the State and county buildings; and upon High street, the next west of the square, stands the Presbyterian church, now in its seventy fourth year. It is a substantial brick building, with a fine steeple, and would do no discredit to any ordinary builder of the present day. Surrounding it is a spacious and well filled church yard; where mingles the dust of many successive generations. The edifice, inside, has been partly modernized, but some relics of the olden time still remain. Here, at a little distance from the south wall of the church, are the family graves of the old pastor. Those of Joseph, the infant, and Benjamin are no longer visible: every vestige of them has disappeared. Two large horizontal slabs, elevated upon substantial brick work, cover the remains—one of the father and mother, buried in the same tomb; the other of their son John, the army surgeon

---

[1] In June, 1864.

of the Revolution. In 1841, these tombs, being much dilapidated, were reconstructed from the lowest foundations. The remains of Mr. Miller and his son John, the only ones examined, were in a remarkable state of preservation. With the remains of each, was found a middle sized key, which had evidently been deposited in the coffin. Near at hand, are the graves of Mary and her second husband, Major Patten, presenting the same general appearance. The earlier church was a frame edifice, standing with its eaves to the street; and the old pastor and his wife are said to be buried just where the pulpit stood.

Returning to the square, and crossing to its north eastern angle, we come to the jail, in the front yard of which stands what we may hope is soon to be a relic of the past—a whipping post and pillory, ingeniously and compendiously brought under one head. It is a stout, white oak pillar, about five feet high, with iron clasps on the sides, in which the wrists of the culprit, or victim, are securely locked, as he embraces the post, exposing his back to the smiter. Two bars, extending horizontally from grooves in the top, are so arranged as to clasp the neck, and hold their pilloried prisoner in a most constrained, half-hanging posture, the head bowed forward, and an inevitable sensation of choking experienced at every motion. This apparatus seems to be used for slaves alone, or chiefly. As imprisonment would deprive the masters of their service, an off hand, and, at the same time more terrible, species of punishment is employed.[1]

A little further to the west, on the same row, is the plain, old fashioned, red brick dwelling, where lived Doctor Charles Ridgely, eminent among Dover physicians, and the medical preceptor of Doctor Edward Miller. The pupil, alas! fell in love with Wilhelmina, his preceptor's daughter, and she, with all due ardor, reciprocated the attachment. Probably she thought more of the young student's handsome face, well cultivated mind, and other manly attractions, than of his empty purse; but her more prudent, or less discerning, mother forbade her marriage, and the engagement was broken off. Doctor Miller's subsequent success and reputation would have satisfied hopes as high as Mrs. Ridgely could, in reason, have formed; but this was all yet in the

[1] In 1864.

7

unknown future. The result was quite as touching as the veriest lover of romance could well desire. Wilhelmina speedily fell into a decline, and died unmarried. Doctor Miller lived a bachelor to the end—near the close of his fifty-second year. The ladies of New York called him the 'divine Doctor Miller,' to distinguish him from 'Dr. Miller, the divine'; but among them all he does not seem to have found such an angel as he left sleeping in the grave-yard at Dover.

A large part of Delaware, and of the peninsula of which it forms a portion, must have been, in former times, very unhealthy. The old minutes of Lewes Presbytery show a great mortality among its members. Mr. John Fisher, writing from Dover to Doctor Edward Miller, under date of the 15th of March, 1801, says

'This wretched place has brought almost half its inhabitants to their graves during this changeable, capricious winter. De-population bids fair to be its fate, in a short time, either by deaths or removals. Considerable alarms are excited in the minds of many whose constitutions are tottering, and the lives of those in the best health are considered as suspended by a thread. The stout, able-bodied family of the Millesses are all dead within the short period of the past winter, and innumera-ble deaths have occurred in the adjacent country.'

Now let us drive out of the village, to the north, on the Old State Road. Here is Jones's Creek, the bridge over which is a comparatively recent affair. Previously, it was always forded; and there is a tradition that after the pre-sent bridge was erected, old Doctor Morris still persisted in fording, considering the use of the new structure un-worthy of a sturdy gentleman of the old school. Possibly his horse had a say in the matter, and claimed, by prescrip-tion, the privilege of cooling his dusty feet and parched throat in the running stream. A drive of four miles brings us to Parson John Miller's farm. How many thousands of them he drove over this road! Delaware, in old times, seems to have been rather famous for sports of the turf and of the field—perhaps had its full share of the rollicking aristocracy. Dr. Samuel Miller used to tell of his father's coming, unexpectedly, once, as he drove along the high-way, in his quiet, clerical style, upon a crowd assembled for a horse-race. The rival horsemen were approaching

him at full speed, and one of them managed, in his blind
eagerness, to precipitate his courser upon a shaft of the
parson's gig, impaling himself on which, the poor animal
fell dying to the earth.

A friend communicates another tradition, which he heard
from the Rev. Francis A. Latta. The father, 'on a certain
occasion, bestrode the horse of his son John, the Revolutionary surgeon. John was partial to fox-hunting, and
the docile animal had acquired his vulpine tastes. While
the reverend gentleman was riding, at a staid, clerical pace,
a party of huntsmen came into view, the music of horn
and hounds proved irresistible to the mettlesome steed, and
he carried the minister off to the hunt, nolens volens, over
fence and ditch, to his deep mortification, and the huge
amusement of the sportsmen.'

On our road, about a mile and a half from the Pastor's
farm, stands the large, substantial brick mansion, where
his daughter 'Polly' resided with her first husband, Vincent Loockerman, Jr. To the south west of it, a short
distance, in the middle of a large field, is situated the family burial plot, fenced in, perhaps twenty feet square.
Here lie the remains of Mr. Loockerman, with those of
several of his house. We come now to Mr. Miller's farm.
It lies across the road and is nearly or quite a parallelo-
gram, of which the two sides, intersecting the road about at
right angles are much longer than the others. The house
stands on the smaller or western portion, nearly a square,
and is perhaps a hundred yards from the highway. It is
now a plain, bare, box-shaped brick structure, of some
thirty six feet front by eighteen deep; the northern half
evidently an unfinished addition, and said to have been
built by one or more of the sons, after their father's death,
on the foundation of a curb-roofed frame building, which
probably was the original house, the southern brick half
having been added possibly by the father himself, when he
first took possession. Back of this latter half, and connected with it by a bridge or platform a few feet in length,
is a primitive looking frame kitchen, or negro quarter,
of one story, with a loft above, said to have been rebuilt
since the era of the Millers, but after the ancient pattern.
There is a good deal of low marshy ground on the farm
and around it, accounting for the intermittent fevers, which

seem to have been, formerly at least, its most abundant product.

The last time that Dr. Miller visited this home of his childhood, he found it in sad plight, and already fast going to decay. As he opened the front door, a hog rushed out from the parlor, where, in former days he had so often knelt in solemn household worship. He went round to a back window, and looking in, saw only bottles and glasses upon a table, standing from a recent carouse. Sadly he turned away, and afterwards remarked to a friend, that it was his last visit.

Very strangely located, immediately in front of the dwelling, between it and the road, is a small, fenced burial plot, which, however, belongs to the later occupants of the place. Many of the old Delaware families seem to have preferred burying their dead thus in little enclosures upon their own plantations. The idea perhaps was brought from older countries, where landed possessions remain for ages in the same family; and where ancestral pride, thus and otherwise kept alive, carefully watches over the monuments of buried worth or worthlessness. Where as with us, for the most part, families soon are scattered, and disappear from their former seats; and family estates are speedily alienated, the church yard, or the public cemetery, is the only proper place of interment; offering the best, though still uncertain, security for the repose of the sepulchre.

About three miles north-east of Dover is *Tin Head Court*, where Mary Miller, after her second marriage, lived with her husband Major Patten. It is an old-fashioned, curb-roofed, frame building, said to have been a resort, in the Major's day, of all the best society of Delaware. There is so little that is courtly in its present appearance, either inside or out, that the tradition seems credible, only because so well attested

The ancient church of Duck Creek Cross Roads has entirely disappeared; but the burial ground, in which it stood, still remains in the north-western angle formed by the creek and the Old State Road.

2. OLD PAPERS.

Nothing but warm love of kindred, the hope of tracing an heirship, or an antiquarian mania for rummaging and preserving, tolerates old papers. But to patient fingers and reverential minds they often make touching revelations of the past.

A scanty file lies here, labelled, ‘Papers relative to Estate of Rev. Jno. Miller ’—the whole settlement. This ‘ Testamentary Account,’ and the inventory and appraisement which accompany it, show what he left—besides the farm about $2,075. James, the youngest child, whose graduation at the University was yet two months distant, when his father died, received a special legacy of £100, equal to $266.66. Samuel, whose theological studies were incomplete, received a legacy of £70, or $186.66, together with his father's library, valued at $100.

The old pastor's wearing apparel was estimated at eight dollars. Half a dozen table spoons, fifteen tea spoons, a pair of sugar tongs, with possibly some smaller articles, the whole together valued at eighteen dollars, were all the plate which he had possessed. The best chairs, doubtless belonging to the parlor, are inventoried as a ‘ half dozen leather-bottomed walnut chairs,’ worth eight dollars. A wheel for spinning wool, and three for flax spinning, are found among the articles which were certainly for use rather than show ; though, to be sure, King Lemuel has made a show of such things, in his inspired account of the “ virtuous woman,” whose “ price is far above rubies.”[1] Then there is a negro woman estimated at about sixty-six dollars, two others, at about forty, each, and a boy worth twenty one dollars. Mr. Miller's State and county taxes seem to have amounted, annually, to about two dollars and forty cents. His funeral charges were thirty-five dollars. No stones, as we have seen, mark the resting places of the two little children who had died years before. At the father's death the graves of his wife and eldest son, John, seem to have been yet without monuments ; but the heirs at once spent a hundred and twenty-one dollars for the two marble slabs, which have been already described. The residuary shares of five children, who survived the final distribution, were a hundred and seventy-three dollars each.

Now, side by side with this little file of accounts of the settlement of the estate, weighing three ounces, is a huge

[1] Proverbs xxxi., 10, 13, 19.

bundle of college diplomas—not a complete collection—
several are wanting—but a good representation of all. No
wonder the poor country parson left so small a patrimony.
The money had all gone to his children's brains. Of his
sons, as before shown, three were university graduates, a
fourth was just about to be graduated, and the fifth, Edward, had received an equivalent training. Nor had Mr.
Miller regarded his obligation for their maintenance as
limited by their college course. The newly graduated
bachelor of arts had not been turned off at once to be
wholly dependent upon his own exertions, and engage in a
dubious struggle to prepare for his profession or business—
if not to starve, to beg perhaps, or borrow, from comparative strangers, a scanty support during an inadequate term
of disturbed study. Inspired by academical advantages
and degrees with a higher longing for the honors, and a
more delicate perception of the proprieties, of life, each
son had returned from college to his father's house: that
was his home again until he had another—until his profession was secured, and he went forth, not only with a paternal
blessing, but also still dependent upon paternal assistance,
while laboring to establish himself creditably in an honorable calling. Thus, from their father's means, two had
obtained a regular medical training, a third a thorough
preparation for the bar, and a fourth was already far
advanced in his theological studies. The impulse thus
given, with a scant patrimony, sufficed to carry the last
completely through his preparations for the ministry, and
to bring forward to the bar the fifth, James, just about to
leave college. Possibly dollars and cents were held at
about their right value in the old Delaware Presbyterian
manse. And perhaps the patriarch, struggling there with
poverty, bodily infirmity, and heavy pastoral responsibilities,
might be profitably remembered by some clergymen of
modern ideas, who are too poor to educate even their sons
liberally, and hurry them through a "business training," and
thus off their hands, as if at least fully determined that God
shall not call them into the ministry. A third and fourth
generation are now reaping the inestimably precious fruits
of those painfully hoarded investments in literary and religious culture.

The oldest among the diplomas is one dated the 17th of May, 1763, from the College and Academy of Philadelphia, afterwards the University of Pennsylvania, attesting that the degree of Master of Arts had been conferred on the Rev. John Miller.   It seems to have been kept with special nicety.   College honorary degrees have depreciated like the current money, only in a far greater proportion, since those days.

LIFE

OF

SAMUEL MILLER, D.D.

PART SECOND.
NEW YORK CITY.
1793–1813.

CHAPTER SIXTH.

NEW YORK CITY.
1793.

1. The City and its Churches.

At the time of Mr. Miller's settlement in New York, it was a rapidly growing city of about forty-one thousand inhabitants. It had two banks, one insurance company, a daily mail to the south, and northern and eastern mails twice a week, excepting from the 1st of May to the 1st of November, when the eastern mail was triweekly. There were three stage-lines every week-day to Philadelphia, one of them, the mail stage being advertised to leave Powle's Hook[1] ferry stairs at 12 M., with two horses, and travel all night. Four times a week, there were, besides, stage-boats and stage-wagons, forming a line for Philadelphia by Amboy on one side, Bordentown and Burlington, alternately, on the other. Boston and Albany stages ran twice a week in summer, three times in winter.

Columbia College, founded in 1754, the fifth in order of

---

[1] Now, Jersey City.

time within the British Colonies, was still the only college that the State of New York could boast. Dr. John D. Gross, of the German Calvinistic, and Dr. John C. Kuntze, of the United Lutheran Church, were now among its professors, as Dr. McKnight, of the Presbyterian Church, afterwards was.

Besides Bishop Provoost, there were three resident Episcopal clergymen in the city—Benjamin Moore, D.D., Abraham Beach, D.D., and John Bissett. John H. Livingston, D.D., William Linn, D.D., and Gerardus Arantz Kuypers were the clergy of the Dutch Church; and, in addition to these, the Methodists had three clergymen, the Scotch Presbyterians one, John Mason, D.D., and the German Calvinists, the United Lutherans, the Associate Congregationalists, the Independents, the Moravians, the Baptists, the Roman Catholics, and the Jews, one each; making the whole number, with Mr. Miller, twenty-two.

From the brief summaries annexed to the minutes of the General Assembly, we can but approximate to the number of ministers and congregations connected with the Presbyterian Church in the United States, when Mr. Miller settled in New York. The former were, as nearly as can well be determined, about one hundred and seventy-five pastors, and twenty-five without charge. . Some of the pastors ministered to two or more congregations, and above two hundred and twenty-five vacant churches were reported. The number of licentiates was near fifty. The harvest truly was great, but the laborers were few.

The First Presbyterian Church of the City of New York was regularly organized in 1716, by a little company of Presbyterians, who had previously been associated for divine service, according to their own cherished forms— some of them for about ten years. In 1719, their first house of worship was erected in Wall street. This was the only one thrown open to Mr. Whitefield, upon his earliest visit to the city, in 1740; and his preaching was greatly blessed to the increase, both temporal and spiritual, of the congregation. The Rev. John Rodgers,[1] called from the Presbyterian Church of St. George's, Delaware, became their pastor, as colleague of the Rev. Joseph Treat, in 1765. Within a few months it was judged necessary to provide

[1] D.D. from 1768. See 3 Sprague's Annals, 154.

enlarged accommodations; and a second edifice, known as the Brick Church, was erected, was dedicated on the first day of the year 1768, and was soon filled with worshippers. The two assemblies, however, yet remained one church, with but one board of trustees and one bench of elders, two pastors preaching alternately in each house. During the war, the church in Wall street was used as a barrack, the Brick Church as an hospital; and both were left in an almost ruinous condition, while the parsonage had been burned to the ground. Without solicitation, the vestry of Trinity Church generously offered St. George's and St. Paul's Churches to be used alternately by the United Congregations, until their houses were repaired; an offer of which the latter gratefully availed themselves. After several changes in the pastorate, the Rev. John McKnight[1] became, in 1789, the colleague of Dr. Rodgers, and they were thus associated, when Mr. Miller was invited to share in their labors. Dr. McKnight's health becoming impaired, he could no longer preach three times every Sabbath, as had been the habit of each pastor; yet the congregations were unwilling to give up any of the services to which they were accustomed. Hence an additional colleague was needed.[2]

2. COLLEAGUES.

Dr. Rodgers, the senior colleague, was a very uncommon, though not, in the ordinary acceptation of the terms, a very powerful or brilliant, preacher of the gospel. Piously trained, and discovering, from his earliest years, a peculiar solidity of character, he had been apparently converted at the age of only a little more than twelve, under Whitefield's ministry. He was not an intellectual, but might, in his renewed nature, be called a moral and religious, genius. At fourteen he had regularly maintained family worship in the house where he boarded, and his godly conversation had been prized by those much his seniors in both age and Christian profession. Licensed when

[1] D.D. from 1791. See 3 Sprague's Annals, 371.

[2] A history of the "First Presbyterian Church of New York," as it seems still to have been called after it was composed of the "United Presbyterian Congregations," may be found in Dr. Miller's Memoirs of Dr. Rodgers, Chaps. iv. &c.

not quite twenty, he had been greatly blessed in the very
earliest months of his probational ministry; and his pastorate of between fifteen and sixteen years, at St. George's,
had been unusually popular and successful, enlarging the
Church, endearing him in an unusual degree to his people,
attracting crowds often to the house of worship, and extending his influence for good over all classes of the community. Not thirty-eight years of age when called to New
York City, he had entered upon his pastoral labors there
in the vigor of his life and usefulness. At the time of his
settlement, New York had a population of about sixteen
thousand, and but one Presbyterian Church; which, of
course, from its close resemblance to the Reformed Dutch
Church, yet in the ascendancy there, labored under peculiar disadvantages. Its growth, of near sixty years, had
been slow and struggling; but when Mr. Rodgers was
called to it, in 1765, a precious revival of religion was the
almost immediate result of his labors. The congregation
rapidly increased. Crowded audiences attested the impression made by his preaching. Within a few months, as
we have seen, it was found necessary to commence the
erection of a new place of worship, every pew in which,
after its dedication, was speedily occupied. But prior to
our war for independence, and still more during its progress, Presbyterianism, in the Colonies, was subjected to
many depressing influences; and the Presbyterian Church
of New York came out of that seven years' ordeal of revolution in a ruinous condition; its pastors having been,
nearly all the time, exiles from the city. His colleague,
in fact, never returning, on Dr. Rodgers alone devolved,
after the treaty of peace, and the evacuation of the city by
the British, the whole labor of the pastorate for more than
a year, during the resuscitation of the church, and the re-
pairing of the two houses of worship. By the time Mr.
Miller was settled, its number of communicants had largely
increased; and, under the fostering influences of peace,
and a more complete religious freedom, it had become
highly prosperous.

Dr. Rodgers was distinguished for an ardent devoted
piety, and an affectionate earnestness of manner, which
impressed all with whom he came in contact. He spent
much time in secret prayer, often accompanied by fasting.

In pastoral labor—preaching, catechising, visiting—he was most systematic, thorough, and indefatigable. He depended, not on great, adventurous, spasmodic efforts, but upon a steady, every day prosecution of ordinary plans. He seldom entered a house, or engaged in conversation, without dropping a word at least to commend the Saviour. The children of the church uniformly received a great deal of his attention. His sermons, though not highly polished, and in form and diction moulded, with little variety, after old fashioned theological treatises, were full of weighty gospel truth, and were delivered with great animation and unction. Until the failing memory of extreme old age forbade, he preached memoriter, and even his public prayers were often carefully prepared. His fidelity to souls; his single-hearted devotion to the work of the ministry; his watchfulness for opportunities of doing good; his practical wisdom; his prudent management of all his private affairs; his caution, bringing upon him sometimes the charge of timidity; his tender dealing with prejudice and passion; his guardedness against giving offence; his remarkable freedom from envy and jealousy, bigotry and repulsive sectarianism; his large, disinterested benevolence; his liberality and unworldliness; the dignity of his manners, sometimes, perhaps, too formal, but always commanding respect; his habitual cheerfulness; his whole consistent life and ministry, "forever the same"; were constantly conspicuous and most influential for good; constantly illustrated the truth which he preached. Even in his neat, appropriate, spotless, carefully adjusted dress, he was a pattern for every gospel minister.

In his Memoirs of Dr. Rodgers, Dr. Miller afterwards testified of him, as follows:—

"I shall not be surprised if it should be imagined by some, that I have discovered in the ensuing sketch, more of the partiality of friendship, than the sternness of historical justice. I can only say, that it has been my sacred aim to exhibit every feature that was attempted to be portrayed, true to the original. If I have in any case failed, the error was certainly unintentional. But it is a consolation to know, that, even after making the most liberal allowance on this score that can be required, there will still remain a large and solid mass of personal and professional worth, which we can scarcely too often, or too re-

respectfully contemplate. We may say concerning the character in question, what I have somewhere met with as said concerning another—'Take away nine parts out of ten, even of its virtues, and there will be still enough left to admire, to imitate and to love.'"[1]

"The venerable subject [of these memoirs] was never indeed considered, either by himself or by others, as belonging to the class of those extraordinary men, who, by the splendor of their genius, the variety and extent of their learning, or the number of their publications, excite the admiring gaze of mankind. But if solid and respectable talents; if acquirements which enabled him to act his part, in various important stations, with uniform honor; if patriarchal dignity; if sound practical wisdom, and a long life of eminent and extensive usefulness, be worthy of grateful remembrance and of respectful imitation, then the life of Dr. Rodgers is worthy of being written and perused. There is a day coming, and the estimate of Christians ought now to anticipate it, when such a character will appear infinitely more worthy of contemplation and regard, than that of the most splendid improver of human science, or the most admired leader of victorious legions, that was ever immortalized by the historian's pen. In that day it will be found, that bearing the image of Christ, and a gracious relation to his Person, is the highest nobility; and that services done for the Saviour's cause will obtain the only lasting reward."[2]

"—— "Take him for all in all," the American church has not often seen his like; and will not, it is probable, speedily or often "look upon his like again." In vigorous, and original powers of mind, a number have exceeded him. In profound and various learning, he had many superiors. In those brilliant qualities, which excite the admiration of men, and which are much better fitted to adorn than to enrich, pre-eminence is not claimed for him. But in that happy assemblage of practical qualities, both of the head and the heart, which go to form the respectable man; the correct and polished gentleman; the firm friend; the benevolent citizen; the spotless and exemplary Christian; the pious, dignified, and venerable ambassador of Christ; the faithful pastor; the active, zealous, persevering, unwearied laborer in the vineyard of his Lord; it is no disparagement to eminent worth to say, that he was scarcely equalled, and certainly never exceeded, by any of his contemporaries."[3]

To the youthful minister, especially, such a colleague was, doubtless, a great blessing. His example, his coun-

---

[1] P. 5.　　　　　[2] Pp. 11. 12.　　　　　[3] Pp. 344. 345.

sels, and the constraint which his fidelity must have laid upon all around him to be faithful, could not but have improved any one brought into the important and intimate relations of a united pastorate with him.   At the same time, the necessity of following closely in the footsteps of such a man, before two large city congregations, taxed, no doubt, his young colleague's powers heavily.   In fact, as we shall see, the burden was probably too great for, at least, Mr. Miller's physical strength.   He was soon obliged, once and again, to escape, for a season, altogether from pastoral duties, in order to recuperate his health by relaxation and travel.

Mr. Miller's other colleague, Dr. McKnight, about fifteen years his senior, was also an able, earnest, and faithful minister of the gospel.   Called to New York some three years previously, he had entered upon his labors there with great zeal and alacrity; not only preaching three times upon the Sabbath, but also lecturing upon a week day evening, and performing a large amount of other pastoral work.   To stand his ground with such men, and in Christian emulation vie with them for a gracious Master's approval and blessing, involved no small trial of a young minister's gifts and graces.   But kind, considerate men as they were, they could, of course, greatly relieve and encourage him.

CHAPTER SEVENTH.

THE "BOY MINISTER."

1793–1798.

---

1. ORDINATION AND SETTLEMENT.

THE following entries stand next in Mr. Miller's diary:—

'January 3, 1793. This day arrived in New York, in consequence of accepting a call there. O Lord, I have come hither, I trust, with a sincere view and desire to serve thee, and to be made an instrument of advancing thy kingdom on earth. Oh, give me a wise and understanding heart! Oh, give me a single eye to thy glory in all things! Bind my heart to the Saviour in sanctified affection! Fill me with the knowledge of thy will in all wisdom and spiritual understanding; and as my day is, so may my strength be!'

Mr. Miller was taken, as a licentiate, under the care of the Presbytery of New York, upon dismission from the Presbytery of Lewes, on the 16th of January, at South Hanover; was immediately 'examined in Latin, Greek, Geography, Logic, Rhetoric, Natural Philosophy, Astronomy, Moral Philosophy, Divinity, Ecclesiastical History, and Church Government.' The text, Romans iii. 24, was assigned him for a sermon, with which the next session of presbytery, at Orangedale, on the 7th of May, was opened. That, with his "Latin Exegesis," was approved, and the arrangements made for his ordination and installation—Dr. McKnight to preach, Dr. Rodgers to preside, Dr. McWhorter to deliver a charge to the people: no charge to the pastor is mentioned.

'June 5, 1793. After having met the Presbytery of New York twice, and gone through the usual trials for ordination, I was this day solemnly set apart to the work of the gospel ministry, by prayer and the laying on of the hands of the Presbytery. O Lord, I have this day renewedly, and, I hope, with some sincerity, given myself away to thee! I am now emphatically not my own. I am doubly thine—peculiarly thine! O Lord, accept of my dedication! Fill me with thy love; prepare me for thy service; help me to be more and more like Christ, and more and more to glorify Christ! O Lord, I have undertaken a charge which is too great for human strength. How shall I go in and out before this numerous and enlightened people? How shall I discharge the solemn and weighty duties which are incumbent upon me? Oh, the unutterable importance of having the care of precious, immortal souls committed to my hands! Father, give me knowledge—give me wisdom—give me strength, to perform my duties aright. Blessed Saviour, whom I trust I have chosen as the hope of my own soul, may I be strong in thee and in the power of thy might! Oh, help me to live, and study, and preach and act, like one habitually and deeply sensible that he must give account!'

On the 29th of August following, Mr. Miller first had an opportunity of taking his seat in the session; at the next meeting of which he was moderator, as the collegiate pastors seem to have been in turn.

His usual routine of public service seems to have required, at first, and for several years, only one sermon each Sabbath, but that sermon twice delivered. The Thursday evening lecture was maintained by Dr. Rodgers, with occasional assistance from his colleagues, until the autumn of 1799, when the growing infirmities of age induced him to commit it wholly to them.

"From the commencement of his ministry in New York," Mr. Miller "enjoyed a reputation," says Dr. Sprague, "in some respects peculiar to himself. Though Dr. Mason, and Dr. Linn, and Dr. Livingston, and other great lights were there, yet the subject of this notice was far from being thrown into the shade. Besides having the advantage of a remarkably fine person, and most bland and attractive manners, he had, from the beginning, an uncommonly polished style, and there was an air of literary refinement pervading all his performances, that excited general admiration, and well-nigh put criticism at defiance. He was scarcely settled before his services began to be put in requisition on public occasions; and several of these early occasional discourses were published, and still remain as a monument of his taste, talents, and piety."[1]

Dr. Milledoler says, 'We frequently passed each other on the Sabbath, Mr. Miller going to the Brick Church, and I to my charge in Nassau street. Mr. Miller's appearance was very youthful—I had just passed my nineteenth year. Being dressed in full canonicals, not omitting the three-cornered hat, we were called the "boy ministers."' This was in 1795.

About the same time that Mr. Miller settled in New York, James Kent, Esquire, afterwards Chancellor of the State, removed thither from Poughkeepsie, and was appointed professor of law in Columbia College. More than six years Mr. Miller's senior, he had already gained some reputation as a lawyer, and as an active politician of the Hamilton school. He became an attendant upon the ministry of the Collegiate Presbyterian pastors; and on a subsequent page he will appear, in advanced life, recognizing his former relations to Mr. Miller.[2]

2. PUBLISHED DISCOURSES—SLAVERY AND THE FRENCH REVOLUTION.

During the first years of Mr. Miller's pastorate, he seems to have been too heavily burdened with immediate professional duties, to think seriously of authorship. His only

[1] Annals, 600.

[2] A late reminiscent of those times, in a gossiping humor, says, "Grace Church disappeared from the lower part of Broadway, and bloomed out, in beautiful marble, at the upper end. It was a fashionable church then, and it is now. A story is told on this point, which, we trust, will not give umbrage to any parties now living, as it refers wholly to the dead past. When the late Chancellor Kent moved to New York City, the churches were interested in obtaining him as a parishioner. A friend of his, a prominent member of Grace church, invited him to attend service, in hope, of course, of securing his attendance permanently there. Mr. Kent consented. It was a fine day, and the congregation was well represented. All the interior arrangements were not only convenient, but elegant: the aisles richly carpeted; the pews furnished in luxurious style; with gilt and purple-velvet prayer-books; the organ music of the most artistic kind, and the most celebrated opera singers to lead in the choir. The ladies, dressed in the highest style, floated gracefully into their seats, and gracefully kneeled on the provided cushions. The minister rendered the service in an unexceptionable manner, and delivered a short but eloquent essay on some religious topic; and then, amid the pealing notes of the organ, the congregation, with mutual greetings, slowly retired. The whole thing, as the Chancellor's friend believed, was a great success. He had no doubt but his mind would at once be made up. So, as they walked out together, he said —'Well, sir, what do you think of that?' 'That, sir,' he replied, 'is what I should call very genteel worship.' "—*New York Observer of the 4th of July,* 1867. *P. 213.*

publications, for some time, were sermons and discourses called forth by special occasions and circumstances. These, in their proper places, may be briefly noticed, as giving some idea of the requisitions made upon him during his earlier ministry, the estimation in which his services were held, and his characteristics as a preacher, public speaker and writer at this time. On the 4th of July, 1793, about a month after his ordination, he preached a sermon, by request, before the "Tammany Society," an institution originally designed to give relief to the indigent and distressed. The publication of this discourse was asked for, and it was the first of his productions committed to the press.[1] According to a taste more prevalent at that day than at this, the author, in an advertisement, craved allowance for the "indigested and defective appearance" of the work, on the grounds of "very short notice," "many pressing avocations," "great haste," and "want of abilities and experience." It gives, however, a specimen not unfavorable of the popular talent and style of the youthful preacher. Portions of it may be particularly interesting, at the present time, when certain opinions, then almost universal, and now only recalled to general favor, are regarded by some as a novelty, or as an infection from a few enthusiasts and fanatics. As uttered by a slaveholder's son, born and chiefly educated in a slave State, such sentiments as the following may to many seem strange; but they were propounded, at the time, without an idea, apparently, that they were not commonly received, and by almost every hearer and reader cordially approved. There have been popular divines, and other orators, of a much later date, who have proclaimed the same opinions with an affectation of originality and daring, which have only indicated ignorance of the past presumed upon in the hearers, unless actually attributable to the speakers. And it should not be forgotten, that Mr. Miller saw no inconsistency between holding such sentiments, and also holding slaves, of a peculiar class to be sure, as we shall see he did, afterwards, in repeated instances.

[1] "A Sermon, preached in New York, July 4th, 1793, being the Anniversary of the Independence of America: at the Request of the Tammany Society, or Columbian Order. By Samuel Miller, A. M., one of the Ministers of the United Presbyterian Churches, in the City of New York." "Christianity the Grand Source, and the Surest Basis, of Political Liberty."—2 Corinthians, iii. 17.—8vo, pp. 38.

"It is a truth denied by few, at the present day, that political and domestic slavery are inconsistent with *justice*, and that these must necessarily wage eternal war[1]—so that wherever the latter exists in perfection, the former must fly before her, or fall prostrate at her feet.[2]

"Humanity, indeed, is still left to deplore the continuance of domestic slavery, in countries blest with Christian knowledge, and political freedom. The American patriot must heave an involuntary sigh, at the recollection that, even in these happy and singularly favored republics, this offspring of infernal malice, and parent of human debasement, is yet suffered to reside. Alas, that we should so soon forget the principles, upon which our wonderful revolution was founded! But, to the glory of our holy religion, and to the honor of many benevolent minds, this monster has received a fatal blow, and will soon, we hope, fall expiring to the ground. Already does he tremble, as if his destruction were at hand.—With pleasure do we behold many evident presages of the approaching period, when Christianity shall extend her sceptre of benevolence and love over every part of this growing empire— when oppression shall not only be softened of his rigours; but shall take his flight forever from our land."[3]

The same sentiments were expressed still more strongly, if possible, in the fifth of his published discourses, an oration delivered in 1797, before the New York Society for the Manumission of Slaves.[4] This was a voluntary organization dating from about the year 1785, and was designed to mitigate the evils of Negro slavery throughout the State. A standing committee had in charge the enforcement of the laws, both local and national, prohibitory of the slave-trade, whether domestic or foreign; the prevention of kidnapping and the assistance of persons unlawfully held in bondage; with the intellectual, social and religious improvement of the negro population. A flourishing free-school, for children of both sexes, was one channel of this charitable effort. Mr. Miller's discourse was the first consequent on the determination to have an annual oration upon the

[1] The "irrepressible conflict" of a later date.

[2] P. 19.

[3] Pp. 27, 28.

[4] "A Discourse, delivered April 12, 1797, at the request of and before the New York Society for promoting the Manumission of Slaves, and Protecting such of them as have been or may be Liberated. By Samuel Miller, A. M., one of the Ministers of the United Presbyterian Churches in the City of New York, and Member of said Society."—8vo, pp. 36.

topic of slavery.   Dr. Sprague says of it, "it may well be doubted whether a more discreet, unexceptionable, and dignified sermon has been written on the subject since."[1] A few extracts may not be unacceptable to the reader, who, had he found them without date attached, would probably have imagined them a part of some very late production— hardly dreaming that such opinions were uttered in this country nearly three-quarters of a century ago.

"That, in the close of the eighteenth century, it should be esteemed proper and necessary, in any civilized country, to institute discourses to oppose the slavery and commerce of the human species, is a wonderful fact in the annals of society! But that this country should be America, is a solecism only to be accounted for by the general inconsistency of the human character. But, after all the surprise that Patriotism can feel, and all the indignation that Morality can suggest on this subject, the humiliating tale must be told—that in this free country—in this country, the plains of which are still stained with blood shed in the cause of liberty,—in this country, from which has been proclaimed to distant lands, as the basis of our political existence, the noble principle, that 'ALL MEN ARE BORN FREE AND EQUAL,'—in this country there are slaves!—men are bought and sold! Strange, indeed! that the bosom which glows at the name of liberty in general, and the arm which has been so vigorously exerted in vindication of human rights, should yet be found leagued on the side of oppression, and opposing their avowed principles."[2]

"Were it made a question, whether justice permitted the sable race of Guinea to carry us away captive from our own country, and from all its tender attachments, to their land, and there enslave us and our posterity forever;—were it made a question, I say, whether all this would be consistent with justice and humanity, one universal and clamorous negative would show how abhorrent the principle is from our minds, when not blinded by prejudice. Tell us, ye who were lately pining in ALGERINE BONDAGE! tell us whether all the wretched sophistry of pride, or of avarice, could ever reconcile you to the chains of barbarism, or convince you that man had a right to oppress and injure man? Tell us what were your feelings, when you heard the pitiless tyrant, who had taken or bought you, plead either of these rights for your detention; and justify himself by the specious pretences of capture or of purchase, in riveting your chains?"[3]

"But higher laws than those of common justice and humanity may be urged against slavery. I mean THE LAWS OF GOD, revealed in the Scriptures of truth. This divine system, in which we profess to believe and to glory, teaches us, that *God has made of one blood all nations of men that dwell on the face of the whole earth.*"[1]

"While the friends of humanity, in Europe and America, are weeping over their injured fellow creatures, and directing their ingenuity and their labours to the removal of so disgraceful a monument of cruelty and avarice, there are not wanting men who claim the title, and enjoy the privileges of American citizens, who still employ themselves in the odious traffic of human flesh. Yes, in direct opposition to public sentiment, and a law of the land, there are ships fitted out, every year, in the ports of the United States, to transport the inhabitants of Africa from their native shores, and consign them to all the torments of West-India oppression.—Fellow citizens! Is Justice asleep? Is Humanity discouraged and silent, on account of the many injuries she has sustained? Were not this the case, methinks the pursuit of the beasts of the forest would be forgotten, and such monsters of wickedness would, in their stead, be hunted from the abodes of men.

"O AFRICA! unhappy, ill-fated region! how long shall thy savage inhabitants have reason to utter complaints, and to imprecate the vengeance of heaven against civilization and christianity? Is it not enough that nature's God has consigned thee to arid plains, to noxious vapours, to devouring beasts of prey, and to all the scorching influences of the torrid zone? Must rapine and violence, captivity and slavery, be superadded to thy torments; and be inflicted too by men, who wear the garb of justice and humanity; who boast the principles of a sublime morality; and who hypocritically adopt the accents of the benevolent religion of Jesus? O AFRICA! thou loud proclaimer of the rapacity, the treachery, and cruelty of civilized man! Thou everlasting monument of European and American disgrace! "Remember not against us our offences, nor the offences of our forefathers;" be tender in the great day of inquiry; and shew a christian world thou canst suffer and forgive!"[2]

"Perhaps no method can be devised, to deliver our country from the evil in question, more safe, more promising, and more easy of execution, than one which has been partially adopted in some of the States, and hitherto with all the success that could have been expected. This plan is, to frame laws which

[1] Pp. 17, 18.   [2] Pp. 28, 9.

will bring about emancipation in a GRADUAL MANNER; which will, at the same time, PROVIDE FOR THE INTELLECTUAL AND MORAL CULTIVATION of slaves, that they may be prepared to exercise the rights and discharge the duties of citizens, when liberty shall be given them; and which, having thus fitted them for the station, will confer upon them, in due time, the privileges and dignity of other freemen. By the operation of such a plan, it is easy to see that slavery, at no great distance of time, would be banished from the United States; the mischiefs attending a universal and immediate emancipation would be, in a great measure, if not entirely, prevented; and beings, who are now knawing the vitals, and wasting the strength of the body politic, might be converted into wholesome and useful members of it. Say not that they are unfit for the rank of citizens, and can never be made honest and industrious members of the community. Say not that their ignorance and brutality must operate as everlasting bars against their being elevated to this station. All just reasoning abjures the flimsy pretext. Make them freemen; and they will soon be found to have the manners, the character, and the virtues of freemen.[1]

In his first published sermon, Mr. Miller expressed what, at the time, was very common in the United States—the deepest interest in the French Revolution then in progress, together with a high hope of results most auspicious to the cause of liberty throughout the world.

"—— Especially," he asks, "can we view the interesting situation of our AFFECTIONATE ALLIES, without indulging the delightful hope, that the sparks, which are there seen rising toward heaven, though in tumultuous confusion, shall soon be the means of kindling a general flame, which shall illuminate the darkest and remotest corners of the earth, and pour upon them the effulgence of tenfold glory?"

"—— If this wonderful Revolution," he says further, "be, as we trust, a great link in the chain, that is drawing on the reign of universal harmony and peace; if it be occasioned by

---

"[1] It is easy to foresee that many strong prejudices, and many feelings not altogether unnatural, will oppose the execution of this plan. The idea of admitting negroes to a state of political and social equality with the whites, even after the best education they can receive, is not a very pleasant one to a great majority even of those who are warmly engaged for their emancipation. I shall not discuss the reasonableness of such feelings at present. It is sufficient to say, that our political body is laboring under a most hurtful and dangerous disease; and that the most skilful physician cannot restore it to health without the exhibition of some remedies which are more or less unpalatable." —Pp. 31, 2.

christian principles, and be designed to pave the way for their complete establishment, however it may appear to be sullied by irreligion and vice, it is the cause of God, and will at last prevail."[1]

Mr. Miller yet corresponded with his venerated friend and preceptor, Dr. Nisbet; who, from the first, took entirely different views of affairs in France, and expressed them with so much candor, or so little caution, as to bring great odium upon himself and the institution over which he presided.

"In addressing the students of the college, as their official instructor and guide, and even on some public occasions, he warned his hearers against the impiety and the enormous cruelty and licentiousness exhibited on a theatre, from which every channel of intelligence brought the most revolting and heart-rending accounts of bloodshed, and every species of inhuman and anti-christian practice." His view of the whole matter may, perhaps, be sufficiently illustrated by a brief anecdote given in his biography. "Sometime about the year 1794, when he happened to be in Philadelphia, a gentleman of his acquaintance said to him—"Well, Doctor, what are we to think of the French Revolution now?" "Indeed, man," said he, "I can give you a better account of that matter now than ever before. What I am about to tell you is no fable, but a fact that really happened in my neighborhood lately. A poor old woman, who is no politician, but a plain, serious body, who had been for some time in a gloomy state of mind, anxious about the salvation of her soul, (a thing, by the way, that no politician ever thinks of,) dreamed that she died, and went to the bad place. It seemed to her like a great inclosure, surrounded by a high, massy wall. She knocked at the door, when who should open it but his Satanic Majesty himself. The old woman expressed her surprise that he should stoop to such an office, and her wonder that he had not sent one of his imps or understrappers to open the door. 'Indeed, good woman,' said he, 'the devil an imp or understrapper have I left in all my dominions. Hell is completely empty. They have all gone to help on the cause of liberty and equality in France.'""

Dr. Miller adds, "Candour seems to require from the author of this Memoir the acknowledgment, that * * he was among the thousands of his countrymen who regarded the French Revolution, in its early stages, with a favorable eye, as the triumph of the spirit of liberty over misrule and oppression; and

---

[1] Pp. 31, 32

as promising, notwithstanding all the crime and bloodshed with which it was attended, the ultimate reign of freedom and good government. Such were the hopes which he once entertained ; and to which, almost without hope, he clung, long after every truly favorable aspect had vanished."[1]

3.   Devotion and Affliction.

A few journal entries are scattered through this and the following year.

'October 31, 1793. I am this day twenty-four years of age. I spend a portion of it in the exercises of special devotion. O thou God of all grace, prepare me for my arduous work. Increase my faith. Bind me more closely than ever to the love and service of my Master in heaven. As my day is, so may my strength be.'

'June 5, 1794. This is the Anniversary of my *ordination*. I have been one year a consecrated minister of Christ. Oh that I had a deeper sense of the magnitude and solemnity of my office, and of the deep responsibility which it involves! O thou God of all grace, inspire me with wisdom, gird me with strength, and prepare me to go forth from day to day in a manner acceptable to thee, profitable to thy church, and to the comfort and edification of my own soul.'

On the 23d of February, 1795, he writes to Dr. Green,

'I inclose you proposals, lately issued, for printing, by subscription, a magazine. They will explain themselves in the most ample manner.   *   *

'The editors are to remain behind the curtain. They are all clergymen, friends of the doctrines of grace, and acquaintances of yours.

'The design of sending the inclosed to you is, that you may interest yourself in procuring subscriptions ; but, especially, that you may, as soon as possible, contribute something to the matter of the publication. I am confident the editors would feel peculiarly obliged to you for any communications for this purpose ; as the first number is generally the hardest to furnish, and, at the same time, involves, more than any other, the character and success of such a work.'

About two months later, Mr. Miller lost his younger brother James. In 1786, his preceptor, Dr. Matthew Wilson had written, 'I am well pleased with James Miller's

<hr>

[1] Memoirs of Dr. Nisbet, 248, 250, 251.

genius. I think it a very good one. He has read too closely and too much for his age, which I suppose has hurt his constitution, as he is at least somewhat consumptive. *   *   *   Mr. James had better eat cough pills with me for a while, to strengthen his lungs. *   *   *

'P. S. Mr. James Miller is Poet Laureate to day, by writing the best description.'

A friend says, '[the Rev. Francis] Latta alleged that James was the brightest gem in a social circle where all were bright. He seemed to consider him, in intellectual gifts, as superior to the others, as they to ordinary men. But James died with the halo of youth about him, when its freshness, effervescence, and fervor gave additional brilliancy to his mind; and I think it probable his partial friends overrated his abilities.'

Here is an old, dingy letter—perhaps the only remaining relic of this brother, and youngest child—nearly two years and nine months younger than Samuel. In pulmonary consumption he went to South Carolina, fondly seeking restoration in a southern climate. He must have left home about the beginning of November, as he had been absent more than two months when this letter was written. It is dated the 12th of January, 1795. He says,

'I staid in Charleston about three weeks. I then spent two weeks with Dr. Richard Waring, who knew brother Edward in Philadelphia, by his pressing invitation. He resides thirty miles from Charleston. I then rode up here. Statesburgh is a small town in the high hills of Santee, about a hundred miles from Charleston. Its situation is pleasant, high and dry, and the air pure and wholesome. On these accounts it was recommended to me, and chosen by me, as a place of residence for some time. I have been here about a month.' Next he gives a particular account of his health, and of his regimen. Poor fellow! he was evidently flattering himself with the hope of recovery, although speaking of his disease, too, as probably consumption. Pecuniary considerations also seem to have troubled him. His accommodations were costing him 'about a guinea a week,' and he mentions a draft upon Colonel McLane, as something which he would gladly have avoided, but necessity required. Doubtless brothers and sisters were gladly supporting his expenses during this vain pursuit of health.

9

To all of them the letter is addressed within, though to his brother Joseph without. Alas! his hopes, like those of the consumptive characteristically, were doomed to disappointment. How, for a while, encouragement and despondency alternated we may easily conjecture; but about three months more ended the struggle: he died the 15th of April among strangers; yet these very attentive to him. In the family of Dr. Waring he was treated as a son and brother, and the last offices of kindness and respect, in his dying moments, and to his wasted remains, were tenderly paid.

About three months before the death of James—in January, 1795—Mr. Miller's sister, Mrs. Mary Loockerman, after a widowhood of nearly five years, had married Major John Patten, whose residence, Tin Head Court, near Dover, has been before mentioned.[1]

Mr. Miller writes in his diary,

'June 5, 1795. Anniversary of my *ordination*. Day of retirement and devotion. It is impossible for this day to recur without humiliation and mourning. Lord, give me grace to be more wise and faithful in time to come. Two years ago I was solemnly invested with the sacred office. In the presence of a great human assembly, and, above all, in the presence of God and angels, I took on myself the solemn vows of an "ambassador of Christ." How have I discharged the duties of that awful office? O Lord, thou knowest how unfaithful I have been. It becomes me to lay my hand on my mouth, and my mouth in the dust, and to cry, "Unclean! Unclean! God be merciful to me a sinner!" Oh for a stronger faith, a more ardent love, and a more indefatigable diligence, in the work of faith and labor of love to which it has been my privilege to devote myself!"

4. Published Discourses—Masonry.

Mr. Miller's second publication was a sermon preached before the Masonic Grand Lodge of the State of New York, in 1795;[2] which if it does not mark, as most natu-

---

[1] See p. 76

[2] "A Discourse delivered in the New Presbyterian Church, New-York: Before the Grand Lodge of the State of New York, and the Brethren of that Fraternity, assembled in General Communication, on the Festival of *St. John the Baptist*, June 24th, 1795. By Samuel Miller, A.M., One of the Ministers of the United Presbyterian Churches, in the City of New York."—Ephesians II. 20. 21.—8vo. pp. 32.

rally it might, advanced maturity of mind, and actual improvement in thought, diction, and literary taste, certainly gives evidence of more leisurely and careful preparation than the one previously published. Before this date, probably soon after his settlement in New York, Mr. Miller joined the Masonic order; he seems to have taken, for years, an active part in its proceedings, and a deep interest in its prosperity; and he reached the dignity of a Royal Arch Mason. His discourse seems to prove, that his confidence had been already shaken, if not in some of the principles of the order, at least in its practical results. But whatever may be thus inferred as to his views of Masonry at this time, certain it is that subsequently—perhaps from the date of his removal to Princeton, where there was no Masonic lodge—he renounced all connexion with the order; at least never attended their meetings; and that he distinctly, carefully, and emphatically advised his sons not to become Masons. Whether the abduction of Morgan, in 1826, which brought a reproach upon the institution from which it has never recovered, and probably sealed its doom in the United States, had any influence, even to deepen his disapprobation, cannot now, perhaps, be determined. But probably his more mature reflections satisfied him, that such a secret order was incompatible with the spirit of good civil government, and especially of our free institutions; and that too easily it might be made a cloak for disorderly, seditious, and treasonable designs; might be abused to base party purposes; might become the active enemy of sound morals, pure Christianity, and the Church of Christ; while it must, naturally, ever prove, in some sort, and in a greater or less degree, a rival of that Church, by proposing its own principles as a sufficient religion, drawing men away from church intercourse and worship, and suggesting, by its very existence, that the institutions of Christianity were not adequate to the fulfilment of the grand philanthropic purposes, for which they were founded. If this order might interfere with the normal workings of the commonwealth, it might interfere much more with those of the Redeemer's visible kingdom.

Only ten days after the delivery of his Masonic discourse,

Mr. Miller preached a Fourth of July sermon, which was also published.[1]

5. VALETUDINARIANISM.

It is very evident from the fewness and brevity of the entries in Mr. Miller's diary, during these earlier years of his ministry in New York, from his despondent dissatisfaction with his own performances, and from the speedy failure of his health, that the burden laid upon him was, indeed, almost too great to bear. It will be seen, hereafter, that the collegiate nature of his charge, though affording, on the one hand, some relief, increased on the other, and, perhaps, in a much greater degree, pastoral cares, anxieties, and toils. A city congregation, of the size of either of those to which he ministered, must always tax most severely the energies of any, and especially of a very young, pastor. It may well be doubted, whether such a charge should ever be laid upon any one, or ever should be accepted, without previous experience in the pastoral office, for a few years at least, in a place of less responsibility and altogether lighter burdens. Moreover, Mr. Miller had chosen the most laborious and oppressive method of preaching. His week-evening lectures were generally extemporaneous, with only the assistance of a brief skeleton; but his Sabbath and other more formal sermons were fully written, then delivered memoriter: he had before him on the desk, at most, only a slip of paper, with the first words of each paragraph upon it, for the help of recollection. Very few have tried this method of pulpit preparation, who will not testify to its pressing heavily upon the mind and spirits.

In a contemporaneous 'Record of Preaching,' we find the entry, 'October 25, At Newark (N. J.)—unwell—did not preach;' probably indicating that ill-health occasioned the absence from home mentioned in the following extract from Mr. Miller's Journal.

'October 31, 1795. From home: still journeying and in the

[1] "A Sermon delivered in the New Presbyterian Church, New York, July 4, 1795, being the 19th Anniversary of the Independence of America; at the Request of, and before, the Mechanic, Tammany, and Democratic Societies, and the Military Officers. By Samuel Miller, A. M., one of the Ministers of the United Presbyterian Churches in the City of New York."—Exodus xii, 14.—8vo. Pp. 33.

midst of fatigue and company. Not very favorable to a birth-day celebration. Oh to be placed in circumstances more friendly to a devout, humble, grateful spirit!'

To Dr. Green he writes, on the 2d of November following,

'The malignant fever which has for some time afflicted us, you will learn, from various sources, is almost entirely extinguished. To-morrow evening, our usual service will be connected with thanksgiving and praise for its removal. You will join me in grateful acknowledgements to the benevolent Father of the universe, for this signal favor. Oh, that there were satisfactory appearances of this dispensation's having a suitable effect on the minds of our citizens!

'Through the goodness of God I have been spared. My exposure to infection has been great; but my life is mercifully prolonged to this time. May it be devoted, with greater diligence, and with more disinterested and ardent zeal, than ever, to the glory of God.

'Be pleased to make my best compliments to Mrs. Green. I must hastily conclude.

'I am, reverend and dear Sir,

'Your friend and humble servant,

'Samuel Miller.'

Valetudinarianism was still seriously interrupting Mr. Miller's pastoral labors; and soon, as his diary indicates, he was obliged to leave home again for relaxation and invigoration.

June 5, 1796. The return of this day brings to my recollection the solemn scene of my ordination in 1793. I am now in Philadelphia. From the beginning of February to the first of June, this year, I was in bad health, insomuch that I did not preach during that time more than three or four sermons. My complaint was a weakness of the breast, which threatened consumption, and rendered speaking painful. I took a long journey on horse-back of near one thousand miles, visiting, in the course of it, Dover, my native place, Philadelphia, Lancaster, Baltimore, Annapolis, Alexandria, Georgetown, Mount Vernon, etc. Returned toward home, thus far, yesterday. For nearly three months I did not preach at all. To-day I have preached in this city (Philadelphia) for the first time in three months; and ventured to preach twice without sensible injury. Oh that this season of painful weakness may be found to promote the glory of God, and my own personal good, as a professing christian and a minister. I ought to take warning of the shortness and uncertainty of life, and how soon all my plans of study and of usefulness may be cut short by death. Great Giver of my life and time, Oh give me grace so to number my days, that I may apply my heart unto wisdom. I feel that I greatly needed a rebuke and chastisement from God. I had been, for months, in a deplorably backsliding state. Blessed be the Lord who hath corrected me in righteousness. Oh may I have the wisdom to improve it well.'

6. DOCTOR EDWARD MILLER IN NEW YORK.

Within a few years after Mr. Miller's settlement, he prevailed upon his brother Edward, practising Medicine at that time in Dover, to join him in New York. Of this, in his "Biographical Sketch" of the latter, he gives the following account :—

"It was in the year 1796, that Doctor *Miller* removed to New York. It is with mournful pleasure that the writer of this sketch recollects his own agency in inducing his lamented brother to make this removal. The malignant epidemic of 1795 had removed by death a number of physicians, whose characters were respectable, and whose medical practice was large. At the close of that awful visitation, when health was restored to the city, and when new plans began to be formed to fill up the chasms which death and desolation had made, the writer, then residing himself in the city, began to turn his eyes towards a brother whom he tenderly loved; whose company he never entered but with improvement ; and from whom he had long lamented his separation. In the month of November of that year, he proposed to him, and urged, an immediate removal to *New York*. Doctor *Miller* received the proposal in the most affectionate manner ; but, with that delicacy and prudence, for which he was always remarkable, he thought himself bound, before deciding, to consult such members of the Faculty in *New York* as he numbered among his friends. He, accordingly, addressed letters to Doctor *John R. B. Rodgers*, and Doctor *Mitchill*, on this subject, frankly explaining his views, and soliciting their judgment in the case. Their replies were such as might have been expected from enlightened and liberal friends, who felt disposed to encourage a professional brother. He determined to make the experiment ; immediately entered on the adjustment of his concerns in *Dover* ; and in the month of September, 1796, found himself fixed in *New York*."[1]

[1] Pp. xxvii, xxviii.

"His success in this city was much greater, and, particularly, more speedy, than he had anticipated. Among the many practical and instructive maxims which the writer of these pages has had the privilege of receiving from the lips of his lamented brother, and which he now recollects with mingled emotions; one, often repeated, was, that no professional man can, ordinarily, expect to succeed in life, without obtaining the general respect and confidence of his professional brethren. He thought that this remark applied to all the learned professions with peculiar force; that divines, physicians, and lawyers are, generally, held in a degree of estimation, by the mass of their fellow-citizens, proportioned to the degree of that which they enjoy among those of their own corps. His own character and history certainly went to the verification of this maxim."[1]

There can be no doubt that Dr. Edward Miller's settlement in New York proved very beneficial to his brother's health, which the journal of the latter shows to have long remained distressingly infirm.

'December 11, 1796. This evening is the first time that I have been in the pulpit for six weeks. Towards the close of October last, I was seized with a severe illness—an inflammatory fever—which brought me very low. I was, for nearly a fortnight, confined to my bed, and was much reduced. After a slow convalescence, I was so far recovered as to be able to preach a short sermon in the Wall street church this evening. Thus the Lord has again most mercifully admonished me. I still feel that I need chastisement. I have not had one stroke laid upon me that was not necessary for my good. "Lord, make me to know mine end, and the measure of my days, what it is; that I may know how frail I am. Behold, thou hast made my days as an handbreadth, and mine age is nothing before thee: verily every man at his best estate is altogether vanity." My attacks are so frequent, and my constitution appears so exceedingly frail, that my friends, as well as myself, seem to be impressed with the persuasion that my time here cannot be long. God of all grace, prepare me for thy will, whatever it may be. Whether my ministry be longer or shorter, Oh that it may be to thy glory, and the advancement of thy kingdom. If I am not deceived, I desire to be in thy hands. Make me "a chosen vessel" "meet for the Master's use," and then dispose of me according to thy sovereign pleasure.'

[1] P. xxiii.

7. Missions.

The royal charter of the Plymouth Company, under
which the Pilgrim Fathers settled in New England, mentions, as one motive for colonization, "the reducing and
conversion of such savages, as remain wandering in desolation and distress, to civil society and Christian religion."
And, for nearly two centuries, the North American Indians were the only heathen for whom the Colonists, in
any part of this country, attempted missionary effort.
The policy of the British government did not permit the
incorporation of societies in America for the work of
missions; and not until after the Revolution did the first
association of this kind receive a charter. It was instituted in Massachusetts, in 1787, and called "The Society
for Propagating the Gospel among the Indians and Others
in North America." Gradually it passed into the hands
of Unitarians. The second was "The New York Missionary Society," formed in the City of New York, the 1st of
November, 1796. In its organization Mr. Miller took a
very lively interest. The following letter to Dr. Green
refers, by anticipation, to this measure:—

'New York, August 14, 1796.

'Rev. and dear Sir,

    'You have, no doubt, been informed of the societies
which have been lately formed, in London, Edinburgh and
Glasgow, for sending and supporting missionaries among the
heathen. The remarkable encouragment which these societies
have received, and the numerous circumstances attending their
establishment, which promise, under the smiles of heaven, the
most brilliant success, cannot have failed to fill your mind with
the highest pleasure. What will be the event, God only knows;
but this is certain, that a prospect like that at present exhibited
in Britain has rarely been seen in the Christian Church.

'A few of the ministers of this city, who cordially agree in
the doctrines of grace, have lately had a meeting, to consider
of the practicability of instituting a similar society in this
country, and of the propriety of attempting some measure of
the kind. The result of this meeting is, that we have des-
patched a circular letter to eighteen or twenty ministers in the
vicinity of this city, belonging to the Presbyterian and Dutch
churches, whose sentiments we can rely on, begging their
advice and concurrence in the case, and requesting their general attendance at another meeting, to be held here on the 23d

instant. At the proposed meeting, the subject will be taken into more deliberate consideration, and something probably decided upon.

'The news we have received and the measures proposed on this subject seem to stir up the pious people among us, and to fill them with a fervent desire to do something. If we may judge by the aspect of things in our corner of the American vineyard, such an institution would probably meet with ample pecuniary and other encouragement. As it is proposed, however, to make the institution thought of a *national affair*, it will become desirable to hear the sentiments of friends to such a measure, in different parts of the continent.

'I write these lines, not at the request of the above mentioned meeting, but from a desire to communicate to you, thus early, what we have thought of, and to hear your opinion on the subject.

'The parts of our country destitute of the gospel are numerous, besides those occupied by the Indian tribes. They are all, however, contemplated in the scheme in question. How happy, if we, who profess to know the value of evangelic truth, should be made the humble instruments of disseminating it among those who sit in darkness and the shadow of death!

'My health is considerably better since my return home. Indeed, I am now nearly as well as usual. Our city, in general, is uncommonly healthy. You may be assured of this, notwithstanding all reports to the contrary.

'Be pleased to make my best compliments to Mrs. Green.

'I am, Sir, with every sentiment of respect and esteem,

'Your affectionate friend,

'Sam'l. Miller.'

The New York Society embraced several Calvinistic denominations. "That the world may be satisfied," said its founders, "as to the religious principles which they embrace for themselves, and resolve to propagate among others, their view of the great outlines of the doctrine of salvation is exhibited in the following propositions:"—a brief Calvinistic creed subjoined. Among its officers, the Presbyterian Church was represented by Dr. John Rodgers, Dr. John McKnight, and Mr. Miller; the Reformed Dutch, by Dr. John H. Livingston, Dr. William Linn, and the Rev. Messrs. John N. Abeel and Gerardus A. Kuypers; the Associate Reformed, by Dr. John M. Mason; and the Baptist, by Dr. Benjamin Foster. Upon the day of its organization, Dr. Alexander McWhorter, pastor of the Presbyterian church of Newark, preached before the Society in the Middle Dutch Church, a sermon entitled "The Blessedness of the Liberal," and a handsome collection was made. The proposed field of missionary effort embraced the frontier settlements and Indian tribes of the United States; but to the Indians, it is evident, from subsequent reports, attention was almost, if not quite, exclusively directed; so that the missions prosecuted were "foreign missions," according to a usual distinction of the present day.

On the 18th of January, 1798, the Society adopted a "Plan for Social Prayer," very much like the Monthly Concert, now so widely observed. We find it resolved,

"That the second Wednesday evening of every month, beginning at candle light, be observed, from February next, by members of this Society, and all who are willing to join with them, for the purpose of offering up their prayers and supplications to the God of grace, that he would be pleased to pour out his Spirit upon his Church, and send his gospel to all nations; and that he would second the endeavors of this Society, and all Societies instituted on the same principles, and for the same ends."

These meetings were held, in rotation, in the Wall street Scots', New Dutch, First Baptist, Brick, and North Dutch churches, the minister of each presiding in his own church, and where there were collegiate ministers, these in turn.

As early as 1794, the Synod of New York and New Jersey had recommended a quarterly concert in prayer for the same great object,—the Advancement of the Redeemer's Kingdom,—to commence on the first Tuesday of January, 1795.

8. DESPONDENT ACTIVITY.—LITERARY PROJECTS AND PASTIME.—POLITICS.

A pastor, especially one oppressed with work and ill health, is often a poor judge of his own labors, which, indeed, brought to the standard of God's perfect law, must ever prove grievously deficient. Diary entries, of which the following is a specimen, attest Mr. Miller's occasional despondency, as well as his orthodoxy.

'June 5, 1797. This is the anniversary of my ordination. Four years ago, this day, I was set apart to the work of the holy ministry. I am trying to recollect it with a devout, humble, penitent spirit. Oh, that I might be more deeply impressed, than ever I have yet been, with a sense of the infinite importance of the trust then undertaken; and be made more deeply humbled than ever with a sense of my exceeding weakness, unworthiness, and shortcomings. Oh Lord, I have come short in everything! My preaching, my devotions, my deportment have all been, alas! very little conformed either to the nature of my office, the character of my Master, or the excitements to faithfulness which I ought daily and hourly to feel. O Lord, make me, by thy grace, more wise and more faithful.'

From his 'Record of Preaching' we find, that Mr. Miller was journeying in Connecticut during a large part of this month of June. On the 18th, he preached twice in Hartford, on the 21st, in Windham before the General Association of Connecticut, and on the 25th, twice at Stamford. The occasion of this visit was his appointment by the General Assembly, on the 19th of May preceding, with the Rev. James F. Armstrong and the Rev. James Richards, to represent the Assembly in that Association.

Mr. Miller had been settled in New York but about three years, when it became apparent that a third Presbyterian church was necessary. The two edifices already in use were crowded, and the inhabitants, particularly of the north-eastern portion of the city, which was rapidly growing, could not find church accommodation. When the project for another house of worship had begun to take a definite shape, Henry Rutgers, Esquire, a wealthy and liberal member of the Reformed Dutch Church, presented the trustees with an ample lot, at the corner of Rutgers and Henry street, where they erected the new building. Early in the spring of 1797, Dr. Rodgers laid the corner stone; and on the 13th of May, 1798, when the edifice was opened for divine worship, he preached the dedication sermon. The greater part of the pews in this "Rutgers street Church," as it was appropriately called, were taken at once, although, for several years, the enterprise advanced but slowly. In fact, Dr. Rodgers was becoming quite feeble; soon after this he was obliged to relinquish part of his long accustomed labors; and the pastoral force became then evidently insufficient to meet the demands of three such congregations. Yet, until 1805, the way did not seem clear for increasing the number of pastors.

On the 31st of October, 1797, Mr. Miller writes in his diary,

'This is my *birthday*. Lord help me to remember it with gratitude and humility. With gratitude, that I have been thus far protected and preserved; that I have been raised up from sickness, guarded amidst dangers, and brought to the twenty-eighth year of my age in peace and in outward prosperity. With humility, because I have been so unprofitable a servant.'

One reason why Mr. Miller's labors pressed so heavily upon him, and his health suffered, was, doubtless, that to his pastoral toils he was adding a somewhat extensive correspondence, and, perhaps, too free an indulgence of mere literary tastes. Among his papers are found long Latin letters of 1796 and 1797 from Dr. Broerius Broes, a minister of the Dutch Church at Leyden, giving information of the state of religion and learning in Holland; in return for which he seems to have communicated similar intelligence from this country. Mr. Miller commenced the correspondence, and probably had some definite object in view, which cannot now be determined. His earlier tastes and habits of study, his associations in New York and elsewhere, and his repeated publications of an ephemeral kind, were evidently inclining him more and more to literary labor and to authorship. He had kept up his acquaintance with Dr. Jedediah Morse, of Charlestown, distinguished, in those days, not only as an evangelical minister of the gospel, but also as a geographer and historian. The following letter to Dr. Morse reveals a part of the influence exerted upon him through such associations.

'New York, November 27, 1797.

' Rev'd and dear Sir,

' In consequence of our conversation on the subject, I began, a few days after you left this city last, to collect materials for a history of this State. The work, I find, will require great labour and patience. These, however, if nothing else, I can engage to bestow, if life and health should be spared me.   I communicate this design to you, by way of preface to a request.

'It has occurred to me as probable, that in the course of your geographical and historical investigations, some curious facts and papers may have occurred to you which relate to the history of this State.   You would confer a great favor on me, ·by informing me whether this is the case; and whether it would be inconsistent with any of your designs to furnish me with the whole, or any part, of such documents.   You are too well acquainted with the subject to need even a hint, that the most trifling facts, anecdotes, and papers would be a valuable acquisition to me in my pursuit, and that nothing scarcely can be too small for a collector of materials for history.'

After speaking of the probable necessity of sending to Holland for materials, and asking for information of any persons in the United States likely to render assistance, Mr. Miller says,

'I have only farther to add, that, considering the present stage of my undertaking, and the uncertainty of its ever being accomplished, it will not be proper for me to make even my design extensively public.

'With my best compliments to Mrs. Morse, and with sentiments of the highest respect and esteem,

'I remain, rev'd & dear Sir,
'Your humble servant,
'Samuel Miller.'

This letter is endorsed by Dr. Morse, 'Answered January 10, 1798, with some valuable MSS. and printed documents, to be returned.'

To further this historical project, Mr. Miller petitioned the legislature of New York, to allow him to search the records of the various public offices of the State for information, and to make copies of important papers, without being subjected to the payment of the ordinary fees.   A special act, introduced by Dr. Samuel L. Mitchill, and passed without a dissenting voice, on the 19th of January, 1798, granted fully his request.   DeWitt Clinton, then a member of the State Assembly, appears to have assisted in the management of this matter for him, and under date of the 25th of January, sent him a certified copy of the act, with promises of further assistance.   Political sympathies, and association in the Masonic lodge, had doubtless

10

brought him into closer intimacy with Mr. Clinton, who wrote from Albany,

'There are very valuable materials in the Clerk's office of this county. The Chief Justice, who is the only man here that is thoroughly acquainted with them, has promised to contribute with all his exertions. The Surveyor General will also render you any assistance. Be pleased to put your ideas in the shape of queries, and send them to me, as it will greatly promote your object. * *

'It will give me great pleasure to assist you, by obtaining information, in the important work you have in hand. You now stand pledged to the public; every man of letters has an usufructuary property in your labors, and feels, I am persuaded, confident that you will not disappoint well-grounded expectation.'

This project also led to a correspondence and literary exchange with the eminent geographer and historian, Professor Christopher Daniel Ebeling, of Hamburgh, which was kept up for several years. Dr. Ebeling's letters are in English, but, like those of Dr. Broes, long and closely written; exemplifying the patient drudgery to which European, especially Dutch and German, scholars are, characteristically, willing to submit. Upon this history Mr. Miller labored long in a desultory way; he seems hardly to have abandoned the idea of writing it before he removed to Princeton in 1813. Something further of his social and literary connexions at the time it was undertaken, he has himself told us in the following paragraphs :—

"Soon after his establishment in *New York*, Doctor *Edward Miller* became a member of a literary association, which had been for some time known to those who participated in its pleasures and advantages, by the unostentatious name of "the Friendly Club." The meetings were held in rotation at the respective houses of the members, on the Tuesday evening of each week. Of this association, one of its members speaks in the following terms.* Never was a place of appointment, of this nature, repaired to with greater avidity, or the pleasures of unshackled intellectual intercourse more highly enjoyed. All form was rejected by the "friendly club," and but one rule adopted, which was that the member who had the pleasure of receiving his friends at his house, should read a passage from

"* Monthly Recorder, vol. I, p. 8, &c."

some author, by way of leading conversation into such a channel as might turn the thoughts of the company to literary discussion or critical investigation.   This was, for the greater portion of the time it existed, truly a "friendly club"; but after a
continuation of most perfect and cordial communion for a few
years, the demon, whose infuriated and blasting influence is un-
ceasingly exerted to mar the blessings of our envied country,
party politics, found his way among the "friendly club," and
the institution died a lingering death.   Yet I believe the surviving members feel a brotherly affection towards each other,
and a regretful remembrance of those days, the more endearing
as the knowledge that they can never return becomes more impressive, from the ravages of time and the unsparing strokes of
death."

""The associates of Dr. *Miller* at this invaluable period, the
first years of the club, were *William Dunlap*, then manager of
the New York theatre; *James Kent*, the recorder of the city,
and now chief justice of the State of *New York; Anthony
Bleecker*, attorney and counsellor at law and master in chancery;
Charles Brockden Brown, the author of Wieland; *William
Walton Woolsey;* Doctor *Elihu Hubbard Smith; George Muir-
son Woolsey;* Doctor *Samuel Latham Mitchill; John Wells*,
attorney and counsellor at law; *William Johnson*, attorney and
counsellor at law, and reporter to the supreme court of the
State of *New York;* and the reverend *Samuel Miller*, D.D.""[1]

In January, 1801, Mr. Miller addressed a memorial to
the legislature of New York, setting forth, that since its
last session, he had 'been gradually making progress in the
collection of materials for his proposed history,' and praying that the Dutch records in the Secretary's office might
be translated, at the expense of the State, for historical
uses.

The 9th of May, 1798, had been appointed by the President of the United States, Mr. Adams, as a general fast-
day.   At this time, the country was greatly agitated by
the prospect of hostilities with France—hostilities very un-
popular with the Republican, or Democratic party, between
which and the Federalists strife was running high.   The
latter were charged by their opponents with being in the
interest of Great Britain, then at war with France; and
with plans of alliance with the one against the other.   Mr.

[1] Biog. Sketch of Doctor Edward Miller, xxix.

Miller preached upon the fast-day mentioned, and the sermon was afterwards published[1] with this advertisement:—

"The following discourse, hastily composed, is published at the request of many who heard it delivered. The author is not accustomed to carry political discussion into the pulpit, nor to deliver his sentiments, in his public ministrations, on several points, connected with politics, which are glanced at in the following pages. He supposed, however, that the occasion permitted, and even dictated, some deviation from his ordinary habits in this respect. Viewing the present crisis in the point of light which he does, he could not reconcile it either with religion or with patriotism to be wholly silent on the subject. It appears by the result, that some of his friends concur with him in opinion; * *"[2]

This apology itself, perhaps, demonstrates that Mr. Miller was indeed very far from being a *pulpit* politician; and he protests against being so regarded in the passage which contains the strongest, nay, almost the only, allusion to the politics of the day, and which simply deprecates all foreign alliances as entangling and dangerous. It must be remembered, however, that, at the time, no alliance, excepting with Great Britain, was in question. Hence opposition to European alliances, however generally and abstractly expressed, could not but be regarded as distinctive of Republicanism.

On the anniversary of his ordination Mr. Miller writes,

'June 5, 1798. Once more am I brought, in the gracious providence of God, to the anniversary of my ordination. Solemn day! Solemn recollection! I have great reason to-day for humble, tender thanksgiving; but much more for the deepest self-abasement. I have preached many sermons, and made many parochial visits, in the course of my last ministerial year; yet I know not that I have done any permanent good. May God, for Christ's sake, forgive my multiplied sins and short comings, and give me grace, in time to come, to live and act more as becomes one charged with the most solemn of all offices, engaged in the most delightful work in the universe, and bound to glorify God in my body and in my spirit which are God's.'

[1] "A Sermon, Delivered May 9, 1798, Recommended, by the President of the United States, to be observed as a Day of General Humiliation, Fasting, and Prayer. By Samuel Miller, A.M., One of the Ministers of the United Presbyterian Churches in the City of New York.—2 Tim. iii. 1.—8vo. Pp. 46.

[2] P. 3.

CHAPTER EIGHTH.

THE YELLOW FEVER.

1798.

Upon first settling in New York, Mr. Miller simply took boarding, and successive city directories place him at the corner of William and John streets, in 1793, at No. 23 Market street, in 1794, and at No. 23 Maiden lane, in 1795, 6 and 7. Afterwards, the two brothers kept house, first at No. 158 Broadway, and, subsequently, at No. 116 Liberty street. Singularly enough, during a part of their bachelor-hall experience, their house keeper was a Mrs. Miller, whose name could hardly have been part of her recommendation to their service.

During the latter years of the last, and the earlier of the present, century, New York and Philadelphia, with occasionally some smaller towns in the vicinity of these cities, were repeatedly visited by epidemic yellow fever. Its first appearance in New York is said to have been in 1791,[1] although it was not very alarmingly prevalent there until 1795. In 1793, it had raged fearfully in Philadelphia; and in 1798, it visited both cities with terrible malignity. Let us trace, briefly, its ravages, during the latter year, in New York, following Mr. Miller and others in their accounts of their own observation and experience. The former says,

"—— Doctor" *Edward* "*Miller* had been residing two years in the city, and had found his medical practice considerably increased. As he believed the Yellow Fever to be neither *imported* nor *contagious*, and as his residence was in the most healthy street in the city, he early resolved to commit himself to the care of Providence, and to remain at his post. He did so, and was mercifully preserved. The writer of this sketch also remained in the city, during that melancholy season, and

[1] 1 Medical Repository, 303.

spent the whole of it under the same roof with his brother; and never shall he forget either, on the one hand, the persevering and almost incredible labours of that beloved Relative; or, on the other, the gloom and horror of the general scene. Doctor *Miller* visited all who sent for him, without discrimination or reserve. The rich, who were able to remunerate him, had chiefly left the city: his professional labors were, in a great measure, devoted to the poor and forsaken, from whom no recompense could be expected. Yet he attended them with unceasing assiduity; though he often exhibited such marks of fatigue, exhaustion, and mental depression on account of the scenes through which he passed, as could not have been described, or easily conceived, without personally witnessing them."[1]

Mr. Miller's older brother, Joseph, had removed to Wilmington, Delaware, and was established there in legal practice, when, in 1798, the yellow fever extended to that place. Though not so fatal in the smaller, as in the larger, more crowded, towns, the victims everywhere within its range were numerous enough to fill all hearts with dismay. But a few months before, Joseph Miller had married Elizabeth Loockerman, half sister of his brother in law, Vincent Loockerman. Both he and his bride were seized with the fever: she recovered, but he died on the 4th of September. The prevalence of the disease in New York City, their own critical circumstances, and, probably, the quarantine regulations which rendered travel difficult or impossible, forbade the presence of his brothers, Edward and Samuel, at his dying bed. To others they must be indebted for every idea of the melancholy scene. Joseph was in his thirty-fourth year.

A life-like picture of the harrowing and fearful experience of those, who, in the interest of humanity and religion, braved the ravaging pestilence, may be taken from the letters of a sojourner, at that time, in New York—Charles Brockden Brown. He was a native of Philadelphia, descended from Quaker ancestors, companions of William Penn. Educated for the Bar, but wholly averse to its public conflicts—of a diffident and gentle nature, and deeply enamored of the Muses—he relinquished forensic practice, to the great disappointment and mortification of his friends.

[1] Biog. Sketch, lviii, lix.

Dissatisfied with himself, and with gloomy prospects, but to escape importunities and reproaches, he rambled away from home, and, without, apparently, any definite object, visited New York. With Dr. Elihu H. Smith he had formed an intimate acquaintance in Philadelphia, where the latter had studied medicine. Dr. Smith introduced him to William Dunlap and other members of the Friendly Club, which Mr. Brown joined; and for several years he passed a large part of his time, first in the family of Mr. Dunlap, afterwards with Dr. Smith and William Johnson, Esquire, in an establishment—a bachelor's hall apparently—set up by these three in partnership. Upon the appearance of the yellow fever, the members of his own family wrote to him urging flight immediately. A few extracts from his replies will best explain his position and surrounding circumstances.

On the 4th of September, he says,

""As to the malignity of the disease, perhaps its attack is more violent than ordinary, but E. H. S., to whom I read your letter, answers for me, that not more than one out of nine, when properly nursed, die; and that its fatality, therefore, is much less than the same disease in Philadelphia."" [1]

On Sunday, September 17th, after noticing the increased prevalence and malignity of the fever, and its extension to the highest and most respectable classes, which had previously escaped its attack, Mr Brown writes,

""On Tuesday last, an Italian gentleman of great merit, and a particular friend of E. H. S., arrived in this city from Philadelphia. The disease had already been contracted, and admission into the boarding houses was denied him. Hearing of his situation, our friend hastened to his succour, and resigned to him his own bed. A nurse was impossible to be procured, and this duty therefore devolved upon us. * * The disease was virulent beyond example, but his agonies have been protracted to this day. He now lies in one apartment of our house, a spectacle that sickens the heart to behold, and not far from his last breath, while, in the next, our friend, E. H. S., is in a condition but little better.

""Extreme fatigue and anxiety could not fail of producing a return of this disease in Elihu. * *

"Sunday evening. Our Italian friend is dead, and Elihu is

[1] 2 Dunlap's Life of Charles Brockden Brown, 4.

preparing to be transported to ——'s, whose house is spacious, healthfully situated, and plentifully accommodated." "

"Brown had been himself attacked by the first symptoms of the fatal disease, and was removed to the house of the same friend who now received the unfortunate Smith. Brown's symptoms yielded to medicine, not so his friend's; —— * * the efforts of his medical friends Miller and Mitchill were utterly unavailing; he saw the last symptom of the disease, black vomit, pronounced the word "decomposition," and died."[1]

Mr. Miller, referring afterwards to the same melancholy scenes, wrote,

"Among the victims of this wasting disease, in the season of which we are speaking, Doctor MILLER was called to lament the loss of his affectionate friend, and able colleague,[2] Doctor ELIHU H. SMITH, who, in the morning of life and usefulness, and in the midst of professional exertions, as honorable to himself as they were beneficial to others, was sent to a premature grave. * * Never can the writer of these lines forget the funeral of Doctor SMITH. It was when the ravages of pestilence had become so tremendous, as to drive almost every individual from the city who was able to fly; when scarcely any passengers were to be seen in the streets, but the bearers of the dead to the tomb; and when it appeared as if the reign of death must become universal;—it was in circumstances such as these, that Doctors MITCHILL and MILLER, accompanied by two or three other friends, bedewed with their tears, and followed to the grave, the remains of a Young Man, in some respects one of the most enlightened and promising that ever adorned the annals of American science."[3]

"Upon the removal of Dr. Smith from his own dwelling to the house of a friend, Mr. Brown resigned to him the chamber he had occupied in that friend's house, and by invitation removed to Dr. Miller's."

Here, on Tuesday, September 20th, the day before Dr. Smith's death, he wrote to his brother:—

" " My excellent friend, Dr. Miller, dissuades me from going to you. * *

" "The number of Physicians is rapidly declining, while that of the sick is as rapidly increasing. Dr. Miller, whose practice, as his skill, exceeds that of any other physician, is almost weary

[1] Life of C. B. Brown, 7, 8.
[2] Doctors E. H. Smith and Samuel Latham Mitchill were associated with Doctor Edward Miller in the editorship of the *Medical Repository*.
[3] Biog. Sketch, lx.

of a scene of such complicated horrors. My heart sickens at the perpetual recital to which I am compelled to be an auditor. * *

"" Thursday morning. * * In the opinion of Miller, the disease, in no case, was ever more dreadfully and infernally malignant." "[1]

After the dreadful scourge had disappeared, the clergy of the city of New York recommended the observance of a day of thanksgiving, humiliation and prayer. On that day Mr. Miller preached a sermon, which was afterwards published.[2]

In this discourse, in singular, yet perfectly legitimate, connexion with a tribute to those who had remained to minister to the sick and dying, stands the following argument to show, that most of the fugitives were undoubtedly right in escaping from the scenes of death.

" It is pleasing to find, that the scruples, which were formerly prevalent and strong, against flying from pestilence, are now entertained by few. There seems to be no good reason why those, who consider it sinful to retire from a place under this calamity, should not have the same objection to flying from famine, from the ravages of fire, or from war, which are equally judgments of God. And yet those who reprobate the former never think of condemning the latter. In fact, if it be criminal to retire from a city in which the plague rages, it must be equally criminal to send for a physician, or to take medicines, in any sickness; for they are both using means to avert danger to which the Providence of God has exposed us.[3] It is hoped, therefore, if Providence should call us to sustain a similar stroke of affliction in future, there will be a more general agreement than ever, in the propriety of immediate removal; and that all will escape without delay, who are not bound to the scene of danger by special and indispensable ties. Had all the inhabitants of New York remained in the city, during the late epidemic, probably four or five times the present number, on the lowest computation, would have been added to the list of its victims.

---

[1] Life of C. B. Brown, 10.

[2] " A Sermon delivered February 5, 1799; Recommended by the Clergy of the City of New York, to be observed as a Day of Thanksgiving, Humiliation and Prayer, on account of the Removal of a Malignant and Mortal Disease, which had prevailed in the City some time before. By Samuel Miller. A. M., one of the Ministers of the United Presbyterian Churches in the City of New York. Published by request.—Psalm ii, 11.—8vo. P. 34.

[3] " See Jeremiah 21. 6–9."

As every diseased individual or family adds force to the malignity of the atmosphere, it appears that the most benevolent
principles conspire with the selfish, in prescribing immediate
and general flight."[1]

The city had, in 1798, somewhere about fifty thousand
inhabitants. At least half of these fled from the scene of
pestilence. Of the twenty-five thousand left, more than
two thousand were swept into the grave between the 1st of
August and the 10th of November. From the two Collegiate churches one hundred and eighty-six persons died,
and Mr. Miller was himself twice slightly affected with the
disease. His journal records some additional facts and
reflections.

'October 31, 1798. Never have I had more occasion to bless
God for the return of my birth-day than now. I have just passed
through the most awful scene of epidemic sickness and mortality that I ever witnessed. The *Yellow Fever* has been raging in the city for more than two months past. From the
middle to the 25th of this month was the most mortal time.
Though the city was deserted by, perhaps, two-thirds of its
regular inhabitants, more than two thousand persons fell victims to the disease. Most of the clergy, as well as of the other
inhabitants, had left the city. I remained with a brother—a
beloved brother—a practitioner of medicine—a bachelor as
well as myself. We were both mercifully borne through the
raging epidemic without any serious attack. Our housekeeper
died of it, and I attended her funeral between midnight and
day. To attempt to describe the scenes of mourning and
horror which this epidemic presented—I dare not. The task
transcends my power of expression. I preached every Sabbath;
but only a few attended public worship; and I know not that
any sensible—certainly no conspicuous—good was done. The
people appeared to me to emerge from this calamity as hardened, as careless, as ungodly, as they were before. I have not
heard of a single instance of conversion, which can be traced
to this awful dispensation of divine providence. Is it not a
humiliating fact, in the history of man, that seasons of great
sickness and mortality have seldom, if ever, been followed
with—what might naturally be expected—a revival of religion? How is this to be accounted for? "If they hear not
Moses and the prophets, neither will they be persuaded though
one rose from the dead." I wish to speak of it, not as a de

[1] Pp. 35, 36. Note.

cided point, but as a matter to be inquired into, whether times of great sickness and mortality have ever been attended, or followed, by great outpourings of the Holy Spirit.

'But the most humiliating part of the story, so far as I am concerned, yet remains to be told. I look back with amazement at the state of my own mind during the last two months. As I observed the frequency of funerals, and the constant presence of the memorials of sickness and death, to produce a very hardening effect on the minds of others; so I found that they had too much of the same effect on my own mind. Such scenes became so familiar to me, that they passed by as common things, without any salutary influence. I mourned over this hardening effect, but still it continued. Truly, "the heart is deceitful above all things, and desperately wicked." O Lord, soften, and enlighten, and try my heart, and lead me in the way everlasting. I think I have learned more of the hardness and desperate wickedness of the heart, within the last two months, than in any similar length of time before.'

Mr. Brown had devoted himself to literature, and was chiefly distinguished as a prolific writer of novels; which, though some of them were well-received at the time of their first appearance, the rather because an American *littérateur* and novel-writer was then almost a novelty, have since passed into oblivion. One of these works of fiction was founded upon the horrors of pestilence through which he had just passed. That his religious ideas were, at best, not particularly well defined, we may conclude from his notice of a sermon he heard in New Haven, in 1801. " " Yesterday, in the morning, we went to church, and heard Dr. Dwight preach an ingenious sermon, to prove the reality of good and bad angels, or genii. A very agreeable doctrine, in which the fancy is more disposed to acquiesce than the understanding." "[1]

After the yellow fever had passed away, Mr. Brown's friends in New York, the Friendly Club in particular, busied themselves to find him employment, and a means of support, agreeable to his literary tastes. He was accordingly encouraged to establish "The Monthly Magazine and American Review," the first number of which bears the date of April, 1799. We find Mr. Miller writing, December, 24, 1798, to Dr. Morse, to solicit his influence in behalf of this proposed publication. He says,

[1] Life of C. B. Brown, 56.

'You may rest assured, this is not an ordinary, nor a catch-penny, plan. The principal editor is a gentleman of undoubted learning and taste, who will devote a large portion of his time to the work; and he will be supported and assisted by an association, which includes some of the first literary characters in this city; so that I think you may, with confidence, recommend the work to the patronage of your friends, as one that will be ably conducted, and as one that will be decidedly favorable to the interests of morality and religion. I have no doubt that it may and will be rendered honorable and useful to the United States.'

Dr. Morse demurred, expressing his fears, as it would seem, that the work might be too Democratic in its bearing. To this Mr. Miller replied, April 3, 1799,

'The principal editor of the American Monthly Magazine is a Mr. Charles B. Brown, lately of Philadelphia. You may, I believe, fully confide in him as a Federalist. Of his learning and taste there can be no question. There is a society, or club, of some ten gentlemen, who meet once a week to consult about the magazine, and concert plans to make up its contents and to promote its interests. Of these ten, seven are decided Federalists; the other three are a little Democratic, but remarkably mild and moderate men. I am not at liberty to mention their names, but am persuaded you need be under no apprehension respecting the work in a political point of view.'

The Fever must have been still raging, or had scarcely abated, when Mr. Miller received a unanimous call from the Market-street, or First Presbyterian, Church in Philadelphia. His answer to this invitation has not been preserved, but a letter of the 8th of November to Dr. Green, alludes to it.

'You will, probably, have been informed, before you receive this letter, that I have given a negative answer to the call from Market street Church. The grounds of this decision were numerous and left no room for hesitation; but it is impossible, in the compass of an ordinary letter, to enter into the details of the subject. I hope my determination is right, and approved by the great Head of the Church.

'I thank you for your kind sympathy under the late bereaving dispensation of Providence in our family. I have lost an affectionate, and, unless I am deceived, in many respects a valuable brother. But it is the Lord: let him do what seemeth to him good! It is my duty, and I hope it is my desire, to be still and know that he is God. I have, as you heard, been twice ill with the fever—once severely so ; but, having obtained help of God, I continue unto this day. Unless I deceive myself, it is my wish and aim to devote the life which has been spared, to more activity and usefulness. May that power, which alone is able, strengthen, continue and realize these wishes !

'As I write in the midst of much hurry, I have only time to add my best compliments to Mrs. Green, and an assurance that I am, dear Sir, with much respect and esteem,

'Your friend and brother,

'Samuel Miller.'

To an introductory letter of the 14th of December, 1798, he adds, 'N. B. I give you joy on the President's delivering so decent a speech. I think it the best public communication he ever made. I know of nothing in it, which I do not approve of substantially, which is going pretty far for a *Democrat.'*

This call to the Market street church was a call to be the colleague of Dr. John Ewing, who united his pastoral office with that of Provost of the University of Pennsylvania. A colleague was soon found in the Rev. John Blair Linn,[1] who, surviving his senior, continued in his relation to this church until 1804, when his early and lamented death made way for the long and very popular pastorate of the Rev. James P. Wilson, D.D.

[1] 4 Sprague's Annals, 210.

11

CHAPTER NINTH.

POLITICS AND PROJECTS.

1799–1801.

1. Death of Washington.

In 1799, Mr. Miller, doubtless, in his already feeble state of health, to avoid the Yellow Fever, was absent from New York most or all of the time for about two months —from early in September till near the middle of November. In December he preached a sermon, afterwards published, on the occasion of the death of General Washington.[1] An unfeigned admirer of the "Father of his Country," he lavished encomiums upon his military skill and success, "his dignified prudence, soundness of judgment, firmness and self-command," his unsullied patriotism, the universally confessed purity of his motives, and his undeviating rectitude of intention. He represented him as "not indeed endowed with those brilliant and dazzling talents, which many erroneously imagine to be alone estimable;" but as possessing a mind of the higher order, and as raised, "without the tinsel ornaments of titled nobility—without the advantage of what is called distinguished and honorable birth"—"raised, by the Governor of the world, to a degree of greatness of which the history of man had furnished few examples."[2]

It might seem remarkable, that so little is said in this discourse about Washington's religious character. Beyond

[1] "A Sermon, Delivered December 29, 1799; Occasioned by the death of General George Washington, late President of the United States, and Commander in Chief of the American Armies. By Samuel Miller, A. M., One of the Ministers of the United Presbyterian Churches in the City of New York. Published by Request."—Chronicles xxix, 12.—8vo, Pp. 39.

[2] Pp. 28, 33.

the warm commendation of his private and public virtues,
it is only observed, "On the providence of God he took
every opportunity of expressing a firm reliance; and to
divine goodness and aid he never failed of ascribing the
glory of every favorable event."[1]　And it is but right to
add, that, in after life, Dr. Miller often spoke, with sadness,
of the doubt clouding his own mind as to Washington's
piety.　How was it possible, he asked, for a true Christian,
in the full exercise of his mental faculties, to die without
one expression of distinctive belief, or Christian hope?[2]—
a most pregnant question, the profound pain inspired by
which is, however, partially relieved, by the consideration
of the great hero's prayerful life; his unusual, but uniform,
and apparently deliberate, reticence on the subject of personal religion; the brevity of his last illness, of less than
twenty-four hours; and his difficulty, from the nature of
the attack, in making himself understood.

This sermon led to a correspondence with the Honorable
John Jay, first Chief Justice of the United States under
the Federal Constitution, but at this time Governor of the
State of New York.

'Albany, 28 February, 1800.

'Sir,

'Accept my thanks for the sermon on the death of General Washington, which you were so obliging as to send me.
In my opinion it abounds in excellent sentiments, well arranged and well expressed.

'Writing thus freely, I think it candid to observe, that in
some instances, ideas are conveyed, which do not appear to me
to be correct.　Such, for instance, as "our glorious *emancipation* from Britain."　The Congress of 1774 and 1775 regarded
the people of this country as being *free;* and such was their
opinion of the liberty we enjoyed so late as the year 1763, that
they declared the Colonies would be satisfied, on being replaced
in the political situation in which they then were.　It was not
until after the year 1763, that Britain claimed to subject us
to arbitrary domination.　We resisted the stamp-act with energy and success; and when, afterward, she attempted to bind
us in all cases whatsoever, the same spirit of resistance animated our councils and our conduct.　When she recurred to
arms to put a yoke upon us, we recurred to arms to keep it off.
A struggle ensued, which produced the Revolution, and ended

[1] 1 P. 34.

in an entire dissolution of the political ties which had before subsisted between the two countries. Thus we became a distinct nation; and I think truth will justify our indulging the pride of saying, that we and our ancestors have kept our necks free from all yokes, and that the term *emancipation* is not applicable to us.

'Speaking of the measures of General Washington's *civil* administration, you observe, and so is the fact, "that there is less unanimity among his countrymen with respect to these, than with respect to his military services." But do facts warrant our ascribing this diminution of unanimity entirely to doubts respecting the wisdom of those measures?

'The Revolution found and left only two parties; viz.,—the Whigs, who succeeded; and the Tories, who were suppressed. The former were unanimous in approving the leading measures, both civil and military, which gave them victory. When the adoption of the new constitution afterwards came into question the Whigs divided into two parties, one for, and the other against it. The party for the constitution prevailed; and they have, with as great unanimity, approved of General Washington's civil, as of his military measures. The party opposed to the constitution disapproved of the government established by it; and there are very few of the important measures of that government, which have escaped their censure.

'I take the liberty of making these remarks from the respect I have for your talents, and an opinion, that, with due circumspection, they will promote the great interests of truth, virtue, and rational liberty. Receive them, therefore, as marks of the esteem with which I am,

'Sir, your most obedient servant,

'The Rev. Mr. Miller. John Jay.'

To the foregoing letter Mr. Miller replied as follows:—

'New York, March 14, 1800.

'Sir,

'Your very polite letter, dated the 28th of last month, came to my hand a few days ago.

'While I receive, with great pleasure, the general approbation you are pleased to express of the sermon which I did myself the honor to send you, I feel equally obliged by the free and candid remarks, which you thought proper to subjoin. Even if they were less agreeable to my own views, they would, from their nature, and the manner in which they are communicated, demand my respectful acknowledgments.

'With respect to the word *emancipation*, as applied to the

dissolution of the ties which connected us with Great Britain, I admit your remark, without hesitation, as perfectly just. Although the word has been often used, in popular harangues, to express the idea for which I employed it; yet it is certainly not strictly correct.   I am the more pleased with your remark on this point, and more fully appreciate the benevolent motive which induced you so candidly to state it, when I reflect on my having undertaken, should my life be spared, to lay before the public some account of the great event to which the expression alluded to relates ; in representing which it would be unfortunate to use language, either erroneous, or liable to be mistaken.   .

'With respect to your observation on the manner in which I took notice of General Washington's services as President, though I receive it, and consider the motive by which it was dictated, with profound respect; yet you will pardon me if I hesitate to adopt your opinion in this, in the same unqualified manner, as in the preceding instance.

'On the occasion on which the sermon was delivered, I was unwilling to touch upon any string connected with party animosity.   Had I, therefore, perfectly agreed with you in sentiment, with regard to the parties which have, for several years, divided the citizens of the United States, it would not have been thought proper by me, to introduce such sentiments, or, indeed, any others involving the political polemics of the day, into a pulpit exercise.

'But, Sir, I had a more powerful reason for speaking as I did. To avoid giving offence to an audience will always, I hope, be a secondary object with me, to the duty of a candid expression of my sentiments, when such expression is demanded.   I am one of those who do not entirely approve the measures of the late venerable President.   And, although I am persuaded that multitudes have opposed them, from a principle of fixed hostility to the Constitution, and in a very unreasonable and criminal manner; yet, after as impartial an examination of my own mind as I am able to institute, I cannot believe that my disapprobation arises from any other source than "doubts of the wisdom of those measures."   My doubts, indeed, may be wholly groundless; and give me leave to say, that few things have more frequently tempted me to suspect that this might be the case, than a recollection of the splendid talents, and (in my view) the unquestionable uprightness, which have been engaged in carrying on the measures referred to.   Still my doubts exist; though I hope they are entertained and generally expressed, without obstinacy, and without malevolence.

'With respect to the last idea suggested in your letter—that the party who originally approved the Constitution have unanimously continued to approve the government established by it —I am ready to admit, that, as a general remark, it is just; but many exceptions are certainly to be found. As I was a lad of seventeen years of age, when the Constitution was adopted, it would be improper to speak of my own sentiments at that time. I was then residing in Delaware, my native state. In that state, you recollect, the Constitution was adopted promptly and unanimously. Among the number of its earnest admirers and supporters were my relatives and particular friends; and in the same class I have, ever since, considered myself to be. It is, moreover, beyond all question true, that a large proportion of the first characters for talents, virtue and property, in that state, who then took side in favor of the Constitution, with great decision; and who have uniformly professed themselves to be its friends to the present day; are now to be ranked with what is called the opposition. I have taken my examples from Delaware, as being better able to compare the different parts of the conduct of its principal citizens for the last twelve years, than to do the same with respect to my adopted state. I am well aware that such conduct is charged with being a dereliction of former principles, and a change of ground. That some have given reason for bringing this charge against them, and for suspecting their motives, I do not deny. But that disapproving the administration, as to some of its measures, always implies enmity to the Constitution, I cannot, at present, concede.

'You will perhaps be surprised at my taking the liberty to trouble you with these expositions and details of my sentiments. I am sensible it is of little importance what my political opinions are. They have been generally held in a moderate and inoffensive manner; and both my profession and inclination forbid me to take any active part in the civil concerns of my country. It is, indeed, my wish to abstract myself more and more from party politics. But several reasons induced me to acknowledge the receipt of your remarks; and, in doing this, my first resolution was to be unreserved. You had given an example of candor too flattering and instructive not to be imitated.

'I have only to add, that, if I do not deceive myself, my highest ambition is to promote "the great interests of religion, virtue and rational liberty;" that, if any of my sentiments have a different tendency, I shall readily abandon them on making the discovery; and that he who corrects any of the errors into which I may fall, will always be considered by me as my truest friend and benefactor.

'I have the honor to be, with sentiments of very high respect,

'Your Excellency's much obliged
'and humble servant,
'Samuel Miller.'

2. CITY LIFE—SOCIAL, LITERARY AND POLITICAL.— THOMAS JEFFERSON.

The occasional entries-found in Mr. Miller's diary during the year 1800 are marked by very much the same tone with those previously given.

'June 5, 1800. I am permitted to see another *ordination* day. Oh how good is God! And how ungrateful and unworthy am I! My health has been frequently interrupted, and always delicate, during the past year; but instead of being animated by this consideration to greater diligence in all my labours, not knowing when they may come to an end; to a more humble, tender anxiety to redeem the time, remembering that my days are evil, and may be very few; it seems as if every feeling of zeal were chilled; every sacred desire blunted; every principle of love, getting colder; every disposition to do good, sinking lower and lower. Lord, help me! Vain is the help of man! Oh, let me not ever live, and ever labor, "at this poor, dying rate!" Lord, quicken me by thy good Spirit; take away, Oh, take away, these miserable, earthly, grovelling dispositions and habits, which draw me down to earth! O Lord, help me so to number my days, as to apply my heart to . wisdom.'

'October 31, 1800. My *birth-day*. Thank God that it is a day of tranquillity, and a day of leisure. I would humbly improve it as a day of serious reflection, self-examination and prayer. I am to-day thirty-one years old. Oh that I had made proportional progress in wisdom, zeal and devotion to the best of Masters! My health has been very delicate and frail for a year and more past. Oh, why am I so slow to learn, from such a consideration, that I ought to be more engaged in working the work of Him who sent me into the world, while it is day; knowing that the night cometh, when no man can work? Alas! my own strength is but weakness; my own wisdom is but folly; my own efforts and resolutions all fruitless, without divine aid. All my help must come from on high. Oh that I may be constantly looking, longing, praying, for that help, until it is vouchsafed to the glory of my Master in heaven!'

The position which Mr. Miller occupied in New York gave him, at once, the freedom of that society to which he was naturally attracted by his cultivated literary and social tastes. His brother Edward, sharing these tastes, added many of his own professional friends to the number of their mutual associates; each brother, in fact, had the circle of his intercourse thus considerably enlarged. No doubt both, in this way, received a new impulse to their earnestness in general study, and to improvement as to various elegant accomplishments. But neither can it be doubted, that such society was not altogether favorable to a gospel minister's spiritual advancement, to his growth in grace and in the knowledge of Jesus Christ, or to his highest usefulness in the Church. In later years Mr. Miller seemed to look back at his life in New York, as having been, in more than one respect, a life of sore temptation; and no one can recur to its remaining records, imperfect as they are, without concluding that he could not have escaped entirely unharmed, from influences far too worldly, by which he was surrounded. The choice of a history of New York as the first great task for his pen, though a task never completed; and his subsequent actual preparation of two volumes of a general "Retrospect of the Eighteenth Century," clearly prove, that he had not yet learned to give himself wholly and rigorously—an absolute condition of great spiritual success —to his bare gospel work. Oh, that ministers of the word were not so slow to learn the secrets of true eminence in winning souls! A curious illustration of the temptations to which he was exposed, and to which, doubtless, he too far yielded, is found in his joining, perhaps helping to organize, as we have seen, a literary club, which embraced some very doubtful characters, as the intimates of a clergyman.

But especially Mr. Miller erred, under the influence of his associations in New York, in becoming far too much of a party politician. This, in after years, he expressly declared; nay, left it so carefully on record, in more than one form, as a warning to other ministers in like circumstances, that withholding any important illustration of the simple truth on this subject, would do serious injustice to his own matured convictions. The brothers had inherited from their father—perhaps both parents—a lively interest in political, as well as ecclesiastical, affairs. Edward was, evidently, a warm politician. A number of the clergy, too, around them, were not only still warmer in their partizanship, but even became electioneering pamphleteers. Mr. Miller's near clerical associates, Dr. John M. Mason and Dr. William Linn, published, each, one "campaign" pamphlet, at least, against Mr. Jefferson. On the other hand, his venerable colleague, Dr. Rodgers, took no part in politics. With the whole body of the Presbyterian clergy, he had been, through the Revolution, a decided Whig; but, subsequently, he was not accustomed even to vote. In fact he was, pre-eminently, a man of peace, shunning not only political, but also religious controversy, both in and out of the pulpit.

During Washington's administration, the two great political parties—Federalists and Republicans—had sprung up; and although, in 1797, Mr. Adams took the presidential chair, the severity of the struggle which resulted in his election by the Federalists, foreshadowed the speedy triumph of Republican democracy. This struggle gave only new vigor to the beaten party; their candidate, Mr. Jefferson, became, under the original provisions of the Constitution, Vice-president; and his adherents were gathering strength, constantly, for the next political contest. Mr. Miller espoused the cause, not alone of the Democracy, but of Mr. Jefferson, with earnest warmth. Though perfectly aware of that great statesman's infidelity, he made, for a time, such a distinction between political and religious character, as to persuade himself, that the latter was, in matters of civil government, of comparatively little importance. The greatness of this mistake he, afterwards, sadly acknowledged. Indeed, it might be called a temporary hallucination rather than a mistake; for, in sermons previously published, he had said,

"The author is not one of those who imagine political liberty to consist in freedom from all restraint, even that of morality and law. He, therefore, considers the man who opposes religion, and who fights against christianity, (the only genuine system of divine truth,) as an enemy to his country. He is persuaded that nothing has so great a tendency to promote and establish real liberty, as the practical influence of this system.

He never expects the happy arrival of the period of UNIVERSAL EMANCIPATION, until the triumph of evangelic truth shall become universal also.—How far, then, the floods of infidelity and vice, which are pouring in on every side, forbode well to the liberties and happiness of this country, he leaves to the consideration of his fellow-citizens."[1]

And again,

"My brethren, consider then, the men who would rob you of this religion, as your enemies, and the enemies of all social happiness. Be assured, whatever may be their motives, and whether they realize it or not, they are madmen, *scattering firebrands, arrows and death.* They may tell you, "that in casting off religion, you will only free yourself from chains which cramp your faculties and degrade your nature; that you will never rise to the true sublimity of the human character, till you throw from you the cumbrous load." They may tell you this; and they may believe it all. But, O fellow mortals! examine well before you commit yourselves to their delusive guidance. Are you patriots? and will you embrace principles which tend to dissolve all the ties of social order? Are you fathers of families? and will you adopt a system, which prostrates every law of domestic happiness? Are you accountable beings? and will you choose a road which conducts to *the chambers of death?* No, brethren. Whatever difficulty or trouble may arise, *hold fast to the profession of your faith without wavering. For the name of the Lord is a strong tower. The righteous runneth into it and is safe.*"[2]

The letter from which the following extract is taken was addressed to the Rev. Mr. Gemmil, of New Haven.

'New York, December 7, 1800.

' My dear Sir,

' Your kind letter by Mr. Broome came duly to hand. I will endeavor to answer it as explicitly as I can. Few things have given me greater mortification and shame, than the use which has been and continues to be made of religion, in the present electioneering struggle for President of the United States. That mere politicians, who despise religion, should thus convert it into an engine of party, is not strange ; but that men professing to love it, and especially its ministers, who ought to be its wise, prudent and wary defenders, should consent to do the same, is to me strange. If I do not totally mis-

---

[1] Sermon, (4th July, 1795,) 29, 30. Note.
[2] Fast Day Sermon, (1798,) 43. 44.

take, they are acting a part, calculated to degrade religion, to bring its ministers into contempt, and to excite in the minds of thoughtful and observing men a suspicion that, even in America, the idea of ecclesiastical encroachment and usurpation is not wholly destitute of foundation. I am mortified—I am humbled at the scenes which have passed and are passing before me.

'I profess to be a Christian. I wish all men were Christians. We should have more private, social and political happiness. But what then? Because Mr. Jefferson is suspected of Deism, are we to raise a hue and cry against him, as if he ought to be instantly deprived of his rights of citizenship? If he be an infidel, I lament it for two reasons : from a concern for his own personal salvation, and that a religion, which is so much spoken against, does not receive his countenance and aid. But notwithstanding this, I think myself perfectly consistent in saying that I had much rather have Mr. Jefferson President of the United States, than an aristocratic Christian.

'But what are we to think of the consistency of the federal party? I hear men, whom I know to despise religion, bellowing against the republican candidate for his supposed want of it. And I hear on the other hand, Christian ministers inveighing against one for infidelity, and ready to embrace another, and straining every nerve to exalt him, when his religion is equally questionable; nay, making no objection to men openly and infamously immoral. Can charity itself believe that religion is the sole motive in this case?'

In explanation of the last foregoing paragraph, and as some palliation, too, of Mr. Miller's adherence to the cause of Jefferson, it may be added, that the candidate of the Federalists for the Vice-presidency—Charles Cotesworth Pinckney—was currently charged by his opponents with infidelity and immorality.

Long afterwards Dr. Miller wrote,

'There was a time, (from the year 1800, to 1809, or 1810,) when I was a warm partisan in favor of Mr. Jefferson's politics and administration as President. Before his death, I lost all confidence in him as a genuine patriot, or even as an honest man. And after the publication of his posthumous writings, in 1829, my respect for him was exchanged for contempt and abhorrence. I now believe Mr. Jefferson to have been one of the meanest and basest of men. His own writings evince a hypocrisy, a selfishness, an artful, intriguing, underhand spirit, a contemptible envy of better men than himself, a blasphemous impiety, and a moral profligacy, which no fair, honest mind, to say nothing of piety, can contemplate without abhorrence. * *

'I am so far from having any grounds of personal animosity against Mr. Jefferson, that the contrary is the case. While I sided with him in politics, he was remarkably polite and attentive to me; wrote me a number of respectful letters; (one of which is published in his posthumous writings;[1]) and said and did many things adapted to conciliate my personal feelings. Nor did anything *personal* ever occur to change those feelings. * *

'I renounce, and wish unsaid and unwritten, everything that I ever said or wrote in his favor.   'Sam'l Miller.'
'Princeton, June, 1830.'

Still later, Dr. Miller, as if very intent upon leaving his matured opinions upon this whole subject on record, wrote again,

'* * I look back on that whole part of my early history with entire disapprobation and deep regret. On two points I totally disapprove my own conduct. In the first place, I was wrong in suffering myself to be so warmly and actively engaged in *Politics* as I was during that period. For though ministers have the rights and duties of citizens, and, probably, in most cases, ought to exercise the right of voting at elections; yet when party politics run high, and when their appearing at the polls cannot take place without exciting strong feelings on the part of many against them; and when their ministry among all such persons will be therefore much less likely to be useful, I cannot think that their giving their votes can have an importance equivalent to the injury it is likely to do. I think I was wrong in talking, and acting, and rendering myself so conspicuous as a politician, as I did. I fear I did an amount of injury to my ministry, which could by no means have been counterbalanced by my usefulness as a politician.

'But I was, if possible, still more wrong in pleading with so much zeal the cause of *Mr. Jefferson*. I thought, even then, that he was an infidel; but I supposed that he was an honest, truly republican, patriotic infidel. But I now think that he was a selfish, insidious, and hollow-hearted infidel; that he had little judgment and no moral principle; that he was a hypocritical demagogue; and that his partisans rated his patriotism far higher than was just. I have long thought that his four volumes of posthumous works disclose a degree of

[1] 4 Vol., 106. This letter will appear on a subsequent page.

meanness, malignity and hypocrisy, of which the friends of his memory have reason to be ashamed. The tradition is, that Mr. Jefferson himself, with minute care and absolute authority, selected all the parts of that publication, and left nothing to the discretion of his grandson, the editor. If it was so, his worst enemies could hardly have made a selection more unfriendly to his memory.

'True, I am now, as I was then, a sincere and honest Republican. But I totally mistook the real character of the leader of the nominal Republicans, who triumphed in the country at that time. I was gulled by hollow, hypocritical pretences, and did all I could to honor and elevate men, whom I now believe to have been unworthy of public confidence.'[1]

---

[1] This language in regard to Mr. Jefferson may, to some persons, seem, if not wholly unjust, at least too strong and objurgatory. It would not have been here inserted, however, without the deepest conviction, after careful examination, that every charge might be fully sustained. Mr. Jefferson had resided in Paris more than five years, the last four of them as our minister plenipotentiary; and returned to the United States in the Autumn of 1789, blindly enamored of Jacobinism, his head full of the worst French revolutionary ideas. (1.) He was not only an infidel, but a bitter, blaspheming infidel. (2.) He was a gross flatterer of the people—an unscrupulous demagogue past redemption. (3.) He was an apologist for insurrection and rebellion, and not in their more dignified form of secession, but in the vulgar shape of sedition and riot. (4.) As President, he was the originator of the incalculably mischievous doctrine, that public offices are the rightful "spoils" of a victorious party; and (5.) of the "policy" of vituperating a co-ordinate branch of the government, (the judiciary in this case,) which was not subservient to his will. (6.) He was father of the doctrine of the repudiation of public debts. (7.) He was an insidious enemy and accuser of General Washington, at the very time when professing for him the sincerest regard. (8.) He was a high priest of that political creed, which justifies the means by the end, counting truth as secondary to the safe and plausible disparagement of personal and party opponents. (9.) In fine, his undoubted talents and acquirements only aggravated the littleness, meanness, insincerity, dishonesty, and malignity, which ought to consign his memory to everlasting shame and contempt. The evidence of all this is found, chiefly, in his own memoirs, letters, and memoranda, carefully preserved by himself, and published posthumously, but doubtless by his direction. He had fallen to that pitch of moral depravation, in which men lose their delicate sense of the difference between right and wrong; boast of their obliquities as praiseworthy; of their low cunning, as deserving the repute of sagacity and statesmanship; and treasure up against themselves, as honorable distinctions, the clear proofs of their debasement.

(1.) See Jefferson's Correspondence, Vol. i. p. 327. ii. 174. iii. 461. 463. 468. 469. 478. iv. 138. 194. 205. 206. 300. 301. 321. 322. 325. 326. 327. 349. 353. 358. 360. 564. 365.

(2.) iii. 317. 348. *Et passim.* Comp. iii. 315. 402.

(3.) ii. 87. 267. 268. 276. iii. 307. 308. 328.

(4.) iii. 456. 464. 467. 471. 475. 476. 477. 483. 484.

(5.) iii. 458. 478. 487. iv. 71. 72. 73. 74. 90. 91. 101. 102. 103. 337. 345. 352.

(6.) iii. 27–32. iv. 196–198. 291. 396. 397.

(7.) iii. 202. 307. 319. 320. 324. 325. 327. 328. iv. 452. 453. 485. (10 Sparks's Writings of Washington, 522. 523.) 467. 468. 478. 491. 512. ii. 439, 463. 464. iii. 46. iv. 185. 235–237. 406. 419. 420. 453.

(8.) iii. 461. iv. 503. 505. 508. (10 Writings of Washington, 159.) 17. 18. 23

12

3. POLITICS AND THE CLERGY.

Before, during, and immediately after the Revolutionary war, the clergy of this country, of perhaps every denomination, took far more interest, or, at any rate, a far more active part, in politics, than they do at present. The very circumstances of those times may, in some measure, account for the fact; while the example of the clergy of Great Britain in such matters had been, doubtless, most influential with their brethren on this side of the Atlantic. There a church establishment, and the spectacle of a bench of bishops in the House of Lords have evidently inclined the clergy to become politicians. And, during our colonial existence, the exclusive political claims of the Episcopalians, with the vigorous opposition to·those claims made by other denominations—by none with stronger purpose than by Presbyterians—rendered the Church the very theatre, often, of political strife. Since the Revolution, the ministry of the gospel has, in this country, become, gradually, more and more disentangled from politics; nay, to an alarming extent, has aimed often at dissevering those ties, which, naturally and most properly, bind up every interest, religious as well as social, with the common interests of the nation. Of course, whenever unusual occasions of political excitement arise, some ministers will be hurried into an excess of partisanship; but while we deplore this, there is scarcely less reason to deplore the indifference which others frequently manifest—in which they have merely indulged, or, from mistaken views, even schooled themselves—as to national affairs. The reproaches or plaudits, which unscrupulous party men lavish, according to their selfish fears or hopes, upon clergymen who step into the arena of politics, are not worth regarding; but, doubtless, it is the common sense of a Christian people, that the clergy ought not, in ordinary circumstances, to become active politicians; and that every Christian who mingles in party strife exposes himself, on account especially of ever prevailing political corruption, to very great danger of harmful reproach, if

24. 169. 170. ii. 88. iii. 315. 316. 324. 330. 539. 378. 402. 404. 407. 465–477. 483. iv. 87. 98. 109. 110. 113. 144. 145. 164. 182. 183. 195. 446–448. iii. 444. 445. iv. 74.

(9.) iii. 315, 316. 330. 364. 369. 400. 414. 416. 429. 440. 444. 338. 340. 343. 344. 345. 409. iv. 69. 407. 408. 428. 413. 487.

not of serious moral contamination. Where, then, is the
line to be drawn between a proper and improper participation, on the part of gospel ministers, in political affairs?
Perhaps the great principles which should govern us, as to
this matter, are simple and obvious enough. The difficulty
lies in their application to particular cases, ever varying
with the state of the country, and with individual relations
and circumstances. No citizen can, by mere self-dedica-
tion to the special service of God, free himself from his
natural obligations. The clergyman may relinquish the
natural rights, but not neglect the natural duties, of citizenship for the sake of his profession. On this principle,
our Saviour once condemned the teaching of the Pharisees;[1]
and, on this principle as well as others, all true Protestants
entirely disapprove of a monastic life. Of course, a miracu-
lously demonstrated call of God may justify casting off ordinary obligations: here it is only a higher natural duty—
the duty to obey special rather than general commands—
that takes the place of a lower. The natural duties of a
citizen are either personal or official. In our country, it is
the official duty of every qualified person, as one of the
sovereigns, to vote; as one of the subjects, to obey the
laws. Personal duties are not so definite, not in form so
obligatory. It is the personal duty of all to do and say
whatever they can, consistently with other duties, for the
welfare of the country, and the success of those measures,
and therefore of that party, which they approve. And,
doubtless, in times of special danger to the state, ministers,
on this ground, may properly engage in political strife with
greater freedom. But, ordinarily, they can *benefit their
country more* in another way—by conciliating all parties
to themselves, as Christ's ambassadors, and, for the gospel's sake, avoiding unnecessary political entanglements
and alienations. For them to talk of the Saviour will have,
usually, a better *political* effect, than to talk of party men
or measures. And, herein, they will not be neglecting
their duty, but really accomplishing it more completely,
and in the better way. Such appear to have been substantially the views in which Mr. Miller settled down, after
much, and some of it painful, experience. The duty of

[1] Mark vii. 11.

voting he seems, always, carefully to have fulfilled; although sometimes, perhaps erroneously, expressing the doubt, whether a clergyman's circumstances might not occasionally justify a different course.

4. - PROJECTS AND CORRESPONDENCE.

About the time of Mr. Jefferson's election, Mr. Miller, perhaps as an offset to his support of an infidel candidate for the presidency, seems to have planned a pamphlet, if not a larger publication, in the shape of letters to the Republicans, or Democrats, of the United States, upon the importance of Christianity. Notes and collections for such a work are found among his papers. He proposed to defend his party, as a party, from the charge of infidelity, and to stigmatize infidel sentiments as the bane of human society. The plan, however, remained unfulfilled.

From the very commencement of his ministry, his life long, Mr. Miller's mind was teeming with projects of writing and publishing. Perhaps no man of like cultivation and opportunity, breathing too an infected atmosphere, especially after once experiencing the sensations of being "put to press," has ever escaped this *cacoëthes scribendi*. And the wisdom of such men must be looked for in their not executing, rather than in their not projecting: we must judge the deed instead of the will. About the time which we have now reached in his history, Mr. Miller's thoughts seem to have been particularly busy with schemes of book-making. Possibly the religious works which he designed were to be a professional balance to his literary undertakings. The following extracts from his note-book exemplify what we mean:—

'This day, August 9, 1800, resolved, through divine assistance and direction, to keep in view, and as soon as possible to execute, the plan of writing and publishing the following religious works:—

'I. A set of Sermons on Regeneration.
'II. A volume of Letters to the Young *Men* of my Charge.
'III. A volume of Letters to the Young *Women* of Do.
'IV. Brief View of Scripture Doctrines.
'V. Two volumes—Select Sermons.'

A few pages further on, in the same note-book, he

writes, 'For a striking extract for my proposed work on the Lord's Supper, see &c., &c.'

Not one of these projects was ever fulfilled, unless the second and third, partially, in some of Dr. Miller's after-writings for the young. In fact, the scheming literary brain seldom overtakes one in ten of its avant-couriers. And, in the present instance, a heavier undertaking soon weighed every energy down to a more sober working frame. Then, providential circumstances, rather than mere taste, gave shape and substance to the book-making of many years.

Mr. Miller's foreign correspondence has been already, in part, noticed. From its commencement, it rapidly extended, until, with diminishing zest, it must have become a heavy burden. His active interest in the New York Missionary Society, his projected history, his subsequent plan of a Retrospect of the Eighteenth Century, hereafter to be noticed, and other causes, some of them now unknown, brought him into epistolary communication in 1799, and a few subsequent years, with the Rev. John Erskine, D.D., the Rev. John Jamieson, D.D., and Sir Harry Moncrief, of Edinburgh; the Rev. Robert Balfour, D.D., of Glasgow; the Rev. Wm. L. Brown, D.D., of Aberdeen; the Rev. Robert McCulloch, of Dairsie; the Rev. Andrew Fuller, D.D., of Kettering; the Rev. Thomas Scott, D.D., the Rev. Thomas Haweis, D.D., the Rev. Adam Clarke, D.D., the Rev. Hugh Worthington, William Wilberforce, Esquire, and Philip Sansom, Esquire, London; the Rev. John Ryland, D.D., of Bristol; the Rev. Benjamin McDowel, D.D., of Dublin; the Rev. Robert Black, of Londonderry; the Rev. Mr. Hamilton, of Armagh; the Rev. Dr. John Wernerus Herzog, Professor at Basle; Frederick Schiller, Esquire, Professor John Heinrich Jung Stilling, and Baron Von Shirnding, of Germany; the Rev. William Carey, D. D., the distinguished missionary, and others. Some of the letters from these gentlemen are interesting, but too far aside from the object of this work to be inserted. Mr. Miller's zeal in this foreign correspondence was no doubt stimulated by the example of his brother, who, together with Doctor Samuel L. Mitchill, had, in 1797, been induced by Doctor Elihu H. Smith, to undertake with him the conduct of the *Medical Repository*, a quarterly journal commencing with the number for August in that year, the earliest in this country devoted to the interests of the medical profession, and introducing its editors to an extensive correspondence with eminent physicians and others in both Europe and America.   This work was continued for many years—even after Dr. Smith and Dr. Miller had been removed by death.   Mr. Miller's home correspondence, at the same time, was so extensive, that of itself it must have been an oppressive load.

CHAPTER TENTH.

1801.

THE marriage of Mr. Miller's sister, Mrs. Mary Loock-erman, to Major John Patten has been already mentioned. Major Patten died on the 26th of December, 1800, and his wife survived him only until the 13th of March following. Their mortal remains lie in the same grave in the church-yard at Dover, under a stone upon which the Major is said to have "distinguished himself as a brave and useful officer during the Revolutionary War, and afterwards served his country with honor, at different periods, as a member of the American Congress."

In May, 1801, Mr. Miller attended as a commissioner, for the first time, the General Assembly, sitting that year in Philadelphia. He was chosen one of the temporary clerks. The most important measure, perhaps, adopted during its sessions was the "Plan of Union," which occasioned eventually so much discord, but was designed, originally, to promote harmonious co-operation between Presbyterians and Congregationalists in the new settlements. In regard to this matter, the General Association of Connecticut had taken the initiative, at its meeting in June of the previous year, by appointing a committee of three, to confer with a similar committee of the Assembly. The latter, instead of a committee of conference, appointed one to draw up a definite plan, which was presented and with entire unanimity adopted: at least, no dissent appears of record. This was in May, and, in June following, the General Association concurred unanimously in the arrangement. Dr. Jonathan Edwards, a Connecticut man, then president of Union College, and a commissioner from

the Presbytery of Albany, took a prominent part in this
proceeding, being chairman of the committee, and, doubtless, draughtsman of the plan. This subject will be adverted to hereafter. At the inception of the measure, no
one appears to have dreamed of the difficulties which it
afterwards occasioned; and, in fact, those difficulties arose
less from the plan itself, clearly unconstitutional as it was,
than from the rise, in New England, of both a new theology and a new spirit, which resulted in its becoming, on
that side, an engine of proselytism and the dissemination
of error within the bounds of the Presbyterian Church.

Dr. Miller, toward the close of life, remarked,

'In looking back on the origin and object .of the "Plan of
Union," (this 25*th of November*, 1847,) I cannot take the retrospect without sorrow and shame. Never, I suppose, did a large
body of ministers act from purer motives, or with more entire
fraternal harmony, than did the members of the General
Assembly, in adopting this measure. The avowed and the
sincere object of it was to avoid discord, and to promote and
establish peace. But it was a most unfortunate measure. It
led eventually to an amount of abuse and to conflicts by no
means anticipated by either Presbyterians or Congregationalists. The truth is, acting under the guidance of our form of
government, we had no right to make the concessions which
that plan included. But these concessions, while altogether
unauthorized and disorderly in themselves, were perverted and
abused in a manner by no means intended or foreseen; until
they produced an amount of evil which rendered necessary the
painful separation of 1837.'

To this Assembly also came as a commissioner the Rev'd
Archibald Alexander, from the Presbytery of Hanover;
and here first became acquainted the two young men and
ministers, who afterwards were to be so long and so intimately associated as the first two professors of the first
theological seminary of the Presbyterian Church in the
United States. Being in ill health, Mr. Alexander prolonged his journey, after the meeting of the Assembly, to
the northward and eastward, and visited New York City;
where he renewed and improved his acquaintance with Mr.
Miller. On his way, he visited Princeton, and spent a
night there—"the first time," he wrote long afterwards,
"I ever saw the place where I have already spent above

thirty years of my life, and where I shall in all probability lay my bones. Such a view of futurity as should have presented to me the events of my life, would then have appeared very strange."

But there was another "plan of union," which Mr. Miller had under serious consideration, at the same time that the Connecticut Congregationalists were so assiduously, warmly, and successfully wooing the General Assembly ; and, doubtless, this plan, if not more important, was far more anxiously debated with himself than the other. His duties as a commissioner, to which those of the temporary clerkship were probably a serious addition, must have occu- pied a large part of his time, and confined him a good deal to the First Presbyterian Church, then in Market Street, and to his lodgings, at Col. McLane's ; but we have his own authority for saying, that he spent all his leisure hours at a place much more pleasant to him than either of those just mentioned. This was the residence, at the north-west corner of Arch and Seventh streets, of Mrs. Elizabeth Sergeant, daughter of the Mathematician and Astronomer, David Rittenhouse. Here the latter had died in 1796, and here his daughter, left a widow three years earlier, was residing with her family—three children and several step- children. Of the latter, the oldest sister—she had one brother older—was named Sarah ; and she rather than any supposable relics of the old astronomer, or any respect to his scientific fame, was the grand attraction for our New York assembly-man. When and where he was first introduced to Miss Sergeant cannot now be ascertained ; but he had met with her twice in the previous month of March, probably in Philadelphia, when upon an excursion to Del- aware, and travelling for several weeks, in quest, it is not unlikely, of health.

It may be reasonably conjectured, however, as Mrs. McLane was one of the chief officers of a benevolent so- ciety, of which Miss Sergeant was the secretary, that the former, in her watchful care for her brother's interests, had recommended the latter to his notice. At the second of the interviews above mentioned, he had formed the de- sign of endeavoring to win her hand. He may not have seen her again, until he visited Philadelphia, about the middle of May, under the heavy responsibilities of his first commission to the Assembly, but the still heavier weight of a determination to make himself as agreeable as possible to Miss Sergeant.

On the 27th of July, after a short visit to Philadelphia, we find him writing, 'I thank you, my dear Sarah, for that candor and confidence in me, which disposed you to remove my fears, and send me away a happy man.' So this visit settled the matter: a "plan of union" of very momentous consequence to many, but which resulted in no excision or schism, and was never abrogated, had been finally agreed upon.

In the letter from which a quotation has just been made, Mr. Miller says,

'I communicated to my brother [Edward,] as far as was proper, the success of my journey, my prospects and my happiness. His answer was—"I give you joy of your prospect: you have reason, in my opinion, to consider yourself one of the most fortunate of men. You could not present me with a sister, of whose character, in all respects, so far as my acquaintance extends, I more highly and fully approve. Bring her along as soon as you please, and she will find a brother proud and happy to acknowledge such a relationship." I confess this language gave me high pleasure. Coming from such a brother; delivered under circumstances so indicative of impartiality; and pronounced with such prompt frankness; it made an impression which at once flattered my pride, and confirmed my prior opinions.'

Another extract from one of Mr. Miller's letters, dated August 7th, will give an idea of some of the expedients of the city clergy of that day, for bodily and mental recuperation.

'On Wednesday week last, I went down with a large party of gentlemen, (twenty-six in number,) to amuse myself with fishing on the sea-bass banks. These banks are in the ocean, about twelve or fifteen miles to the southward of Sandy Hook, and nearly opposite Long Branch. The company was pleasant, the fishing delightful, the bathing highly refreshing, and the mirth and jollity of the party, notwithstanding the presence of several clergymen, so great, as almost to border on being excessive. We returned the next evening; and I think I felt ten per cent., at least, better for the jaunt. Contrary to all my expectations, I escaped sea-sickness; though my wish was, for the sake of its salubrity, to experience that painful disorder.'

Mr. Miller was married to Miss Sergeant on the 24th day of October, 1801, by the Rev. John Ewing, D. D., Provost of the University of Pennsylvania, her half uncle by marriage. The yellow fever was, at the time, prevalent in New York, though not so alarmingly as in some previous years; and the Health Committee of Philadelphia were imposing a quarantine of fifteen days upon all visitors from the former city. Here was a dilemma, but love triumphed; a dispensation from the Committee, which Mr. Miller wrote for, seems to have been obtained; and, not impossibly, as he appears to have gone without the wedding day's having been fixed, the supposable difficulty of getting a second dispensation, within any reasonable time, somewhat precipitated the marriage.

Dr. Ewing was now in his seventieth year, and was thought to exhibit a little of the forgetfulness of old age. Lest he should fail to remember the time of the wedding, or his duty to keep it a profound secret, the matter was confided to his wife only: she, without informing him who the parties were, was to see that he was ready for the summons. Old Hans, a clever negro coachman, who had long been in Mrs. Sergeant's family, was sent with the carriage at the appointed time. Hans was never more in his element, than when mimicking the Provost for the amusement of the children, or waiting upon him with a droll obsequiousness. He had been let into the secret, and enjoyed, hugely, mystifying and surprising the old gentleman. "Where are we going?" asked the latter. "Just a few squares," replied Hans; and directly he stopped at Mrs. Sergeant's door. Dr. Ewing entered briskly, and revenged himself for the ruse, by declaring, for a while, that he would not perform the ceremony until Mr. Miller promised—it was Saturday evening—to preach for him the next day.

The newly married couple spent the first Sabbath, and perhaps several days, in Philadelphia; for Mr. Miller was seized with an alarming illness of a few hours, which it was feared might be the yellow fever. The next Sabbath, however, they were at Abington, Pennsylvania, where the Rev. William M. Tennent was then pastor of the Presbyterian church. Mr. Miller did not preach, but assisted in the communion service. The following Sabbath he preached in New York. In answer to a congratulatory letter from his warm friend, Mr. Dickinson of Delaware, he writes on the 23d of November,

'The friendship with which you have long and uniformly favored our family is a subject of frequent and very pleasing recollection to me; and the manner in which you have been pleased to recognize it on the present occasion is peculiarly gratifying. To be remembered by those whom my parents loved and honored is a pleasure too valuable in itself, and connected with too many interesting considerations, to be received without the deepest sensibility.

'The late change in my situation was made deliberately; and I hope the result will prove that it was made wisely, and for the lasting happiness of both parties. It has pleased a kind Providence to bestow upon me, in a wife, such a degree of good sense, improvement, loveliness and moral excellence, as can scarcely fail of securing, through the divine benediction, our mutual felicity.

'I cannot refrain from offering to you my cordial congratulations on the continued prosperity and progress of Republicanism in our country, and on the prospect of returning tranquillity in Europe. May these events prove important means, in the hands of the supreme Governor of Nations, of promoting the dignity and happiness of man!

'I am, dear Sir,
'With sentiments of very high respect,
'Your obliged friend and servant,
'Sam'l Miller.

'John Dickinson, Esquire.'

Sarah Miller.

CHAPTER ELEVENTH.

1778–1803.

———

1. ANCESTORS—BIRTH.

MRS. MILLER'S father, Jonathan Dickinson Sergeant, was the son of Jonathan Sergeant, who resided first at Newark, afterwards at Princeton, New Jersey. His name and descent may be traced back to Jonathan Sergeant, his great grandfather, who is mentioned among the early settlers of New Haven, in 1639, and of Branford, Connecticut, in 1646. He died in 1652, leaving at least two sons, Jonathan and Thomas. The former was among the Branford people, who settled Newark, and signed "The Fundamental Agreements" for that settlement in 1667; although he seems not to have removed thither before the next year. An old Newark record, for the 25th of January, 1669, says, "Accommodation was granted to him, according to his estate, * * if he will abide in the town and follow his trade." What this "trade" was is unknown. "The Fundamental Agreements" bound the subscribers to· provide carefully for the maintenance of the purity of religion, as professed in the Congregational churches of Connecticut; the migration having been determined partly, if not wholly, by dissatisfaction with the choice to civil offices of men who were not professing Christians. Jonathan Sergeant, son of the Newark settler, was father of the Jonathan first above mentioned; and of his younger brother, the Rev. John Sergeant,[1] born in 1710, graduated at Yale College in 1729, and well known as a missionary, from 1734 until his death in 1749, to the Mohegan Indians at Stockbridge.

---

[1] 1 Sprague's Annals, 388.

The older brother, Jonathan, married Hannah, daughter of James Nutman, justice of the peace; and, after her death, Abigail, daughter of the Rev. Jonathan Dickinson,[1] of Elizabethtown, first President of the College of New Jersey. In 1758, he removed to Princeton, whither the College, in the prosperity of which he seems to have been greatly interested, had been transferred in the Autumn of 1756. Here he probably was engaged in farming. In Newark he had held, from time to time, several public trusts, and had employed himself, occasionally, at least, as a conveyancer, and probably as a surveyor. By his second wife he had two children, Jonathan Dickinson, and a daughter, Elizabeth, who married Edward Fox.

Jonathan Dickinson Sergeant was born at Newark in 1746, and graduated at the College of New Jersey in 1762. He studied law in Princeton with Richard Stockton, one of the signers of the Declaration of Independence; and there, first, practised his profession. In 1776 he was elected to the Continental Congress, and took his seat a few days only after the Declaration had been executed. A short time before, he had married Margaret, daughter of the Rev. Elihu Spencer[2] of Trenton, previously of St. George's, Delaware. Mr. Sergeant, on going to Congress, left his wife and infant son at Princeton, either with his father, or in a new house which he had lately built upon the same lot, on another portion of which, forty years afterwards, Dr. Samuel Miller erected his dwelling.

Mrs. Sergeant was descended from a well known New England ancestry. Her father was a son of Isaac and Mary (Selden) Spencer of East Haddam, Connecticut. But a little younger than the missionaries, David and John Brainerd, he could trace back his descent and theirs to a common great grandfather, Jared Spencer, of Cambridge, afterwards Lynn, Massachusetts, and subsequently of Haddam. Moreover, his two brothers, Samuel and General Joseph Spencer had married, the former, Jerusha, and the latter Martha, Brainerd, sisters of the missionaries.

Mr. Sergeant as a member of Congress, Mr. Spencer as

---

[1] 3 Sprague's Annals, 14.

[2] D. D. from 1782. For sketches of Dr. Spencer's life see 3 Sprague's Annals, 165, etc., and Dr. Hall's "History of the Presbyterian Church in Trenton, N. J.," pp. 208-289.

a Presbyterian clergyman, and both for their ardent patriotism, and active efforts in the cause of independence, were particularly obnoxious to the British authorities and troops. Indeed, the latter having gone on a mission to North Carolina, and perhaps other neighboring States, to inform the remote settlers of the ground of the war, and to arouse them to self-defence, a reward of one hundred guineas had been set upon his head. This was known to the American officers, and one of them, probably General Mercer, sent a messenger to him one night in December, 1776, to say that the British army was near, and that he must fly for his life. At two o'clock in the morning, a friend of Mr. Sergeant's, Dr. Bainbridge of Princeton, aroused Mrs. Sergeant, informed her of the enemy's approach, and insisted upon her hastening, immediately, in her carriage, with her sister and infant, to a ferry on the Delaware, where her husband had agreed to meet her, in case she were compelled to fly from the British soldiery. Mr. Spencer was hurrying for her from Trenton to Princeton, when he met Dr. Witherspoon, who told him she had already fled, and that he must return and remove his own family at once. Having returned, he locked up his dwelling with all its contents, left his cattle without having been able to provide any care for them, set out immediately, with the entire household, in a large carriage, and took them that night four miles to Howell's Ferry on the Delaware. Leaving them there, he went on, sixteen miles further, to McConkey's Ferry, where he found Mrs. Sergeant's party. To this point he then brought the others, and here they all crossed. Dr. Spencer's youngest daughter,[1] often described, in after days, the scenes at both ferries. 'To my youthful imagination,' she said, 'they called up the day of judgment: so many frightened people were assembled, with sick and wounded soldiers, all flying for their lives, and with hardly any means of crossing the river. We were unspeakably delighted when we got over safely, and into a little hut, where we spent the night with a company of American soldiers, on their way to join General Washington. We stayed at McConkey's Ferry for two or three weeks, until General Mercer sent my father word that he was not safe there. This was the Sunday

---

[1] Mrs. Lydia Biddle, of Carlisle, whose reminiscences have supplied this whole account.

before the battle of Trenton. He preached that day at Newtown. Afterwards, he went on slowly to Fagg's Manor, where he remained until the people of St. George's, Delaware, hearing that their former pastor was a fugitive, and being themselves without one, sent for him.' He accepted their invitation, and, on his arrival, found a house ready, well supplied with furniture and provisions, the wood cut, the fires made, and everything prepared for the comfort of his family. Here they remained until the July following, when St. George's being sickly, and Trenton free from the British soldiery, he returned home. He found his house empty and somewhat damaged; its contents, including all his papers, the Hessians had burned. The loss of his sermons so discouraged him, that he never wrote another, but preached, thereafter, from short notes merely. Mrs. Sergeant had not left her father, as her husband was still in Congress, sitting then at Baltimore. Meantime his new house at Princeton had been burned by the enemy, and his father had died of small-pox. The following winter, however, his wife spent with her widowed mother near Princeton, where her second child, Sarah, was born on the 1st of January, 1778. In the spring, she went to Pittsgrove with her father, whose position in Trenton was considered unsafe, while Philadelphia was in possession of the British troops; and they did not return until after the evacuation of the latter city, and the battle of Monmouth. In September of the same year, Mr. Sergeant was appointed Attorney General of Pennsylvania, and thenceforward resided with his family in Philadelphia.

2. YOUTH—MEMOIRS.

A few years after Mrs. Miller's marriage, she undertook, for her own improvement, the satisfaction of her husband, and the possible benefit of her children and other near relatives, to commit to writing some brief memoirs of her previous, particularly her religious, life. In 1807, she began this work, but, although the narrative was never extended beyond that year, she did not complete it before 1823. From time to time, she put her reminiscences on paper, frequently amended them and added something, returning to her task frequently after long intervals of neglect. She says at length, 'I have written over and over again many parts, and have not now satisfied myself with it.' She evidently wrote and rewrote under a strong impression of the difficulty of giving a correct narration of religious experience.

A portion of these memoirs, relating to her life before marriage, will perhaps be more interesting and profitable than any account which could otherwise be offered of her early years. The whole is addressed to her husband.

'* * Indeed, my dear Friend, we are too reserved on these subjects: you and I have both acknowledged this fault many times, and have both resolved to do differently in time to come. We suffer ourselves to be, in some measure, drawn into that delusion, which causes us to feel as if the great interest of religion were the only one which silence and reserve could not injure; when, as, in the first instance, "faith cometh by hearing," so we help to establish one another in this precious faith, by conversing together about the interests of our Master, and our joint interest with him. * *

'Thus, actuated by a desire to have my own hopes confirmed and strengthened, to impart to my husband my reasons for indulging such strong ones, and to be the means of doing, if possible, some good to those relatives, who are living "without God in the world," I have resolved to collect together and commit to writing those circumstances which have impressed my own mind, made religion appear to it what it really is—the "one thing needful," and made me conclude, in some of my best moments, to live as if it were so; that have, I trust, been the means of preparing the way of the Lord in my own heart, and, at length, of forming him there "the hope of glory"; and I intended, when this arrangement should be completed, to commit all to my best earthly friend.

'Since the veil which concealed from my mind the true light has been, by divine influence, in some measure removed, one of my most delightful mental exercises has been that of endeavoring to recollect my earliest religious impressions, so as to form a series, which should connect my own ideas on this subject in some order, and make them more intelligible to others. The first impressions, which this exercise has revived in my mind, I think, from the combined recollection of scenes and events, must have commenced between the ages of seven and nine. More than once, whilst engaged in play with my companions, my mind has been suddenly abstracted from these objects, and fixed on creation at large, through the medium of surrounding scenes, and these queries have internally arisen: There must have been a point when these things had a beginning: what was before them? These objects do not occupy boundless space: what is beyond them? The incapacity of my mind to fathom boundless space or duration rendered these questions distressing to me: they produced an awful state of feeling, from which I found relief only by engaging more devotedly in play. I think I perceive the divine benignity in the choice of the time for these impressions. I am persuaded, from the organization of my mind, that, if they had engaged it in a state of vacuity, the conception would have been overwhelming. In this season of pastime they were made, as a means of improvement for a future time, to be nurtured and expanded at leisure. How much pain would I have been spared, if I had attended to these invitations of the Spirit!—for now I recognize whence they were. If my Father had found these to answer, harsher methods might have been omitted. If then, when God was "working in me," I had endeavored to "work out my own salvation," how many misspent years might have been usefully engaged; how many scenes of vanity avoided; how great acquisitions of knowledge and virtue might have been acquired! Oh that the Lord would make me to redeem the time, and that he would overrule all for good!

'It might be asked, had I never been instructed in the doctrines of Christianity? Had I never read the Bible? Had I never been called to observe God in creation and providence? The peculiar doctrines of the Gospel, as a system, had never been presented to my mind, and formed no part of the education which was given me. Where then was the child thus educated? The Bible I read at school as children generally do, and in the same unprofitable manner, without retaining in my mind, or having my heart engaged in, any truth contained in it. I was brought up to a punctual attendance at church, and have ever, in consequence, felt it an indispensable duty on the Sabbath. For this I have unspeakable reason to be thankful! Besides these advantages, I had sometimes a word from my mother, which drew my attention to an overruling Providence. I remember once, in particular, when some wild fanatic had predicted, that, on a certain day not far distant, there was to be an earthquake, or a comet; or that the end of the world was at hand; which, as usual, had terrified the ignorant and children to a great degree, I was trembling under serious apprehension, when my mother said to me, "If this dreadful event should occur, it will do you no harm, if you are a good girl." This conveyed to my mind, I believe, some of the first impressions of a

God of Providence, in whose hands was the disposal of all events—at least some of the first which were lasting. Until the present day, although there is scarcely another incident of that part of my life alive, I can, when this is recalled, recollect the seat which I occupied at the dinner-table, and other minute circumstances of the time. How often have I been thankful, that my mother, instead of endeavoring to subdue my fears by ridiculing the cause of them, directed my attention to Him who is able to preserve from every danger, and overrule every event for good! How much better is it, to take advantage of such excitement in the minds of children, as a means of impressing upon them the solemn truth, that there are dangers and objects of terror, which may present at every step, and at the same time of directing them to their only hope of protection and deliverance.

'Various changes took place in our family circle in the course of a few years. In 1787, when I was nine years old, my mother died, and two years afterwards my father married again. During this interval, and until my fifteenth year, I was sent from one boarding school to another, and through this medium became acquainted with the sentiments and practices of the world, as far as my age, and the slight restraints made use of in these places, would permit; and becoming also weaned from home, I acquired a taste for rambling. In this time, I do not recollect that one religious impression was experienced; religious feeling was quenched by the breath of an opposite influence, and was not renewed within me until the poison began to be eradicated by severe trials. The association of unsanctified human nature, in any way, excites to sin and increases its prevalence. The evils resulting from this in mere common schools is very great; but the result of evil is incalculable in boarding schools, where children are constantly together. Nothing can be said in their favor, but that they are less injurious than some homes, where example and influence are still more pernicious, and from which children may be sent to them with impunity.

'I had just passed through these scenes of folly and temptation, and come abroad into the world, to engage in its pursuits and pleasures, as far as my father's plain habits would permit, —for without being restrained by the principles of religion, he seemed to have an inherent aversion to worldly amusements, and only permitted them in his family from a desire to indulge his children,—when the first visitation of yellow fever took place in our country, and fixed upon Philadelphia as the scene of its devastation. Whatever others, who were involved in the miseries which took place in consequence of this pestilence, felt,

I am persuaded that I needed some solemn check to my worldly career; and it laid a foundation which enabled me to withstand, in some little degree, the torrent of temptation which assailed me afterwards.

'Of my father I would say a little more: he well deserved it. His descent was no common one. He was from both sides of his house a Puritan child—a descendant of some of the best men in the Church, and men high in office—himself one of the first in his profession as a lawyer—inheriting the promise to the seed of the Church, included in the Second Commandment.

'The revolutionary spirit had sprung up in France, and given rise to those movements which preceded and commenced the bloodshed and disorder, continuing for many years in that country, and driving so many of its inhabitants to seek an asylum under other governments. The iniquity of their devoted land had become full, according to Scripture expression; and the Lord had begun his controversy with it. One of the inconveniences of that liberty, in which we had so rejoiced, was then experienced. These outcasts, even the royalists, flocked to this land of freemen, and brought with them an example and influence likely to involve us in all the iniquity which was under such severe judgment in their own country. The enemy was coming in like a flood; but this favored land, which had been in a great measure populated, many years before, by an influx of a very different kind—the persecuted believers of the old world—experienced the fulfilment of the consequent promise —The Spirit of the Lord lifted up a standard against him. It was a standard indeed of affliction; but "the Lord hath his way in the whirlwind and in the storm"; and although the yellow-fever has continued to waste our cities, from time to time, ever since, it was part of that storm which precedeth the still, small voice of mercy, which has been heard in the hearts of so many, and hindered, no doubt, at the time, the current of vice and folly.

'Now that the frequency of this visitation has enabled us to learn so many meliorating circumstances with regard to it, those who saw not that time can scarcely imagine the panic which agitated our city. It might emphatically have been said, "all faces are turned into paleness." My father, moved by compassion at seeing the multitudes who must suffer, if all who were able to render assistance fled, would have remained in the city; but the entreaties of his family at length induced him to remove to a small farm of his, at such a distance from it as would allow of his devoting every day to the sick and suffering. He connected himself with the Board of Health, and by this means we were kept awake to almost every peculiar and distressing circumstance of this calamity.

'Being, after our removal, relieved from that overwhelming fear which had assailed me in the city, but solemnly impressed with the apprehension of still existing danger, a realizing sense was induced, for the first time, of the frailty and uncertainty of human life, and the need of something more than this world can afford, to render us safe in it, or willing to relinquish it. I had, from education, a *superstitious* dependence on the Bible; and when this trial arose, to the Bible my mind involuntarily turned, from choice—if that can be called choice, which was produced by the presence of affliction. I read it formally, and felt as if there was a righteousness in the mere perusal. It was certainly not that seeking, to which the promise—"ye shall find"—is annexed; and it remained a sealed book to me. With this attention to the Bible, I engaged in prayer also in a different manner from that to which I had been accustomed. Besides the habitual prayers learned and continued from my childhood, frequently the pressure of *present circumstances* drove me to this duty; and they made the subject of my petitions. When my father was taken ill, to this means I resorted for relief. And this spirit of prayer continued through all the sins, and follies, and scepticism of many years of self-indulgence.

'When my father died, anxiety for his everlasting welfare agitated my mind, and I found relief only in hoping, that he had been prepared for his change in some manner by his latter works. In my ignorance I thus encouraged myself. I have rather hoped since, that his apparently disinterested benevolence was the evidence of a better preparation, and have been strengthened in this hope, by recollecting that it was observed of him, in his last moments, by his attendants, and I trust by him who loves to hear the voice of prayer—"Behold, he prayeth!"

'After my father's death, and after the yellow-fever had disappeared, I continued serious and attentive to religious reading for some time. The recent calamitous season had made so deep an impression, that former follies but gradually returned. What, however, tended, in some degree, to lengthen this season of seriousness, was the same solemn bias of mind in M——.[1] The distresses which she had witnessed and experienced had cast, indeed, a deeper gloom over her spirit, which saddened every object on which it rested; and as religion was, at present, this object, it received the gloomy tinge of her mind, and was, as in many similar instances, stigmatized as the cause

[1] A dear friend.

of that, which it was probably assisting to alleviate. Her
friends, although they were attentive to the forms of religion,
and respected it, were afraid she was too much occupied with
it, and would sink into melancholy. I cannot help, when re-
tracing my own steps, calling to mind M——'s also, especially
as they appear to have been, for some time, considerably inter-
woven. * * We were the only persons * * who appeared to have
had recourse to the Bible for relief, at this awful season ; and
although her seriousness continued somewhat longer than mine,
we both began to decline, in a short time, from the truth, or
rather from the means of obtaining it. My father's death had
left me my own mistress, and gaiety and dissipation spread
their lures for me, whilst error and infidelity ensnared M——.
She had, probably, been wavering for some time, when Dr.
Priestly preached in Philadelphia. She was amongst his hearers, and soon became a proselyte. Some friend, about this time,
or soon after, lent her ——, [an infidel work,] which she read
with much pleasure. —— ——, [another infidel work,] followed this, either casually, or by design, as a means of saving
her from gloom and despair, and powerfully assisted her progress into a gulf of unbelief, which has, I fear, stopped little short
of Atheism, and from which, we may emphatically say, a God of
mercy alone can deliver her. She seemed to have become herself
persuaded that the Bible was her worst enemy, and seized with
eagerness, and read with avidity, every plausible work, which
had a tendency to weaken, or subvert, its influence. Religion
has been a favorite subject of discussion with her ever since ;
she has, indeed, been a laborer in the field of infidelity ; has
appeared to be endeavoring to overthrow the truth in her own
mind, as well as in the minds of others, by every argument
which infidelity has opposed to it ; but has evidently not been
able to effect this even in her own ; and thus has but a tolerable existence in this world, while endeavoring to subvert the
best hopes for another.

'I would bless the Lord, who brings good out of evil, and
makes the wrath of man to praise him, that the cavils of M—
have been overruled for good to me. The opposition which she
made to the Bible involved considerable discussion of its doctrines, and led me, though only as an idle caviller, to its interior ; and, in the midst of worldly attractions, has kept some
impression of it on my mind.

'In May, 1795, our family were divided ; my mother, with
the five younger children continued together ; the others went,
some to college, and some to boarding with Mrs. —— a lady,
who from an unexpected failure, from some unknown cause,

when her husband died, of all her expectations of a sufficiency,
found herself compelled to earn her own and her children's
support. She concluded to receive into her family young
ladies, either going to school, or wishing to have the advantages
of a city life—that is, to enjoy the amusements and gaiety of
the world. Here was my next and dreadful temptation. I
was one of the number, who, upon leaving my father's house,
entered into the scene of dissipation and folly which Mrs. ——'s
family presented. We lived as if the object of life was self-
gratification; and I recollect having, at one time, internally
concluded, that it was our privilege to seek this in every way,
and that it ought to be our pursuit. Without recognizing it at
the time, I was an Epicurean in sentiment, and preparing to
rush into many of the follies of such a faith. In the course of
the five succeeding years, I was often sporting the lax sentiments of M——, more from neglect of thinking, and the desire
of being thought to have an independent spirit, than from
knowledge or inquiry; for I had only the random arguments,
which I heard casually dropped, and no settled ideas on this
great subject. I desire to be thankful to Him who has the
hearts of all flesh in his hands, that I was never permitted to
make this a subject of ridicule, which always shocked me, and
arises, I am persuaded, from a hard heart that is seldom changed.
During those years, I was suffered to engage in almost every
kind of dissipation, but in what fashionable people call a
moderate way. The theatre was the most attractive scene at
first; but repetition satiated, and its fascination was soon over.
Balls, and parties, and the company which they involved, while,
indeed, they consumed and perverted much time, took, in themselves, comparatively little hold of my feelings. But they were
a preparation for deeper and more entangling snares. With
regard to these amusements it may be said, that although they
murder precious time, which is given as a preparation for
eternity, and of which we know not what moment may be the
important one, on which hangs the destiny of our immortal
souls: for the poet's words may be applied spiritually, with
more meaning than temporally—"There is a tide in the affairs
of men, etc.": yet the deliverances from them are a thousand-
fold, compared with those from other fascinations, something
similar to the intoxicating draught, from which few will rejoice
forever in their deliverance. The amusements in question frequently involved a game of cards, of which old and young
partook. I, at first, seldom, if ever, participated in this, although it was not allowed to be called gambling, because it
was said that the trifle of money implicated was only to make

it interesting; a confession, which, had we perceived its spirit, would have convicted us of one dreadful idol.

'Against this fearful snare, I had a habitual prejudice: an impression of the sin of gambling had been formed by all my early education, and I steadily refused, for several years, every approach to it in company. But a family party offered a temptation more seducing than any which fashionable circles would have presented. It had a specious appearance of innocency, because it was at home, Aunts, and cousins, and other relatives, made up the greater part of the circle, and I recognized no harm that could arise amongst them. In this way my prejudices against gambling were shaken. I did not at first perceive how my feelings were becoming entangled. Three or four nights, every week, were employed at the fascinating table; and hour after hour passed away, each one finding us more unwilling to leave it: it was becoming quite indispensable to my comfort: every evening not thus employed was vacant and tedious. I was arrested by irresistible conviction in the midst of this dangerous course. Conscience imperiously said, This is a ruinous consumer of time, unworthy of so large a portion of the attention and devotion of a rational being, and I am sinking deeper and deeper into the snare. I must break off instantly, or the temptation will become irresistible. I felt the weakness of any resolution which I could form for this purpose; I knew how often my best formed ones had failed; and in order to enforce a compliance with what I thought reason dictated, I knelt before that God, to whom like the unknown God of the Athenians, an altar had been erected in my imagination, by early impressions, and by the pressure of circumstances, during the prevalence of yellow fever; and to whom I had conscientiously and regularly addressed the voice of prayer ever since, notwithstanding the influences of infidelity which surrounded me—I knelt and promised never again to engage in cards, unless drawn in by necessity. I could not clearly discover what this necessity could be, but I was induced to make the exception, from a kind of fearfulness about this solemn transaction, and the horror which the thought of ever failing in my promise inspired. I believe, however, that this reserve was a snare to me, and prevented a firm adherence to my determination. Now that I would acknowledge God in all my ways, I recognize his influence in bringing me to such a resolution. It arose from that concentration of thought, which I have since felt to be the operation of the Holy Spirit; and if I had known then the precious doctrine of this gift to sinners, and had in faith called in his aid, my victory would, probably, have been complete. I did immediately desert this social game, and adhered steadily to my purpose for three or four years.

'Notwithstanding all the dissipation and all the folly of this time, the word which I heard preached sometimes reached my conscience. I resolved frequently, under its influence, to attend more to the things which belong unto our everlasting peace, but the impression and resolution vanished together at the first touch of the world. All my reading, too, was calculated to weaken any right impression, and strengthen infidel sentiments. Besides novels and the popular works of the day, the works of fashionable French authors formed a considerable part of my amusement. Covering their hostility to the truth, with the broad and popular term, *philosophy*, they insinuate their views into the minds of the unthinking, and form a hindrance which only the Spirit of God can overcome. The effect of an infidel work I particularly remember. It [an infidel work] produced on my mind a wretched suspicion of every form of religion, without directing to anything satisfactory as a substitute. I trace back to this, as well as other causes, the restless wretchedness which at length came upon me, "as an armed man." The effects of such reading I feel to this day, notwithstanding the perfect demonstrations which I have had of the truth. I find, however, that every shock which it now gives, serves, under divine teaching, to establish me more firmly, and make my standing more secure.

'In the summer of 1800, I left Philadelphia to spend a few weeks in Princeton, intending to live again with my mother when I should return. Although I was weary of the noise and confusion of a large and mixed family, such as Mrs. ——'s, and in a great measure disgusted with fashion and dissipation, I still clung to these things as the only good, and hoped by engaging in them at my mother's, in a more select way, to find that enjoyment which they had failed to give heretofore. About this time, the question often arose in my mind, What eventual good is to result from them? For even then a conviction was felt, that only the end could justify the means. My heart sickened at the question, and I continually drove it from me. I was not willing to look to consequences, but submitted to voluntary blindness, endeavouring to enjoy the present, leaving the future, after the manner of the world, to take care of itself.

'In the comparative retirement of Princeton, with my mind, probably, more than usually exercised, in view of my intended change of residence; in a happy season, chosen by him, I trust,

14

who cannot err, the doubts of M——, the importance of the subject about which they were agitated, my own everlasting interest in this question, and the utter impossibility that I should ever obtain the truth of myself, unitedly pressed upon my mind, and concentrating all its energy, brought me, I believe, "in Spirit and in truth,"[1] to the feet of him, who only could effectually teach me, to ask his teaching, and implore that I might know the truth in regard to the Christian religion. Blessed prayer! inspired and answered by thee alone, my Father and my God! And although it has been answered by means of suffering; although the entrance of light has been after a dark night, I give thee thanks sincerely, thou God of my salvation! And although this light is but as the dawning of the morning, which has not assumed strength enough to dispel entirely the vapors of the night, I trust it is that light which shall shine brighter and brighter "unto the perfect day."

'Before I returned to Philadelphia, I visited Long Branch, with some friends from Princeton. At this resort of the fashionable folly of our country, and especially of our city, I first broke my promise with regard to cards. There arose, as I thought, that necessity which I had anticipated. The friends with whom I had gone were indisposed, and retired early to their chamber; my gay acquaintances whom I met at the Branch surrounded the card table; and no means of occupying my time, which would prevent passing a dreary, unsettled hour, occurred to set aside this powerful temptation: I yielded with but little struggle, and made one at the table. I was deceived, when I sat down, as to the amount for which the company were playing, and had lost, before I understood their arrangements, nearly all the money in my pocket. At this crisis the party separated. I felt ashamed of having been so entangled, and unwilling to acknowledge to my friends the dilemma in which I was; and was unable to meet any call for money. The infatuation of gamblers seized upon me. I resolved to sit down with the same company the second evening, and concluded that the knowledge of the management of the game which I had obtained, would enable me to replace my money. There is one fact which probably lessens the apparent madness of this step. I had a relative at the Branch, boarding not far from us, to whom, in case of failure, I had determined to apply for a loan. The success, however, of the second night more than answered my expectations: the sum which I had lost was more

---

[1] Mrs. Miller evidently uses this Scriptural expression in a modified sense—not as implying a renewed heart.

than restored, but without a restoration of my tranquillity. I
was suffered, in violating my promise, so solemnly given, to
trespass so far on early habits and the principle of my education, to go so far beyond my own previous doings, that the
retrospect agitated me with an unusual uneasiness. I was not
satisfied with myself, and felt disgraced in the eyes of the
world: in spite of the conviction which my knowledge of the
fashionable world gave me, that this was rather an honour than
a disgrace in their eyes, I lost all dependence on my own resolutions, since I had failed in my engagements to him, who was
my only resource against myself; and I was given up to irreso-
lution and distraction of mind: for although the effect was
gradual; although a disease, which occurred some days after
my return to Princeton, was more ostensibly the cause; I felt
that the mental distress, with which I labored for many years
afterward, must be dated from this time. From this time,
feeble nerves, with all their attending miseries, commenced
their operation; and the world rapidly lost all its attractions,
and realized to my view the wilderness which the word of truth
represents it to be. I had partly enjoyed, and partly ascertained by inference, as I thought, all that it was capable of
giving of real enjoyment. From this time, for several years
afterward, I was like a drowning wretch, ready at every instant
to perish, but still catching at some floating straw in hopes of
finding aid; and, although failing more, and sinking deeper,
at every effort, still buoyed up by some unknown cause, until a
persuasion was induced, that I should yet be delivered.

'After becoming domesticated again in my mother's family,
public amusements, and even cards, occasionally engaged my
time and attention—an evidence of the danger of the first deviation from the direct course. But I engaged in them now, not,
as formerly, for gratification, but for relief; and should, at this
period have fallen a snare to any infatuation which would have
afforded that, even to the use of laudanum, or other excitements of the same kind, if I had not soon discovered that such
stimuli rather increased, even at the present, than relieved, my
distress. I had recourse also to the Bible and prayer. I concluded to read, or rather study, the Scriptures through, and
even committed to memory parts that were difficult to retain ;
but I had no friend, no director, like Philip, at hand, to say,
"Understandest thou what thou readest?" and, by means of
the word, to point out the way of salvation ; and my occupa-
tion was dull and tiresome. Profane thoughts often mixed
with the Scriptures in my mind, and produced distressing
anxiety, a sense of guilt which was almost overwhelming, and

hindered my progress.   My weakness under these circumstances
was remembered, like that of the Athenians, when Paul taught
them by means of their own poets.   A quotation from Milton,
which I met with in some book I was reading at that time,
was a great relief to me.

> " Evil into the mind of God or man
>   May come and go, so unapproved; and leave
>   No spot or blame behind."[1]

Such help frequently occurred.   A year or two afterwards,
when in peculiarly trying circumstances, and under a consequent weight of depression, I found another passage from Milton, in Hayley's life of that poet, which gave a strength which
it could have given only under divine influence.

> " But thou, take courage, strive against despair,
>   Shake not with dread, etc."[2]

Had I been familiar with Watts at that time, I should have
found many passages in his Psalms and Hymns, more consoling
and applicable, and more under spiritual influence, as I have
since discovered.

'M—— said, " As long as you pore over the Bible so, you
will be miserable ; " and the noise of a distracted woman in the
neighborhood, whose insanity was ascribed to the influence of
the Methodists, gave a pang to my heart which I cannot describe.   But the expression of my inmost feelings was, " What
shall I do ? "   An arm of flesh, I felt, could not relieve me,
and by the only means accessible to me, I was seeking for spiritual assistance.   I had nowhere else to go, and the mere expectation of aid from this source, kept me from absolute despair.   Had my mind sunk under its morbid pressure, religion
would, probably, have borne the imputation of being the cause,
an imputation which it has often suffered with as little justice.
Blessed refuge, which even sin itself does not hinder us from finding! How often is our extremity the point at which mercy begins.
Many times, when all seemed lost; when I have felt as if one
painful thought more would overwhelm me; have I been encouraged to press on by more than human influence.   Every
account which I heard of the evils prevailing in the world,
every recital of trouble or wickedness, entirely unnerved me.
But all was overruled for good, and prepared the way for the
deep conviction, which I experienced at that time, that some
radical defect in man had been the procuring cause of all his
woe; and thus laid a foundation in my mind for the great
gospel doctrine on this subject.

<hr>

[1] Paradise Lost, v. 117-119.   [2] Dublin Ed. (1797), 12.

'Thus passed my days—tedious days, succeeded by disturbed nights! How often have I laid me down, with a half formed wish, that I might never rise again! To M— I owe much. As far as mere human effort would answer, she exerted herself. She exhorted me against yielding to my feelings, and was a means, under Providence, of rousing me from my first distress. Could she have been the means of binding up my broken spirit with the consolations of religion, what a finish, under the influence of the Holy Ghost, might have been given to her efforts. But the blind cannot lead the blind, and this was and is her pitiable condition. Glorified Saviour, can she not, touched by thy grace, be an instrument in thy hands of good to precious and immortal souls? Oh, that I may yet see her a fellow-worker with thee, and of the household of faith !

'Sometimes the being and nature of God, with a confused set of metaphysical questions, perplexed my brain. At other times practical duties equally agitated me. I thought of withdrawing from the world ; of mortifying myself by a total change of dress and life ; ready, as Herod, to do many things to relieve my present distress. I believe I was just in that state of mind, which would have made me a convert to any sect of Christians, to which individual friendship had attached me, or under whose influence I had fallen by any providential occurrence, if they had discovered zeal and sincerity. I am persuaded that this is the crisis, in that experience which precedes true faith, at which we are the most exposed to the influence of errorists ; and at which many have turned aside and been lost forever. It is a state in which we have especial need to ask, and seek, and knock.

'In this state of anxiety and distraction, the question between revelation and infidelity took a direct form in my mind ; as if Elijah, or one greater than Elijah, witnessing their contrary influence, had said, "How long halt ye between two opinions?"—Make up your mind which you will adopt, and take that as your object of attention and search. I cannot describe the agitation which, for a few minutes, followed. My countenance was presented in a glass before me, and evidenced the emotion within. The paleness of death overspread it, and every muscle was in action. I resolved on the Lord's side, and the tumult gradually ceased. I have often reflected on this season, and wished to understand it. I have sometimes thought, that I had been exercised with a suggestion of the enemy, for the purpose of making me rest in a formal assent. At other times, these exercises have appeared as of the operation of the true Spirit, to bias me on the right side, and make a mere arbitrary resolution a means of good. Whatever the influence, here I was not permitted to rest.

'About this time, the useless life which I led was presented impressively to my mind. I realized that I had lived to little purpose in the world, and began to desire to be useful, and concluded that, as a married woman, I might have more means and opportunity for this. My thoughts were directed to a gentleman, who had been a student and friend of my father's, and on that account, I fancied, ought to be recommended to me. He had visited us for some time, and I knew had serious intentions with regard to myself. He had large property, and I had already formed plans of universal benevolence, which were enlarged by becoming connected with a benevolent society in Philadelphia, the first of the kind, and just then formed for the relief of the poor. But, besides other objections, this gentleman was probably double my age, and, had I married him, it would have been without any feeling of affection, as I deeply experienced at every interview. In the firm persuasion, however, that this step was duty, I knelt and prayed for direction and aid, not doubting but that both would be given in favor of my plans with regard to this object. How often since have I been called to consider the perils which assailed me! I was allured, not driven, from this dangerous error, into which I certainly should have plunged, had not one who engaged affection as well as judgment been presented. My mind was perplexed, for some time, about giving up what I had so conscientiously considered to be duty; but happily nothing definite had been proposed to me, until after another had offered; and I was under no previous engagement. How are the merciful circumstances of this time increased in my view by every renewed recollection of them! One of the most ensnaring books which had been lent to M— * * was from this gentleman's library; and his own mind, I have much reason to believe, was entirely poisoned by such productions; and, after a year or two of probably lonesome wretchedness, without a friend in this world or another, he was permitted to put an end to his own life: a specimen of many like tragedies, I am persuaded, which will, one day, be brought to light!

'How different was the wealth which appeared in your family, my dear Friend, from that which I had anticipated in a different connexion! Instead of the riches of this world, the Word of Life was presented in every form that could heal a wounded spirit such as mine, and give relief—a spirit of which the Bible emphatically inquires, "Who can heal?"—evidently to lead our expectations away from all human means immediately to him who is the Father of our spirits. Had I sooner improved the advantages which surrounded me, years of anguish might have been spared. I say anguish, because I do not believe that, on the face of the earth, there were many more wretched than myself, when I became your wife. For more than a year my mind had been enveloped in some of the deepest shades of melancholy, beset with dreadful imaginations, and in that state of almost desperation, which hurries many a wretch to an untimely grave. On the borders of insanity, I had just reason enough left, to be the means of discovering to me the precipice on which I was tottering; and how often I have shuddered at the view God only knows. My imagination seemed to have overleaped almost every barrier, and to be employed in nothing but horrid anticipations.

'At this representation, my dear Friend, I know that you will experience emotions little short of amazement; and especially when I add, that this state of mind and feeling continued, and even increased in bitterness, until the Spring of 1806. If my senses and memory at all serve me, the whole of what I have said is certainly true; and this distress was the powerful means, in the hands of the Lord, of extricating me from the fatal delusion, in which the world had involved me, and of preparing me for that strong hope, which, notwithstanding all my sins and all my infirmities, I now cherish.

'I know the questions which will arise in your mind, upon being informed of these trials. Was the wife of my bosom thus agitated and I unconscious of it? What could have produced such a state of disorder? Under its first influence I was not able, silently, to endure the shock. My mother, as far as human means could go, was firm and faithful. She tried to persuade me, that my state of feeling was not a new one; that she herself had experienced it in some degree; that it required determined and unwearied resistance; and advised especially that I should avoid making it a subject of conversation, or even of thought, as far as possible. I took her advice and began a violent struggle, which continued many years afterward, and so far succeeded, as to enable me to put on the appearance of peace, when all was panic within. The influence of the world also operated powerfully to keep me silent; for it had obtained an ascendancy, which no mental shock appeared to have weakened, and which was now, perhaps, overruled for good. I was afraid that the result of my agitations would be insanity, and was sure that if my state of mind was known, I should already be considered as an insane woman, and become a spectacle. I sometimes fancied myself on the point of perpetrating some horrid act; and the bare idea almost drove me to desperation; and, after rising a little above the suggestion, the thought of such a possession again reduced me to agony. I look back myself with astonishment at the fact, that not one external.symptom indicated the disorder of my spirit. He that was for me was greater than he that was against me; and although my silence has sometimes appeared like want of confidence in my husband, I have learned more entirely the sufficiency of God, and to resort, with purpose of heart, more immediately to him at all times.

'The other question—What could have produced such a state of disorder?—has agitated my own mind many times. In the midst of that season of intellectual bewilderment, when a moment of calmness has been granted to me, and the past and present have been presented in connexion to my mind, I have internally exclaimed, Is this indeed so? Am I awake? I was an enigma to myself. The same scenes surrounded me, that had engaged me from my childhood; and I was still in the circle of those friends, whose society had been habitually endeared to me; but all within was changed; a dreadful panic possessed me; and my feelings were better expressed in those few words —"a fearful looking for of judgment"—than in any that I can combine. And now, in comparing the experience of that time with the language of inspiration, how appropriate the Psalmist's description appears—"The sorrows of death compassed me, and the pains of hell got hold upon me." [1] But I trust I feel some measure of gratitude to that God, who made this valley of Achor a door of hope to me.

"My fear and agitation did not arise from any clear or sensible convictions of sin. I was like the jailor, whose mind the earthquake and its attendant circumstances had entirely unhinged; and having lost all expectation from the world, or myself, I saw no sure resting place short of an all-seeing and all-powerful God, who was willing to undertake for me. I felt like a lost creature. Thus was my mind preparing for just such a revelation as God has given of his Son; and, as the gospel unfolded to my view, I perceived, that a firm belief of its truth, and of my interest in it, with the assistance of a Spirit who knew and could influence every thought, was my only rational dependence for deliverance. I therefore sincerely desired that the Christian system might be true, and wished to be a believer in it. I thought that habit would produce faith within me. My early convictions had received a shock from M——'s cavils, and I hoped to have this kind of faith more

---

[1] Ps. cxvi. 3.

than revived, by living with believers, and hearing the truth of the gospel taken for granted every day; and, above all, I counted much on the faith of the great and wise men of the earth. Sir Isaac Newton was a believer. Dr. Johnson was a believer. A cunningly devised fable could not have deluded such men as these. I felt the snare that there was in this kind of faith; the doubts of a great man on the other hand, and, above all, the apostasy of such an one, shook every fibre; and if my husband, and those who surrounded me, professors of religion, had denied the faith, habitual belief would have been annihilated. Thus much, however, I certainly had realized, that in the gospel there was a sure resting place for even my mind, if I had but perfect confidence in it. How to believe the gospel was the question. "The natural man receiveth not the things of the Spirit of God."[1] I have sometimes of late been inclined to doubt my hope, because my exercises did not reach the popular standard; but I am directed to the fountain for relief, and always find it there. A heartfelt conviction of sin, and a real sorrow for it, have followed faith in Jesus Christ, and I now feel the difference between a legal and childlike fear.

'In the first place, I believe that constitutional, as well as accidental, or rather providential, circumstances concurred in producing that state of mind and feeling. In recollecting former years, many little facts are brought to remembrance, which convince me that I was naturally prone to melancholy. I recollect strange fancies which beset me, and deep and unaccountable glooms that pervaded my mind, even when, generally speaking, my days were the happiest. I was, probably, raised above these weaknesses, for some time, by good general health, and by varying scenes and circumstances. Perhaps it may be, that the gay life which I led, like opium, preserved me from their oppressive influence. But, alas! the period came, when vanity, and gaiety, and everything else, lost their upholding power; and I believe a short reprieve was purchased at the expense of much additional suffering. And now, what reason have I to be thankful, that these vain preventives did not continue through life!—that I was discovered to myself to be not only exposed to wrath in the world to come, but poor, and wretched, and in want of everything for this life—solitary in the midst of friends!

'Against such a constitutional weakness, I feel now what only could have formed a radical guard—an early education which would have cultivated principles with more than this

____
[1] 1 Cor. ii. 14.

world as their object; which would have drawn out the mind
to view, beyond this transient and perishable scene, an end
worthy of all our ambition, and all our exertions, and to which
all sublunary views ought to refer: I mean mere human teaching of this kind, or rather a full indoctrinating in the peculiarities of the Christian religion. Such a religious foundation
would, I am persuaded, have saved me years of anguish; and
when the grace of God had sanctified this culture, how much
more useful might my life have been. Oh, my dear Friend,
when I realize this, how doubly awful does our responsibility
for our children appear. If it were merely for the purpose of
saving them so much temporal suffering, how ought we to strive
and pray; but especially how ought we to wrestle for them, if
they may be made the means, by a well directed education, of
more effectually pulling down the strongholds of Satan, and
building up more abundantly the Redeemer's kingdom. Instead of such an education, what an unprofitable, or rather
mischievous, one was mine! Or perhaps I ought to say, How
was an expensive education, well directed as far as the common acceptation of this word goes, marred by adventitious
circumstances! I was not only without instruction in the
sober truths of the gospel, but some of my earliest years were
devoted to the unlimited perusal of novels, to which, in the
second place, I ascribe the violence of my mental malady.
Their highly wrought pictures of human character and manners gave me a distaste for real life; and their dark and mys-
terious wonders filled me with superstition; thus laying a
foundation for an utter separation of feeling from the world
which I inhabited, and forming an almost insuperable barrier
against entrance into a better—the sad fruit which I reaped
when the infatuation had subsided. I said, like many others
who know not their own hearts, I have received no injury from
these condemned publications. But even when the pleasure
which arose from reading them was diminished in some measure,
they had left their baneful poison in my mind. All that senti-
mental feeling which they exhibit, and which is so blended with
fashionable folly, had formed to my fruitful imagination a
terrestrial paradise, which was to be found in connexion with
such a character as every novel depicts, aided by riches, and
splendor, and fashion, and family, and all that assemblage
which accompanies such a character. And, although sober
reason sometimes humbled me, by applying to conscience a
question of my deserving such an assemblage, from any co-
incident claims, yet the play of fancy again led away my
better judgment. Boarding-schools and the fashionable ac-

complishments of the day were not calculated to deliver from this wretched delusion; and I came forward into the world, with the hope of finding that perfect happiness here, which, in some form or other, is the end of all our natural expectations, and with no alternative for the hour of disappointment. I looked upon the world around me, and saw not a person who appeared to me to have obtained this happiness; but imagination triumphed over reason and impelled me on.'

In the foregoing narrative, Mrs. Miller does not perhaps give as strong an attestation, as she sometimes gave to her children, of the republican simplicity of her father's habits, and his aversion to many of those fashionable luxuries, extravagancies, amusements, and indulgences, which even religion, so-called, is, often, in our day, easily wheedled into allowing and encouraging. She frequently expressed the conviction, that had he lived to guard her a few years longer against the temptations of the gay world, she would have been spared many of the painful steps by which she had been brought back from her wandering.

Her remarks about boarding-schools, had she given herself space to enter at all into particulars, would probably have excepted one school, at least, of that class, which she ever remembered with peculiar interest. In 1789, her father placed her at the Moravian female seminary at Bethlehem, Pennsylvania, doubtless because it was distinguished for that plainness and simplicity which he approved. Mrs. Miller always spoke with affectionate remembrance of that institution, and particularly of Sister Kleest, one of the teachers, under whose special care she had been, and who afterwards married a missionary to the Indians.

3. Married Life.

To the bachelor's hall in New York, No. 116 Liberty street, Mr. Miller took his bride, whose presence at once changed the whole character of the establishment. Dr. Edward Miller remained to welcome them, and, for a short time, probably, continued with them; but the affectionate delicacy of his feelings, admitted of no assurance that it was better for him to participate in their domestic comforts, and he soon removed to other lodgings, though he still sat at their table. His brother quickly returned, with new zeal and activity, to his pastoral and literary labors; which, in spite of freshened interest and ardor, were all too oppressive for his slender health. To the chief literary results of about three years, commencing nearly a twelvemonth before his marriage, we shall come, after a few paragraphs—chiefly extracts from his diary, and explanations of those extracts.

In April, Mr. Miller preached the annual sermon before the New York Missionary Society, which, by request of the latter, was published.[1] It appears, from the report printed as an appendix to this discourse, that he was, at the time, secretary pro tempore.

This sermon is no doubt a favorable specimen of Mr. Miller's preaching at the time, and fully equals, if it does not surpass, in real merit, any which he had before committed to the press. Very much like his other productions, earlier and later, it contains no thoughts particularly brilliant, or strikingly original; no display of imagination; but is a perspicuous, scriptural, enforcement of plain gospel truths, in style polished and rhetorical, and rising, at times, to somewhat of dignity and power. Committed to memory, as it doubtless was, and delivered with the freedom which the memoriter mode of preaching may secure, and the propriety of tone and manner, which the preacher had always assiduously cultivated, it no doubt fulfilled in a good degree its important design—to recommend to hearer and reader the great work of missions.

Here are two extracts from the diary :—

'September 29, 1802. This day my *first child* was born—a daughter. I am a father! What tender, solemn, complicated feelings attend the first consciousness of the parental relation! I cannot express them.

'Thank God, my wife is doing well! May this dear child be made a subject of God's grace and a blessing to her generation.'

Afterwards he added, 'We call the name of this child *Margaret*. My own mother and my beloved wife's mother both bore this name.'

<hr>

[1] "A Sermon, delivered before the New York Missionary Society, at their Annual Meeting, April 6th, 1802. By Samuel Miller, A. M., One of the Ministers of the United Presbyterian Churches in the City of New York. To which are added, the Annual Report of the Directors, and other Papers relating to American Missions."—Habakkuk ii. 3.—8vo. Pp. 81.

'October 24, 1802.   This is the first anniversary of my *marriage*, which I desire to observe as a special season of thanksgiving and praise.   One year has elapsed since I was happily united to Sarah Sergeant. * *   And now, when the ardent feelings and the sanguine expectations of a lover may be supposed to have yielded to the more calm and reasonable views of a married man, I desire to record my gratitude to God for the precious gift which he has been pleased to bestow upon me. My beloved wife was not a professor of religion when I married her, nor is she yet one.   But her natural and moral qualities are such as have more and more endeared her to me, and impressed me every day with a deeper conviction of the wisdom and happiness of my choice.   She has a profound reverence for religion; a firm belief in the reality and importance of piety of heart; and as strong a desire to become possessed of that treasure, as one who does not already possess it can be supposed to have.   A variety of appearances inspire me with hope, that the time is not far distant, when she will be able to unite with her husband in the hopes and joys, as well as the duties, connected with membership in the Redeemer's kingdom.'

We have seen that Mr. Miller had been accustomed, before marriage, to observe the anniversaries of his birth and ordination, as seasons of special prayer with fasting; to these we now find him adding each anniversary of his wedding-day, for particular thanksgiving and praise; and, to the close of his life, the three observances were continued with an unwavering conscience.   After removing to Princeton, he often noticed in a similar manner the return of the date of his arrival there; while not unfrequently he observed Mrs. Miller's birth-day, and she several of his special days of religious exercise.

Herein they were walking in the footsteps of the most pious men of preceding generations; who had never discovered that fasting was not a Christian ordinance, or that times of special devotion were justified only by "extraordinary dispensations,"[1] in a sense forbidding all anniversary or other stated observances, whether public or private.   They believed that great mercies should call forth life-long gratitude; that great responsibilities and short comings demanded unceasing humiliation before God; and that the appointment of regularly recurring seasons for the

---

[1] Directory for Worship, Ch. xiv. 2.   The expression is referred to, not as at all objectionable in itself, but as sometimes wrested and abused.

15

special performance of these duties, to refresh the memory, and give a new impulse* to the heart, was both reasonable and scriptural. At the same time, they carefully distinguished all such days of human, from the one only day of divine, appointment. The former were not to be imposed upon the conscience, were not to be regarded as holy days, unless, in a qualified sense, to him who might, for himself, *set them apart*, and dedicate them to the exercises of devotion. No man was to judge his neighbor as to any day but the Christian Sabbath. And Mr. and Mrs. Miller were careful not to lade themselves with burdens grievous to be borne; not to regard with superstitious reverence the anniversaries which they observed, nor to permit a human dedication of time to become a plea for neglecting divinely indicated obligations. They endeavored, with care, to guard these seasons of special devotion, as they did daily closet hours, from intrusions of the world; but were not regardless of providential hindrances, or calls to higher duties.

In Dr. Miller's last published work, he said,

"I take for granted that every candidate for the ministry, and every minister of the gospel, will, every year, observe days of special prayer and humiliation, accompanied, at proper seasons, with fasting. Such days will ever be found important in nurturing a spirit of piety, and will not be neglected by him who wishes and studies to grow in grace."[1]

A number of extracts from Mr. Miller's Diary have been already given to the reader, and others will be found scattered through the following pages. In after years he was accustomed to recommend strongly the habit of keeping a diary, as both a means of self-improvement, and a source of pleasure. This led, after his decease, to an anxious search among his papers for such a record of his own life. But nothing of the kind has been discovered, beyond a few brief, occasional paragraphs; little more, possibly, having been written, or, probably, much more having been destroyed. What we have is chiefly of a devotional character, and found partly in a bound book, partly upon loose sheets and slips of paper; and with whatever was written at the dates which the several entries bear,

[1] Thoughts on Public Prayer, 300.

subsequent reminiscences are sometimes so interspersed and incorporated, that it is impossible to distinguish between the original records and these additions. It is evident that Mr. Miller's diary and all that accompanies it, were written without any continuous plan, but according to the purposes and suggestions of the hour. For the most part, evidently, self-recollection and examination were the object; at times, doubtless, he wrote for the gratification of surviving members of his own family; and, as he was repeatedly called upon, by literary collectors, to give an outline of his life, he may sometimess have desired to gather materials for any sketch to be attempted either before or after his demise. These scanty records were penned chiefly upon the three anniversaries already mentioned—his birth-day, his wedding-day, and his ordination-day, and throw light mainly upon his habits of private devotion. A fuller, more connected, and more varied diary might have lightened very much the biographer's task : the want of it was more to be regretted on that account, perhaps, than on any other.

'December 5, 1802. This day my beloved wife sat down, for the first time, at a sacramental table, and placed herself among the professing people of God. She has been, ever since our marriage, becoming more and more serious. She now cherishes a hope that she has given herself to Christ. God grant, that her dedication may have been sincere, and the work of grace in her heart genuine and deep! She is not wholly without doubt concerning herself; but, on the whole, thought it her duty to go forward. May the Lord bless and help her!'

In 1803, Mr. Miller's record of preaching shows that he was absent from New York nearly the three months, August, September, and October; and one entry seems to indicate that two of the three Collegiate Presbyterian churches of the city were closed during the same time. "About the 18th of July," says a contemporaneous writer —probably Dr. Edward Miller[1]—"the Yellow Fever began

[1] In 1803 he was appointed by the Governor and Council of the State, Resident Physician of New York City, one of three officers, who, under an act of the legislature, were to adopt measures for guarding the city against malignant epidemics. This office he hel⟩ until his death, excepting about a year, a change of politics in the Council having, in 1810, occasioned his temporary removal.

to excite attention in this city, and continued to prevail, more or less, till the close of October. During that period, the deaths from this disease were between six and seven hundred. The alarm and flight of the inhabitants were very suddenly produced; and the suspension of business and desertion of the city on this occasion far exceeded what had been ever experienced in former seasons."[1] Mr. Miller's own ill health doubtless incapacitated him for active duty among the sick, while it would have increased his danger from the pestilence; yet he seems to have preached every Sabbath—once in New York City, on other Sabbaths at Perth Amboy, Fordham, Albany, Troy, and 'in a sloop on the Hudson;' but oftenest, and in fact the whole of October, at Mount Pleasant. On the 26th of December he wrote to the Rev. Eliphalet Nott, of Albany, 'I have been repeatedly indisposed since my return home; and never was any man more oppressively busy. But if I could be convinced that I am doing some little good in the world, I should be comforted under every inconvenience.

Mr. Miller never knew how to swim, and used to relate, that he had once fallen overboard from a sloop, but had been buoyed up by a large cloak he had on, until assistance could be rendered. Not improbably it was when he was 'in a sloop on the Hudson,' that this casualty occurred.

[1] 7 Medical Repository, 178.

CHAPTER TWELFTH.

"RETROSPECT OF THE EIGHTEENTH CENTURY."

1804–5.

----

1. Preparation of the Work.

As an author, Dr. Miller became most widely known, and gained, perhaps, the chief part of his reputation. Beginning to publish quite early, he continued, until very late in life, to address the public through the press. Eight discourses, which appeared within the first nine years of his pastorate, have been already noticed. We must now glance at his earliest more extended work, which, indeed, was the most voluminous single production of his pen. This was "A Brief Retrospect of the Eighteenth Century,"[1] published in January, 1804. The following extracts from the preface will here serve to introduce it to the reader.

"A simple history of this publication will best unfold its design, and will form the best apology for its numerous imperfections. On the first day of January, in the year 1801, the author being called, in the course of his pastoral duty, to deliver a sermon, instead of choosing the topics of address most usual at the commencement of a *new* year, it occurred to him as more proper, in entering on a *new century*, to attempt a review of the preceding age, and to deduce from the prominent features of that period such moral and religious reflexions as might be suited to the occasion. A discourse, formed on this plan, was accordingly delivered. Some who heard it were pleased to express a wish that it might be published. After determining to comply with this wish, it was at first intended

----

[1] "A Brief Retrospect of the Eighteenth Century. Part the First; in Two Volumes: containing a Sketch of the Revolutions and Improvements in Science, Arts and Literature during that Period. By Samuel Miller, A.M., one of the Ministers of the United Presbyterian Churches in the City of New York, Member of the American Philosophical Society, and Corresponding Member of the Historical Society of Massachusetts."—8vo. Pp. xvi. 544, vi. 510.

to publish the original discourse, with some amplification; to add a large body of notes for the illustration of its several parts; and to comprise the whole in a single volume. Proposals were issued for the publication in this form, and a number of subscribers gave their names for its encouragement.

"Little progress had been made in preparing the work on this plan, for the press, before the objections to such a mode of arranging the materials appeared so many and cogent, that it was at length thought best to lay aside the form of a sermon, and to adopt a plan that would admit of more minuteness of detail, and of greater freedom in the choice and exhibition of facts. This alteration in the structure of the work led to an extension of its limits; materials insensibly accumulated; and that portion which was originally intended to be comprised in a third or fourth part of a single volume gradually swelled into two volumes."[1]

"It will probably be remarked, by the intelligent reader, that a due *proportion* between the parts of this work, according to the relative importance and extent of each subject, is not always preserved. Had the manuscript been completed before any part of it was sent to the press, faults of this kind would, no doubt, have been, in some degree, avoided; but the truth is, that the first pages of the manuscript were put into the hands of the printer before a single chapter of the work had been fully written; and each successive sheet was prepared, from the materials previously collected, at the call of the printer, and amidst the hurry of incessant professional labors. It is scarcely necessary to add, that this race with the press frequently rendered impossible that laborious investigation, and that careful correction which were highly desirable: nor could the author excuse himself for conduct so manifestly indiscreet, had he duly considered beforehand the nature and magnitude of the engagement. But it must be acknowledged, that as he entered on the work without duly appreciating the arduousness of his undertaking, so every step in the pursuit convinced him more and more of its extent and difficulty; that in the prosecution of his task he wished a hundred times he had never undertaken it; and that now it is brought to a close, few readers can be more sensible than he is himself of its numerous and great defects.

"It will be observed, that *three* parts of the original plan yet remain to be executed. Whether the execution of the whole will be attempted depends, in some measure, on the reception which shall be given to this *First Part*. The author is particularly

[1] Preface, vii. viii.

desirous of completing the fourth and last division; viz., that which relates to the Literature, Science, Revolutions, and principal Events of the Christian Church during the last age; and even if he should be compelled to abandon the two intermediate divisions, he cherishes the hope of being able, if his life should be spared, to lay something before the public on this favorite subject." [1]

This preface, no doubt, is quite too deprecatory and self-detractive, if not for truth, at least for good taste and sound policy. But with the feelings by which it was prompted we can hardly sympathize, without passing through a like ordeal of authorship, and coming, with like embarrassment, before the bar of public opinion.

The assistance which Mr. Miller received, in preparing the Retrospect, from his brother Edward is thus noticed in his Biographical Sketch of the latter :—

"In the year 1801, the writer of these memoirs undertook a work, which was published soon afterwards, under the title of *A Brief Retrospect.* * * The tolerable completion of his plan obliged him to attempt an exhibition of the principal discoveries and improvements in *Medicine,* during the period which was to be delineated. When he came to that part of his work, his Brother, with that affection for which he was always distinguished, offered to furnish the requisite materials, and to give any other assistance in his power. This offer was accepted, and was more than realized. The readers of the "Retrospect" have, doubtless, observed, that the chapter on "Medicine" is by far the best part of the work. Its matter, its arrangement and its style, are all superior to those of any other in the volumes. The truth is, that three-fourths of that chapter were written by Doctor *Edward Miller;* a few pages only of the latter (and certainly the inferior) part being written by the author of the main body of that publication. Permission was earnestly and repeatedly requested from him to state this to the public in a note, at the commencement of the chapter in question; but he pointedly and perseveringly refused. His native modesty shrunk from such an obtrusion of his name on the public notice. He had written in haste, and considered the sketch which he had furnished, though adapted to the place which it was intended to occupy, as by no means sufficiently digested to be sent abroad under the name of a physician. And, what probably operated with no less force, such was his uniform and tender affection for

1 Pp. xiii. xiv.

his Brother, that he was willing to transfer to him whatever credit in public estimation might be attached to that part of the work. That brother, however, who feels a confidence founded on the opinion of much better judges than himself, that the chapter in question, the more it is examined, will be found more distinctly to bear the marks of the vigorous, comprehensive, well-stored, and polished mind, by which the greater part of it was produced, considers himself as now at liberty to give the history of its composition. He takes more pleasure than he can well express in perusing that chapter as a memorial of his relation to one to whom he feels, next to his Parents, more indebted than to any other mortal; and whose numberless monuments of fraternal affection he cannot contemplate without the tenderest emotions."[1]

2. RECEPTION OF THE WORK.

The Retrospect was dedicated to "John Dickinson, Esq., LL.D., late President of the State of Delaware, and President of the Supreme Executive Council of the Commonwealth of Pennsylvania"; whom the author thus addresses:—

"Dear Sir,

"In finding your name prefixed to the following pages, without permission, I trust you will feel no emotion more unfavorable than that of surprise. I know not, indeed, to whom I could dedicate such a work as this with more propriety than to an elegant scholar, a comprehensive observer of a large portion of the century attempted to be reviewed, a master of so many of its literary and scientific improvements, a conspicuous actor in some of its most memorable and important transactions, an able and eloquent defender of his country's rights, a munificent patron of American literature, and (if personal or local feelings may be allowed to intrude) a uniform and affectionate friend of my honored parents, and one of the most illustrious of those who owe their birth to my native State."[2]

Further on, the author expressed his happiness in the assurance that Mr. Dickinson perfectly coincided with him in certain views presented in the work, especially those respecting the "harmony between the RELIGION OF CHRIST and genuine Philosophy," and respecting the "theories, falsely called philosophy, which pervert reason, contradict

---

[1] Pp. lxi. lxii.
[2] P. iii.

Revelation, and blaspheme its divine Author"; and classes him with those who "contemplate every department of human affairs through the medium of Christian Principles."[1]

Upon receiving a copy of the Retrospect, Mr. Dickinson wrote a letter of hearty thanks, in the course of which he says,

'In the particular notice taken of me, it is easy to discern the marks of friendship. Yet, to tell the truth, even these biased commendations, from such a man, give me pleasure.

'However they have been dictated, I will try to be animated by them to the warmest exertions for approaching nearer to the character that has been formed so much to my advantage.'

'One circumstance recorded in thy address comes, I am sure, from thy heart, and goes directly to mine: the friendship between thy honored parents and myself.

'It commenced in my youth, and held on, unabated, uninterrupted, up to their removal into another world. Nor did the connection then die. Their children caught the mantles that fell from them, and, in my advanced years, I am still favored with a continuance of the same kind spirit towards me.

'Delighted as I am with the contemplation of this subject, I am also highly gratified by thy publishing, "*without permission*," my belief in Revelation. I humbly rejoice in this unexceptionable testimony to my faith, and that I am not "ashamed of the Son of Man, or of his words." I had rather be a *Christian*, than sovereign of the world.'

'Any expressions I can use would be imperfect interpretations of the affection with which I am thy obliged friend ——'

A glance at the table of contents[1] will show the comprehensiveness of the plan of this publication. Not the least important portion of it was that devoted to the literature of

[1] P. iv.

[2] INTRODUCTION. PART I. On the Revolutions and Improvements in Science, Arts and Literature, during the Eighteenth Century. Chap. I. Mechanical Philosophy. § 1. Electricity. § 2. Galvanism. § 3. Magnetism. § 4. Motion and Moving Forces. § 5. Hydraulics. § 6. Pneumatics. § 7. Optics. § 8. Astronomy. General Observations. Chap. II. Chemical Philosophy. Chap. III. Natural History. § 1. Zoology. § 2. Botany. § 3. Mineralogy. § 4. Geology. § 5. Meteorology. § 6. Hydrology. Chap. IV. Medicine. § 1. Anatomy. § 2. Physiology. § 3. Theory and Practice of Medicine. § 4. Surgery and Obstetrics. § 5. Materia Medica. Chap. V. Geography. Chap. VI. Mathematics. Chap. 7. Navigation. Chap. VIII. Agriculture. Chap. IX. Mechanic Arts. Chap. X. Fine Arts. § 1. Painting. § 2. Sculpture. § 3. Engraving. § 4. Music. § 5. Architecture. Chap. XI. Physiognomy. Chap. XII. Philosophy of the Human Mind. Chap. XIII. Classic Literature. Chap. XIV. Oriental Literature. § 1. Hebrew Literature. § 2. Arabic Literature. § 3. Persian Literature. § 4. Hindoo Literature.

the United States, as one of the "Nations lately become literary." This section embraced more information about the men of letters, the institutions of learning, and the literary productions in general, of our country than had before been brought into one view. The whole work, indeed, though since often imitated, and, in many respects, surpassed, was then novel, and perhaps unexampled. It was well received on both sides of the Atlantic, and was republished in London—a compliment not doubtful in that day, when it was still the fashion, in Great Britain, to sneer at everything like American learning or literature.

It was perhaps a kind providence, which, after the publication of two volumes of the Retrospect, prevented the further prosecution of the plan, involving the delicate, difficult, and exciting subject of Politics, as well as the Subjects of Theology and Morals; and turned Mr. Miller's pen, for the rest of his life, in a direction more strictly professional. But the work certainly had the effect of adding to his reputation in the literary world. Among its more immediate fruits, were his reception from Union College, on the 4th, and the University of Pennsylvania on the 6th, of May, 1804, of the degree of Doctor of Divinity, and his unanimous election, on the 29th of June following, upon motion of Dr. Adam Clarke, the commentator, as a corresponding member of the Philological Society of Manchester, England. It was republished, in London, in three octavo volumes, with some corrections and additions by Dr. Miller himself, and some slight modifications by an English editor, in about eighteen months after its appearance in New York. Of the honorary degree Dr. Sprague says,

§ 5. Chinese Literature. General Observations. Chap. XV. Modern Languages. § 1. English. § 2. French. § 3. Italian. § 4. German. § 5. Swedish. § 6. Russian. General Observations. Chap. XVI. Philosophy of Language. Chap. XVII. History. Chap. XVIII. Biography. Chap. XIX. Romances and Novels. Chap. XX. Poetry. § 1. Epic Poetry. § 2. Didactic Poetry. § 3. Moral and Devotional Poetry. § 4. Satirical Poetry. § 5. Descriptive Poetry. § 6. Pastoral Poetry. § 7. Lyric Poetry. § 8. Elegiac Poetry. § 9. Drama. General Observations. American Poetry. General Reflections. Chap. XXI. Literary Journals. Chap. XXII. Political Journals. Chap. XXIII. Literary and Scientific Associations. American: (1) Societies and Academies of Arts and Sciences; (2) Historical Society; (3) Medical Societies; (4) Agricultural Societies. General Observations. Chap. XXIV. Encyclopædias and Scientific Dictionaries. Chap. XXV. Education. Chap. XXVI. Nations lately become Literary. § 1. Russia. § 2. Germany. § 3. United States of America. Recapitulation. Additional Notes.

"He was honored with the Degree of Doctor of Divinity, from the University at which he was graduated, in the year 1804. At that day it was uncommon, if not unprecedented, for a person so young to receive that honour; and he used sometimes, in sportively referring to it, to relate the following anecdote:—

"He was travelling in New England with a clergyman who was well acquainted there, and they called, at the suggestion of the Doctor's travelling companion, to pay their respects to a venerable old minister, who lived somewhere on their route. The Doctor's friend introduced him as Dr. Miller, of New York; and as the old gentleman knew that there was a distinguished medical practitioner of that name living there, and as he had not heard that the clergyman had been doctorated, and perhaps it had never even occurred to him that so young a man as he saw before him *could* be, he took for granted that it was the medical doctor to whom he had been introduced; and, after a few minutes, wishing to accommodate his conversation to the taste and capabilities of the stranger as well as he could, he turned to him, and asked him whether he considered the yellow fever, which had then just been prevailing in New York, contagious. Before the Doctor had time to reply, his friend perceiving the old man's mistake, said, "This is not a medical doctor, Sir, but a Doctor of Divinity." The venerable minister gathered himself up, as if in a paroxysm of astonishment, and lifting up both hands, exclaimed, with a protracted emphasis upon each word, "*You don't!*" "[1]

Lindley Murray, the Grammarian, residing at this time at Holdgate, near York, seems to have been in familiar correspondence with Dr. Miller, and to have taken a sincere interest in the success of his work. On the '30th of 7th mo., 1804,' he writes,

'In reading the Preface to the Retrospect, it occurred to me, that the author had expressed too much diffidence of his own abilities, and too great apprehension of the imperfections of the work. Modesty well becomes an author: but when he, who best knows the nature and merits of his production, and who may be supposed to have a natural partiality for it, speaks disrespectfully of what he has produced, many persons will be disposed to admit his opinion, and spare themselves the trouble of reading the book; and others will peruse it with little expectation, perhaps with unfavorable prepossessions. To make a

[1] 3 Annals, 601.

good impression, at the outset, is of consequence ; and therefore the author should appear to possess *proper* confidence in himself, and a proper sense both of the importance and the execution of his undertaking. I was the more struck with the apologies of the Preface, because the execution of the design appeared to me to be at direct variance with them ; and because there was no necessity for them, if the merit of the publication had been problematical.'

Here is a crabbed, patronizing letter from the well-to-do, indifferent English publisher, determined that the American adventurer in the field of letters should recognize his full obligation for the risk run in bringing a transatlantic author into notice.

'Reverend Sir,   London, April 8, 1805.
    *   *   For a considerable time I was in great doubt how to act. It immediately occurred, that a work embracing so much, and so long a period, and composed without the assistance in many cases, which a writer here would have, must frequently be defective and erroneous ; and that the best way would be to cut the work into parts, and divide it between a number of literary friends, giving to each the subject in which he was most conversant. What think you was the consequence? Month after month passed away, and nothing done. I discovered what I should have thought of before—that we are alive only to *our own* whims. Thus disappointed, I determined to give it to the press, under the direction of a general scholar, to correct whatever appeared erroneous. Nothing has been added, or scarcely anything ; you have not been made to say anything more, or give a different opinion ; but some passages have been struck out, which, if you had studied more, with better information, would probably never have appeared. More of this mischievous work would have been done, if more leisure had offered. Had you written a work addressed to your own congregation or party, it might have passed ; but you have undertaken a history ; and the requisites of a historian will be expected by the intelligent among your readers. They will look for a fair statement of facts and opinions to enable them to form a judgment, and not for oracular dogmatism : that men who have enlarged the boundaries of knowledge, and extended the sphere of mental improvement, should be treated with high respect, not disposed of in a line of censure. I wish every historian to imbue his mind with the spirit of Lardner. But enough and more than enough to seal my doom with you.
    '*   *   I forgot to say, that if I had read your pre-

face, the first thing a man ought to read, I honestly confess that I should have been deterred from reprinting.

'As to a compliment for sending immediately a copy to me, nothing can be said till its fate be known.

'*   *   believe me, Rev'd Sir,

'Your obliged and obedient servant,

'J. Johnson.'

Dr. Miller was no doubt by this time cured of the self-depreciative spirit of preface writing. What excited Mr. Johnson's ire as "oracular dogmatism" is explained by the following extract from his letter of August 14, 1805, sent with a copy of the English edition.

'Please to receive a copy of your book in its English dress, lopped indeed of a few severities, which I trust you will not take amiss, and with some corrections. The time I hope is not very distant, when thinking men will be as liberal in America as in England; and when it will not be necessary to embrace any set of opinions, in order to obtain the good will of the orthodox.'

Dr. Edward Miller, while his brother was absent from home, on the 21st of September, 1806, wrote to Mrs. Miller,

'Since my brother's departure, I have seen one of the British reviews, (Aikin's Annual Review,) from which he expected, on account of its religious principles and customary arrogance and intolerance, the most severe treatment. On the contrary he treats the Retrospect with great deference and distinction. He offers some criticisms, several of which are not unfounded, but always with civility and respect. And he concludes the review in the following manner: "But it were ungrateful to require perfection, where so much has been performed. It is flattering to Great Britain, that the celebrity of her authors should so soon cross the Atlantic; and it is honorable to America that literary curiosity should be there so alert and so comprehensive. Mr. Miller has deserved well of both worlds."—Is not this pretty well for an American writer?'

16   .

---

1. Miscellaneous Topics.

The opening years of the present century were prolific, in the United States, of grand schemes for the advancement of the Redeemer's kingdom, and of theological and ecclesiastical controversies. The country had rapidly recovered from the physical prostration occasioned by the Revolutionary War; and, especially since the adoption of the Federal Constitution, had made astonishing progress as to all its important material interests. With commerce, manufactures, and the arts in general, learning and religion had commensurately advanced; and, national prosperity assured, leading minds, on this side of the Atlantic, were busying themselves more and more with the great problems of social and religious improvement; while truth and faith found no excuse for slumber in any diminished activity on the part of error or superstition. The awakening of a fresh zeal in the hearts of many for the prosecution of gospel missions has been already noticed. Divinity schools for the United States had begun to engage serious attention. The Hopkinsian controversy was assuming new importance among Congregationalists and Presbyterians. Unitarianism was lifting its head ominously in Boston and elsewhere. High Churchism, in its Anglican form, was preparing for a new and vigorous attack upon the distinctive doctrines of the Reformation. To all these subjects we find Dr. Miller alluding, from time to time, in his correspondence, from which some extracts will next be inserted.

On the 9th of August, 1804, he writes to the Rev. Edward D. Griffin,[1]

---

[1] See 4 Sprague's Annals, 26.

'Most cordially do I reciprocate your wishes for a further
and more intimate acquaintance. It has long been my desire;
and I hope a few months will bring with them better opportunities of gratification, in this respect, than I have hitherto
enjoyed. Little did I think, when you settled at Newark, that
I should be, all this time, so slightly acquainted with a fellow
presbyter, with whom I have so strong a disposition to "fra-
ternize." We shall manage things better, I hope, in future.'

In January, 1804, met, in the city of Philadelphia, the
"Ninth American Convention for promoting the Abolition
of Slavery, and improving the Condition of the African
Race." To this convention "The New York Society for
promoting the Manumission of Slaves" sent seven delegates,
of whom Mr. Miller was one.

About the issue of the duel between Hamilton and Burr,
which was just then agitating the whole nation, he writes
to the Rev. Eliphalet Nott,[1] the 14th of August,

'As the murder was not committed in our State, I have
doubts, whether either the principal or either of the accessories
could be seized under a charge of this sort, before the State of
New Jersey has taken any steps to have the culprits brought
to justice. And, as Governor Bloomfield is Mr. Burr's particular friend, and, I am told, vindicates his conduct, it is by no
means likely, in my estimation, that Jersey will ever take any
such steps at all.
'My friend! I have no words at command to express my
feelings on this subject. Will nothing put a stop to that wicked,
unnatural, barbarous, infamous practice, which has been so
long the disgrace of our country, and which has lately cut off
the greatest man which it contained? I begin really to fear,
that all our hopes from human laws, on this subject, must be
given up.'

Of Burr Dr. Miller was accustomed to say, Such was
his plausibility, that he might enter a room where there
were a dozen gentlemen, who all believed, from the bottom
of their hearts, that he was a vile scoundrel; and yet, that
from an hour's interview, so great would be the power of
the man, they would retire ready to shout, "Hurrah for
Aaron Burr!"

To Mr. Griffin he writes again,

---

[1] Afterwards D.D.

'New York, August 31, 1804.

'Dear Brother,

'I returned from Staten Island on Monday, fully expecting the pleasure of your company the next morning; but I had been only a few minutes in the house, when your letter was put into my hands. I trust it is not necessary to assure you, that I received it with pain, and that I hope you will take the earliest opportunity that occurs, of paying us a visit with Mrs. Griffin.

'I find that the great body of the letters of Cowper, lately published, are directed to Mr. Newton and to Mr. Unwin, Jr.; and a very few to two or three other persons. They are excellent, but do not furnish so many additional incidents concerning the writer as I hoped to find. It is not yet certain whether they will be republished here. Do come and see them; and we will lay our heads together more closely and leisurely, respecting the best means of gratifying your laudable curiosity to know more of our favorite poet.'

It is very evident that the Collegiate Churches in New York were careful not to call any one, without his having made full proof before them of his ministry. They were not satisfied with the evidence of one Sabbath's preaching, but insisted upon a long trial of each candidate, if possible, as the following letter, of the 15th of October, to Dr. Green, shows.

'This letter will be handed to you by * * Mr. ——, who has preached four times in our pulpits, and is highly acceptable to our people. Our church session had a meeting last evening, and, with great unanimity and cordiality, requested Dr. Rodgers to write to your presbytery, for the purpose of obtaining a portion of Mr. ——'s time, in the course of the ensuing winter. * * There appears to me a high probability, that our people will be prepared, in a short time, to give him a cordial and affectionate call to be one of our ministers. * * If he can come next week, or the week after, so much the better. As to the length of his stay here, I hope he will not think of less than ten or twelve Sabbaths. And, if he can reconcile it with his views to stay longer, pray urge it.'

To Dr. Green again, on the 12th of November, Dr. Miller writes,

'Much information, concerning the character and proceedings of Mr. H——, had reached me before the receipt of your letter. I was early led to believe, that he intended to establish an Independent church in your city. And it has occurred to me as a very difficult question, how he ought to be treated by you and your Presbyterian brethren. My information respecting minute circumstances (often of great importance in these cases) is too scanty to enable me to form a decided opinion; but, if I mistake not, the course of true policy is, to take him by the hand and treat him politely. If he should eventually decline in weight and reputation, you will have a new Presbyterian church established by his instrumentality; and, if it should prove otherwise, the course above mentioned will, I suspect, make such an impression on your own congregations, as greatly to diminish his power to do mischief. This deportment towards Mr. H—— appears to me to be best calculated, also, to counteract the delusive and mischievous system of lay-preaching. Unless I am deceived, you will be able to combat this system with more force and effect, while you are not suspected of being on ill terms with its principal promoter. * *

'Mr. H——, from what I can learn, appears to be an Independent *in principle.* He certainly has a right to go to Philadelphia, and (if he can get people to hear and support him) to stay there. What, therefore, would be a gross irregularity, and even a just ground of suspension or deposition, in me, can scarcely be denominated an irregularity in him. It is easy to see that opposition to such a man, in such circumstances, in the face of public sentiment, (even supposing this sentiment to be, by no means, unanimously embarked in his favor,) would be made under great disadvantages, and perhaps with impolicy. And whether there is any proper medium, in this and similar cases, between decisive opposition and decisive politeness, I much question. If, therefore, with my present views, I were a minister in Philadelphia, I believe I should open my pulpit to Mr. H——, and studiously avoid every public testimony of disapprobation. Treated in this way, he will soon find his proper level, and attract no more attention than his character entitles him to receive.

'Pardon my troubling you with these remarks. I have thrown out what occurred to me, without ceremony, assured that, whether right or wrong, it will be candidly received.

'Mrs. M. joins in respectful and affectionate regards to yourself and Mrs. Green, with, dear Sir,

'Your sincere friend & brother,
'Samuel Miller.

'Dr. Green.'

Toward the close of the year 1804, Dr. Miller was invited to edit the theological lectures of his honored preceptor, Charles Nisbet, D.D., but felt obliged to decline the

16*

undertaking. He agreed, however, to prepare a sketch of Dr. Nisbet's life, to be prefixed to the work. Some extracts from a letter on this subject, to Alexander Nisbet, Esquire, of Baltimore, will disclose the state of his health, and the heavy pressure of his engagements. It is dated the 25th of December.

'I feel honored by that friendly preference which you and your family have given to me, in selecting an editor for the proposed publication; and it gives me great pain to think of declining the undertaking. But I am compelled to do so, without hesitation. My reasons are—

'1. The numerous and pressing avocations which necessarily belong to my professional duty in this place. These are so numerous and so oppressive, as to leave me, for weeks together, scarcely a single hour of leisure for literary pursuits.

'2. My health is feeble; and it is with much difficulty that I read and write enough for my pulpit preparations, without injuring myself. I suffer so much from sedentary occupations, that it has become an essential point with me to curtail them as much as possible.

'3. My eyes are weak, and easily hurt by the perusal of obscure manuscripts and proof sheets. I have already suffered much from this source.

'4. The expense of printing is from ten to fifteen per cent. more in this city than in Philadelphia, and I presume that it is higher than in Baltimore. The price of the mechanical labor is higher, and the price of paper much more so. * *

'Agreeably to your request, I have drawn up a short address to the public, intended to accompany the proposals. It is of great importance, that everything of this kind should be short and comprehensive. * *

'While I decline myself to take the charge of conducting the proposed publication, I should consider it indelicate in me to name another person. * *

'You will see in the proposals a promise of a "Life and Character of the Author," to be prefixed to the publication. I am willing to undertake this, provided it will be agreeable to you, and provided you will, as soon as convenient, furnish me with such facts and dates, * * as will enable me to draw up a connected narrative.'

2. SERMONS ON SUICIDE.

In February, 1805, Dr. Miller preached two sermons on suicide, which, by request, were published shortly afterwards.[1] The occasion of these discourses is thus stated in the former of the two by the author himself.

"It is my design, from this passage, to offer some remarks on the crime of SUICIDE—a crime of the deepest dye—a crime which has become alarmingly frequent in our land, and in our city—a crime, therefore, against which it becomes those who would declare the *whole counsel of God* to bear public and solemn testimony."

In a note he adds,

"It is believed, that within three months immediately preceding the delivery of these discourses, at least nine cases of suicide occurred in the city of New York. This number, in a city, the population of which does not exceed 70,000, must be considered as enormous and alarming."[2]

In May, 1807, Dr. Miller received an anonymous letter from Boston, his answer to which was, by absence from home, ill health, and various pressing duties, delayed until the 9th of July. This correspondence will illustrate how bread cast upon the waters may be found after many days.

'Rev. Sir, * * I have no doubt it will give you pleasure to be informed, that you have been the means, through the blessing of God, of saving a miserable creature from perpetrating the horrid crime of suicide. * * My misfortunes were great; I have been reduced from a respectable standing in society to the most embarrassed circumstances; and I supposed I had not the courage to live and see those connected with me suffer; in consequence of which I had determined to quit the world. Already were my last, parting communications to those who were dear to me finished; the fatal implement of death was within my reach; and, just on the brink of eternity, by accident, I took up a paper, published this day, containing an extract from your excellent discourse on Suicide. Had you known every circumstance of my life, had you known my present situation, you could not have made an address more applicable. It had its effect. Every sentence struck me to the heart. Yes —I assure you, had I perpetrated the crime I was about committing, I should indeed have embittered the evening days of my beloved parents, and brought down their grey hairs with

[1] "The Guilt, Folly and Sources of Suicide: two Discourses preached in the City of New York, February, 1805. By Samuel Miller, D.D., One of the Pastors of the United Presbyterian Churches in said city.—Job ii. 9, 10.— 8vo pp. 72.

[2] P. 13.

sorrow to the grave. I should have precipitated an amiable partner into the deepest affliction. I should have left my tender babes fatherless; and by my desertion, they would have been exposed to all the dangers of an unpitying world. I should have left brothers and sisters to share in the grief and disgrace of my unworthy conduct. I should have left some friends, I trust, who would have wept for me; but, no doubt, would have found themselves wounded by my folly and sin. I should have tortured the bosom of sensibility. I should have defrauded my creditors. I should have plunged a friend in difficulty. In short, I have no conception what misery I should have inflicted on those I should have left behind. It appeared as if every sentence in the extract was intended for me. I paused—I reflected—I threw the murdering instrument aside, and determined to live. I will still struggle through the world; and, perhaps, may yet bless the propitious moment, that put the paper in my hand; and may yet have the pleasure of personally thanking you. I have often had the pleasure of hearing you in public, and conversing with you in private circles.' * *

A comparison of the foregoing letter with Dr. Miller's first discourse,[1] will show that the acknowledgments of the former took their mode of expression very much from the latter. He replied,

'It would be difficult for me to describe the emotions which your letter excited. To be made the means of doing any good, however small, to any individual, would, I trust, always give me unfeigned pleasure. But to be made the instrument of so great a deliverance, to the head of a family, to one who stands in so many relations in society, did, indeed, fill me with joy indescribable. But I desire never to lose sight of the humbling truth, that, whenever we do good, it is only as instruments in the hand of infinite wisdom and benevolence. God can make the humblest and feeblest means effectual to the accomplishment of the most important ends. In this case, he has thought proper to employ a small production of mine for accomplishing a most merciful purpose. While my bosom swells with gratitude at this gracious dispensation, I hope I shall always feel disposed to say, *Not unto me, O Lord, not unto me, but unto thy name be all the praise!*

'You say you have often heard me preach, and conversed with me in private. Though this general information affords me no clue to discover who you are, it is another circumstance which adds to my deep and tender interest in your welfare. It

[1] Particularly p. 24.

would gratify me to take by the hand a man, to whom I am bound by such a tie as this event has created; but to think of our meeting, and spending a happy eternity together, in a better world, is a still more delightful and interesting thought. May we keep it in view; and may it be gloriously realized!

'You discover a deep conviction, my dear unknown Friend, of the guilt of suicide, and of your own crime in having meditated such an awful deed. In this I rejoice. No language is strong enough to express the folly and the sinfulness of such a step; and the more just your views, the more shocking it will appear to you. But I feel anxious that you should have something more than a deep conviction of the folly of *that* crime. It is my earnest desire that the dispensation may be sanctified to your spiritual and eternal welfare; that it may be a means of convincing you, more than ever, of the unsatisfying nature of all earthly things; and of leading you to that practical acquaintance with the blessed gospel, as a system of holy obedience, and of divine consolation, which is the only genuine and adequate source of happiness to sinful mortals.

'I know not, my dear Sir, what have heretofore been your views of religion, nor in what point of light you now consider the gospel of Christ. But viewing, as I do, all mankind as fallen and depraved creatures; convinced as the Scriptures declare, that there is no salvation but through the atoning sacrifice and perfect righteousness of the Lord Jesus Christ; and assured that none (among those to whom the gospel is offered) can have an interest in its rich blessings, but those who unfeignedly repent of all sin, and cordially embrace the offered mercy, I cannot forbear recommending this gospel to you, as the only foundation of hope, and as the only source of happiness. Rest not satisfied, I beseech you, with deliverance from the despair into which you were plunged, and from the dreadful crime which you meditated. Consider yourself as no longer at liberty to love and pursue this deceitful world with the same ardor as before; but as loudly called to seek a better portion; to become acquainted with that God, who alone can give you real and continued peace; and to dedicate yourself to him as your rightful and gracious sovereign. Perhaps you have already formed this happy resolution. Perhaps you are already enjoying the delightful consolations arising from such a choice. If this be the case, you will be so far from feeling displeasure at these suggestions, that you will consider it my duty to have made them. If this be the case, you will never regard it as unreasonable to recommend to you that Saviour, *whose blood cleanseth from all sin,* and whom to *know aright is life eternal.*

'But if you are yet a stranger to the character of a real and practical Christian, let me entreat you now, while your mind is humbled and softened by the happy dispensation which prompted you to address me, to begin the work of religion; to make that blessed choice, without which you can have no hope. If you look for justification, before God, on any other ground than through faith in the atonement of Christ, you will be disappointed. If you have any other dependence than the righteousness of Immanuel, it will assuredly fail you in the day of trial. But, if your trust and confidence be in him, you will never be put to shame. Excuse this freedom. You cannot suppose, that I mean to hurt your feelings; as I have not even a conjecture who it is I am advising.

'May you be enabled, my dear Sir, to make a due improvement of the great deliverance which you have experienced! May the divine goodness, so remarkably manifested, lead you to sincere and evangelical repentance! May the holy benediction of a gracious God rest upon you and your family! And may you have reason to say, not only now, but through eternity, that even the attempt to destroy yourself was made to *work for your good!*

'I am, dear Sir, with every wish for your temporal and eternal welfare,   Your sincere friend,
                                        'Samuel Miller.'

About a week later, Dr. Miller received a second letter from his correspondent, disclosing his real name, and stating that he was in prison for debt. There are no traces of any further correspondence, or of the subsequent career of the person in whose providential rescue from suicide it originated.

3.   EPISCOPACY.—THEOLOGICAL EDUCATION.

After the foregoing anticipation, to complete what relates to the discourses last noticed, the following extracts from Dr. Miller's correspondence and diary may restore us to the chronological order of events. Writing to Mr. Griffin, on the 11th of February, 1805, in regard to a call the latter had received from the Dutch Church of Albany, he says,

'Another consideration most important is, that the Episcopalians of this city have lately begun to employ a language and act a part, which indicate a wish to get the mastery over every other denomination in the state, and particularly in the city;

and their immense wealth will enable them to do much towards
the accomplishment of their object. It appears to me, and to
others, that, among the means to be employed for repelling
these claims, and for maintaining the respectability of the non-
Episcopal part of our state, it is of the utmost importance that
the minister to be placed in the Dutch Church of Albany,
should be a man both able and zealously disposed to coöperate
in all just and liberal measures for this purpose.'

Again, on the 7th of March, he writes,

'I thank you most cordially for your remarks on my "Retrospect." It is somewhat curious, that I entirely agree with
you in almost every one of them. Is the critic or writer entitled to most credit for this? I must again thank you for
your two sheets. They contain a number of very valuable
remarks; and, if my book should ever reach a second edition,
(which, alas! is not very likely at present,) I shall profit much
by your communication. I make this acknowledgment as
candidly as you have made your remarks.

'Three weeks ago, I rather leaned to the opinion that you
ought to accept the Albany call. I confess this opinion is
now somewhat shaken. I find it is the judgment of some
judicious persons, that your sentiments about the sealing ordinances would probably tend to diminish your comfort there;
and I am not without my suspicions that your Hopkinsian
sentiments generally may be considered as an offence against
the Dutch Church!! I throw out these things rather as hints
for cogitation than as advice. If I were in your situation, I
should be much at a loss; but it appears to me that I should
rather incline to avoid a more northern exposure. * *

'I inclose the prospectus of a new magazine. The members
of our clerical association are to be the editors. As you have
pledged yourself to patronize the Assembly's Magazine, we
cannot expect you to do much for this. But perhaps you can
get some clerical subscribers in your part of New Jersey. I
mention clerical subscribers more particularly, because the
work will probably contain much discussion on the Epicopal
controversy and other subjects specially interesting to clergymen.'

In a letter to Dr. Green, of the 12th of March, 1805,
Dr. Miller speaks of the Episcopalians of New York City
and State as having grown rapidly within two years, not
so much in numbers, as in their arrogant claims and high-
church principles.

'Within the last year,' he says, 'they have made many publications, in the form of sermons, tracts, and much larger works, in which the high-toned doctrines of Laud and his successors in opinion are exhibited, and most strenuously contended for. We, at first, thought that the state of public opinion was so utterly repugnant to these principles, that our true policy was to treat all their exertions with silent contempt. But things have lately occurred of so flagrant and offensive a nature, that we have determined, at length, to defend our Presbyterian opinions, and to put our people on their guard. * * It has been judged best, after mature deliberation, to establish a magazine, as a vehicle for conveying to the public what we may choose to write on this subject. As the Episcopalians have already a magazine, which they employ as an engine to promote their views; and as controversial pieces will, perhaps, be least likely to give offence, or excite alarm, in this form, (being mixed up with much practical matter,) it is probably the most eligible plan on which to engage our adversaries.'

In the same letter he adds,

'I have long thought of addressing you on a suject, which appears to me most intimately connected with the interests of religion generally, and of our church in particular. We have, if I do not mistake, a melancholy prospect, indeed, with respect to a supply of ministers for our churches. Cannot the General Assembly, at their next sessions, commence some plan of operation for supplying this deficiency? I know that there are difficulties to contend with—prejudices, narrow views, want of money, etc., etc. But it is of the utmost importance that something decisive should be done. Am I not right in supposing, that, at least, two hundred more ministers might, at this moment, be advantageously employed, within the bounds of the General Assembly; and that near half that number are imperiously demanded? It appears to me, that we ought, forthwith, either to establish a new theological school, in some central part of our bounds; or direct more of our attention to extend the plan and increase the energy of the Princeton establishment. On the latter part of the alternative many doubts occur to me; and, with respect to the former, I know difficulties of the most formidable kind will arise. I can think of no person in the United States, who has so good information of the state of the Presbyterian Church as yourself, or who is so capable of devising and putting in motion the plan best adapted to our situation. I hope, therefore, you will devote your leisure time between this and the meeting of the Assembly to the consideration of the subject, and the preparation of some plan to be acted upon by them.'

In a letter, dated the 12th of April, 1805, to Dr. Nott, just made President of Union College, and accompanying some copies of his discourses on suicide, Dr. Miller remarks, 'I wish to do as much good as possible; and doing good to the young has always appeared to me as, humanly speaking, doing it on the largest scale.'

To Dr. Morse, the 13th of April, 1805, Mr. Miller writes,

'I am gratified, my dear Sir, to hear of the noble stand which you have lately made against the public sanction given to heterodoxy by the choice of professor of Divinity in Harvard College. For this intrepid faithfulness you are entitled to the thanks of all the friends of piety in the United States. I feel myself under obligations to you for it.'

The following is from Mr. Miller's Diary:—

'May 12, 1805. A very interesting event has occurred to my beloved wife. About two years and a half since, she united with the church, in the hope that she had given herself to the King and Lord of the Church. She now thinks that she was then deceived with a false hope, and that she never has, until this time, had genuine discoveries of herself and of Christ, and enjoyed a "good hope through grace." There seems to be some reason to believe that it is even so. She now appears to have clear views and a firm hope. A sermon preached in the Wall street church, by Dr. Nott, seems to have been specially blessed to her; and the weekly lectures of our excellent friend, Dr. Abeel, have also been sensibly useful. Oh, how important to be resting on a firm gospel foundation!'

Mr. Griffin was a member of the Assembly of 1805, which convened in Philadelphia on the 16th of May. In a letter of the 13th, Dr. Miller says to him,

'I wish you to have a full and free conversation with Dr. Green, our mutual and highly esteemed friend, on two important subjects:—

'I. The ambitious designs and artful proceedings of our Episcopal brethren. Since I saw you, I have received increasing conviction, that they are taking unwearied pains, upon a large scale, to disseminate their high church doctrines much beyond the bounds of this city and state. Every minister of the Presbyterian Church ought to be apprized of their designs, and to be particularly armed on the subject of Church Government, and the history of Presbyterian and Episcopal ordination.

'II. The great scarcity of ministers, and the indispensable

17

necessity of adopting speedy and vigorous measures for increasing their number. I consider our prospect on this score melancholy and alarming. If we go on, according to our present system of measures, I do not believe that the funds of the Assembly will be prepared for any effective plan in less than ten or fifteen years; and to wait so long without doing anything, it appears to me would be madness. It is probable that little can be done at this Assembly farther than to digest and begin a vigorous system of measures. And for this purpose, every member of the Assembly ought to have a fire kindled in his mind, that should not cease to burn till the purpose shall be accomplished.

'I throw out these hints: make such use of them as you please. But, at all events, embrace Dr. Green for me, and give him my cordial love.

'The great Head of the Church bless you, my Brother, and, wherever you are, make you useful and happy!

'Ever affectionately yours,

'Sam'l Miller.'

In a letter of May 13, 1805, to Dr. Green, he recurs to the subjects of Episcopalian aggressions and theological education.

He says, 'they are printing, and distributing through the United States, very large editions of books, both polemic and practical, replete with high church doctrines.' The advocates of these doctrines he represents as employing every method, 'both in public and private, to impress upon the minds of the people a belief of the invalidity of all ministrations, excepting those of men who are episcopally ordained.'

'Ought not,' he asks, 'every Presbyterian minister in the United States, to be apprized of these designs and exertions? And ought not the subject of church government generally, and especially the controversy respecting Presbyterian ordination, to be more attended to and better understood, than it commonly is among our brethren. I throw out the foregoing remarks for your consideration. * *

'I cannot help again mentioning my anxiety about the scarcity of ministers in our connexion. It appears to me, that to wait for that slow increase of the Assembly's funds, which may be expected in consequence of any measures heretofore adopted, ought not to satisfy us. I cannot help thinking that measures more speedy and vigorous ought to be contemplated. Besides all the ministers wanted in the middle and Atlantic

country, a few of talents and piety might, probably, extend the
Presbyterian Church in the Southern and Western regions, to
a degree of which none but those who have travelled in those
regions can have any adequate idea. I feel anxious on this
subject—perhaps too anxious. If anything can be done, I
know of no individual either likely or able to do a tenth part
so much as yourself in this very interesting matter.'

In accordance with Dr. Miller's reiterated suggestion,
Dr. Green, though not a member of the General Assembly
of 1805, sent in an overture to that body, which was spread
at large upon the minutes,[1] laid over for consideration at
the next meeting, and recommended to the particular attention, meanwhile, of the Presbyteries. This overture represented the need of ministers as urgent and increasing;
advised that measures should be taken to remove existing
discouragements to entering the ministry; and proposed
that the Presbyteries should be enjoined severally to select
and train up suitable young men, within their bounds, for
the sacred office. Dr. Green says, there was thus "originated a system of measures in the General Assembly which
were continued for several successive years." Then—evidently forgetting Dr. Miller's letter of the 12th of March,
already given, and his letters of the 10th and 14th of May,
1808, written, respectively, nine and five days before the
Assembly met, and to be found on a subsequent page—he
adds, "Still nothing was said about a theological seminary
till some time afterward, when Dr. Alexander, after he had
been Moderator of the General Assembly in 1807, mentioned it in the opening sermon of the following year."[2]

The biographer of Dr. Alexander gives the following
passage from the sermon of the latter at Dr. Miller's
funeral :—

"It may be remarked, that no man in the Church had
been more zealous and active in founding this Institution,
than Dr. Miller. He and Dr. Green may more properly
be considered its founders than any other persons. Others
aided by their counsels and occasional exertions, but these
two devoted themselves with untiring zeal to the prosecution
of the object, and had the pleasure of seeing their exertions
crowned with success. At this time, Dr. Miller, so far as

[1] P. 341, etc.

[2] Life of Dr. Green, 332, etc.

I know, was not thought of as a professor; and I am persuaded the thought was entirely foreign from his own mind."[1]

In October 1805, the Presbytery of New York, appointed a standing committee of five ministers and five elders, to attend to the recommendation of the Assembly (really of Dr. Green's overture) as to the education of candidates for the ministry. Dr. Miller was the second named of this committee, and he and Mr. Griffin were directed to draft an address to the churches, to pious parents, and to pious youth, upon the subject. This address was reported the next day and adopted; it was resolved that three hundred copies of it should be printed; the pastors were recommended to read it from the pulpit; and subscription papers for an education fund were ordered to be prepared and distributed. A quotation of a few lines will show how alarming, to the minds of some persons, the destitution of ministers had become.

"While the population of our country has been rapidly extending; while new settlements have been forming; and new churches in quick succession rising to view; the increase in the number of ministers has been slow, and altogether incommensurate with the increasing demand for their services. This deficiency has become serious and alarming. Important congregations, which have long enjoyed the ministrations of the gospel, when they become vacant, are, with the utmost difficulty, supplied with pastors. Large districts, within the bounds

[1] Life of Dr. Alexander, 580. 581.

The Associate Reformed Church had the honour of establishing the first Protestant Theological Seminary on this side of the Atlantic. John M. Mason, D.D., seems to have had more to do than any other man with its establishment. As early as 1796, he presented an overture to Synod, which resulted in the creation of a synodical fund, one object of which was to assist "pious youth, who, from poverty, could not comfortably and successfully pursue their studies; and the establishment of a Professorship of Theology for the instruction of such as designed the Holy Ministry." At the meeting of Synod five years later, in 1801, the question of the increase of the ministry, and of the erection of a Theological Seminary, was referred to a committee; and, upon their report, Dr. Mason was sent to Great Britain, "to procure a number of ministers and probationers, and, more especially, to solicit donations in money and books" for the proposed Seminary. The latter he made his principal object, and collected about $5000. In 1804, he was appointed Professor of Theology, and upon the first Monday of November, 1805, the regular exercises of the institution commenced in the City of New York. "In 1809, the Rev. James M. Mathews, D.D., was chosen Assistant Professor of Biblical Literature and Church History. He continued in the office until 1818. Dr. Mason labored as the principal Professor, without interruption, (except during one session when absent in Europe on account of his health,) from 1805 until 1821, when the loss of his health, which for several years had been declining, compelled him to resign."—*Hist. of the Seminary,* (1840,) *P.* 8.

of old settlements, in which churches might easily be planted, and where ministers would meet with a cordial welcome, are lying waste for want of their labors; and more than one thousand congregations, on the extensive frontier of the United States, as well informed persons have asserted, are able and willing to support spiritual teachers, but cry for them in vain.'[1]

4. Valetudinarianism.—Miscellaneous Topics.

Dr. Miller's health began to fail him again in the spring of 1805. His 'Record of Preaching' shows that, from the last of April onward, he had frequent help in the pulpit, and during a large part of June was absent in Philadelphia and Princeton, and able to preach but little. Early in September, the yellow fever renewed its ravages in New York. In his feeble condition, and with so little prospect of strength for active labor, it would have been madness for him to have exposed himself; and, in an extremity, he accepted Mr. Griffin's kind invitation to his house in Newark, and thither removed his family. On the 11th he writes to Alexander Nisbet, Esquire,

'And to crown all, ever since my return from Philadelphia, I have been in such bad health, that I have hardly had strength or spirits, for a week together, to perform any professional duty. I have not been able to preach for three Sabbaths past; and, for five or six Sabbaths before, was not fit to be in the pulpit. * * Being now on the eve of departure from the city, (which is fast evacuating on account of pestilence,) I embrace the opportunity of dropping you a hasty line.'

On the same day, he writes to Mr. Griffin,

'You may expect us at your house to-morrow in the forenoon, with the leave of Providence; but whether to spend our exile with you or not, is still undetermined. After every exertion, we have not been able to get such a servant woman as we thought could be relied on. * *

'The continuance of my indisposition, and the feeble state of my health generally, demand immediate attention. It is therefore my purpose, after disposing of my family in a comfortable manner, to spend a considerable portion of my exile in riding on horseback, and visiting some parts of New Jersey which I have not yet seen. This will probably render several little journies, of four, five, or six days each, necessary for me. * *

'In this situation, my dear Brother, we resort to you. The

P. 4.

only reluctance we have felt, in accepting your fraternal offer, has arisen from a fear that Mrs. Griffin's health might suffer from an addition to the number and noise of her family. The difficulty about another servant woman, I am in hopes of being able to obviate after getting to Newark. If this should prove impossible, I should consider myself as doing an injury to Mrs. Griffin's health, not to insist on seeking other quarters. But, if this difficulty can be removed; if you will consent to treat us without ceremony; and without making the least alteration in your ordinary family arrangements; if you will suffer us to consider ourselves at home from the first moment we enter your house; and if you will (as I would be done unto in similar circumstances) consent to receive a just pecuniary compensation for all the additional trouble and expense we may give you, we shall consider ourselves greatly and lastingly obliged.'

Dr. Miller fulfilled his purpose of spending a considerable portion of his exile in riding on horseback over some parts of New Jersey. He did not return to New York until near the end of October.

Shortly after his return, Dr. Milledoler was added to the number of the collegiate Presbyterian pastors. Dr. Miller, in his Memoirs of Dr. Rodgers, says,

"The ministrations requisite for carrying on the stated service of *three* churches becoming, every day, from the natural increase of the city, more extensive, multiplied, and laborious, it was judged expedient to call a *fourth* minister. Accordingly, after the usual preliminary steps, the congregations were convened, in joint meeting, on the 5th day of August, 1805, when they unanimously made choice of the reverend Doctor *Philip Milledoler*, then pastor of the Third Presbyterian church in the city of *Philadelphia*, to be one of their collegiate pastors; with a view, however, to his taking the church in *Rutgers*-street under his more particular care, and being considered, if a separation of the churches should ever take place, as its sole pastor. The call for Dr. *Milledoler* was regularly prosecuted before the Presbytery of *Philadelphia*; and he, having accepted it, was installed, in the church in *Rutgers*-street, on the 19th of November following,"[1] Dr. Miller preaching upon the occasion.

The new pastor proved very efficient and successful; and in less than seven years, the church of which he had taken particular charge, though small and feeble at the time when he was called, grew to be the largest of its denomination in the United States, numbering between five and six hundred members.

P. 269, etc.

In 1805, Dr. Miller, associated with Dr. J. M. Mason, Dr. Abeel, and Mr. McLeod, took part in establishing a select grammar school, of a superior kind, in New York. "We designed it," said Dr. Mason, "as an experiment towards the melioration of our system of preliminary education, and it succeeds admirably. There is not a rude or idle boy in it. Two of us visit it monthly, and not only mark their progress, but their manners, and blame or praise, reward or disgrace, according to the evidence of a public ledger, on which every day's deportment and diligence are marked."[1]

To Dr. Nott Dr. Miller wrote,

'Rev'd and dear Sir,   New York, January 22, 1806.

'The object of this letter is to call your attention to the literary and theological merit of our friend, Mr. Griffin, of Newark, and to ask whether a *doctorate* might not be procured for him, from Union College, at the next annual commencement.

'I would be understood, my dear Sir, as making this suggestion with all that caution and humility which the nature of the subject requires. I am sensible how often those who preside over literary institutions are pestered by officious meddlers like myself; and how often justice, or policy, or prudence requires, that their applications be rejected. And if, in the case proposed, you should think the honor unmerited, or should consider it as difficult to be obtained, be pleased to burn this letter, and think no more of its contents: in which case, much as I love Mr. Griffin, and highly as I respect both his literary and religious character, I shall silently and most respectfully acquiesce. But, if you think that any thing ought to be done, and can be done, towards decorating him with the proposed honor, I shall feel cordially gratified and personally obliged.

'I am rejoiced to hear that Union College flourishes under your Presidency. May your most sanguine expectations be more than equalled; and may the richest of heaven's blessings rest on you, and on your labors in behalf of learning and piety!

'I am, Rev'd and dear Sir,
'With much respect,
'Your cordial friend and servant,
'Samuel Miller.'

Mr. Griffin did not get his doctorate 'at the next annual commencement,' but it was given to him in August, 1808 —two years later.

[1] Memoirs of Dr. Mason, 241, 2.

On the 3d of February, 1806, we find Dr. Miller, in his correspondence, mentioning his very bad health ever since the previous May, which had rendered it extremely difficult for him to pursue his ordinary avocations. But he was now decidedly convalescent, and well was it that he had partially recovered strength; for, on the 28th of the same month, he tells Mr. Griffin, that he is performing, as far as possible, in addition to his own duties, those of Dr. McKnight, who, on account of sickness, has preached once only within six weeks. He adds,

'We are all in good health, except myself, who am yet infirm and frequently complaining—very liable to take cold, and under the necessity of exercising habitual caution. We call our little boy Edward Millington. The first name is borne by my brother in this city, and by several very dear friends.[1] The second was the maiden name of my mother. Without any compliment to the living, I will venture to say, that if he should possess half the sweetness and half the grace of that glorified saint, whose name I can never pronounce but with the mingled emotions of veneration, gratitude and love, he will be an honor to his parents and useful to the world.

' We do not propose to remove into our new house until about the middle of April—just time enough to receive you and yours comfortably at Presbytery.'

The addition of Dr. McKnight's duties to his own does not seem to have been attempted with impunity; for, from the middle of March to the middle or end of June, we find Dr. Miller again suffering from ill health, and able to preach very little.

The 'new house' was one which Dr. Miller was having built for himself in Dey street—No. 27; and which, according to contract, was to have been completed by the first of the previous November, 'provided there was no fever to stop the workmen.' But two months of pestilence had given license for three times as long a delay.

5. Theological Education.

In 1801 and 1803, Dr. Miller had been commissioned to the General Assembly. He was again a commissioner in 1806, and was chosen moderator. He no doubt took as active a part as the presiding officer could properly, in re-

---

[1] Mr. Griffin himself among the rest.

commending the substantial adoption of the plans of Dr. Green's overture of the preceding year, which now came up for discussion. Most of the Presbyteries reported, that they had seriously considered, and that they highly approved, those plans. The minute finally adopted, as not too stringent, yet determined by "a most gloomy prospect" as to the supply of ministers, concludes as follows:—

"—the Assembly do hereby most earnestly recommend to every Presbytery under their care to use their utmost endeavors to increase, by all suitable means in their power, the number of promising candidates for the holy ministry: to press it upon the parents of pious youth, to endeavor to educate them for the Church; and on the youth themselves, to devote their talents and their lives to the sacred calling; to make vigorous exertions to raise funds to assist all the youth who may need assistance; to be careful that the youth they take on their funds give such evidence as the nature of the case admits, that they possess both talents and piety; to inspect the education of these youth, during the course of both their academical and theological studies, choosing for them such schools, seminaries, and teachers, as they may judge most proper and advantageous; so as eventually to bring them into the ministry, well furnished for their work. And the Assembly * * do hereby order, that every Presbytery under their care make annually a report to the Assembly, stating particularly what they have done in this concern, or why (if the case so shall be) they have done nothing in it; and the Assembly will, when these reports are received, consider each distinctly, and decide by vote, whether the Presbyteries severally shall be considered as having discharged or neglected their duty in this important business."[1]

Prior to the establishment of the Theological Seminary at Princeton, in 1812, the Presbyterian Church in this country was indebted to individual and sectional efforts for the training of a learned and pious ministry. The "Log College," at Neshaminy, established, soon after the year 1728, by the Rev. William Tennent, sen., was, for its humble pretensions, singularly blessed in carrying on this work. After the Church was divided, in 1741, the "New Side" soon established the College of New Jersey, with particular reference to the education of ministers; while the "Old Side" patronized the academies at New London, Pennsylvania, and Newark, Delaware, and the College and Academy

[1] Pp. 366, etc.

of Philadelphia, afterwards the University of Pennsylvania. The efforts made by the College of New Jersey in behalf of a theological, in addition to a classical education, seem to have been stimulated afresh by Dr. Green's overture; for the faculty, through Dr. Smith, the President, issued a communication on the subject, which was read to the General Assembly of 1806. A few lines from this will show what that 'Princeton establishment' was to which Dr. Miller had referred, distrustfully, in his letter of the 12th of March, 1805, to Dr. Green. Says Dr. Smith,

"The College of New Jersey was originally founded with a particular view to promote the interests of religion, as well as learning, by training up men of piety and talents for the ministry of the gospel. The Trustees of the institution have ever been attentive to this great object, and have made the most generous provision for the support of theological students. * *

"All persons who are actually engaged in the study of Theology, at whatever institution they may have received the preliminary parts of their education, may, on producing proper testimonials of their character, pursue their further studies here, at the moderate charge of one dollar a week for board, and enjoy the assistance of the President and Professor of Theology, without any fee for instruction. This Professor gives lectures to the theological students twice in the week; and, at each succeeding meeting, examines them strictly on the subject of the preceding lecture. His course of lectures embrace Divinity, Ecclesiastical History, Church Government, Christian and Jewish Antiquities, and the duties of the pastoral office. He instructs those who desire it in the Hebrew language, so useful and almost indispensable to a good divine.

"At every meeting, one or more of his pupils submits to his criticisms and remarks an essay or sermon on a subject previously assigned. The Professor, together with the President of the College, holds a Theological Society once in the week, for the discussion of important questions immediately relative to the science of divinity.

"The emulation and encouragement communicated by a variety of fellow students, the opportunity of cultivating any branch of science, and an access at all times to a large and well selected Theological Library, are other advantages of no small consequence."[1]

On the 31st of May, having just returned with his

[1] Minutes of the Gen. Assembly, pp. 362, 3.

family from Philadelphia, after the meeting of the General Assembly, Dr. Miller wrote to Mr. Griffin,

'You have probably been informed, that the overture respecting the education of young men for the ministry was acted upon and carried *nem. con.* As many as eight or nine Presbyteries have already begun to act; and it is hoped that the greater part of those within our bounds will begin soon.'

6. MISCELLANEOUS TOPICS.

To Dr. Nott, on the 17th of July, 1806, Dr. Miller wrote,

'Mr. & Mrs. McKesson have mentioned, since their return, that you intend to visit this city toward the last of this month. Is it so?—or do they mistake? It is not necessary, I trust, to add, that to find them correct would give us very great pleasure. When you come to New York, (let it be when it may,) come directly to my house, and regard it as your permanent home. I have no notion of your wandering geniuses, who have no fixed place of lodging, when they visit a distant city. Such a practice is contrary to the fitness of things, and leads to multiplied mischiefs. * *

'P. S. How is your health now? Do you take exercise enough, and dissipate sufficiently? I hope you have not forgotten my numerous exhortations on these points.'

The facilities enjoyed for a trip from New York to Albany, in 1806, may be understood from the following passage in a letter from Dr. Miller to Mr. Griffin, dated the 9th of August.

'I find there are three vessels going on Monday next. At least I find three, the captains of which *assure* me they will certainly sail on that day. One proposes to sail at 10 o'clock A. M.; a second at 4 P. M.; and a third at 8 or 9 P. M. The first and third of these I think are the best sloops; but any one of them, in my opinion, would do extremely well. I shall therefore expect you and Mrs. Griffin with Louisa, on Monday morning, to remain at our house, until you shall be ready to go on board, *and to make yourself contented until that time shall arrive.* For it is very possible, though I have done all that can be done, that it may be sometime on Tuesday before either of the above mentioned vessels may actually sail. You are sensible that, in all naval enterprizes, much depends, in spite of every effort to be punctual, on wind and tide.'

From the middle of March, 1806, throughout the spring,

summer, and opening autumn, so much enfeebled was Dr. Miller's health, that his pastoral labors were frequently and seriously interrupted. Within twelve weeks from the date first mentioned, he was able to preach but three times. On the 4th of September, he writes to Mr. Nisbet, 'I propose to set out on a journey of four or five weeks on Monday next. The principal object of this journey is to lay in a good stock of health against the winter.' We find him accordingly travelling, for even a little longer time than he had mentioned, in New England and the State of New York, with evident benefit.

He spent successive Sabbaths at Litchfield, Connecticut, Brattleboro', Vermont, Dartmouth College and Walpole, New Hampshire, Troy and Harlem, New York. Mrs. Miller and the children had gone in the opposite direction, and were whiling away the time at Mr. Griffin's in Newark, at Judge Kirkpatrick's in New Brunswick, and among their relatives in Philadelphia, successively. From Newark, the 11th of September, she wrote to her husband,

'Mr. Griffin was well enough to come down stairs on Monday evening, and has been pretty well ever since, not complaining more, I think, than is usual for those of his calling: it would be quite unclerical, you know, to be very well. I hope, however, my dear Samuel, to find you unfashionable enough, for some time after your return, to use this term in perfect truth.'

From New Brunswick she wrote, on the 19th,

'Our children are delighted with their present situation: they have become so absorbed in the little girls, *their* tables, and chairs, and other toys, as to care comparatively little for their mother. They have cessation of amusement enough, sometimes to inquire for their father, and wonder when he will return: I believe they will be highly delighted to see you. Edward has grown fatter, I think, since we left the city; and Bessy is certainly much better: her cheeks have acquired more rotundity, and a brighter hue. Margaret is the admiration of all persons of genuine taste, and is considered a perfect beauty. We met, at Woodbridge, Mrs. Rush and Mrs. Stockton, with their respective daughters: they exclaimed most vehemently at her beauty, and I was in hopes would have frightened her so much, as to prevent a worse effect from extreme praise; but the little gipsy understood the matter perfectly well, and was very desirous of meeting with them again on our journey; and *I*, really, was somewhat pleased myself with the effect her appearance had produced. How shall we avoid being led into the general infatuation on these occasions?

'Mrs. Kirkpatrick and the Judge are as kind and attentive as ever. Their children are certainly better than children in general, and agree perfectly well with ours.'

Dr. Miller was again, in 1807, a Commissioner to the General Assembly, appointed, according to custom, as the moderator of the previous year, who always opens the next Assembly with a sermon. He preached from Philippians iii. 8: "Yea, doubtless, and I count all things but loss, for the excellency of the knowledge of Christ Jesus my Lord."

18

CHAPTER FOURTEENTH.

---

1. HISTORY OF THE CONTROVERSY.

DR. MILLER had hitherto been a voluntary, toilsome worker for the press, at the prompting, too much, of scholarly taste, and of surrounding social influences. Nevertheless, his labors had evidently, in God's providence, been overruled to prepare him, as to habits of study, style of writing, the courtesies of literature, reputation and influence, for subsequent more strictly professional and more important undertakings. He had scarcely thrown off the Retrospect, and relapsed, perhaps, into the fever of historical research, when he was restored, by Providential circumstances, to a proper theological diathesis. We have already found his letters recurring, frequently, to the subject of Episcopal aggressions. It is time to show that his representations and apprehensions upon this point were not groundless; and the leaves just now opening before us exhibit an important crisis in his history; a coloring which more or less marked the whole of his subsequent life.

The prevailing spirit of the Episcopal Church, in this country, has always been a spirit of arrogant pretension and exclusiveness. During our colonial existence, the establishment of religion in England was extended to some of the colonies with more or less rigor; and, in all of them where it existed, Episcopacy claimed peculiar preëminence as the state religion of the mother country. Its influence, during our Revolutionary struggle, was cast, predominantly, in favor of England; its connexion with the English Church being generally thought too important an advantage to be

206

lightly severed.   When, however, the colonies became independent, Episcopacy had in reserve still other grounds,
on which to demand that its communion should be recognized as *the* Church, and all other bodies of Christians stigmatized as dissenters and schismatics.   It now gave new
prominence to the claim, long before advanced, of an exclusive apostolical succession ; and while acquiescing in the
results of the Revolution ; nay, joining in the general ac-
clamation of victory, yielded nothing of its own lordly as-
sumptions.   Still, the effect of our independence was, for
a time, naturally enough, to depress the Episcopal Church.
By her substantial adherence to the mother country, in our
great struggle, she had lost prestige ; and about a whole
generation passed, before she recovered in either character
or influence.

The chief opponents of Episcopacy in the colonies had
been the Presbyterians ; whose opposition, moreover, had
been so persistent, and, in many respects, so successful, as
to widen, lastingly, the distance in feeling between the two
denominations.   Until after the Revolution, all the efforts
of the Episcopal Church in this country, to secure an
American Episcopate, had been defeated, mainly through
Presbyterian influence ; an influence wisely and skilfully
exercised, to prevent the aggrandizement of an ecclesiastical power, which had been, in repeated instances, unhesita-
tingly exerted, to annoy and oppress so-called dissenters.
Nevertheless, from the return of peace to about the beginning of the present century, the two denominations in New
York City lived together in unwonted harmony.   The war
having left both the Presbyterian churches in an almost
ruinous condition ; until one of them could be repaired—a
period of more than six months—Trinity church, as we
have seen, with unsolicited and distinguished kindness, gave
to the united congregations under Dr. Rodgers the use of
St. George's and St. Paul's churches, alternately, for their
worship.   Of this period, and of what immediately followed,
Dr. Miller has thus spoken :—

"For more than twenty years after the establishment of
American independence, the Presbyterians of New York dwelt
in peace and harmony with their Episcopal neighbors.   They
well recollected, indeed, the long course of oppressions and
provocations which they had suffered, by means of Episcopal

influence, prior to the Revolution. They recollected that, for more than half a century, besides supporting their own churches, they had been forced to contribute to the support of the Episcopal Church, already enriched and strengthened by governmental aid. They recollected in how many instances the fairest and most laudable exertions to promote the interest of their denomination, were opposed, thwarted and frustrated by the direct interference of the same favored sect. But when our national independence and equal rights became established; when all denominations of Christians were placed on the same footing, with respect to the state, and left to enjoy their privileges together, the Presbyterians were disposed to forget every injury; to cover every former subject of uneasiness with the mantle of charity; to dwell in equal concord and love with their brethren of every name. It was not supposed, indeed, during this period of tranquillity, that Presbyterians and Episcopalians were *agreed* in their views either of evangelical truth, or of ecclesiastical order; or that they considered all the points in which they differed as of small importance. But while both thought for themselves, and pursued their own views of doctrine and worship, they avoided an *unnecessary*, and, especially, an *irritating* and *offensive* obtrusion of their points of difference; and, above all, never seem to have thought, on either side, of that system of proscription and attack, which our Episcopal brethren have since chosen to commence.

"The formal and open commencement of this system may be dated in the year 1804. Previous to that period, indeed, several sermons and other fugitive pamphlets had evinced a disposition on the part of some individuals, to revive and urge certain claims, as unfounded in Scripture as they are offensive to liberal minds. But in that year there appeared, in the City of New York, the first of a series of larger publications, which evidently had for their object a system of more bold and decisive proscription than had been ventured upon for a considerable time before. These publications, among other doctrines, were professedly intended to maintain and disseminate the following; viz., "That the power of ordination to the Christian ministry is, by divine appointment, vested exclusively in Diocesan Bishops; that where these Bishops are wanting, there is no authorized ministry, no true Church, no valid ordinances; that, of course, the Presbyterian and all other non-Episcopal churches and ministers are, not only unauthorized and perfectly destitute of validity, but are to be viewed as institutions founded in rebellion and schism; and that all who are in communion with such non-Episcopal churches are "aliens from Christ," "out of the appointed road to heaven," have no interest in the promises of God, and no hope but in his "uncovenanted mercy," which may be extended to them, in common with the serious and conscientious heathen." Books, containing doctrines of this kind, had been published and sent abroad with much assiduity, for more than a year before any Presbyterian came forward to refute them, or to vindicate primitive simplicity and order; and, since that time, similar books have been printed, re-printed, new-modelled, and circulated, especially in the city and State of New York, with a degree of zeal and perseverance altogether new and extraordinary.

"Nor is this all. These books have been put into the hands of non-Episcopalians. Presbyterians have been personally addressed on the subject, and attempts made to seduce them from their church, on the express allegation, that they were totally destitute of an authorized ministry and of valid ordinances. And, that nothing might be wanting to fix the character and purpose of these treasures, they were accompanied with declarations, that a state of warfare with the Presbyterian church, on the subject of Episcopacy, was earnestly wished for, and considered as one of the most probable means of promoting the Episcopal cause.

"It was not possible for one denomination of Christians to act in a more inoffensive manner towards another, than *we* had uniformly done towards our Episcopal brethren. We had never attempted to unchurch them. We had never, directly or indirectly, called in question the validity of their ministrations or ordinances. We had never, on any occasion, obtruded our particular views of church order, as essential either to the *being* or *prosperity* of the body of Christ. On the contrary, whenever we had occasion, from the pulpit or the press, to instruct our people on those points in which we differ from Episcopalians, it was always done in a manner respectful, and conciliatory, and perfectly consistent with acknowledging them as a sister church; a sister by no means, indeed, in our estimation, free from error; but yet sufficiently near the primitive model to be regarded as a church of Christ. All this, however, did not secure us from the treatment of which you have heard.

"Under these circumstances; when we were virtually denounced and excommunicated; when the name of a Christian church was denied us; when our people were warned to abandon the ministry of their pastors, under the penalty of being regarded as *rebels* and *schismatics* both by God and man; when more than insinuations of this kind were presented and reiterated, from the pulpit and the press, on every practicable occasion, and in almost every possible variety of form; when, by the frequency and the confidence with which they were brought forward, some in our communion were perplexed, others, more discerning and better informed, rendered indignant, and all appeared to feel the propriety of vindicating the abused ordinances of Christ; it became at least *excusable* to say something in our own defence. It was no bitterness against our Episcopal brethren; no love of controversy; no restless ambition; no desire to intrude into another denomination for the purpose of making proselytes; that dictated an attempt to justify our principles. The attempt was purely defensive, and was demanded by every consideration of duty to the souls of men, and of fidelity to our Master in heaven."[1]

In the foregoing extract, reference is made to "Sermons and other fugitive pamphlets," preceding the larger volumes, in which the controversy in New York originated. Published sermons seem to be intended; but there was one, apparently never published, which, however, was more than once mentioned in the course of the controversy, though not perhaps by Dr. Miller. The Rev. Mr. Wright, on the ordination of a deacon in St. Paul's church, had preached a discourse, containing, in substance, the following passage:—

"The man who affixes a seal to an instrument, unauthorized thereto, not only gives no validity to the instrument, but is guilty of forgery. So the man who undertakes to administer the Christian sacraments of Baptism and the Lord's Supper, without authority from our Holy Mother Church, is guilty of impiety, sacrilege, and blasphemy."

Dr. Rodgers, who had been particularly invited by one of the Episcopal clergy to attend the service says,

"On hearing this declaration, I could not help saying to myself, what I afterwards repeated: That it was, in my judgment, a piece of insolence in Mr. Wright, to tell his Bishop to his face that he was an unregenerated man, and no member of the Christian Church; and that he bore the brand of forgery, impiety, sacrilege and blasphemy." Dr. Provoost, bishop of the diocese at that time, had been baptized by a minister of the Reformed Dutch Church, Mr. Dubois, who had, of course, no "authority" from Mr. Wright's "Holy Mother Church."[2]

[1] Continuation of Letters concerning the Constitution and Order of the Christian Ministry (1809), 14-18.

[2] 2 Christian Magazine, 435.

2. THE REV. JOHN HENRY HOBART.

In the year 1800, the Rev. John Henry Hobart[1] was called to be an assistant minister of Trinity Church, in the City of New York. With his coming, there seems to have been a marked revival of High-churchism in that city. The "series of larger publications," mentioned by Dr. Miller, commenced with him. "The strong attachment of Mr. Hobart," says his biographer, "to the distinctive principles of the Episcopal Church, and his bold, active and persevering defence of them, at all times, through good and through evil report, were striking peculiarities in his character and life. He was constantly endeavoring to rouse others to a sense of their importance; and by his indefatigable labors, his noble enthusiasm, even in the cause of soberness and truth, and the influence of his talents, character and station, he revived the languid zeal of Episcopalians, gave a new tone to their sentiments in this diocese, and stamped the impress of his own mind and feelings on thousands throughout the Church at large."

In the month of May, 1804, Mr. Hobart published his work entitled, "A Companion for the Altar." In the fall of the same year, he gave to the public another volume— "A Companion for the Festivals and Fasts."

Some extracts from these works will serve to verify Dr. Miller's account of them.

"These sacraments are both *necessary* to *salvation*. *Baptism* is *necessary*, being the ordinance whereby we are regenerated, that is, are translated from our natural state into a state of grace, and *born again* to a title to all the privileges of the gospel covenant. The *Lord's Supper* is necessary, because it conveys that spiritual food by which we are nourished to everlasting life. * * These ordinances the church considers as only *generally*, not *absolutely*, necessary to salvation."[2]

"Am I a member of the Church of Christ, which he purchased with his blood, which he sanctifies with his Spirit, and which, according to his sovereign pleasure, is made the channel of his *covenanted* mercies to a fallen world? * *

" Do I keep up my communion with this Church, by devout submission to the ministrations of its *priesthood* in the orders of Bishops, Priests and Deacons, deriving their authority by regu-

---

[1] See 5 Sprague's Annals, 440.
[2] Companion for the Altar, 13, 14.

lar transmission from Jesus Christ, the Redeemer and Head of the Church, who has promised to be with the ministers of apostolic succession, "alway, even to the end of the world?" * *

"In this regenerating ordinance, [baptism,] fallen man is born again from a state of condemnation into a state of grace."[1]

"The mercy of the Saviour is co-extensive with the ruin into which sin has plunged mankind. And "in every nation he that feareth God and worketh righteousness, is accepted with him." But where the gospel is proclaimed, communion with the church, by the participation of its ordinances at the hands of the duly authorized priesthood, is the indispensable condition of salvation. Separation from the prescribed government and regular priesthood of the church, when it proceeds from *involuntary and unavoidable ignorance or error*, we have reason to trust, will not intercept, from the humble, the penitent, and obedient, the blessings of God's favour. But when we humbly submit to that priesthood which Christ and his apostles constituted; when in the lively exercise of penitence and faith, we partake of the ordinances administered by them; we maintain our communion with that church which the Redeemer purifies by his blood; which he quickens by his Spirit; and whose faithful members he will finally crown with the most exalted glories of his heavenly kingdom. The important truth which the universal church has uniformly maintained, that, to experience the full and exalted efficacy of the sacraments, we must receive them from a valid authority, is not inconsistent with that charity which extends mercy to all who labour under *involuntary* error. But great is the guilt, and imminent the danger, of those who, possessing the means of arriving at the knowledge of the truth, *negligently* or *wilfully* continue in a state of separation from the authorized ministry of the church, and participate of ordinances administered by an irregular and invalid authority. Wilfully rending the peace and unity of the church, by separating from the ministrations of its authorized priesthood; obstinately contemning the means which God in his sovereign pleasure hath prescribed for their salvation; they are guilty of rebellion against their Almighty Lawgiver and Judge; they expose themselves to the awful displeasure of that Almighty Jehovah, who will not permit his institutions to be contemned, or his authority violated, with impunity.

"Let it be, therefore, thy supreme care, O my soul, to receive the blessed sacrament of the body and blood of thy Saviour,

---

[1] Companion for the Altar, 143.

only from the hands of those who derive their authority by regular transmission from Christ, the divine head of the church, the only legitimate source of power in it. Thou wilt then enjoy the assurance, that this holy sacrament, which derives all its efficacy from the accompanying power of Christ, administered by those to whom he has given his commission and authority, will be acknowledged and blessed by him to thy comfort and salvation; will, if humbly and devoutly received by thee, be the means and pledge of his pardoning mercy and strengthening grace. By preserving thy communion with the authorized priesthood; by revering that ministerial authority, and submitting to those institutions which thy Saviour established; thou wilt maintain the *unity of the church*, and thus fulfil the high injunction of Christ and his apostles often repeated and earnestly enforced."[1]

"The Christian Church is not a mere *voluntary* society; but one whereof men are *obliged to be members*, as they value their everlasting happiness: for it is a *society appointed by God*, with enforcements of *rewards and punishments.* * * Now, as God, by instituting this society, and annexing such rewards and punishments, has sufficiently declared his will, that men should enter into it, all men are *obliged to become members of it;* and it can in no other sense be called a voluntary society, than as it is left to every man's choice, whether he will be forever happy or miserable."[2]

"The *obligation* of *communion* with the Christian Church is founded on its being a society established by God, to which he has annexed all the privileges and blessings of the Gospel covenant. Of course, in order to partake of these privileges and blessings, we must be *admitted* into the Christian Church, and maintain *communion* with it."[3]

"The uniform testimony of all the apostolic and primitive writers establishes the general conclusion, that whoever was in communion with the bishop, the supreme governor of the church upon earth, was in communion with Christ the head of it; and whoever was not in communion with the bishop, was thereby cut off from communion with Christ."[4]

3.   HIGH CHURCHISM.

In these works, Mr. Hobart ignored, entirely, the common Protestant distinction between the Visible and the

<hr>

[1] Companion for the Altar, 202.
[2] Festivals and Feasts, 15, 16.
[3] Id., 55.
[4] Id., 59.

Invisible Church; and it was but a logical consequence of this, to represent non-Episcopal pastors as mere laymen, the ordinances which they administered as wholly invalid and worse, and the people attending upon their ministry as having no covenanted right to the salvation of the gospel. But this, under another name, was the very core of Romish error. True, those who, in the Church of England, and in the Protestant Episcopal Church of this country, have maintained and propagated high-church opinions, have stoutly denied them to be Romish; or, to use a word more common in this controversy, *Popish*. But the latter word affords the only real pretext for a denial. If Popery implies adherence to the Pope, as the self-styled Chief Bishop, Visible Head of the Church, and Vicar of Christ on Earth, then all High Churchism cannot justly be charged with it; although thousands, it is well-known, have been led thereby, and that most naturally, direct to Romanism, and the fullest acknowledgment of the Pope's claims.

But if High Churchism itself be the very foundation error, the real $\pi\rho\tilde{\omega}\tau o\nu$ $\psi\varepsilon\tilde{\upsilon}\delta o\varsigma$, of the Papacy, as undoubtedly it is, then is it in vain for high churchmen to deny their affinity to the Papists. The recognition of the Pope is only a specific difference: generically, Romanism and High Churchism are the same. Their common heresy embraces three essential points of doctrine: *First*, there is no earthly, or in part earthly, invisible Church of Christ: the only Church on earth is a visible, external communion: *Secondly*, all Christ's promises to his people, his Church, including the promise, or covenant, of salvation, belong, therefore, to a visible communion, and that alone: *Thirdly*, this visible communion, within the pale of which, alone, covenanted salvation is to be found, depends essentially for its existence, upon an outward succession of prelatical bishops:—the Romanist says, the succession from Peter of the Bishops of Rome—the Popes:—the Protestant high churchman says, an unbroken, tactual succession, of prelates simply, from some one or more of the Apostles. The former contends, that there is no covenanted salvation out of the Church of Rome; the latter, that there is no covenanted salvation out of a communion which has prelates with unbroken, tactual apostolical succession. The conse-

quences of this dogma are tremendous. As to this country, the Romanist tells you, that there is no covenanted
salvation out of his own little communion. The Episcopal
high churchman tells you, that there is no covenanted salvation out of his, and, perhaps, the Moravian, and the
Romish communions ; and upon the last he often throws
doubt on the ground of some Tridentine corruption. Of
course, high churchmen are found, so called, of every
grade ; but high churchism, properly speaking, is what has
just been described. It derives its name from this heretical exaltation of the Visible Church, or a part thereof,
which it puts, in fact, nearer than Christ to both saint and
sinner. Christ says, " Come unto me." High Churchism
says, "Come to our Visible Church, or you can never
properly, or certainly, reach Christ."

The Reformation of the sixteenth century is often said
to have turned upon the doctrine of Justification by Faith
—"the article of a standing or falling church." In appearance, it may have been so, but not in reality. The
Reformers, digging through the overlaying mass of Romish
corruptions, down to the great doctrines of the gospel,
which they brought once more to light, did not reach first,
as indeed they could not, the very foundations of truth.
They recovered, both theoretically and experimentally,
the doctrine of Justification, and were rejoicing in it, " as
one that findeth great spoil ;" when Rome launched her
excommunications and anathemas upon their heads. Out
of *the* Church they were lost ! The very thought was terrible, and it carried some faint hearts back in a hurry to
the Pope's fold by the door of submission. Not so, however, with those who knew best the Scriptural foundation,
and the Scriptural power of justifying faith. They were
only set to delving deeper into the doctrine of Christ.
They had, perhaps, the witness in themselves that they belonged to him—were the sheep of his fold : what did it
matter whether they belonged to the Pope or not ? Happy
thought ! Now came to light the great gospel truth of an
Invisible Church, the whole company of true believers,
past, present, and future, united to Christ, and through
him to one another, by faith, and heirs of every promise,
every covenanted blessing. The Church of Christ, it was,
henceforth, against the Church of Rome: that was the

grand corner doctrine of the Reformation; which, alas! has been "a stone of stumbling," and a "a rock of offence," to so many calling themselves Protestants. Every great struggle for the faith has brought to clearer view, and more definite expression, some momentous truth. The doctrine of the Invisibility of the True Church was the main doctrine battled for and successfully maintained by the Reformers: the denial of it really lay at the foundation of every Romish heresy.

4. DR. MILLER'S "LETTERS."

In the summer of 1805, the Rev. Dr. William Linn published, in "The Albany Centinel," under the title "Miscellanies, No. IX," a few strictures upon the extravagant claims set forth in Mr. Hobart's volumes. He was met at once, in the same newspaper, by "A Layman of the Episcopal Church," or Thomas Y. How, Esquire, afterwards the Rev. Mr. (finally Dr.) How; and the controversy was continued in this manner, by the gentlemen already named, Dr. Linn adopting, for different articles, the different signatures "Clemens," "Umpire," and "Inquirer;" and by "Cyprian," or the Rev. Frederick Beasley, rector of St. Peter's Church, Albany; "Cornelius," or Bishop Provoost; "An Episcopalian," or Bishop White; and "Detector" and "Vindex," signatures both employed by Mr. Hobart—five against one; either the temptation of such extemporaneous newspaper debate, or distrust of each other, multiplying thus the champions of Episcopacy. At length, as usual, the publishers interposed, saying the public had become weary; and, not satisfied with the result, Dr. Hobart[1] republished,

---

[1] Bishop Hobart, after all, was not a high-churchman of the straitest sect. The statements most likely to give offence in his "Companion for the Altar" and "Festivals and Fasts," he subsequently very much modified, or almost explained away. He had said, to be sure, that participation of the Church's ordinances, "at the hands of the duly authorized priesthood," was "the indispensable condition of salvation." But, for the latter clause, he substituted, in another edition, "the prescribed method of salvation," contending that he meant only "a condition with which men had no right to dispense." (4th ed. 156, etc.) He had quoted, with apparent approbation, the "uniform testimony of all the apostolic and primitive writers," as establishing "the general conclusion," that "whoever was not in communion with the bishop was thereby cut off from communion with Christ;" but in his "Apology," he says, this was but a statement of the "*historical fact*, that such WAS the opinion of the APOSTOLIC AND PRIMITIVE WRITERS;" that he must not be held responsible for the language at least; and that his own understanding of the doctrine

in 1806, the whole controversy in a volume, "with additional notes and remarks." "My republishing the "Essays on Episcopacy,"" he says, "was a defensive measure. * * Many of the assertions of the author of "Miscellanies" remained unanswered, which it was necessary, therefore, to notice in a separate publication."[1]

It would seem to have been in fulfilment of the plan of issuing a magazine, of which, in the spring of 1805, Dr. Miller's letters speak, that, about the beginning of the year, 1807, "The Christian's Magazine" was commenced, in New York City, under the editorship of the Rev. Dr. John M. Mason, with the assistance of other clergymen. Among religious articles of various kinds, it embraced a review, by the editor, of the recent Episcopal controversy. This speedily called forth Dr. Hobart again : he replied to the review, as far as it had gone, in a work issuing from the

was, that *visible*, not *spiritual*, communion with Christ depended upon communion with the bishop. (Ed. 1844, pp. 64, 5.) He had represented baptism as a "regenerating ordinance," in which "fallen man is born again from a state of condemnation into a state of grace;" but in his "Apology" remarks, " Episcopalians maintain *baptismal regeneration* in this sense, that the *baptized* person is *born again*, not in the affections of his soul, but into a *new state*, in which he receives conditionally a title to the blessings of the gospel covenant." (4th ed., p. 230.) He had been accused of "holding up Episcopacy as of primary, and faith in Christ as of secondary importance;" but replied, "I make, of course, faith in Christ of more importance than communion with the bishop. This communion with the bishop can take place only through baptism and the Lord's Supper, dispensed by ministers Episcopally ordained. And for baptism in the case of adults, and for the Lord's Supper, faith is a preparatory, an essential qualification. As, therefore, on my principles, faith *precedes* communion with the bishop, it is *distinct from* this communion, and *independent* of it." The modern editor thinks this a dangerous concession, and adds, in a note, " This is doubtless in a certain sense true. But if, through "communion with the bishop," we enjoy the highest *fellowship with Christ;* and if this followship be designed to exalt and perfect within us the essential graces of the Christian character, may it not be questionable how *far* or how *long* we can have the *gospel faith* without "communion with the bishop," or through him with CHRIST the divine head of the Church, which the gospel enjoins as so important a means of grace? Ed." Pp. 67, 68.

Bishop Hobart, doubtless, did more than any one on this side of the Atlantic, before, or any other during, his time, to promote High-Churchism; but that his disciples, many of them, have gone beyond their master is nothing unprecedented or remarkable. Besides, he never relaxed his grasp of the essence of the system—that there is no church on earth which is not visible, no visible church without a prelatical bishop, no covenanted salvation without communion with such a bishop. This is the very corner-stone of Romanism; and although the Papal, differs, no doubt, in some important respects, from the mere prelatical, superstructure; both are, however, upon exactly the same foundation. Modern Puseyism is simply an attempt to bring the Episcopal high-church system into more complete conformity with the Roman, and to make them ultimately one and the same throughout.

[1] Hobart's Apology (3d ed.), 49.

press in June, 1807, entitled, "An Apology for Apostolic Order and its Advocates." About a month later, in July, Dr. Miller published the first volume of his "Letters concerning the Constitution and Order of the Christian Ministry."[1] It was written without any reference to Dr. Hobart's "Apology," as the dates just given sufficiently prove.

Of this volume the author afterwards wrote,

"Mr. *How*, for reasons which he himself best understands, has thought proper to assert, that my *Letters* "are well known to be the result of several years of laborious attention to the subject which they discuss."[2] Another writer, in the Churchman's Magazine, has made a similar assertion; and boasts that the advocates of the Episcopal church will not require as much time to answer, as was employed in writing them. I cheerfully yield to these gentlemen the palm of celerity and copiousness in writing; and even if the statement respecting the time employed in preparing my publication were true, it is not easy to see how it bears on the argument. What would it avail a culprit to show that the collection of the testimony which seals his conviction was the work of a month instead of a day? But the statement is not true. My attention to the Episcopal controversy had been very small, perhaps culpably so, until within a few months previous to the publication of my Letters. When the printing was begun, not more than one third of the volume was written; and the greater part of it was actually composed during the *three months* which were consumed in passing the sheets through the press. But though the work was chiefly written with that haste which every one who has run a race with the press well understands; and amidst the feebleness of an habitual valetudinarian, as well as the distraction and fatigue of multiplied professional labors; it affords me some satisfaction to reflect, that, after the maturest deliberation, I see no cause to retract a single argument, or materially to alter a single statement. On the contrary, further reading and reflection have convinced me, that every argument and every statement, notwithstanding all the contemptuous sneers and confident assertions of my opponents, are capable of being irrefragably fortified."[3]

[1] " Letters concerning the Constitution and Order of the Christian Ministry, as deduced from Scripture and Primitive Usage; addressed to the Members of the United Presbyterian Churches in the City of New York. By Samuel Miller, D.D., one of the Pastors of said Churches. New York. 1807." 12mo. Pp. 355.

[2] "Letters, 5."

[3] Continuation of Letters, 25, 26.

This passage has been copied, not to justify Dr. Miller's plan of writing and publishing as an example; but as part of the history of the work, and to illustrate the pressure, at this time, of his various employments, which were impairing his health, and preventing that leisurely and thorough investigation, which he himself had regarded his subject as imperatively demanding from every Presbyterian clergyman. It should be remembered, however, that, obvious as are the advantages of long study, the most useful men that ever lived have often, perhaps generally, been the most incessantly hurried in their labors; and the most effective works of the brain have not always been those, which, in their production, have occupied the longest time. In fact, the brain, characteristically, needs driving to its highest achievements: we labor best at a white heat.

5. OPINIONS OF FRIENDS.

The opinion of Dr. Miller's friends in regard to his "Letters" may be gathered from the following communications.

On the 3d of August, 1807, Dr. Wm. Linn wrote to him from Albany,

'As soon as I heard of your "Letters," I purchased a copy, and have read them with much satisfaction. In my opinion, the moderation, the candour and the research which you have shown, do you honor. I cannot see how a candid Episcopalian can read your work, and not receive perfect conviction of the unfounded nature of the exclusive claims which have been set up.'

The writer of the following letter had, in 1806, left the bench of the Supreme Court of the State of New York, to take his seat upon that of the Supreme Court of the United States.

'Bloomingdale, 8th August, 1807.

'Reverend and dear Sir,

'I have read, with very great pleasure and instruction, the Letters of which you were so good as to present me a copy. Although their subject was not new to me, I had never before seen it treated in a way so well calculated to produce conviction. The proofs are arranged with much skill, and the remarks on them are often new and always judicious. The arguments of our opponents are also very fairly stated, and examined with candor and temper. What must please every one is, that you have not indulged in any of that acrimony, which too frequently finds its way into writings which should breathe only a spirit of charity. No one, ever so little accustomed to weighing evidence, and whose mind is free from the influence of opinions already formed, can hesitate, after an attentive perusal of this work, to yield a full assent to the points which it is intended to establish. He will be compelled to acknowledge, that diocesan Episcopacy, instead of being of divine origin, owes its institution to man; that rank among gospel ministers has no foundation in Scripture; and that the Presbyterian form of church government departs little or nothing from that introduced in the time of the apostles.

'Upon the whole, I consider Presbyterians very much indebted to you for this valuable performance. While it reflects great credit on its author, if regarded in no other light than as a highly classical composition, and as an evidence of deep research, industry and judgment; it not only furnishes every Presbyterian with a reason for his faith, but must satisfy the most wavering, that he is not obnoxious to the penalties denounced against him by a few of his less charitable Episcopal brethren, for his separation from the pale of their church.

'Accept of my best thanks for it, and of my most fervent wish, that your useful life may be long preserved, a blessing to your family and the world.

'With every sentiment of esteem and regard, I am, dear sir, your very obedient servant and friend,

'The Rev'd Doctor Miller.　　Brockholst Livingston.'

'Sir,　　　　　　　　　　　New Haven, August 10, 1807.

'The copy of your "Letters," which you were so obliging as to send me, and for which please to accept my acknowledgments, I have read with much satisfaction and profit. My principles had been engaged on the same side of the question, not by careful researches into Church History, but by a general view of the true interpretation of Scripture. You have given a summary of the facts and inferences on that subject, which, as far as I can judge from an ex parte hearing, leaves no room in the candid, unbiassed mind for hesitation. Indeed, the facts and arguments in favor of Presbyterianism are far more numerous and pointed, and less disputable, than I had supposed. I regret, with you, the existence of the controversy. The distraction of opinion which is produced by polemical controversy always weakens the faith of doubting Christians, furnishes new weapons to the infidel, and impairs the cause it is intended to maintain, at least with men of a sceptical turn of mind; not to mention the inroads it makes upon private friendship. But it is always lawful to defend our opinions as well as our persons and property. * *

> 'Accept my best wishes for your welfare,
> 'and believe me, very respectfully,
> 'Your obedient servant,

'Rev'd Dr. Miller.   N. Webster.'

The writer of the following was at the time Chief Justice, though since better known as Chancellor, of the State of New York.

'Dear Sir,   Albany, September 1st, 1807.

'I return you my thanks for your book on the Constitution of the Christian Ministry. I have read it with attention, with pleasure, and with great instruction. The subject was certainly not familiar to me, and you have awakened my astonishment at the *weak* and *contemptible* foundations of the Episcopal claim to the divine origin of diocesan Bishops. I may express myself too strongly; but the truth is, I have, carefully and *without the least prejudice*, followed your argument, and I think the performance a finished one, and perfectly conclusive on the question. I was as much pleased with the style and temper of the book, as I had reason to admire its logic and learning. It will be eminently useful, not only against the arrogant pretensions which gave birth to it, but against innovations upon the Presbyterian model from Independent sects.

'That your health may grow firm and enable you to prosecute your studies and your duties, is the sincere wish of

> 'Your friend and obedient servant,
> 'James Kent.'

The following extract is from a letter of the Rev. Evan Johns, dated "Berlin, November 23d, 1807."

'My dear Friend,

'At last I sit down to write the letter which I promised you, respecting your publication on the extravagant and impudent claims of the Episcopalians; but my observations must be very few, because you would not wish me to abound in your praise; and be assured, that is nearly all the subject matter which presents itself; though I have read the book twice, in the free exercise of all the critical acuteness I could command. The style is, in my opinion, much superior to that of any former production by the same author. Simply elegant, and very accurate, it is highly gratifying to correct taste. The *spirit* which animates the whole performance is excellence itself. Every argument used possesses irrefragable cogency. The two properties just mentioned are indeed so conspicuous, as that the author may be said to possess and exercise the art of knocking a man down without offending him.   When attending Commencement at New Haven, I was happy to find that Dr. Miller's Letters were getting into extensive circulation, *with great effect*, in those parts of Connecticut most abounding with Episcopalians.'

Two passages of a letter from Ebenezer Hazard, Esquire, may be added.

'Dear Sir,   Philadelphia, December 23d, 1807.
      'I have lately read your pastoral Letters, which have afforded me much entertainment.   What the advocates for diocesan Episcopacy will do with them I know not; but I think they will not easily refute your arguments.   They will at least be obliged to treat you as a gentleman, because you have managed the business so *suaviter in modo;* or they will lose ground in the public opinion.   *   *

'The following assertion by Mr. Hobart is one of the most extraordinary I have ever met with : Pp. 168, 169 : "You cannot open an ecclesiastical writer, either of the present or primitive age, who does not stare you in the face with the fact, that there were *Bishops, Presbyters* and *Deacons* in the primitive Church.   Yes, Sir, *such Bishops as we have in modern days*, with Presbyters subject to them."

      *   *   He may easily find, and, no doubt, has often seen, ecclesiastical writers who contradict him ; and if he will consult Suicer's Thesaurus Ecclesiasticus, Art. ἐπίσκοπος and Πρεσβύτερος, he may receive abundant evidence upon this subject.'

The well known author, James K. Paulding, Esquire, wrote, on the 4th of September,

'*   *   It will afford me an opportunity to express the peculiar satisfaction I feel in the mild and Christian spirit which pervades every part of your excellent Letters, and the clear, logical and conclusive manner, in which, in my opinion, you have conducted the argument.   *   *

'I cannot, my dear Sir, conclude this letter, without offering you my warm approbation of the style which characterizes your Letters.   It has been one of the very serious misfortunes attending religious controversies, that they were prosecuted with the warmth of personal animosity, rather than that of conviction; and with the spirit of rivalry, rather than with that philanthropic good will, which should actuate all men to go hand in hand in the great cause of discovering truth.   If truth can ever be bought too dear, it is when she is purchased at the price of heart-burnings and divisions among those who have been solemnly adjured to live together as brothers.

'I delight to see that your work displays nothing of this sanguinary spirit of controversy; but that, while its precepts carry full conviction to the mind, its example is calculated to produce the most beneficial effects, by demonstrating that the strongest reasoning, the warmest sentiments of piety, and the Christian spirit of forbearance may be beautifully combined; and that controversy may be so conducted, as to wound no man's feelings, to hurt no man's good name, and injure no man's belief in the existence of Christian charity.

'Let me now drop the critic and assume the friend.'

The Rev. Conrad Speece,[1] of Virginia, in a hurried letter of the 28th of January, 1809, wrote,

'Accept my renewed thanks for your *Letters on the Ministry.* Had I time, I think I could hardly resist the impulse of my heart to say a great deal in praise of that work. I *will* say, that I am much delighted with the *Christian spirit* in which you have written; a spirit unhappily very rare in controversial works, to the reproach of the disciples of a meek and benevolent Saviour. In point of *argument*, I deem the work most decisive. It ought to be read by all our clergy, and especially by our young candidates for the ministry; not excluding the people at large.'

6. RECEPTION BY OPPONENTS.

What the opponents of Dr. Miller thought of his "Letters" may be gathered, perhaps, best from the number who rushed forward to meet him in the breach, and from the spirit and temper in which they carried on the contest. That which a polemic lacks in argument, he not unfrequently attempts to make up by confident assertion, and personal abuse. All, of course, cried out, that they had been attacked: it was the old story, that the poor lamb below had muddied the waters of Christian fellowship. Dr. Miller gives the following account of the matter, which any intelligent reader may easily verify.

"Such a manual appeared to me to be much wanted; a manual which was intended to present a concise view of the whole subject, without the useless appendages, and the offensive recriminations which have been too frequently admitted. In composing this work, it was my sincere aim to render it as free

[1] In 1820, D.D.

from everything personal or irritating as possible. Accordingly, I attacked no particular writer. I avoided even mentioning the name of any American who had written in opposition to that apostolic truth and order which we maintain. My arguments were stated, as far as the nature of the undertaking admitted, in the abstract; and a studious care was exercised to exhibit the whole in language of the most mild and conciliatory character. In all this it was not supposed that offence could reasonably be taken by any, and least of all by our Episcopal brethren. As they had been in the *habit*, for several years before the appearance of my volume, of publishing and distributing, even beyond the bounds of their own society, books, in which the Episcopal doctrine was warmly urged, and Presbyterian principles loaded with opprobrious epithets; it was supposed that they would scarcely think it very consistent or decent to attack with violence, if at all, a publication so moderate, so respectful, and so exclusively intended for Presbyterians. It was, therefore, my prevailing expectation, that the work would be considered as not belonging to the polemic class, and would be suffered to pass without a reply.

"But in this I was mistaken. With all the mildness and inoffensiveness of their character, my *Letters* no sooner made their appearance, than murmurs of resentment, and threats of overwhelming refutation were heard from various quarters. These threats had not been long proclaimed, before attempts were made to fulfil them. The first who presented himself before the public, as an assailant, was Mr. *Thomas Y. How*, (since the Rev. Mr. *How*, of *New York*,) who, in about six months after the publication of my volume, produced an angry and vehement pamphlet, which he announced as *introductory* to a more full discussion of the subject. Mr. *How*, after an interval of six months more, was followed by the Rev. Dr. *Bowden*,[1] *Professor of Moral Philosophy, Logic and Belles Lettres in Columbia College*. This gentleman, who had been long versed in the Episcopal controversy, and who, more than twenty years ago, stepped forth as a champion of the hierarchy, did me the honour again to take the field against me, and undertook in a work, at least formidable in *size*, to give a complete refutation of all my arguments, and to prostrate the Presbyterian cause. About the same time with Dr. *Bowden's* two volumes, there appeared, on the same side, and with the same object, the first of a series of Letters addressed to me by the Rev. Dr. *Kemp*,[2] *Rector of Great Choptank*, in *Maryland*.

[1] 5 Sprague's Annals, 304.

[2] Bishop of Maryland, 1814-27. See 5 Sprague's Annals, 371.

And, finally, with this number, the Rev. Dr. *Hobart* has united himself as an occasional remarker on my *Letters*, in the *Churchman's Magazine*, published in the city of *New York*, for the contents of which he acknowledges himself, both as Editor and Proprietor, to be responsible.

"To be fallen upon by so many assailants, and with so much vehemence, is a compliment as great as it was unexpected. My thanks are due to these gentlemen for conferring on my work a degree of importance, and unwittingly disclosing that it has made a degree of impression, which I had never ventured to anticipate or to claim. I have also to thank them for another favour. Their violent attacks, and their numerous cavils, have induced me to examine the subject with more care, and to pursue my inquiries respecting it to a greater extent, than I should probably otherwise have done. The result is a deeper conviction than ever of the weakness of their cause, and of the Apostolic character of our church."[1]

"Mr. *How* also endeavours to represent my work as an *unprovoked attack* on the Episcopal church, and to throw upon it all the odium of *aggression*. To those who are acquainted with the incontrovertible facts stated in the beginning of this letter, such a representation will appear something more than strange! If to state and defend the principles of my own church, after they had been frequently and violently attacked; if a calm and respectful plea against a sentence of excommunication from the church of Christ; if an attempt to show, that we, as Presbyterians, are not *aliens from the commonwealth of Israel, and strangers to the covenant of promise;* if a work designed to prove that our ministry and ordinances have as fair a claim to divine warrant as those of our Episcopal brethren; and that they, in denying us the character of a church, and in consigning us over, with the heathen, to the uncovenanted mercies of God, act wholly without warrant— if these things constitute an unprovoked attack on the Episcopal church—then, indeed, I have been guilty of such an attack. * *

"Another charge which these gentlemen concur in urging, is no less unexpected and extraordinary. It is, that I have written with great *bitterness*, and that even my moderation is *affected* and *insidious*. This is a point concerning which no man can be an impartial judge in his own case. But, after receiving so many respectable suffrages in favour of the mildness and decorum of my style; after receiving the acknowledgments of so many moderate and candid Episcopalians in differ-

---

[1] Continuation of Letters, 18, 19, 20, 21.

ent parts of the United States, both clergymen and laymen, that I had avoided asperity and bitterness to a very unusual degree ; it is impossible to avoid suspecting that these gentlemen (who, so far as I know, stand alone in making this charge) have felt irritated by statements which they could not deny, and by arguments which they could not refute ; and that they have mistaken both for bitterness and abuse.   Dr. *Bowden* and Mr. *How* never discover so much wounded feeling and irascible temper, as when they meet with intimations of any affinity between some of their high-toned doctrines, and those of *Popery.*   The intimations of this kind which my book contains, were made neither lightly nor with passion ; but with a conscientious persuasion of their correctness.   This persuasion remains with undiminished, or rather with increased, force. And it happens, unfortunately for these gentlemen, that similar charges of popish origin and tendency, have been brought against several of the same doctrines by some of the most pious and learned Bishops of their own church.   Nor can I forbear to add, that the pointed resentment which my opponents manifest at every suggestion of this kind, is calculated to excite the suspicion, that they feel it more easy to *rail* at such intimations than to *answer* them."[1]

"These gentlemen, in the course of their strictures, have allowed themselves frequently to employ language of which I cannot forbear to exhibit a specimen.   Dr. *Bowden* charges me with "contemptible cavilling ;" with "contemptible puerilities ;" with "misrepresentations gross to excess ;" with writing "nonsense," "palpable nonsense," etc., etc., etc.   Mr. *How's* pamphlet abounds with language, which I hope he will reconsider, in his cooler moments, with shame and regret.   He charges me with "a continued strain of misrepresentation ;" with "an outrage on decency itself ;" with a construction "as puerile as it is disingenuous ;" with "fanatical absurdity ;" with "violations of the plain language of Scripture, as presumptuous as are to be met with in the entire annals of fanaticism ;" with "talking like a deranged fanatic ;" and with advancing allegations which I "ought to know, and cannot but know" to be groundless.   In fact, he frequently imputes to me, in terms a little indirect and softened, known and deliberate falsehood.   And, on one occasion, he permits himself to address me thus : "You could not possibly have adopted a mode of address more calculated to sour the minds of your readers, or better fitted to indulge the bitterness of your own heart.   It is indirect and insidious, covering, under the mask of moderation and kind-

[1] Continuation of Letters, 26, 27, 28.

ness, all the loftiness of pride, and all the rankling of passion."
P. 16.   Dr. *Hobart* represents me as writing with great "arrogance" and "bitterness," and even with *insidiousness*, a term which, no intelligent reader needs to be told, implies *dishonesty*. I regret that such language has found its way into this controversy. * *

"But these gentlemen not only employ, on their part, what I must consider as exceptionable language; they also impute to me language scarcely less offensive, or exceptionable than their own.   Dr. *Bowden* says, that I pronounce Episcopacy an *antichristian usurpation*.   Vol. I. p. 245.   And Mr. *How* asserts, that I "brand prelacy as *the detested offspring of ecclesiastical fraud and tyranny*."   I can only say, that no such expressions are to be found in my book; and that whatever there is in them which bears an opprobrious or indelicate character, is to be ascribed, not to me, but to the invention of my accusers."[1]

[1] Continuation of Letters, 32, 33, 34.

CHAPTER FIFTEENTH.

CORRESPONDENCE.

1807, 1808.

---

1. MISCELLANEOUS TOPICS.

DR. MILLER had been a trustee of Columbia College since the latter part of the year 1806. On the first of October, 1807, he was elected a trustee of the College of New Jersey, at Princeton, in place of Dr. Rodgers, who had resigned. On the 6th of April following, he "appeared, and having taken and subscribed the oaths required by law, took his seat at the Board." He seems to have been, from the first, a very active member, deeply interested, as he had indeed become long before, in the welfare of the institution. The year 1807 was memorable in its annals for a great rebellion, just after which, on the 8th of April, he wrote to Mr. Griffin,

'Have you heard the terrible news from Princeton? What is the great Head of the Church about to do with that Seminary? Is it about to be purged and elevated?—or totally destroyed? God grant that the latter may not be the case!'

On the 4th of July, he writes to Dr. Green,

'I promised to prepare a biographical memoir of Dr. Nisbet, to be prefixed to the first volume.' [Of his lectures, the immediate publication of which was then contemplated.]

'For writing this I am miserably furnished with materials, to say nothing of capacity to put them together. I have collected one thing or another, which I hope will enable me to eke out a decent account—say one hundred, or one hundred and twenty, pages; but still I am sadly in want of more matter. I wish you would take the trouble to commit to paper everything that you can recollect concerning the Doctor's history and character, either in Scotland or America. In short, my desire is, that you should write me a letter of three or four sheets at least, (less or more, however, as you please,) *   *   with appropriate anecdotes as they may occur to you, *   *   and throwing the whole into a form that will make it proper to be published in the body of my memoir. I wish this for two reasons:—

'1. It will gratify me to have my little effort adorned with a communication from you, more especially as a monument of that friendship which I consider as one of my honors, and which I wish to be increased and cemented.

'2. Such a letter introduced into the body of the narrative will relieve the reader from my monotonous composition, and will greatly enrich the whole: particularly, as it is my firm belief, that there is no man in this country so well qualified to draw the character of Dr. Nisbet as yourself.'

On the 17th of August Dr. Miller writes to Mr. Griffin, that he is better, though his cough is still very troublesome, and adds,

'Adieu, my dear Brother. My last interview with you has riveted my affections more closely to you. Let us love and pray for one another more and more!'

2. ANDOVER AND BOSTON.

The old Calvinistic and Hopkinsian clergy of New England were becoming deeply interested in the idea of a theological seminary, to maintain their views in common, and train a Congregational ministry, which should be of one heart in opposing Socinian heresies. Dr. Leonard Woods, writing in 1816 to Dr. Samuel Spring, reminds the latter of his having thought of Dr. Romeyn, Dr. Miller, and others, and finally fixed upon Dr. Griffin, for professor of Sacred Rhetoric in this institution.[1] To that project and another Dr. Miller refers in the following letter of the 24th of November, 1807, to Mr. Griffin.

'Dr. Morse wishes me to converse with you on two points. The *first* is a *Theological Seminary* in Massachusetts. When he last saw you, that institution existed only in design. Now, very large funds are actually secured, and its organization is commenced. There are five professorships—one of Natural Theology, one of Christian Theology, one of Biblical Criticism, one of Ecclesiastical History, and one of Sacred Eloquence.

Two of these chairs are already filled. A Mr. Woods[2] of Andover (where the seminary is placed) is Professor of Chris-

[1] 2 Dr. Gardiner Spring's Pers. Reminiscences, 315.
[2] D. D. from 1810. See 2 Sprague's Annals, 485.

tian Theology, and a Mr. Pearson (lately of Harvard College) is Professor of Biblical Criticism. The three others remain to be appointed; and these it is the wish of the gentlemen who take the lead in this business to get from the Middle or Southern States.

'The *second* subject is this. Some wealthy and influential gentlemen, devoted to the interests of evangelical truth, propose to build a large and handsome church in the heart of Boston, and to call one, if not two, decidedly able, evangelical and decisive men, to undertake the pastoral charge; and to make this, like the Seminary, a centre of orthodox operations. The persons concerned also wish to get a pastor for this church from the southward.

'Dr. Morse and his friends, before he left Boston, had conversed respecting several southern gentlemen for the above places. When he came to New Haven, he and Dr. Dwight had a particular conference on the subject. The result of the whole was a determination to turn their eyes toward the following gentlemen—Mr. Griffin of Newark, Mr. Romeyn of Albany, and Messrs. Abeel and Miller of New York. You have now the whole matter before you.

'Dr. Morse is much engaged on these subjects. He informs me that the funds for both undertakings will be ample; that the temporal provision made for the support of the gentlemen who may be elected will be of the most liberal kind; and that discerning and pious people think they see, in these undertakings, great and permanent benefit likely to redound to the interests of religion in Massachusetts, in New England, and perhaps through the United States. He considers every friend of piety, who may be called upon to take a part in these enterprizes, as having a call of the most solemn kind, which he cannot easily or lightly put aside.

'The evangelical men in Massachusetts are also about to organize a General Association, between which and our General Assembly they mean to propose a system of intercourse and cooperation. All these may be considered as parts of one great whole, the object of which is to promote the interests of truth.

'The plan of establishing a new church in Boston is not, at present, in a situation to be freely and undisguisedly spoken of. You will please, therefore, to consider this part of my communication as made in confidence.

'Think of this whole subject—sleep on it—pray over it—and then write to me.   *   *

'P. S.   I rejoice with you, my Brother, that God is still continuing his glorious work among you. We sometimes have a trembling hope, that he is about to pour out his Spirit on our poor city. Let me again ask you to pray for us without ceasing. I should be glad to visit you frequently, and to preach on Thursday evening; but we have our hands full and cannot leave home, and have a public service always on that very evening.

'P. P. S. S. Dr. Morse earnestly wishes you to visit Charlestown and Boston as early as possible.'

To the Panoplist, a religious Magazine established by Dr. Morse of Charlestown, Dr. Miller was an occasional contributor; but very few of his contributions can now be identified. On the 22d of December, 1807, he writes to Dr. Morse in regard to one of them, and other matters already noticed,

'My review of Dr. Griffin's sermon you will find on the first page. It is short, as I supposed that a single sermon ought not to occupy more room. I have been obliged to do it in extreme haste: I trust you will be able to read it, with all its blottings and interlineations.

'That I might have as little fatigue as possible in writing, (by which my health is daily impaired,) I have abridged Mr. Griffin's life of Dr. McWhorter in a new manner. You will learn what this manner is by looking at the pamphlet.

'I had an interview with Mr. Romeyn, of Albany, on the business respecting which you wished me to confer with him. He spoke in terms of warm approbation of the plan, most heartily wished it success, and expressed an opinion that it is a plan of immense importance; but, as I expected, could not see how it was possible for him to detach himself from his present charge.

'Mr. Griffin speaks in the same manner. He is now, as you have, no doubt, heard, in the midst of a most animating revival, with which it has pleased God to favor his church. This absorbs his attention and binds him to Newark, to a degree which he never experienced before. You will not wonder, therefore, that he views his removal from his present station as next to impossible. I received a long letter from him a few days ago. He considered your plan as a grand one—a plan, which, if it can be executed with energy, will form a grand era in the history of the American churches. He says, however, that before he can come to an absolute decision, he must receive many details of information, which have not yet been given him. He laments that it is not possible for him to visit Massachusetts this winter.

'I really fear, my dear Sir, that you will find it difficult to secure any suitable characters from the South. If there were not a dearth of ministers among us, we might abandon our present stations with less scruple; but who now would supply our places? I do not see that it is possible for Dr. Abeel or myself to think of leaving New York. '

'Has it not occurred to you, that strangers would be more apt to incur odium and violent opposition, than natives of your own State? And is it not questionable, whether your plan might not be more satisfactorily prosecuted by gentlemen already on, or near, the ground, than by persons from a distance? Is Mr. Woods (your professor of Christian Theology) an *Old Calvinist*, or a *Hopkinsian*, or between the two? What is the nature of the connexion between the Old Calvinists and the Hopkinsians? Is it of a kind to promise a permanent and energetic system of operation?

'I have only time to add, that I am, with cordial wishes for your personal welfare and happiness, and for the prosperity of the great plans in which you are engaged for the Redeemer's kingdom,

'Your friend and brother, * *'

On the 28th of December, Dr. Miller wrote to Mr. Griffin in relation to these New England schemes,

'* * You ask—

'1. "What distribution of the places is contemplated, and what part is assigned to me?" A. I do not know. The four gentlemen named to you have been mentioned *in cumulo*, for the places *in cumulo*. I know not that any distribution has been decisively made, even in the minds of any of the managers.

'2. "How extensive are the funds secured for the Seminary?" A. $100,000 are actually in hand; as much more is considered as certainly secured; and Dr. Morse thinks that from $400,000 to $600,000 may be counted on, with confidence, as the ultimate amount of the funds.

'3. "Have the Hopkinsians been prevailed on to unite in this object?" A. I am told they have; but how far, and on what terms, I know not.

'4. "Shall we be Presbyterians still?" No, certainly not. I take for granted we should be expected to be good Congregationalists. And, if a change in favor of Presbyterianism should hereafter be made, it is, probably, not at all in the calculation of those who engage in the business.

'Your remarks are important and interesting; yet I have some doubts about the soundness of several of them: e. g.

when you say, that, "if the object be obtained, it must be by the aid of gentlemen from the Middle and Southern States," I hesitate—the position appears to me extremely doubtful—I have even questioned, whether the indifference, as it would be called, of gentlemen from the South, might not excite an odium and an opposition, which the same things, done by natives of their own state, would not excite. At the same time I think there is a degree and a kind of assistance which we can and ought to give. This, if I live to see you, shall be more fully unfolded.

'Again, immensely important as the proposed seminary really is, you seem to me to assign to it, in your mind, a station which it cannot, at present, fill. Should it ever be erected and organized under the most favorable auspices, I take for granted it never can be the seminary of the Presbyterian Church, as such. Our General Assembly will, doubtless, in a few years, institute a seminary of its own, unless Princeton College should be placed on a better footing. Nor do I suppose, that the Massachusetts seminary can be expected to command, at once, even the students, the influence, and the funds of New England. But, if rightly managed, it will command them all in seven years, and will be the centre of everything great and good to the eastward of New York. This is assigning to it quite as much consequence as ought to be thought of. And when we recollect how important that section of our country is; how constantly its citizens are migrating to every part of the Union; and, of course, how much influence its institutions must have on the religious taste and character of the United States, I think the plan ought to be considered as of immense magnitude.

'The evangelical interests of this country can support three or four great theological institutions, not only without difficulty, but with advantage. I have always been of the opinion, that, if the Presbyterian Church, the Dutch Church, Dr. Mason's, and the Congregationalists of New England, would set to work and each erect a grand theological seminary, in the heart of her territory, the plan would be infinitely better than to endeavor to make one for all; even if we could command any men we chose, and any amount of funds for the purpose. More would be done in the former case than in the latter.

'I perfectly agree with you, that we cannot rely on the biased judgment, or the sanguine expectations of any individual, however respectable, in this business; and that we must have a great deal more information, from different sources, before we can decide what to do.

'I have no hesitation in giving you abundant light as to my "propensities," and those of Dr. Abeel, on this subject. You are sensible that all four of us occupy stations, at present, among the most important in the United States. I do not see that it is possible for me, consistently with duty, to quit New York. If my usefulness in another place were like to be greater than it is here, I ought to make any sacrifice and go to that place. But I am, at present, far from being satisfied that such a probability exists. This is also precisely the state of Dr. Abeel's mind.

'I do not know what Mr. Woods's sentiments are, excepting that a general assurance that they are evangelical has been given me. * *

'We still hope that God is about to revive the hearts of his people in our city; but we hope with trembling. * *

'P. S. Can you not visit us in a short time? I wish, with all my heart, you could do us this favor. When you come, make a point of spending a Tuesday evening with us, as we have, on that evening, a large praying society in our school room. Our people would be rejoiced to hear you.'

On the 4th of March, 1808, Mrs. Miller wrote to Mrs. McLane,

'It is a long time since I have written to you, * * but I must, as in all other cases of a similar kind, where an apology has been necessary, present our little family, with all their wants and all their attractions, and let them plead for their mother their mother's cause. They can tell you that one was sick, and another peevish; one wanted clothes, and another nourishment; one a little coaxing, and another a little whipping; and that nearly the whole time was consumed in satisfying these and other numerous demands. Indeed, my dear Sister, I have scarcely had time to be interested beyond our own dwelling; and even the present delightful appearances with regard to religion have not, I fear, had their due effect upon me.

'We hope and believe that a great work is beginning amongst us. Mr. Miller has seen nothing like it, in this city, since he has been an inhabitant of it; and the same God who has aroused his people, has renewed his strength, and, according to the promise, made it equal to the burthen which is put upon him. I wish you could see him—how well he looks, and how animated with present appearances. As to any exact account of this small revival amongst us, I am afraid we can give you but little satisfaction.'

The first Presbyterian church organized in New York City outside of the collegiate relation, after that relation had been established, was the Cedar Street Church, formed in 1808. The Rev. John B. Romeyn,[1] pastor of the First Presbyterian Church of Albany, a very popular preacher, of growing reputation, accepted a unanimous call to the pastorate. Upon hearing of his decision, Dr. Miller wrote to him, the 4th of October,

'Seldom, very seldom, have I received a letter which gave me so much pleasure as this. I most cordially rejoice in your decision, my Brother, and hope and believe that you have been directed to it iu mercy to all concerned. My solicitude on the subject was real and great, partly, I will confess, from considerations of personal comfort, but much more, if I do not deceive myself, from a desire to see the growth and prosperity of the Redeemer's kingdom. The result is highly gratifying to us all. May we have reason permanently to rejoice in it as a blessing to the Church!'

Adverting, long afterwards, to the Cedar street enterprise, as an illustration of the benefits of church extension by colonizing, Dr. Miller said,

'When the men, who left the Wall street and Brick Churches to form that congregation, had given up their pews to assume a new station and responsibility, their places were soon filled; they were really not numerically missed; and larger numbers than ever were brought within the sound of the gospel.'

3. PRESIDENT JEFFERSON.

Mr. Jefferson was approaching the commencement of his last year in the Presidency, when Dr. Miller wrote to him a letter, and received a reply, in regard to which, after the lapse of twenty-five years, the latter made the following memorandum :—

'I never can read this letter [Mr. Jefferson's] but with regret and shame. At the time in which it was written, I was a warm and zealous partizan in favor of Mr. Jefferson's administration. I substantially agreed with him in *political* principles, without being aware of the rottenness of his *moral* and *religious* opinions. I had written to him, urging him to recommend to the nation a day of *religious observance*, on account of the peculiarly solemn and interesting circumstances, in which we were placed as a people. I informed him that a number of serious persons, (clergymen and others,) of different denominations, had thoughts of formally addressing him on the subject, and, as a body, re-

[1] From 1803, D.D.

questing him to appoint a day of special prayer. I stated that I was very desirous of his appointing such a day, and had thought of uniting in the effort to secure a joint address; but that, before doing so, I wished to know, whether it would be disagreeable to him to receive such an application; assuring him that neither I, nor my associates in this plan, had any wish to embarrass him; and that, if it would give him pain to be thus addressed, I would endeavor to prevent the adoption of the proposed measure. To this communication his letter was an answer.

'I *now* (1833) feel, that I was utterly wrong in thus writing; and, if I had known the real character of the man, I should never have done it. It was wrong for a minister of the gospel to seek any intercourse with such a man. It was wrong so far to consult his feelings, as to oppose a formal and joint address, that he might be spared the pain of refusing.' * *

'Sir,   Washington, Jan. 23, '08.
'I have duly received your favor of the 18th, and am thankful to you for having written it; because it is more agreeable to prevent than to refuse what I do not think myself authorized to comply with. I consider the government of the U. S. as interdicted by the Constitution from intermeddling with religious institutions, their doctrines, discipline, or exercises. This results, not only from the provision that no law shall be made respecting the establishment, or free exercise, of religion, but from that also which reserves to the States the powers not delegated to the U. S. Certainly no power to prescribe any religious exercise, or to assume authority in religious discipline, has been delegated to the general government. It must, then, rest with the States, as far as it can be in any human authority. But it is only proposed that I should *recommend*, not prescribe, a day of fasting and prayer: that is, that I should indirectly assume to the U. S. an authority over religious exercises, which the Constitution has directly precluded them from. It must be meant, too, that this recommendation is to carry some authority, and to be sanctioned by some penalty on those who disregard it; not, indeed, of fine and imprisonment, but of some degree of proscription, perhaps, in public opinion. And does the change in the nature of the penalty make the recommendation the less a *law* of conduct for those to whom it is directed? I do not believe it is for the interest of religion, to invite the civil magistrate to direct its exercises, its discipline, or its doctrines: nor of the religious societies, that the general government should be invested with the power of effecting any uniformity of time or matter among them. Fasting and prayer are religious ex-

ercises; the enjoining them an act of discipline. Every religious society has a right to determine, for itself, the times for these exercises, and the objects proper for them according to their own particular tenets; and this right can never be safer than in their own hands, where the Constitution has deposited it.

'I am aware that the practice of my predecessors may be quoted. But I have ever believed, that the example of State executives led to the assumption of that authority by the general government, without due examination; which would have discovered, that what might be a right in a State government, was a violation of that right when assumed by another. Be this as it may, every one must act according to the dictates of his own reason; and mine tells me that civil powers alone have been given to the President of the U. S., and no authority to direct the religious exercises of his constituents.

'I again express my satisfaction, that you have been so good as to give me an opportunity of explaining myself in a private letter; in which I could give my reasons more in detail, than might have been done in a public answer. And I pray you to accept the assurances of my high esteem and respect.

'Th. Jefferson.'

4. ANDOVER.

On the 12th of February, Dr. Miller wrote to Mr. Griffin,

'I want to talk with you about many subjects, and have something to say about Boston and Andover among the rest. I had a very full conference with Dr. Dwight on this subject, when he was here a week or two ago.'

And again, on the 18th of April,

'Dr. Morse has written to Dr. Abeel, that a kind of formal organization of the Theological Seminary will take place on the 18th of May, and that he very much wishes Dr. Griffin, Dr. Mason, Dr. Abeel and Dr. Miller to be present and to grace the solemnity; requesting that all the gentlemen might be informed of his wishes. He also says, that the ordination of Mr. Huntington, as colleague with Dr. Eckley, will take place about the same time; and that the general election will be the week following; making a cluster of great occasions at once, well worthy the attention and the presence of such men as *you* and I!

'What is implied in the organization then to take place; how far the professorial chairs are filled, and by whom; whether they are still looking out, and expecting, or hoping, to get one of us there, I know not. It is not in my power to answer any of these queries. I only know, that, if it were possible, I should

be much gratified to be present on the occasion. But it is out
of the question. As one, and perhaps two, of my colleagues
will go to Philadelphia to the Assembly, it would be high treason against the interests of religion in our congregations, for me
to be absent a fortnight, or three weeks, at that time. I wish,
with all my heart, you could be there.   *   *

'I was mortified, my dear Brother, the last time I saw you,
to hear you say, in our conversation respecting the review in
the Panoplist, that you sometimes felt as if you were in an
enemy's country, and as if there were a stronger disposition to
view your character with affectionate partiality to the Eastward
than in these regions. Pray do not indulge in such feelings.
They are wrong. Depend upon it, you are beloved and honored, as well as useful, among us—as much, I will venture to
say, as anywhere else. With respect to that review, I could
tell you something,¹ if I chose, which would take off, a little,
the edge of a portion of the feelings which you so frankly and
honorably confess.'

Again Dr. Miller wrote on the 3d of August,

'I feel very solicitous, my dear Brother, respecting the question whether you will leave us or not; and long to hear, what
kind of answer Dr. Green has returned to your letter. * *

'I have nothing new to say on this subject. I have much
anxious thought about it. If you go, I shall consider it as among
the most serious and afflicting personal bereavements I have
ever experienced; and as a melancholy day for this part of
our vineyard. May God direct you to a wise and happy decision! Every feeling of my soul rises up against the idea of
your leaving us.'

Andover Theological Seminary was one of the fruits of
the unsuccessful opposition of Evangelical men to the
appointment of a Unitarian professor of Divinity, Dr.
Ware, at Harvard, in 1805. Two different projects, originating alike in Trinitarian zeal, were combined to establish
the single institution at Andover. Dr. Spring, of Newburyport, who had long taken a deep interest in the education of young men for the ministry, and had received and,
with eminent success, trained a number of them in his own
house, proposed a seminary at Franklin, Massachusetts;
for, as he was a thorough-going, ardent Hopkinsian, he
desired that the celebrated Dr. Emmons of that place

¹ Mr. Griffin did not know, apparently, that Dr. Miller had written it. See
above, p. 231.

should be the first professor of Theology. Mr. William Bartlett and Mr. Moses Brown, parishioners of Dr. Spring, and Mr. John Norris, of Salem, offered liberal contributions toward this important enterprise. In 1778, Phillips Academy had been established, in the interest of sound learning and evangelical religion, at Andover; and Mrs. Phillips, widow of one of its founders, influenced by their known wishes, was ready to endow a theological chair in connexion with that Academy. Here, the views of the "old Calvinists" were predominant. But the two parties at length united the liberal means at their disposal, and made Andover the seat of a single institution, in which both should be represented. Dr. Leonard Woods, the first professor of Theology, was, at the time of his appointment, a decided Hopkinsian, although his views afterwards underwent a considerable modification, and he became rather an old Calvinist. The Seminary was formally opened in 1808.

5. WOMAN'S RIGHTS.

Dr. Miller's only publication during the year 1808 was a charity sermon,[1] printed by request of the female society on behalf of which it was preached. This society had, at the time, under its care one hundred and ninety-four widows, and five hundred and sixty-five children. The subject of the discourse was, "The appropriate Duty and Ornament of the Female Sex." "There is no new thing under the sun:" we find the preacher here, as before, indeed, in the "Retrospect,"[2] ventilating the doctrine of "woman's rights."

"* * I take for granted we shall agree, that Women ought not to be considered as destined to the same employments with Men; and, of course, that there is a species of education, and a sphere of action, which more particularly belong to them. There was a time, indeed, when a very different doctrine had many advocates, and appeared to be growing popular: viz., that in conducting education and in selecting employments, all distinctions of sex ought to be forgotten and confounded; and

[1] "A Sermon, preached March 13th, 1808, for the benefit of the Society instituted in the City of New York, for the Relief of Poor Widows with Small Children. By Samuel Miller, D.D., one of the Pastors of the United Presbyterian Churches in the said city."—Acts ix. 36-41.—8vo. Pp. 31.

[2] 2 Vol., 281-293.

that females are as well fitted to fill the academic Chair, to shine in the Senate, to adorn the Bench of justice, and even to lead in the train of War, as the more hardy sex. This delusion, however, is now generally discarded. It begins to be perceived, that the God of nature has raised everlasting barriers against such wild and mischievous speculations; and that to urge them is to renounce reason, to contradict experience, to trample on the divine authority, and to degrade the usefulness, the honour and the real enjoyments of the female sex." [1]

The author says afterwards, " In the volume of Revelation she is represented as the equal, the companion and the helpmeet of man." [2]

This sermon was republished, by permission, in 1852—after the author's death—in a volume, entitled " The Princeton Pulpit," made up of representative Sermons from a number of the clerical professors, and other ministers, and published for the benefit of the Second Presbyterian Church, of Princeton.

6.   PRESBYTERIAN THEOLOGICAL SEMINARY.

The following letters, before referred to, were written to Dr. Green :—

'New York, May 10, 1808.

'My dear Sir,

'Having a few moments leisure, I do not know that I can better dispose of them, than by writing a few lines to you, on a subject concerning which I know that you, in common with myself, take a deep and serious interest.

'Just before we parted at Princeton, in the course of the conversation which occurred in the college yard, you expressed a doubt whether the friends of a theological seminary ought to wait for a favorable change in that college, and, indeed, whether, supposing such a change to have taken place, it would be expedient to locate the seminary for theological instruction at Princeton. Perhaps you did not mean to suggest the latter doubt: at any rate, the conversation alluded to has given rise to a train of thought in my mind, the substance of which I will frankly lay before you.

'Is it not time to do something decisive towards establishing a Presbyterian divinity school? Is any time likely to occur, within eight or ten years, in which fewer difficulties would

<hr>

[1] Pp. 10, 11.

[2] P. 12.

probably attend such an undertaking, than at present? If it be judged proper to undertake anything, ought it to be set on foot by individual ministers; or, after being talked over and digested by individuals, ought the plan to be adopted and issued as an act of the General Assembly? If a school be organized, ought it to be placed at Princeton? or would any advantages attend making it an entirely separate establishment, and at a different place? With respect to the last question, I am, on the whole, in favor of a separate establishment and a different place, for the following reasons:—

'1. Nothing can be done at Princeton at present, and perhaps not for ten years. I doubt whether a divinity-school there, with ever so able and eminent a professor at its head, could be made, in the present state of the college, to command the confidence and patronage of the Presbyterian Church.

'2. Under the most favorable arrangement of the college that can be expected, I fear the theological students would not be the better for habitual intercourse with the students in the arts.

'3. If the theological school should, in a few years, become extensive, and a faculty of several professors be formed, would there not be danger of clashing between this faculty and that of the arts?

'4. Would not the president of the college, and the president of the theological faculty be rivals, and, of course, be placed in a situation calculated to interfere with their personal friendship?

'5. It appears to me that it would be ineligible to have a large and important divinity school under the care of the board of trustees of the college as now constituted. I think many difficulties would arise from this. Wherever the divinity school is fixed, there must be a separate board of visitors to watch over and conduct it. Considering how many questions of doctrine and discipline would inevitably arise in conducting such a seminary, I think none ought to be members of the board, vested with the government of it, but ministers and elders of our own church.

'6. In order to guard against the degeneracy, both in principle and practice, to which such institutions are liable, and which most of those in Europe have actually exhibited, I think every Trustee ought to subscribe our Confession of Faith, before taking his seat, in a very formal and solemn manner, and perhaps to do this every fifth or sixth year thereafter. But this obviously could not be done by all the trustees of Princeton College.

21

'In short, if it be desired to have the divinity-school uncontaminated by the college, to have its government unfettered, and its orthodoxy and purity perpetual, it appears to me that a separate establishment will be on many accounts advisable.

'If, then, it be advisable to erect a seminary altogether separate from Princeton College, why wait an hour for a favorable change in that institution? Precious time is wasting, valuable opportunities are passing away, and the interests of the church are languishing. God has been pouring out his Spirit, for some months past, on various parts of our church. Ought not this to be considered, not only as a token for greater good, but also as a favorable period for exertion?

'Dr. Mason thinks, that every theological school ought to be in a large town, because the students will have a better opportunity, in such a place, of contemplating a variety of talents; better means of becoming acquainted with the world; and be better guarded against that foolish haste in forming matrimonial connections, which is promoted by a small circle of acquaintances and ignorance of human nature. I suspect he is wrong, and that while very great advantages would result from a more retired situation, most of the evils which he speaks of might be avoided by prudent management. The same funds would, in the country, educate nearly twice as many young men as in the city. And by selecting a populous and genteel village, and giving the students an opportunity, twice a year, to see our principal cities, everything might be accomplished, that a longer stay in them could give.

'I do not suppose that anything decisive can be done at the approaching assembly. But, if it be necessary to bring the subject, at first, before the Assembly at all, might not a committee be appointed, this spring, to digest and report a plan to the Assembly of 1809? And, if the embargo should be raised in a few months, would you not be willing to undertake a journey, in the course of the next year, to beg for such a seminary? I merely throw out the foregoing hints. Think of them, and, after having done so, either throw the letter in the fire, or take such order respecting its contents as you may judge best.　　　　　　　I am, dear Sir, cordially yours,

'Sam'l Miller.

'P. S. I am encouraged to write, by recollecting what took place in 1805; when, in consequence of my writing a hasty and crude letter, on the subject of educating pious young men for the ministry, you were prompted to think of it, and to propose a plan which has already done much good. I take no part of the credit of that plan to myself. It is wholly different from any that ever occurred to me, and greatly superior to any. I scarcely deserve so much of the honor as belonged to "P. P., Clerk of this Parish," who plumed himself greatly, you remember, on having suggested a text, on which the rector formed an excellent sermon. May the great Head of the Church enable you to take such enlarged and just views of the subject, as to propose a course of procedure that will meet all sentiments, and be productive of countless and permanent blessings!   S. M.'

'Rev'd and dear Sir,   New-York, May 14, 1808.

'Your letter of the 11th instant is now before me. The perusal of it has given rise to much anxious reflection, the substance of which I will endeavor to throw out without delay or reserve.

'The prejudices, to which you refer, against divinity schools, I was aware of; and I am very sorry also to know, that they exist much more strongly in the minds of clergymen than of laymen; no doubt for the reasons which you have mentioned. But I did hope that we might venture to encounter and resist these prejudices, in the open field, with confident hopes of victory. If you, however, after much longer experience, much more extensive acquaintance with the ministers of our church, and much more comprehensive views of the subject, think differently, I am ready to yield to your opinion, and to unite in promoting the next best plan.

'If we cannot have a single great school, then I am clearly of opinion that one in each synod holds the next place on the scale of expediency. And I also fully agree with you that the adoption of this latter plan, in the beginning, may prove the best means of ultimately establishing the former. But, if this wished-for effect should fail of being produced, shall we not run the risk of having our church divided into seven or eight parties, or separate interests, with some enterprizing, ambitious man at the head of each, and thus weaken, if not destroy, it? A situation in some degree like that which I have supposed, is, at this time, the distress and the curse of the Dutch Church. Every system that is likely to have an unfavorable operation on the unity of the Church ought to be, if possible, avoided.

'Again, I have some doubts about the plan of instituting a seminary for educating young men from the first, as well as in their theological learning. Shall we systematically abandon the idea of requiring our young men to produce a diploma from some college? Shall we erect a new college? In either case, will not Princeton College take offence at the measure, as calculated, in its ultimate operation, to form a rival institution?

Besides, if we form an institution for carrying out the whole of the education of young men, we must have, at least, two instructors, if not three, besides the theological instructor. This will treble, if not quadruple, our expenses.

'On the whole, I feel perplexed and divided between two plans. The one is to bring forward an overture of the kind you have suggested in your letter. The other is to do nothing more at the ensuing Assembly, than to appoint a committee, "to consider and report to the next assembly, what further measures may be necessary for increasing the number of able and pious ministers in our church." I, on the whole, lean to the latter expedient for two reasons:—1. Because the state of our public affairs does not appear favorable, at present, to exertions which involve the raising of funds. But little time, therefore, will be lost on this plan. 2. Because it is a matter of so much consequence that we should begin wisely, that, perhaps, it ought to be deliberately talked over, in a leisurely and confidential manner, before any system be brought forward.

'If, however, you, after revolving the subject further in your mind, and mentioning the matter to such as it would be proper to consult, should, on the whole, still prefer the former plan, I shall make no objection, but heartily do all in my power to promote it. I leave it with God and you. May unerring Wisdom dictate the determination!

'If a committee, in pursuance of the latter plan, should be appointed, it will require some address to get a good one. It will readily occur to you, that much will depend on this. * *

'I have only room to add, that I am, dear Sir, unfeignedly and affectionately yours,
'Rev'd Dr. Green.   Sam'l Miller.'

7. CALL TO DICKINSON COLLEGE.

A few years previous to Dr. Nisbet's death in 1804, the prosperity of Dickinson College had seriously declined. Another principal was not immediately chosen. Meanwhile the professors—one of them the Rev. Dr. Davidson, Vice-Principal, and pastor of the Presbyterian Church in Carlisle—conducted the affairs of the institution. At length, in 1808, a benefaction from the legislature of Pennsylvania determined the Trustees to appoint a principal. On the 5th of July, Dr. Miller received a very kind letter from his friend, Dr. Benjamin Rush, of Philadelphia, urging him to allow his name to go before the Board. Some of the Trustees proposed to fix a salary, and rely

upon the reviving prosperity of the college for its payment.
Others suggested giving the institution entirely up to the
new principal, allowing him to carry it on at his own risk,
and for his own benefit. Dr. Rush, in his letter, remarked,

'I need say nothing to you of the commanding situation of
the College of Carlisle for unbounded usefulness to Church
and State. But I will suggest, what perhaps may be unknown
to you, that your talents, your present attainments, your love
of knowledge of all kinds, your peculiar and specific manners,
and your high character, qualify you in an eminent degree for
that eminent station. Education in our country stands in need
of a revolution. It should be accommodated to our government and state of society. I know of no man so fit to lay the
foundation of this revolution as Dr. Miller.

'I will mention one reason, of a private nature, for your removal to Carlisle. It will defend your breast from the consumptive air of the sea-shore, and thereby, probably, be the
means of prolonging your life, and continuing your labors and
your honors in the Church for many, many years to come.'

The following was Dr. Miller's reply :—

'My dear Sir,   New York, July 16th, 1808.
        'I received your letter of the 5th instant a week ago,
and should have acknowledged the receipt of it before, had I
not spent the greater part of the last fortnight, with my family,
at a place, a few miles from the city, to which we have re-
treated during the summer months.

'It is scarcely necessary for me to say, that I read your
letter, both on account of its writer and its subject, with much
interest. To find myself thought of for a station so important,
and by a judge of character so enlightened and discriminating,
was as unexpected as it was flattering. And, though I am
conscious that you greatly overrate my qualifications for such
a place; yet by your estimate of them, and by the favorable
terms in which you have been pleased to speak of them to
others, I feel myself highly obliged and honored; and, I will
frankly confess, not a little gratified.

'I am perfectly aware of the commanding situation of Dickinson College, and of the important services which, under wise
and energetic management, it might be made to render both to
Church and State. But when I consider how long it has lan-
guished; and that when aided with all the learning and weight
of character of Dr. Nisbet, even in his best days, it was not
able to gain more than a small portion of public favor; I

acknowledge I have not self-complacency enough, in my most sanguine moments, to hope that it would be in my power to accomplish more than he did : and, perhaps, with all his peculiarities of character, I ought to calculate on much less.

'The *first* plan founds all its calculations on the talents and popularity of the Principal. On these he, as well as the institution, is to depend for such an increase of reputation, and of students, as will insure support. Would this not be a very precarious dependence for a young man, comparatively but little known; who has never made trial of his powers as an instructor in literature or science; and who, on the most favorable supposition, might calculate on being a number of years in the office, before he could receive such a degree of public countenance, as would place him in comfortable circumstances? A man must have more confidence in his own powers than I can possibly summon to my aid, before he can feel secure in presuming on the success of this plan.

'With respect to the *second* plan, there are many men with whom it would be not only feasible, but, perhaps, highly eligible. But I am not one of those men. It would indispensably require such a vigor, as well as wisdom, of discipline; such a vigilant and incessant attention to the details of economy; and, in short, so large a portion of the active, bustling, mercantile character, that I fear neither my temperament, nor my habits, would bear me out in the undertaking. All this would be necessary to guard against bankruptcy. But there is a more serious difficulty yet to be mentioned. In all seminaries of learning, in which the students are boarded in common, there are continual complaints of the living, arising from the luxurious habits of some, the caprice of others, the personal malice of a third class, and the want of reflection and wisdom in all. These complaints, in ordinary cases, terminate on the Steward, who is expected, both on his own account, and that of the Trustees, to make all his calculations on economical, or, if you please, mercenary principles. But, on the proposed plan, would not the case be entirely changed? Would not the Principal be the butt of every complaint, taunt, or sneer; and almost unavoidably exhibit himself, in the eyes of the students, as a *maker of money*, rather than a dignified minister of religion and literature? Perhaps these difficulties appear the greater to me, for want of more mature reflection on the subject. However this may be, they really strike me, at present, as very formidable.

'Under these circumstances, I am inclined to believe, that I could not remove to Carlisle, with any prospect of either more comfort or more usefulness than my present situation promises; and that other gentlemen might be thought of, much better qualified than myself, to fulfill the wishes of the Trustees, and to promote the interests of the College, on either of the proposed plans.

'The consideration which you suggest, respecting my *health*, is weighty. I have no doubt that the climate of New York is unfavorable to my lungs; and will frankly confess, that, from this consideration alone, I have felt, for several years past, as if a removal to a more inland residence would be a personal blessing to me. But, as frequent changes of residence are neither agreeable to my taste, nor consistent with respectability in my profession, I have thought it my duty calmly to commit this concern to the direction of Providence, and to wait for an offer of removal to some station, which shall promise comfort and usefulness, with as much quietness and stability, and with as much opportunity to pursue my studies without the distraction of temporal cares, as the changing nature of our world will warrant us in expecting.

'On the whole, Sir, I feel it my duty to express a decisive wish, that your views may be immediately turned to some other person; and that my name may no longer be retained in the list of those from among whom a choice is to be made.

'Suffer me again to express my grateful acknowledgments for the friendliness of your communication, and for the honor which it does me; and to repeat my assurances of the great respect with which I am, Dear Sir,

'Your much obliged friend
'and servant,

'Dr. Rush,   Sam'l Miller.'

Dr. Rush replied promptly, expressing his regret, and mentioning the general favor with which the suggestion of his friend's name had been received. The Trustees met early in October, and in spite of the foregoing letter, which had been communicated to them, elected Dr. Miller by a large, unanimous vote. Doctor Rush now, once more, with great earnestness, urged his acceptance of the appointment. As to salary, the proposition finally made was much more promising than any which had preceded it.

'A wide field of usefulness,' said Doctor Rush, 'will now be opened to you. You will become the patriarch of the western churches of the United States. You will have the honor of introducing a system of education into our country, accomodated to the form of our governments, and to our state of society and manners. You will be able to abolish customs and studies, in the College, of monkish origin, and which have nothing but antiquity to recommend them. The present depressed state of the College will serve to heighten your reputation. The difficulties you will encounter at first will give a vigor to your mind that will last through life. Be not discouraged in viewing them. "Hoc est periculum par animo Alexandri." You are more than equal to them.'

'Recollect the text chosen by Mr. Davies for his funeral sermon: "No man liveth to himself." You are called, not to the chair of the President of the United States, not to a throne, but to a station above both of them—to rank with Edwards, Burr, and others of the greatest and best men that have lived in our country; to form young men for time and eternity; to raise up pillars for the Church as well as for the State; and to be no longer a star, but a sun, in the great system of science, morals, and religion.'

On the 10th of October, the action of the Trustees having been officially communicated to him, Dr. Miller wrote to James Armstrong, Esquire, President of the Board, a letter from which the following is an extract:—

'In a letter written, more than two months ago, to a distinguished member of your board residing in Philadelphia, I made a very frank and unreserved exposition of my views on the subject, in reply to some suggestions communicated by that gentleman. That letter I expected and hoped would have prevented the more formal step which has since been taken. Although my views remain unchanged, yet my deep sense of the honor you have done me; and the obligation which I feel to give the subject all that serious and respectful consideration, to which it is, on every account, entitled; induce me, before giving my final answer, to request from you some information on the following points:—'

A number of queries were subjoined. Mr. Armstrong, a fortnight later, gave the information requested. Dr. Miller's final answer was as follows:—

'Sir,   New York, October 31, 1808.
       'Your letter, containing the information which I had desired concerning Dickinson College, came to my hands three days ago. Agreeably to my promise, I embrace the first moment of leisure to communicate my final answer to your application.

'In expressing the state of my mind on this subject, I cannot forbear beginning with a respectful acknowledgment of the honor you have done me, by your call to a station so high and responsible. I shall long retain a grateful sense of this honor; and will frankly confess, that the flattering nature and the unanimity of your choice, joined with the consideration of my having some valued friends in Carlisle, and of my having felt, for many years, a deep interest in the prosperity of Dickinson College, formed a strong plea in favor of my accepting your call. But after the best view of the subject that I could take, I have come to a different determination. Among the reasons which have led to this determination are the following:—

'My present happy connexion with a most indulgent and affectionate people forms an obstacle to the proposed removal, which I know not how to surmount. Unless my friends deceive me, it would not be possible for me, at present, to leave my pastoral charge, without giving more uneasiness, and, perhaps, inflicting greater injury, on a people whom I have every reason to respect and love, than it would be proper to hazard, without the most unquestionable prospect of much greater usefulness, as well as comfort, in another place. That prospects of this undoubted kind would be opened to me in taking charge of your college, under present circumstances, I dare not promise myself.

'Another consideration which weighs not a little with me is, that a removal to Carlisle would compel me to abandon several literary plans, which I have formed within a few years past, and which I still cherish the hope of executing, if my life and health should be spared. I will not trouble you, Sir, or the Board of Trustees, with a detail of these plans. It is sufficient to say, that most of them are so much connected, on the score of convenience, with a residence in a large city, or in the neighborhood of it; and one of them is so closely and almost inseparably connected with a residence somewhere within the State of New York, that I should consider the acceptance of your call as a virtual dereliction of these objects. And, when I recollect that they have employed much of the time and labor of ten years, I feel unwilling, without the most evident and imperious call of duty, to make such a sacrifice.

'But the consideration which appears to me most forcible and conclusive is, that I am persuaded I can never realize the expectations of the Trustees. It is impossible not to perceive, that much of their hope for reviving and establishing the reputation of the College, rests on the talents and character of the Principal. For a station to which such peculiar responsibility is attached, and to which a failure would direct such pointed and inevitable imputations, I candidly declare that I do not consider myself as fitted. With my present views of the subject, I could not acquit myself of the charge of practising a criminal deception on the Board, were I to undertake the task to which they have called me.

'Under these impressions, I beg leave to announce to the Board, (what I trust, from the strain of my former letters, they have been led to expect,) that I cannot perceive it to be my duty to accept of the high and honorable office to which they have elected me.

'In communicating this decision, I beg that it may be distinctly understood, that the amount of the salary offered me by the vote of the Board makes no part of my objection to accepting their call. I am firmly persuaded, not only that the salary is as large as they could wisely or safely promise; but also that my temporal support in Carlisle would be fully equal, all things considered, if not superior, to that which I enjoy in this place.

'With fervent wishes for the prosperity of your college; with respectful salutations to the Board; and with grateful acknowledgments to you, Sir, and to the other members of the committee, for the polite and flattering manner in which you have communicated with me on this subject,

'I have the honor to be
'Your obedient servant,

'James Armstrong, Esquire,   Samuel Miller.
  'President of the Board of Trustees, &c.'

CHAPTER SIXTEENTH.

1801–1808.

MRS. MILLER'S MEMOIRS.

Mrs. Miller's memoirs of her life, to the date of her marriage, have already been given. The conclusion of them, coming down to the year 1808, in which she began to write, claim, chronologically, a place here. It will be remembered that these memoirs were addressed to her husband.

'You advised me, a few months after we were married, to make a sketch of the sermons which I heard, as my recollection might serve, immediately after returning from Church. I followed your advice, and it was the commencement of an undertaking, which was finally made the means of an effectual blessing. This exercise engaged me in hearing more attentively and systematically, and thus wandering thoughts were more and more called in, and vain imaginations more and more subdued; and faith, at length, came by hearing, and that acquaintance with God, and that peace promised from it, to which Dr. Rodgers's sermon, the first of which I took notes, would have been the means of leading me sooner, if it had been suitably improved. The adaptedness of his subject—from the text, "Acquaint now thyself with him, and be at peace; thereby good shall come unto thee"[1]—to my state of mind was remarkable. I had looked to the day on which he preached as the commencement of the exercise which you had recommended; and the Lord had prepared for me what was really a fundamental subject; and I was frequently afterward compelled to remark his dealings with regard to me in this way. * *

'My opportunities in the house of God were, however, far from being uninterrupted. I was as one fighting every inch of the way, and for every word that I heard. It seemed as if my

[1] Job 22, 21.

enemy here had double power; and it was with difficulty, sometimes, that I kept my seat through the service.   *   *   My ignorance of the Scriptures, which arose from the want of early,
enlightened, systematic instruction, I now felt the effects of in
a distressing degree.   I had the most dreadful thoughts and
imaginations mixed with every sermon, and especially on those
occasions when the Lord's supper was commemorated.   I had
made a profession of religion shortly after coming to New York,
and, on these occasions, doubts with regard to my fitness for
the ordinance pressed peculiarly on my mind; and frequently
the suggestions—what if I should not unite with the church at
this time, and if I should give my unworthiness as the reason?—
confused my spirit.   None who have never experienced these
things can imagine the agitation they produced.   *   *

'You also recommended religious books to me, expressing a
desire that I should take notes from recollection of their contents; but I did not find much light or comfort from the regular perusal of any lengthy and labored human performance.
Particular passages have been greatly blessed to me; but the
state of my mind, and the occupations to which I was called,
did not permit me to devote much time to reading.   Sometimes, when a book was returned which you had lent, and remained in the parlor for some days, I occasionally took it up,
and often found a word in season, which was a volume to me.
In this manner I had here a little and there a little of divine
instruction, as some would say by chance, but by what I have
found to have been the sure, unerring influence of a friend, who
was conducting me by regular, though gradual, progress to the
knowledge of himself.

'Wilberforce's *Practical View* was one of the most effectual
helps of the kind I have mentioned, that I have ever had.   His
observations on the influence of evil spirits seemed to throw
light on the state of my mind.   They were the means of convincing me of such influences, and led me to look, with more
purpose of heart, for the only help which could enable me to
resist them.   I learned that the dreadful thoughts which had
perplexed and almost overwhelmed me, were the injections of
an enemy, who took advantage of my sins and infirmities thus
to distract me; and having identified the enemy, I found more
strength in resisting him.   Amongst other books, novels were
sometimes brought in my way, and the fashionable poetry of
Scott and others; but they produced in my mind a sensation
which it is difficult to describe—something like that, I presume, which would be produced in a half starving wretch, by
throwing him bones to satisfy his hunger; and I neglected
them from indifference, or rather something like resentment.

'Besides books, any employment which exercised my mind was greatly beneficial. I had sometimes anticipated the pleasure of instructing my children, and I now looked forward to it as a probable means of relief. But what in anticipation sometimes is pleasant, may be so difficult in practice, that a single effort may discourage all our plans. I found, when —— arrived at an age suitable for instruction, I was doing little more than in intention that in which it was time to be actively engaged; and I should have gone on in this dream, until a public school for her had been the result, had not an admonitory voice said, Now is the season; and the business is of great importance. It was that influence which makes "both to will and to do"; and I set about the work in earnest; and, in the performance of this duty among my children, I have found, besides all the advantages which I hope will result to them from it, a relief to my spirit, which nothing else but a precious word from the Fountain of life has given and by this means such a word has often come. Thus the opportunities of religious instruction which I enjoyed, and employment which had some important end in view, were the only things from which I found permanent relief.

'I had left a numerous family connexion in Philadelphia, for which I found no substitute in New York; for although I shall ever remember with gratitude the kind attentions of the people to whom you ministered, only an acquaintance of years could have produced that familiar intercourse with them, which would have been at all like that existing amongst my relatives. This loss, together with your frequent absence, arising from the necessary claims of your congregation and others, left me to a lonesome wretchedness, which favored the growth of imaginary troubles, and the dread of future horrors. How was I preserved under such accumulated influences favoring entire despair? How, but by more than human means? My realizing impressions of religion were, for some time, few and slight. The strongest which I recollect arose from the fact, that man, who was certain of death, should think and care so little about it; should suffer himself to be led away from reflection on this subject, in which time and eternity were so much involved, by the passing trifles of a day. My convictions on this subject were in unison with the Psalmist's expression—"Surely every man walketh in a vain shew."

'My ignorance of the Scriptures, which arose from the want of early, enlightened systematic instruction, I now felt the effects of in a distressing degree. I had not leisure to supply this loss, and I had a fear of them which hindered my improving the little time I could redeem from other concerns. A kind, persuasive influence had reached my mind, by means of the words in Isaiah—"To the law and to the testimony," etc.,[1] to induce me to search them diligently; but a host of wild fanatics, who had perverted them, and professed to have drawn from them an impulse to all their deeds of darkness, affrighted and kept me from getting much engaged in them. Thus was I distracted between such fears, and the conviction that in the Scriptures was my only hope of deliverance.

'After the birth of —— I experienced, together with much indisposition, new and oppressive anxieties. But there were also new and delightful feelings accompanying this gift. I felt too that my life was of double importance, and my duty to strive against whatever would render it useless greatly enhanced. Some suitable sense of my relative obligations was bestowed with this child, and, for the first time, the claim which my husband and she had upon me affected my heart.

'I had an impression that much reading and study were necessary in order to come to the knowledge of the truth, and, of consequence, much leisure and retirement; I was distracted between this great concern and the constant demands of my family; and when our second child was a few weeks old, and I found that an additional one brought so many additional cares, I said, internally, with a fretful, desponding spirit, Now, all hope of attending effectually to my everlasting concerns is entirely at an end. It is a little remarkable, in view of these perplexities, that the first four or five months after the birth of our third child were chosen as the season for bringing me to the saving knowledge, as I trust, of the truth as it is in Jesus. I had now not only the further cares which another child gave, but the difficulties of a removal to a new house, which was not quite finished, and the task of attending to a number of friends in it, while thus situated, whom the meeting of Presbytery had drawn together. It was so ordered, that the voice of the Lord might be more impressive, which said, When I will work, what shall hinder?

'I labored with melancholy and unbelief, and more ignorance than I was sensible of, until after the birth of this third child; but scarcely had my agony passed, when I was involuntarily engaged in surveying this dear infant, this new-born miniature of man; though so small, perfect in every part; his features, limbs and joints in every respect so wonderful! I was wholly absorbed in this contemplation, until my admiring view was, through it, raised to the more wonderful Maker of this nice mechanism, and I was enabled to believe in my heart, that there was truly a God behind the curtain of creation—

---

[1] Is. 8. 21.

the Creator of all things in heaven and earth. By the light
of this discovery I perceived that I had been little, if any,
more than an atheist, except that I had not realized and
gloried in my unbelief. I had really lived without God in the
world. This delightful conviction of the reality of a First Cause
was so consoling, so exhilarating to my spirits, that it spread
sunshine and joy through almost the whole of my confinement;
I concluded that I had obtained that gift which is the earnest
of future happiness; and, had I been permitted, here would I
have rested. This might have done for a heathen; but what
is the gospel good for if we may rest here? It was, in fact, as
yet a sealed book to me, and my heart was but preparing for
the ingrafting of the written word. Indeed I was not altogether satisfied with my present experience; I felt sometimes
as a learner who had entered only upon the threshold of spiritual knowledge; and I recollect, * * when the world began
again to take possession of me, and arrangements for new-
modelling our family, and producing more order and regularity
in it, when we should remove and occupy a new house, were
forming another idol in my heart—I recollect, under a momentary conviction of my danger, kneeling and praying that I
might not be led away by temptation, but might be continued
and kept in the truth, if it were even at the expense of a repetition of those sufferings which had oppressed me for five years
past. I began to feel that I needed correction, and that I was
stretching toward heaven only in proportion as I was pressed
on the earth. The same blessed Spirit, which opened the eyes
of my mind to discern the truth of an Almighty Maker of all
things, hovered round me. I was, indeed, still distressed with
former fears; but they were restrained, and assisted in urging
me to meditation and prayer; and "a still small voice" seemed
to be endeavoring to allure me into the path of wisdom—the
study of the Bible. * * From the time I left my room my
way was again hedged up; my distress of mind came on with
redoubled violence; distracting cares again beset me; and the
comfort I had experienced appeared like a dream.

'It was about this time that Wilberforce's *View*, which you
had lent to a friend, was returned, and attracted my attention.
But so stupid was I, that, although I was convinced that I had
to strive not only with flesh and blood, but with principalities
and the powers of darkness, and ought to have felt that watchfulness and prayer were my best weapons against them; the
suspension of evil influence for an hour made me careless, and
the world resumed its attractions. Instead of taking advantage of precious freedom to obtain a hope against my besetting

enemy, I thought only of enjoying the present moment, or laying up a store of earthly comfort with which to occupy my mind and heart. Wretched, infatuated mortals! What would become of us if left to ourselves?

'Every circumstance, for a few weeks after this, concurred in bringing my feelings to an extremity. Your frequent absences from home that spring, in consequence of exchanging pulpits with your brethren, left me without my only efficient help, as I then felt; for there was a dependence on you, strengthening daily, which ought to have been placed upon God alone. I realized the snare, but was not able to escape from it. When you were to be absent for two or three days, many previous ones were spent in anxiety and dread; and I was as a wretch who has been released from the gallows, when the time of separation ended. I knew that the performance of duty required these separations, and conscience did not permit me to make any resistance to them. At one time, during this season, when left alone and almost at my wit's end to know what to do, I found the Bible open at Hebrews xii. 11 lying in your study; and it gave comfort to my wounded spirit. I felt as one under severe chastisement, and was encouraged to hope for the annexed promise. At another such season, Dr. Rodgers preached from the text—"Did not our hearts burn within us?" etc.,[1] and the sermon had a word in season for me. It was a powerful means of shaking, and in some measure re-removing, the prejudice which I had against the Bible. Our venerable father, who had, indeed, been a second father to you, seemed to be endeavouring to win some soul to attention to the word. * * The enemy said, The religion of Christ is a religion of fanatics, and has been the cause of war and bloodshed wherever it has come. The "still small voice" said, It is a religion of meekness and brotherly love: when properly understood, it makes man tender-hearted, forgiving, meek; and the sermon of Dr. Rodgers confirmed the latter testimony—that it was a system of purity and righteousness. But when my mind had been fully convinced, that the system was free from these imputations, the enemy took the next stronghold, and I feared that *I* might build upon it a system of delusion and horror. The world has taught us that man may do so, but because he examines it with a perverted understanding, and a heart filled with his own ways. These were the examples which affrighted me. But what made this sermon, and the Psalm, and all, delightful, was the persuasion that an unseen influence was operating upon my mind, opposed to the spirits of darkness

[1] Luke 24, 32.

which had tormented me; and my heart was attracted, before
Christ was formed in it the hope of glory. My feelings were
buoyed above the melancholy, which depressed me, for some
hours after I returned from church; I wrote down as much as
I could recollect of the sermon immediately; and I often look
upon it with wonder now, when I consider its effect, and feel
that it was indeed, though a feeble instrument, in the hand of
an almighty power. Mr. Woodhull, who exchanged with you
shortly after, preached upon that state in which the "worm
dieth not, and the fire is not quenched." My mind had always
revolted at the idea of eternal torment. I could not acquiesce
in a truth so repugnant to human nature. This subject exercised my mind through the week, and was one means of gradually removing the comfort derived from Dr. Rodgers' sermon.
* * My mental cavils against the doctrine of eternal punishment remained for days, in spite of some convictions in favor
of it, and have been but gradually subsiding under the clearer
light of gospel truth. * * I have sometimes thought, however,
that when my mind became engaged in the deep and mysteri-
ous doctrines of religion, although it was perplexed and distressed, there was a relief from the deeper anxiety, occasioned
by imaginary evils, with which I was filled at other times; and
I was certainly preparing to be more sound in doctrine, when
I should be enabled to believe unto salvation. When you returned, I grew careless and inattentive, and the enemy again
beset me with more violence than ever. It appeared to me, at
this time, that I heard more stories of distress and horror than
usual. Several cases of what was called religious melancholy
and derangement occurred in a few weeks, and some within
the circle of my acquaintance; and the deep-felt language of
my heart was—I can no longer struggle! I must sink! But
I had an almighty helper and was sustained.

'On Saturday, the 5th of April, you made an exchange with
Mr. McDowell of Elizabethtown. Perhaps no separation was
ever more trying to me. After you were gone, I hurried into
the street to endeavor to dispel my anguish: I now know that
retirement and prayer would have been far more effectual.
The horrors of my situation pressed upon me. I knew that I
was beset with feelings that had driven many to desperation.
In the evening Christiana Anderson came to attend the exercises of the Sabbath with us, and stay until Monday, when you
were to return. This was indeed a kind interposition of Providence for my relief, and by no means the first of the kind that
I had experienced; and I felt the conviction deepened, that the
providence and grace of the Lord were working together for

my final deliverance. I began this evening to pray in our family in your absence: the effort was a difficult one, but the result has proved a blessing. The foundation was laid, in that season of darkness, for many exertions which I have since thought were the means of much good, and which would probably never have been engaged in, had not the pressure of habitual distress benumbed my feelings with regard to worldly circumstances.

'Mr. McDowell preached, on the 6th of April, 1806, from "The Lord is my shepherd, I shall not want, etc.";[1] and it was a word of comfort to me, which, although it did not raise me from the waters in which I was sunk, kept my head above them, and was one means of preparing the way for more effectual deliverance. It especially weakened the effect of that argument against me, which was sometimes so overwhelming, drawn from the inability of those to resist the pressure of weak nerves and their dreadful consequences, who were far stronger in body and mind than myself. When reflecting on this, I often said in despair, If a Johnson and a Cowper sunk in such circumstances, what shall a poor, weak woman do, whose infirmities and occupations make them tenfold more oppressive? Mr. McDowell said, in connexion with the words—"Though I walk through the valley of the shadow of death, I will fear no evil"—"Let not the Christian pilgrim be discouraged by its being strewed with the bones and skeletons of others who have travelled before"; and pointed to an almighty helper; and there was strength by means of his words.

'A friend seemed now to be with rapid progress gaining access to my spirit, diseased beyond the reach of human skill, who alone knew how to apply a balm for every wound. The certainty that nothing human could save me made me feel like a poor, isolated being alone in a crowded world; and the inquiry was continually present with me—What shall I do? Who will shew me any good?

'Of the week succeeding this Sabbath I have but a faint recollection. My distress of mind increased so, that when you were out but for an hour, I was almost in agony lest some dreadful thing should take place. I have often, when some circumstance has recalled this period, asked in astonishment, Was all this concealed from my husband and every other human being? Do I deceive myself, or was I, to appearance, like the rest of the world, and no distraction perceived? Was I preparing all this week to leave one place of abode and occupy another, with scarcely a thought engaged in the business; and

[1] Psalm 23, 1, et .

did I proceed rationally?   If I did, it was from thine upholding grace, O Lord!

'The next Sabbath, April 13th, I spent at home—I do not know on what account, but probably from indisposition.   It was a restless, wretched day, and I awoke under the pressure of increased weakness on Monday morning, to begin the business of removing.   I was assisting at both houses, sometimes at one, and sometimes at the other, and going backward and forward, as my presence seemed to be required at either.   Toward noon, in returning from Dey to Liberty street, my mind, almost overwhelmed with dreadful images, but still endeavoring to fasten on something that would save it from distraction, still striving to enter into some religious exercise which would draw it off from imaginations of horror, was aided suddenly in its efforts; and, from a course of reasoning which was almost instantaneous, I came to the conclusion, that I would lay aside all my books, even those on religious subjects,[1] that I would assiduously attend to my avocations through the week, and endeavor diligently to listen to the preaching on the Sabbath; recollecting that I had been more comforted by one sermon preached, than by all the labored works which I had attempted to peruse.   This arrangement, which seemed to proceed from the influence of the Spirit upon my mind, composed my feelings, and subdued, in some measure, my fears; and, from anxiety for myself, my desires became immediately engaged for my children.   I began to feel that change of heart, which was necessary as a preparation for any good, and I labored in spirit, for a few moments, for them.   These reflections, which had been rapidly succeeding each other, and which had occupied but as it were a minute, were suddenly succeeded by an illumination of mind certainly supernatural.   It was the light of *character*—that Light which is the life of men—a lovely impression of him, whom the Apostle John represents repeatedly under the image of light in the first part of his gospel. It was a ray of that light from heaven, which rested on the Apostle of the Gentiles; and had no need of a voice to tell me what it was, for my heart had been preparing to hail it as my only hope.   And I can now say with renewed certainty, when one experience after another has confirmed this hope, that "the glory of the Lord shone round about" me.   It shone indeed in darkness, and I can give but a faint impression of its effect upon my mind.   It was something like that which is at times produced by natural objects.   I have seen all nature overshadowed with gloom and obscurity, by the unusual effect

[1] Except the Bible, as she afterwards explains.

of dark, thick clouds; when suddenly, from an opening wholly unperceived before, the sun has darted forth his rays, and thrown light and gladness all around. And as the eye recedes from such a burst of natural light, so did my mind from this beam of spiritual day: it was too vivid for a mind so long wrapped up in gloom to bear. I was afraid of being entirely overcome, and sinking in the street under its influence; but I was enabled to struggle against its overwhelming power, and hurried home still experiencing its happy effects. All my experience since has convinced me, that this was not a vague illumination, a mere chimera of the mind. It was immediately followed by the intelligent fruits of the Spirit. By means of preaching and the Scriptures, I have been led to faith in all the doctrines of the gospel; sometimes as unexpectedly as when this illumination took place; and I have more and more reason to hope, that it was the dawn of an everlasting day.

'I had scarcely reached home, when the enemy of the souls of men again began his attacks, but in a new form. I was in deep distress for a few minutes, at the thought, that light had appeared for my salvation, but I had resisted it. My fears, hitherto, had been all for the flesh: this was the commencement, I believe, of spiritual distress, properly so called. My horror at the thought of my day of grace's being past can scarcely be expressed. But the plea was internally and irresistibly made, that it was infirmity which had opposed, not intention. I was soothed by this suggestion, and the more persuaded that I had experienced what was the dawning of a new day in my heart. It did, indeed, like the dawning of the morning, for some time render the vapors of the night more apparent and terrific; but its increasing strength has been gradually dispelling, and I trust will go on to dispel, them, until they shall all vanish in noon-day glory. The word of God directs us to judge of the operations of the Holy Spirit by its fruits; and I soon had an evidence in my favour by means of this rule. A sight of the greatness and mercy of the Redeemer produced a deep conviction of my own littleness; and at every review of his charming image, my heart involuntarily cried, Why me, Lord? Why me? These words arose from the deepest conviction and feeling. How often did I say, through that day and evening, and for some days after, I will tell my husband what I have experienced: I will tell him that I have a better hope than this world can afford. I am going into a new earthly dwelling, but a better dwelling is in store for me: I shall inhabit those mansions which the Saviour is preparing for those who love him. But words, on this subject,

failed me, and further employment prevented the communication. The Lord would have the whole glory of establishing as
well as renewing. From this time until the 27th of April, was
the most distracting and the darkest that I had ever passed.
Satan knew that he had "but a short time," and made it as
wretched as possible.

'The confusion which took place in removing; the impossibility almost of seizing a moment for meditation and prayer—
the necessary means, as I have since found, of keeping alive
the new-born principle of grace; the weariness which over-
powered me on the Sabbath, and either kept me from church,
or rendered me unfit to be there; all had a tendency to hinder
the means of grace, to which I felt that I was directed for
relief, from taking effect. And it was not until I was enabled
to make a violent effort to rise above these hindrances, that I
experienced the first precious effect from the course which I
had resolved to pursue. The Sabbath[1] previous to the meeting
of the General Assembly this year, Dr. Nott preached in the
morning in the Wall street church. He had been staying with
us, for some days, on his way to the meeting of that body, and
we were to proceed with him to Philadelphia the next week.

'The day commenced and continued with me, as usual, with
agitating fears, and an almost distracted state of mind. Could
I have found any rational plea, I would have staid at home;
but I felt that my duty to attend could not be lightly set aside.
My mind was so bewildered and wretched, that I found my utmost exertion necessary to keep my seat, in church, at all
quietly; and all my hope arose from the possibility of fastening
my mind intently on the sermon. I bent my whole strength to
this, and found more than human assistance in doing so. It
was the most propitious sermon that could have been selected
for me. It contained arguments in proof of the resurrection of
Christ—I should say the most forcible that could be collected,
because they irresistibly convinced me, and set aside all the
cavillings which had been collected in my mind for years. I
was as well convinced, when the sermon closed, that this wonderful event had taken place, as that any one had in my own
life; and that, if this was true, Christ must be the Sent of God,
he in whom we were to believe; and I was willing to place all
my dependence on him. I knew now what faith in Christ was,
and was, in spite of men and devils, in spite of myself, spiritually a believer. Oh, what a bright season it was! I felt indeed like a new creature. The cloud of gloom within me was
rent, and was more and more dispelled from this time; a new

[1] May 11th, 1806.

world of spiritual views opened upon my mind and heart—a
door which has never been closed against me when I had a
heart to enter; and never will be closed, I trust, until faith
shall be lost in sight, and hope in enjoyment. But Oh, how
often does flesh and the world prevent my taking advantage of
this privilege! How often do I sink, like a mere clod of the
valley, into spiritual stupor!—how often, like the beasts that
perish, feel satisfied with the enjoyments of the flesh! From
this time every assault of mental anguish was a means of new
light and a firmer trust; in all I came off conqueror, and more
than conqueror, through him who had loved me; every new
struggle fixed some Bible truth in my mind, or gave me another
animating hope.   *   *

'After this, my attention to the Word arose, not merely from
a sense of duty, and a desire to put aside distressing imaginations, but for a sincere taste for the undisguised truth. Sometimes, when a word in season had reached my heart and shut
out the world, the flesh and the Devil; when I beheld every
object through the gospel glass, and each took its proper and
relative situation in my judgment; when my heart was, I trust,
filled with the love of Christ, and participated, in some measure, in the joys of heaven; I was almost afraid of breathing,
lest this frame should be lost. I realized the fear expressed in
the Canticles,[1] and was unwilling that anything should move
to disturb this enjoyment; and prayer appeared involuntarily
to arise, that I might be preserved from every temptation to
apostacy. It was the prayer of faith, which said, I have no
hope but in thee! At the next step I shall be ensnared, unless
thou uphold me!   *   *

'After I reached Philadelphia, I found the distraction of
mind produced by company, and a constant change of scenes
and objects, very unfriendly to growth in light and knowledge;
but I experienced a strong warfare of the Spirit against the
flesh, as well as of the flesh against the Spirit. I sometimes
was so abstracted from these, as to feel as if I took no part in
the struggle—somewhat as a spectator feels, who is overlooking
two contending adversaries—but not without a faithless, trembling anxiety as to which should be the conqueror; as to
whether it was possible that I could be delivered from such a
powerful enemy, as I had been contending with for so many
years.   *   *   'The passage—"But I tell you of a truth, many
widows were in Israel in the days of Elias, etc.,"[2] was accompanied by the powerful operation of the Spirit, and not only
quieted every agitating fear, but produced that peace and joy in

1 Probably Cant. ii. 7, iii. 4. 5. etc.   2 Luke 4, 25-27.

believing, which the world cannot give, or take away. The doctrine of election, which had so often perplexed and troubled my mind, now entered it with a comfort that I cannot describe. I now learned, that God could and would impart that strength and aid to the weak and foolish, to babes in Christ, which he denied to the wise and prudent; and I felt that I was an inheritor of the promises.

'On our return from Philadelphia, in company with several members of the assembly, either from their conversation, or some other forgotten cause which occurred during our ride, the question as to the divinity of the Saviour exercised my mind. It was not an idle speculation merely; my feelings were engaged; I was in great distress for a few minutes—in that kind of distress which every Christian has, no doubt, experienced, when the things belonging to his everlasting peace have exercised his mind. A sermon, which I had heard from Dr. Priestley, some years before, had convinced me that error had no safe side. If Christ were a man, it was idolatry to honor him as God. Although my judgment was then convinced, I was indifferent as to the result of the question. But now I was alive to all the importance of it. My mind vibrated for a minute; but my faith in Jesus as the Truth—the Sent of God—was fixed, and the infallible word said, Hear him! The recollection of the simple fact, that he had suffered himself to be worshipped, without reproof, delivered me from the fear of being guilty of idolatry, and established his divinity in my mind. For the same infallible word said, "Thou shalt worship the Lord thy God, and him only shalt thou serve." God does not deny himself. Therefore being the Sent of God, he speaketh the words of God; and suffering himself to be worshipped, must be God. Thus * * by means of a moment of agitation, an important truth was fixed in my mind.'

Mrs. Miller closes these memoirs with a description of some of the further conflicts, through which she was enabled to take a stronger hold of the doctrines of the gospel, and obtain a clear assurance of her interest in Christ. She adopted, experimentally, one by one, the great evangelical truths involved in God's entire sovereignty, her own utter unworthiness, and just condemnation, and her helpless dependence upon divine grace. These attainments were made, every one of them, by searching the Scriptures with diligence and prayer, while at the same time she was stirring herself up to run in the way of all duty. Thus she prevailed against the errors of "falling from grace,"

and doubting her own state, because she did not attain
practically that perfection, which theoretically she had
never expected. Thus she got rid of her remaining troubles respecting the doctrine of eternal torment.

'Thus,' she concludes, 'did the Holy Spirit teach me one
truth after another, and with little formal effort on my part;
for my constantly besetting sin was indolence: I was willing to
sit down and count every attainment enough, instead of following on to know the Lord. I would not be a snare to any by
this representation; and should add, that the same Friend
who led me step by step into the truth, saw the necessity of
trial as a preparation; and what I would not labor for was
given me always by suffering. * * When a subject, which
I had neglected to take hold of, took hold of me, my spirit
labored, and my mind was weighing argument even in the
midst of worldly employments. And I feel that I have, notwithstanding all that has been done for me, stopped short, not
I trust of everlasting life, but of being thoroughly furnished for
every good word and work—of making that return which so
much grace demanded; for "unto whomsoever much is given,
of him shall be much required." And I am left with no other
plea than, "God, be merciful to me a sinner!" What has been
sown in weakness, do thou raise in power!

'Thus was I sustained notwithstanding constitutional ten-
dencies, reduced health, and the most unfavorable circumstances; and none need despair.'

CHAPTER SEVENTEENTH.

---

1. History of the Dissolution.

Soon after his settlement in New York, Dr. Miller seems to have become thoroughly convinced, that the union of the congregations, to which he and his colleagues jointly ministered, was a great evil. The church edifice in Rutgers street having been dedicated in 1798, there were three places of worship and worshipping assemblies, with but one board of trustees, one session, and one body of deacons—in fact, but one church. And of this whole church each of the collegiate ministers, until the settlement of Dr. Milledoler in 1805, was a pastor. Preaching, in turn, to each of the three congregations, he was expected to visit and watch over the great body of the people at large. There were, doubtless, advantages attending this arrangement. As it was understood that the sermons preached to one congregation would be repeated to the others, the labor of preparation for the pulpit was abridged, or more time afforded for making that preparation thorough. Moreover, the general supervision of Dr. Rodgers, the senior colleague, was regarded as particularly important; and the whole people, to whom he had greatly endeared himself, as a pastor and friend, were spared the pain of parting with him, or losing any of his ministrations. The evils of the arrangement, however, far overbalanced all its advantages, real or imaginary. If it facilitated pulpit preparation, it greatly multiplied all other pastoral cares. Every family expected and claimed the visits of each pastor—formal, ministerial visits, too, according to the usage of the Church of Scotland. To visit, with the best effect, a single large city congregation; to cherish a proper intimacy between pastor and people; to exert that immediate personal influence, which is so important to a church's stability, growth, and general welfare, is a herculean task, under which many clergymen have sunk down exhausted; and which a far greater number have been able to persuade themselves that they had hardly time or strength to attempt. What, then, must have been the labor of visiting three such congregations in union? It is evident, too, that partialities among the parishioners towards this or that one of their pastors, and such invidious comparisons as some would hardly have refrained from making, must have operated unfavorably upon the people themselves, and presented to the collegiate ministers constant temptations to rivalries and jealousies, very unfavorable to their own comfort, their spiritual improvement, their harmonious co-operation, and their general usefulness. Dr. Miller remarks of his burdensome pastoral duties, that he soon found their full discharge wholly out of the question: his work seemed ever accumulating upon his hands. 'This,' he adds, 'always grieved me. Besides, perplexities and difficulties often arose respecting both the temporal and spiritual concerns of the two congregations. In fact, they were tied together very much as the Siamese twins, and their respective movements embarrassed and impeded very much in the same way. No one who never had any personal experience of these difficulties could adequately feel or estimate them. After struggling with them for a number of years, I became perfectly satisfied, that if the churches could be separated, and each one have its appropriate pastor, the best interests of each would be in every respect promoted.'

Yet of this union many of the church members, especially the older ones, who had longest enjoyed Dr. Rodgers's labors, were so tenacious, that for years after Dr. Miller's settlement, every thought of attempting to dissolve it was discouraged by determined opposition, and by a fear of disturbing the peaceful relations of the people among themselves and to their pastors. Still, the prejudices by which the old system was upheld were gradually dying away; and every year added strength to the growing conviction, that a separation of the "United Churches" would be very advantageous to each of them, tending to the increase of Presbyterianism, and the enlargement of the Redeemer's kingdom. Hence, Dr. Milledoler's settlement as one of the collegiate pastors, in 1805, was peculiar. Though he was to preach to all the congregations, according to the established routine of pulpit services, the Rutgers street people were to be otherwise his particular pastoral charge; and of the latter, it was understood, that he was to be the sole pastor, should a division afterwards be effected.

Dr. Miller, from almost the beginning of his pastorate, had been in the habit of expressing freely his opinion that the Collegiate Churches ought to be separated. With Dr. McKnight, in particular, he had often talked on the subject; finding his colleague's sentiments quite accordant with his own, and that they had once led him to propose the separation to a joint meeting of the elders, deacons, and trustees; who, however, had so summarily, and, as he thought, so offensively, rejected his proposition, that he had determined to have nothing more to do with the matter. But in the spring of 1807, a number of gentlemen, worshipping in the Wall street and Brick Churches, associated themselves with others who had been unable to obtain pews in either, to erect a new Presbyterian house of worship. The Cedar street Church was the result of this effort, and was opened in November, 1808. At the installation of the Rev. John B. Romeyn as its first pastor, Dr. McKnight, in giving the customary charge, congratulated him on being the sole pastor of a single church; noticing, in strong terms, the advantages of such a position, and the disadvantages of the collegiate relation. This, with the entire and happy success of the experiment, greatly diminished the numbers and influence of those who stood out for maintaining the union of the earlier congregations. 'People began to see,' says Dr. Miller, 'that a church was more likely to prosper, which had a single pastor, to whom all eyes and all hearts could be directed, and who had a single people that he could call his own.'

As he began to think more seriously of making the attempt to effect a separation, Dr. Miller conversed more freely with Dr. McKnight; and at length informed him, and him alone, that he proposed making it at the juncture, evidently near at hand, when Dr. Rodgers might be laid aside from active service. But finding, afterwards, that a number of persons in the collegiate churches, who favored the separation, were growing restive under delay, and were disposed to seek another church connexion, he precipitated the attempt. With Dr. McKnight's hearty concurrence, but without mentioning his purpose, beforehand, to another human being,—not even to Mrs. Miller, lest she should be unnecessarily disquieted,—he formally proposed to the session, on the first of December, 1808, the adoption of measures for separating the United Churches. At Dr. McKnight's suggestion, the matter was referred, as before, to a joint meeting of the elders, deacons, and trustees. For nearly four months this subject occupied the attention of the people and their officers, until, about the close of March, the joint body of the latter unanimously recommended separation : Dr. Rodgers, however, was to retain, as long as he lived, his connexion with both churches ; while Dr. McKnight was to be pastor of the Brick Church, Dr. Miller of that in Wall street. This result was the more gratifying to the latter, because he had fully resolved, and had delicately informed the session, in bringing the matter before them, that he must seek another settlement, if the collegiate relation were continued.

Dr. Rodgers had steadily refused to take any part in the prosecution of the measures thus brought to an issue. He freely acknowledged, indeed, many of the evils of the collegiate relation ; but his long connexion with the United Churches, his unwillingness to sever the ties which bound him to any portion of his charge, and the fact, doubtless, that his most active services had been performed before that charge became so overgrown, complicated, and oppressive, seem to have prevented, with him, a full conviction that the change was necessary.

2. TROUBLES.

Evils which have long existed, and have taken deep root, can seldom be eradicated, without violence to the feelings of many persons ; and reformers must ever expect to encounter opposition and incur odium. Perhaps Dr. Miller,

while he had counted the cost in certain respects, had no
idea, beforehand, of the real troubles into which he was to
be brought by his reformatory zeal. In fact, these troubles
could hardly have been anticipated, although most naturally
springing from the measures just as naturally adopted to
separate the United Churches. Dr. McKnight's particular
friends thought that his seniority entitled him to the pastorate of the old Wall street church. On the other hand,
that church deemed itself entitled to make its own choice;
while the New, or Brick, church could not readily brook
the idea of taking just what the other left. Hence, the
apprehended difficulty of making a satisfactory disposition
of things, after the separation, became a serious obstacle to
the separation itself. Some, to remove the difficulty, proposed that Dr. McKnight should, like Dr. Rodgers, continue to serve both churches, or simply to preach for both;
but he was not himself satisfied with the proposal. Others
suggested calling a popular man to occupy this relation, as
a preacher chiefly, to the two. Again, in the Brick Church,
as it must yield the first choice to Wall street, there was a
strong desire, apparently, to call a new pastor, and leave
to others the determination of the question, which of the
two, Dr. McKnight or Dr. Miller, should be settled in Wall
street, and which should be the preacher in common. Dr.
Miller had frankly offered to take either of these positions,
or the pastorate of the Brick church, and had, indeed,
staked all upon the issue. No person seems to have had
the slightest idea of the dismissal of Dr. McKnight. In
fact, more than one of Dr. Miller's warmest and most influential friends had candidly said to him, that if, in the result, either should be dismissed, it ought to be he, as the
younger man, who could the more readily shift for himself.
Probably, too, this was considered but fair, since he had
been the mover in the business, and had counted upon dismission as the possible cost of his attempt.

More than a year before making the formal proposition
to separate the churches, he had written on business to his
friend, Mr. Speece, of Virginia; and, at the request of Dr.
Abeel of the Dutch Church, in which there was a vacancy,
in anticipation also of the wants of the new Cedar street
church, and with the prospect that Dr. Rodgers's growing
infirmity would soon make a new collegiate pastor neces-

sary for the United Presbyterian congregations, had urged him to visit New York, and let himself be heard. But Mr. Speece had not been willing to leave Virginia.

A commission from the same friend to procure a book obliged him to write again, just after the separation had been formally proposed. He was moved to write, moreover, by the facts, that the vacancy in the Dutch Church still existed; that Dr. Rodgers, who actually preached his last sermon some nine months only thereafter, was very feeble; and that an influential officer of the United Churches urged him to write. He had scarce a thought that Mr. Speece would come to the North, yet believed that, if he came, he would prove acceptable as a collegiate pastor, and would himself be likely to prefer the position of preacher to both congregations, should they be separated. He therefore renewed the suggestion of a visit to New York, though without mentioning the project of separation. The answer, however, was the same as before.

At this time Dr. Griffin was widely known and admired as a preacher. Dr. Miller, as his intimate personal friend, was urged by several leading men in the United Churches to write to him, proposing that he should visit New York as a candidate. On a variety of accounts Dr. Miller objected. He supposed, especially, that Dr. Griffin was already committed to the people of Boston, and to the Seminary at Andover. At length, however, he yielded to strong and repeated importunities in behalf, particularly, of the Brick church, concluding that it could do no harm to let Dr. Griffin know the state of feeling towards him in New York; and he wrote first a hurried, afterwards a more leisurely, letter. But Dr. Griffin decided to go to Massachusetts, and Dr. Miller, though painfully affected by it, could not but approve his decision.

With the arrangements for separation Dr. McKnight was not satisfied, and they were followed by new complications and troubles. He charged his colleague with having used unfair influences to secure a settlement in the Wall street church, and stigmatized the project of separation itself, and the letters to Mr. Speece and Dr. Griffin, written though they had been at the urgent suggestion of others, as parts of a plot to get rid of him. No doubt injudicious friends aggravated the misunderstanding. It became evident, at length, that a full authoritative investigation alone could quiet feelings, on this subject, which were becoming more and more excited. Dr. Miller offered to submit the case to Presbytery, or to a joint assembly of all the officers of the two churches, or to other arbitrators chosen by Dr. McKnight, or selected in any manner which he might propose. Finally, it was agreed that each party should choose five arbitrators, and the ten thus appointed five more—in all fifteen, whose judgment was to be final.

Dr. Miller first proposed five names. Dr. McKnight not only expressed entire satisfaction with the gentlemen named, but said that three of them were on his own intended list. The number was completed according to agreement, and, one person declining to act, the rest, by general consent, proceeded with the investigation. Two, at least, of the gentlemen thus appointed were well known to be strongly prejudiced against Dr. Miller, from what they had been told, in private, of the affair; but after each party and his witnesses had been fully heard, the referees unanimously and fully acquitted Dr. Miller; and Dr. Mc-Knight expressed his entire conviction, that they could not, as conscientious men, have done otherwise. Subsequently, in the course of the day on which an attested copy of the decision was delivered to him, the latter 'called on Dr. Miller at his own house, took him by the hand, and expressed a 'desire, that all grounds of uneasiness between them might be, thenceforward, considered as buried and forgotten. On Dr. Miller's expressing a similar sentiment, they again formally shook hands, in testimony of a renewal of their friendship and intercourse. This took place on Saturday. On the following Monday, Dr. Miller returned the visit; when Dr. McKnight again took him by the hand, and received him with as much apparent cordiality as he had ever done.' It should be added, that the referees, while wholly exonerating Dr. Miller, declared that Dr. McKnight's suspicions, though mistaken, had not been unnatural, or unpardonable, considering the imperfect statements he had received, and all the circumstances of the case.

Dr. McKnight, however, under the influence, evidently of mischief-makers, calling themselves his friends, was induced, afterwards, to question the righteousness of the decision; and, undesignedly doubtless, put it in their power to bring the whole matter, as they subsequently did, before the public, in his absence. He seems never to have justified this proceeding, and by the action of Dr. Miller's friends it was promptly put to shame. The latter, to the end of his life, always spoke of Dr. McKnight as a truly honest and pious man, of excellent talents, a sound, orthodox divine, and one of the most instructive preachers he had ever heard; but always averred, that his colleague's suspicions and accusations in the case just mentioned had been wholly without ground, except in an excited imagination.

The decision of the arbitrators was not given until the 2d of June, but, meanwhile, the two congregations had, both separately and jointly, ratified the arrangements made by their officers; and on the 26th of April, Presbytery had consummated the business, by releasing Dr. McKnight, at his own request, from both charges, and dissolving Dr. Miller's connexion with the Brick church, that he might devote himself altogether to that in Wall street. The relations of Dr. Rodgers remained undisturbed, while Dr. Milledoler, according to the original stipulation with him, became sole pastor of the Rutger's street church.

The troubles which have been mentioned were themselves a strong argument against the collegiate arrangement, illustrating, as they did, the unhappy suspicions and jealousies which, not unnaturally, might influence associated pastors. Dr. Miller ever maintained, that the separation of the churches, notwithstanding these troubles, was a great blessing; and he was disposed to regard his efforts in the matter as the most important service which he ever rendered to the Presbyterian Church in New York.

CHAPTER EIGHTEENTH.

1809, 1810.

---

1. Ordination of Ruling Elders.

On the 10th of January, 1809, Dr. Miller, by invitation, ordained ruling elders at Powles Hook, now Jersey City. In regard to such ordinations, and this one in particular, he subsequently remarked,

"The fact, so far as I know, is indubitable, that from the commencement of the Reformation to this hour, in the Reformed Churches of Scotland, France, Holland, Geneva and Germany—all of which were Presbyterian—in short, throughout the whole Presbyterian world of Europe, the ordination of ruling elders by the imposition of hands has been altogether unknown. Upon the same plan our Formularies, as agreed upon by the Presbyterian Church in the United States, in 1788, proceeded. They made no provision for the use of this form in the ordination of this class of officers; nor was it ever introduced into our practice, until about twenty years after the adoption of her present system. Then the first specimen of it, in our, or, so far as he knows, in any Presbyterian Church, was given by the author of this Manual. In the year 1809, being called upon to constitute a new church, in a destitute settlement, he ordained the Elders with the imposition of hands. He was aware, that in our Church, there was no precedent for this proceeding; but so deep was his conviction that both scriptural principle and scriptural example called for this method of setting them apart, that he could no longer forbear to adopt it. He well remembers, indeed, the doubting look and the shaking head which he encountered, on the occasion, from some who considered themselves as peculiarly strict Presbyterians."[1] "Finding, however, that many of his brethren considered it an innovation, and were by no means prepared to introduce the practice; believing that diversity of practice in this matter would be very undesirable; and persuaded, moreover, that the act in question ought not to be deemed an essential in any ordination—he resolved not to repeat it, until it could be used without offence, and with better prospects of edification to the Church."[2] "Since that time, however, the practice has been gradually gaining ground, and seems now likely to obtain general prevalence in our Church."[3]

Dr. Miller's reasons for preferring this method of ordination in the case of ruling elders, were, to state them briefly, these two:—*First*, the rite of laying on hands, especially considering its use in the Church, was as appropriate in their case as in any other; and, *Secondly*, it seemed to be according to Bible example to ordain all strictly ecclesiastical officers in this way. If deacons were so ordained,[4] why not ruling elders?

On the 28th of May, upon ordaining elders in the Wall street church, Dr. Miller preached a sermon on the Eldership, which was published in 1811,[5] and many years afterwards, as we shall see, enlarged into a volume.

2. MISCELLANEOUS TOPICS.

With a review, for *The Panoplist*, of a sermon by Dr. Dwight, Dr. Miller wrote to Dr. Morse, on the 14th of February, 1809,

'The discourse is good—worthy of its author; but it might, it ought to have been better. In such a cause, a man ought to *write for his life*.

'* * I ought to apprize you, that, when I write for the press, I always write *currente calamo*, and depend on correction after the composition gets into type. This is wrong, but it is my

---

[1] Sermon on the Warrant, Nature, and Duties of the Office of the Ruling Elder, (1843,) Appendix, 115, etc.

[2] Essay on the Warrant, Nature, and Duties of the Office of the Ruling Elder, (1832,) 285, etc., n.

[3] Sermon, etc., etc., 117.

[4] Acts 6, 6.

[5] The Divine Appointment, the Duties and the Qualifications of Ruling Elders. A Sermon preached in the City of New York on the 28th of May, 1809. By Samuel Miller, D.D., one of the Pastors of the First Presbyterian Church in the City of New York.—Acts 14, 23.—8vo.

habit; and I hope you will not let the proof sheet of this pass unnoticed.

'If my heart does not deceive me, I most cordially rejoice to hear of the good prospects of your seminary, your Panoplist, and your new church in Boston. May the great Head of the Church continue to prosper and bless them, and bless all who are engaged in promoting them.

'You propose that Mr. Romeyn and myself should come under engagements, as stated contributors to the Panoplist. We cannot either of us possibly think of such a thing. If you knew the feebleness of my health, and the constant pressure of my avocations, you would almost think me mad to promise an occasional contribution. I hope, therefore, you will expect nothing from me, for at least twelve months to come.'

To Dr. Griffin, who had accepted a professorship at Andover, and also an invitation to preach statedly in the new Park street Church, he wrote on the 17th of March,

'It was with a mixture of sensations, which it would not be easy for me either to analyze or to express, that I received your last letter. I rejoice in everything that brings honor to my brother, and, in this view, was gratified to find, that the people of Andover and of Boston felt as if they could not do without you. But when I recollect that all this included your separation from us, and your departure to a distant region, it afflicted, as it continues to afflict me, to a degree that I cannot express. I believe you have decided as you ought—my judgment tells me you have. But, O my Brother, we want you here! and the thought of your going is too painful to be dwelt upon. But the great Head of the Church, I know, will direct all for the best.'

Again, on the 27th of May, he writes,

'I was in hopes I should see you before you left our neighborhood, but it seems I must give up this hope. Farewell, my beloved Brother! May as much honor and comfort, as will be for your good, be heaped upon you while you live! Above all, wherever you are, may the consolations of grace, and the most abundant success in winning souls to Christ, attend you! May the Captain of Salvation arm and strengthen you for the war, and bring you off, in every conflict, a conqueror and more than a conqueror!

'Again, farewell! Write to me as soon as you get settled, and have anything to say. Always recollect, that there lives not a brother in the ministry, who loves you more than myself;

and that I shall always feel a deep interest in everything that relates to you and yours. * *

'I am, dear Brother,

'Yours, inviolably,

'Rev'd Dr. Griffin.   Sam'l Miller.'

On the 6th of April, 1809, Dr. Miller was commissioned by Daniel D. Tompkins, governor of New York, as chaplain of the first regiment of the State artillery, an office which probably added little to his labors, and less to his revenues.

In this year the New York Bible Society was formed—one of the Pioneers of the American Bible Society. We find Dr. Miller actively assisting in its organization, for a time one of its Secretaries, afterward, a Vice-president, and then President.

The New York Historical Society was instituted the 10th of December, 1804, and incorporated the 10th of Febuary, 1809. Dr. Miller was one of its founders and original corporators, all the rest of whom he survived; also its Corresponding Secretary; and the earliest of its collections presents us with a discourse of his, as the first paper after those relating to the Society's formation.[1] As long as he resided in New York he took an active part in its proceedings, and never lost his interest in its welfare. Of the Massachusetts Historical Society, an earlier kindred organization, he was a corresponding member.

The following letter to Dr. Green explains itself:—

'Rev'd and dear Sir,   New York, September 6th, 1809.

I am happy in the opportunity of introducing to your acquaintance the Rev'd President Atwater, lately of Middlebury College, and now on his way to take charge of Carlisle.

'It gives me particular pleasure to find, that President At, water entirely coincides with you and me on the importance of restoring the old puritanical discipline in colleges; and that he estimate the importance of colleges by the degree in which they subserve the interests of the Church. I take for granted that the moment this is known, he will receive the decided countenance and aid of the friends of religion in your state. That he

---

[1] "A Discourse designed to Commemorate the Discovery of New York by Henry Hudson; delivered before the New York Historical Society, September 4th, 1809; being the completion of the Second Century since that event. By Samuel Miller D.D., One of the Pastors of the First Presbyterian Church in the City of New York, and Member of the Historical Society."—8vo. Pp.28.

will have yours, I have ventured to assure him.   The high
character of this gentleman you are already acquainted with.

        'I am, dear Sir,
           'Cordially and affectionately yours,
                    'Sam'l Miller.'

The following letter, was written on the 30th of October,
1809.

'My answer shall be short.   I feel deeply for the establishment and welfare of the church in Boston, and need no arguments to convince me that it is one of the most important and
interesting establishments in the United States, or the world.
But I cannot leave New York, under present circumstances, to
go and take charge of it.   The state of the Presbyterian Church
in New York, generally, and that of my own congregation in
particular; my engagements some time since virtually made
with the latter; the apprehended danger from a change of climate ;—these and several other considerations weigh so heavily
on my mind, that I can recollect no case in which the path of
duty has appeared more clear to me.   And this is the decided
opinion of all, without exception, whom I have consulted (con-
fidentially) on the subject.   Notwithstanding what your friends
say, I do not believe I should enjoy my health in Boston.   But
even if I had no doubts on this point, the ties which bind me
to my present station are such, as, I am convinced, it is not my
duty to break.

'My dear Brother, it would give me more pleasure than I
can express, to spend the remainder of my days near you.
And I ought to be able to say—I trust I can say—that it
would give me still greater pleasure to be made an instrument
of bringing glory to the Redeemer's cause in Boston.   But, until God, in his Providence, shall give me an entirely different
view of the subject from what I now have, I *dare not stir*.   I
speak with perfect frankness, and hope you will receive this as
my final answer.'

'Mr. Codman[1] has been with us two Sabbaths.   We are
very much pleased with him.   For my part, I have not seen a
man, for a long time, whom I more highly esteem or more
heartily love.   I bless God that such a man is near Boston.   I
wish he were in it.

'My family has been out of town during the summer and beginning of autumn.   We have just returned, and are in pretty
good health.   The religious aspect of our city is much as it has
been for a year.   Dr. Romeyn still continues very popular and

[1] See 2 Sprague's Annals, 492, and Memoir and Reminiscences of Dr. Codman,
by Dr. William Allen and Dr. Johusa Bates.

very useful. His church members are rapidly becoming more numerous. *   *

  'I am, my beloved Brother,
   'Your affectionate and devoted
'Rev. Dr. Griffin.   Sam'l Miller.'

To Dr. Green, on the 15th of November, Dr. Miller sends his felicitations :—

'I have been intending, for several weeks past, to address a congratulatory letter to you and Mrs. Green on your late marriage; and have been prevented by nothing but incessant hurry. I embrace this opportunity of tendering to you my cordial felicitations, in which Mrs. Miller affectionately joins. There are few persons in whose welfare we feel a deeper interest than in that of yourself and Mrs. Green. And to find you bearing to each other the relation which you have lately formed, is certainly not calculated to diminish our interest. May that blessing, which maketh rich and addeth no sorrow with it, rest on you and yours!

'You must know that about twenty-four hours after the news of your marriage had reached New-York, (which it was not very tardy in doing,) Mrs. M. and our sister, Miss Sergeant, both dreamed, on the same night, that you and Mrs. Green had just arrived on a visit to us. When we met, next morning at breakfast, (which you know has been the invariable dream-disclosing occasion, time immemorial,) each told her dream, and our conclusion immediately was that you would soon be here. To our mortification, however, we find, so far, that the old-fashioned rule of interpreting dreams must still stand good. If you could make out to set this rule aside, for once, and let us see you and Mrs. Green before the winter sets in, you would give us more pleasure than I can well express.

  'I am, Rev'd and dear Sir,
   'Respectfully and affectionately yours,
'Rev'd Dr. Green.   Sam'l Miller.'

3. EPISCOPAL CONTROVERSY.

In December, 1809—nearly two years and a half after the appearance of his first volume of Letters on the Christian Ministry, Dr. Miller published, in a second volume, "A Continuation" of those letters.[1] This work, as the

---

[1] "A Continuation of Letters concerning the Constitution and Order of the Christian Ministry; addressed to the Members of the Presbyterian Churches in the City of New York. Being an Examination of the Strictures of the Rev. Drs. Bowden and Kemp, and the Rev. Mr. How, on the former Series. By Samuel Miller, D.D., one of the Pastors of the First Presbyterian Church in the said City. 1809."—12 mo. Pp. 428.

continuation of a controversy to which his opponents had chosen to give the character very much of a personal contest, was, of necessity, somewhat different from the former one. It had to deal, not only with certain opinions, but also with men who had fairly subjected themselves to criticism in advocating those opinions, in a variety of appeals to popular prejudice, and by systematic personalities which were, to say the least, no evidence of the strength of their cause. An examination, however, of this volume, from which extracts have already been given, will show that Dr. Miller preserved, throughout the controversy, the general manner and spirit by which his entrance upon it had been characterized. It was a very significant fact, that his opponents, with all their diligence and zeal, could find so little even to allege against him in point of temper and courtesy, that they were driven, as we have seen, to pronounce his "moderation," and "kindness" affected and insidious; nay, only a "mask" to cover the pride, passion and bitterness, which they pretended to discern in his heart.

To the *Continuation* of Dr. Miller's Letters, Dr. Bowden replied in a single volume, published in 1811. Here the formal controversy between these opponents ended. It has been spoken of at some length, because of the important influence which it exerted on Dr. Miller's reputation and subsequent labors. Whatever may have been the real damage which he did to the extravagant claims of ultra prelatists, certain it is that they treated him, thereafter, his life long, as a most formidable adversary. Not content with attempting to answer his arguments, they thought it necessary to reiterate, from year to year, from mouth to mouth, and from pen to pen, that he was a garbler of quotations, and, particularly, in his treatment of their patron saint, Ignatius, had borne a double face. Again and again these allegations, which will be mentioned more particularly hereafter, were shown to be baseless; but it was easy to repeat, without verifying them; and their frequent repetition seems to have been relied upon much more than legitimate argument, to support the Episcopal cause. Another doubtful expedient of these controversialists has been that of mutual laudation. To meet and vanquish an antagonist was not so easy as to tell how triumphantly some one else had already done it. Of this sort of strategy, and of even the still more masterly method of self-laudation, high example was given, and was not hesitatingly followed.

4. THEOLOGICAL SEMINARY.

In May, 1809, the General Assembly received an overture from the Presbytery of Philadelphia for the establishment of a theological school. This overture was referred to a select committee, and, upon their report, the Assembly resolved to submit to the Presbyteries the question, whether *one* great school should be established, in a central location, for the whole Church; or *two*, in such places as best to accommodate both the North and the South; or a school for each of the Synods, of which there were at this time, *seven*. We find Dr. Miller writing still on this subject to Dr. Green.

'My dear Friend,   New York, January 16, 1810.
          'As the object of this letter is single, and as I have not time for a long introduction, I plunge at once into the business.

'Our presbytery will certainly, and, I hope, *unanimously*, offer an opinion to the next general assembly, in favor of a *single* theological school, on a large and liberal plan, in preference to two or more. But I am much afraid that a large majority of the presbyteries will be of a different opinion, and will address the general assembly accordingly; in which case, I suppose, the assembly will consider itself as bound to adopt the plan which a majority recommend.

'I am of opinion, that measures ought to be taken to produce a different result; and that, for this purpose, a pamphlet, of a single sheet, ought to be written stating strongly and clearly the arguments in favor of a single school; that it ought to be written immediately; that it should be anonymous; and that a copy of it should be sent by mail, as soon as possible, to every Presbyterian minister in the United States.

'If I do not deceive myself, you also are in favour of a single school. I am not certain whether this impression has been produced by hearing you say so; or by my knowing, in general, that you are a man of sense. At any rate, I am well persuaded that such ought to be your opinion. And I earnestly hope, that you will undertake to write the pamphlet in question; and that you will do it without loss of time.

'I think that the theological school which shall be instituted ought to be furnished with at least three professors; and that at least one of these ought to be selected from the South or West, in order to conciliate those portions of our church. Such a school would be, in all probability, of incalculable advantage in promoting the union, extension, and energy of our church; whereas two or more schools, I verily think, by dividing and distracting it, would place us in circumstances less eligible than we are at present. I had much rather have none established, for a year or two, than several.

'As for the place of this school, I have no predilections—no anxieties. Feeling myself totally unqualified to take any part in such a seminary, I really feel as if it were a matter indifferent to me where it may be located—within ten miles of me, or five hundred from me.

'I beseech you to undertake to write such a pamphlet as I have suggested. I think it will do good. And unless some measures are taken to secure a majority on the right side, I fear we shall have a sad spot of work.

'Perhaps you will say, "Let A., B., or C. write it." But really I know of no one except yourself who can. My health is so feeble, and my avocations are so numerous, that I cannot undertake it. Dr. Romeyn is quite as unfavorably situated as myself—perhaps more so. We all say, "Dr. Green is the very man!" Pray inform me, by the next mail, that you have set the printer at work.'

In answering this letter, Dr. Green seems to have asked for suggestions as to the matter of the proposed pamphlet; and, on the 23d of January, Dr. Miller replied at some length, giving arguments in favor of a single divinity school. A report, however, which he drew for his presbytery, followed by a few extracts only from the reply to Dr. Green, will present, most favorably, the whole subject. Dr. Romeyn was his active coadjutor in these efforts.

'The Presbytery of New York, after maturely deliberating on the overture respecting THEOLOGICAL SCHOOLS, sent down by the last General Assembly to the several Presbyteries, are decidedly of the opinion, that, of the three modes proposed in that overture, the *first*; viz., the establishment of *One* Great School, ought to be preferred for the following reasons:—

'1. The whole strength and resources of the Church, in this case, would be directed to a single point; and might, of course, be made to operate with more convenience and effect.

'2. By having all the theological students collected in one Seminary, it would be easier for the different parts of the Church to perceive, at a single view, the number and character of the youth destined for the ministry, and to be excited to exertion for increasing their number, than if their attention were divided between a number of seminaries. The Presbytery are deeply persuaded that one of the principal reasons why our churches are not more impressed and alarmed with the scarcity of ministers and of candidates for the ministry is, that those ministers and candidates, being scattered within the bounds of near *forty presbyteries*, are supposed to be much more numerous than they really are.

'3. By devoting all the strength and resources of the Church to a single school, it would be furnished with larger funds, with a more ample library, with a greater number of professors, and, of course, with a more extensive and complete *system of education*, than could be expected, or, indeed, would be possible, if a number of schools were established. The Presbytery are persuaded that no single professor, however great his talents and learning, and however unremitting his diligence, can possibly conduct, with any degree of efficiency and justice, the whole studies of a large class of theological students.

'4. The adoption of the plan of a single school would tend, in the opinion of the Presbytery, more than any other, to promote the *unity* and *peace* of the Church. The youth educated on this plan would be more likely to be united in the same views of evangelical truth and order, than they would if educated at different seminaries. In this case also, the great body of our ministers would be personally acquainted with each other; early and intimate friendships would be formed between them; and in addition to the higher and more important motive of promoting the interest of the Redeemer's kingdom, they would be prompted, by a desire of seeing and conversing with each other, to come together in the higher judicatories of the Church. The Presbytery cannot help believing that to this source we might look, under the smiles of Providence, for a growing diligence and punctuality in our delegation in attending on the General Assembly, that most important bond of union and harmony in our ecclesiastical system.

'With respect to the disadvantages attending the plan of a single school, the Presbytery cannot believe that they bear any proportion to the great and manifest advantages which forcibly recommend it. The inconvenience, arising from the distance of the position of a single school from the extremes of the Presbyterian bounds, would be much more than compensated by the superiority of the plan of education; by the more ample means of improvement, and by the probable provision, an this case, for the cheap, if not gratuitous, education of such is might not possess adequate means themselves.

'In case the *first plan*, or the erection of a *single school*, cannot be carried, the Presbytery would then express an opinion in favour of the *second plan*, or the establishment of *two schools*, in such convenient stations as might be selected.

'And, finally, rather than have a theological seminary established in each Synod, the Presbytery have no hesitation in declaring, that they would, on the whole, prefer leaving the education of candidates for the gospel ministry on its present footing; and are persuaded that the respectability, the comfort, and the unity of the Church would be more promoted by remaining as we are, than by a system so calculated to divide our strength, and distract our counsels, as the erection of a number of independent seminaries.'

In the letter mentioned, the following sentences occur:—

'Our church being scattered over so large a tract of country; embracing people of so many different classes and habits; but a small portion of the ministers being acquainted with each other, and even these seldom coming together; and a variety of sentiments and practices prevailing, with respect to Psalmody, Church Government, Sealing Ordinances, etc.; I verily think, unless something be done to counteract these evils, the harmony, the comfort, the respectability, and even the extent of the Church must, before long, be very seriously diminished. The establishment of several schools will, obviously, have a direct tendency to increase and perpetuate all these evils.'

'[In case a single school is established,] the different habits and feelings at present existing, in different parts of our country, can be consulted, by selecting professors from such different portions of the Church, as will render them, strictly speaking, representatives of the whole.'

'Allow me to add, that, in attempting to make an impression on our Southern brethren, great care ought to be taken to write in such a strain, as to convince them that our great object is to make, not merely a learned ministry, but a fervently pious one, and one favorable to revivals of religion.

'Upon my shewing the above to Dr. Romeyn, he observed, after attentively reading it, that he had only one additional idea to propose, which was, that if there were a number of schools, each professor, feeling himself the centre of a little world, would be tempted to endeavor to extend his fame, by broaching new opinions, and attaching his name to some new *sub-sect*, if the expression may be allowed.   *   *'

Dr. Griffin, after a short term of service at Andover, was called to the Park street Church in Boston, in which he had labored, already, to some extent as a supply.   We find Dr. Miller writing to him on the 6th of March, 1810,

'The call, I think, must come through the Presbytery of Jersey, unless you previously take a dismission.   But it may be sent on by mail as well as by a commissioner.   If, after accepting the call, you should still remain a member of that Presbytery, then I think the installation must be performed by a committee of Presbytery.   At any rate, I feel confident, that this is the only regular way of proceeding.   If you take a dismission, either before or immediately after the presentation of the call, the installation may be performed by a council.   Otherwise, I think this cannot be done, unless the Presbytery agree, in a special case, to dispense with their rules.

'With respect to my preaching the installation sermon, I will, undoubtedly, God willing, comply with your wishes, if the business can be so arranged as to admit of it.   My opinion, indeed, is, that collecting an installation council from three or four distant States will savour a little of the ostentatious, and may be considered as liable to objection on that account.   But if, after taking this and every other matter into mature consideration, you and the church should still wish me to attend, and perform that service, I shall consider it as an honor to have an opportunity of serving a brother, whom I highly love and revere, and of contributing my mite towards the promotion of a cause, which, unless my heart deceives me, I cordially love.'

When the General Assembly of 1810 met in Philadelphia, on the 17th of May, the reports of the several presbyteries, in relation to a theological school, were put into the hands of a committee of five, of which Dr. Miller was chairman, for examination.   Ten presbyteries had pronounced in favor of a single school, ten in favor of a school in each synod, one only in favor of two schools; while six had declared it not expedient to attempt, as yet, the establishment of any school, and nine had sent no reports. These bare facts, certainly not encouraging, were at first simply announced; but the same committee, with the addition of two members, were immediately instructed to consider the subject, and report, "whether in their opinion any thing, and if any thing, what, was proper further to be done."   It was a critical moment for this the greatest enterprise of the Presbyterian Church since its establishment in America; but a happy presentation of the case by the committee won the Assembly to immediate and decisive measures. The second report suggested, in substance, that a clear majority of all the presbyteries favored the establishment of one or more seminaries; that the objections made to a single great institution were several of them founded entirely in misconception, some supposing they would be absolutely bound to send all their candidates to the one school if it were established, and others that the theological professors would be empowered to confer licensure—things never for a moment contemplated; that, upon the whole, therefore, the plan for a single seminary appeared to have "the greatest share of public sentiment in its favor"; and that a second reference to the presbyteries, or any farther delay, was likely to result in serious inconvenience and evil. On these grounds the committee recommended, and the Assembly determined, that a seminary should be at once established. The result, however, was evidently due in this, as in many a case, not to the awakened interest and conviction of the Church at large, but to the enlightened and enterprising spirit of a few adventurous individuals; and hence the difficulty experienced afterwards in raising the funds requisite for so great an undertaking.

A committee[1] was appointed "to digest and prepare a plan," "embracing in detail the fundamental principles of the institution, together with regulations for guiding the conduct of the instructors and the students, and prescribing the best mode of visiting, of controlling, and supporting the whole system"; and to report to the next General Assembly. Several persons, moreover, were named, in each Synod,[2] as "agents, to solicit donations, in the course of the current year, within the bounds of their respective synods." A pastoral letter upon the subject was also addressed to the churches. To prepare this, Dr. Miller and the Rev. James Richards were appointed; it seems to have been penned by the former as chairman; and it was issued in connexion with the report and resolutions previously adopted.[3]

[1] "The Rev. Drs. Green, Woodhull, Romeyn, and Miller, and the Rev. Messrs. Archibald Alexander, James Richards, and Amzi Armstrong."

[2] The agents for the Synod of New York and New Jersey were the "Rev. Drs. Samuel Miller, Philip Milledoler, John B. Romeyn, and Aaron Woolworth, the Rev. Messrs. James Richards, Comfort, and Isaac Vandoren, and Col. Henry Rutgers."

[3] See Bair'"- Digest, (1856,) 406, etc.

As Dr. Miller's family grew up around him, it became a necessity for their health and comfort, that they should spend some weeks or months in the country during the heat of summer, The frequently recurring visits of yellow fever made, of course, a summer retreat all the more imperative. Staten Island, Harlem and other places seem to have been resorted to, successively, until the warm heart and watchful solicitude of Doctor Edward Miller prompted him to purchase a piece of ground at Bloomingdale, and erect upon it a stone dwelling of moderate dimensions which he put, almost unreservedly, at his brother's disposal. In this dwelling, yet unfinished, the latter, with his family, spent the "heated term" first in 1810. Subsequently, until his removal to Princeton, it was their constant and delightful residence for the hot months. Dr. Miller speaks of it as 'seven miles from the scene of his parochial labors.' Ample verandahs, and an unpartitioned attic gave the freest exercise for all, especially the children, even when they could not range over the grounds: the considerate brother and uncle had planned everything with a physician's eye to the promotion of vigorous health. This house, if it were now standing, would face the New York Central Park, being separated from it by only the width of the Street. It was torn down but a few years ago.

From his summer retreat, Dr. Miller wrote to Dr. Green as follows :—

'Rev'd and dear Sir,   Bloomingdale, September 4, 1810.

'I am sorry—very sorry—to have "vexed" you. But, really, you must not be unreasonable. Consider that it is ONLY *two months* since the receipt of the letter which you complain has not been so promptly answered as it ought to have been. Now, if you had but known how much longer I keep many of my correspondents without an answer, I am confident you would not have thought so strange of me. But, to be serious—the removal of my family to this place, instead of giving me more leisure than usual, rather diminishes it; so that I am obliged to neglect every kind of business that is not immediately urgent; and sometimes, no doubt, make an improper estimate of what ought to be so considered. In the present case, I really supposed that you stood so little in need of any communication from me on the subject concerning which you wrote, that I was the more ready to put off writing from time to time, taking for granted, that, whether I put pen to paper or not, everything would be done as it ought to be. * *

'I read the whole of your letter of July 4th and 6th to Dr. Romeyn. He appeared to think favorably of the plan of an academical school in each synod. I am also, on the whole, in favor of it. But my sole reason for being so is precisely that which you mention; viz., that it would probably "add to the popularity of our plan, by giving each synod a direct connexion with it." I think you may very safely, and with great propriety, add that item to your sketch. The only doubt I have is, whether provision for an academical course, at the theological school, ought to be made at the *same time* at which academical schools are established in each synod. I am inclined, however, to answer this question in the affirmative, under the impression, that in process of time, it will be found expedient, if not necessary, to have the academical, as well as every other part of the course, passed through at one great, central school; and the sooner provision is made for it the better.

'* * My brethren, as well as myself, view this business of the Seminary as the most important in which we were ever engaged, and are determined to act with vigor.'

5. NEW WALL STREET CHURCH.

One of the first fruits of the new spirit which the severance of collegiate ties infused into the separated congregations, was the enterprize of erecting, for the Wall street church, a better edifice. " In the beginning of the winter of 1809 and 1810," says Dr. Miller, " the congregation worshipping in *Wall* street, determined to take down their house of worship, which had become too old and tottering to be any longer occupied with safety, and to erect a new one on the same site. The requisite preliminary measures having been taken, the corner stone of the new building was laid on the 21st of March, 1810. On this interesting occasion, Doctor *Rodgers* attended, bending under the weight of years. It had been the earnest wish of many, that in commencing the rebuilding of the original church, to which he had first borne the pastoral relation, and which was surrounded with the sepulchres of those who had called and welcomed him to the city, he should lay the first stone. His infirmities, however, rendered this impossible. It was laid by the writer of the present volume; his venerable colleague being only able to favor the solemnity with his presence and his benediction.

"While the edifice thus commenced was erecting, or rather [beginning] more than three months before the erection of it was begun, the congregation worshipped in the French Episcopal church, *Du St. Esprit*, in Pine street, which, on application, was politely and liberally granted by the vestry for their use. That place of worship was occupied by the Presbyterian congregation from the 1st day of December, 1809, till the 11th day of August, 1811, on the latter of which days, the new edifice in *Wall* street was opened for the Worship of God."[1]

6. Settlement of the Rev. Gardiner Spring.

By the resignation of Dr. McKnight, Dr. Rodgers having been left sole pastor of the Brick Church, it became necessary, at once, to obtain for him a colleague. On the 8th of August, 1810, the Rev. Gardiner Spring, who had been unanimously called to this relation, was ordained to the gospel ministry and installed collegiate pastor. Dr. Milledoler preached, Dr. Romeyn delivered the charge to the people, Dr. Miller presided, made the introductory address, and gave the charge to the pastor. These several discourses were published together.[2] In the charge Dr. Miller said,

"It is none of the least of these, [advantages,] that you are associated in your pastoral charge with an aged and venerable servant of Christ, who has had long experience in the ministry, and whose praise is in all the churches. And, although he is too far advanced in life to admit of the hope that he will diminish your burden by taking an active part with you in public labour; yet, we trust, you will be not a little profited by his fervent prayers, by his paternal counsels, and by the lustre of his long and exemplary life. And when he shall ascend to his Father and our Father, to his God and our God, may the mantle of *Elijah* fall upon *Elisha*, and leave no room to say, *Where is the Lord God of Elijah?*"

Of the congregation he remarked,

"I am persuaded you will find them a harmonious, an affec-

---

[1] Memoirs of Dr. Rodgers, 274, 5, 6.

[2] Dr. Miller's portion of the publication is entitled, "The Address Introductory to the Ordination Service, and the Charge to the Minister. By Samuel Miller, D.D., one of the Pastors of the First Presbyterian Church in the City of New York."—8vo. Pp. 20.

tionate, a kind, and an indulgent people. The tenderness with which they received and treated me, when I came to them an inexperienced youth; the liberality with which they ministered to my comfort; and the more than kind forbearance which they manifested toward the numerous infirmities and defects of my ministry, it were unseasonable to attempt, on the present occasion, to acknowledge; but they will never cease to impress me with gratitude, while I have a memory to recollect, or a heart to feel. Nor can I forbear to felicitate a Brother on being brought into the same interesting relation. * *"[1]

Of the minister's duties he said,

"In preaching the gospel, and in all your ministrations, whether public or private, set the Lord Jesus Christ himself before you, and next to him, his inspired apostles, as your models. Be not afraid to tell men, with all plainness, of their total depravity by nature, and of that state of condemnation and wrath under which they lie while strangers to the grace of Christ. Be not afraid to sound in their ears the thunders of *Sinai*, as well as *the still small voice of Calvary*. Be not backward to proclaim the humbling and self-denying, but most glorious, doctrines of free and sovereign grace, however unpalatable they may be to some, or whatever your fidelity may cost you. Warn men boldly of every danger. Strive to bring them off from every false foundation. Give them no rest till they are brought humbled and trembling to the foot of the Cross: and then, and not till then, pour into their bleeding wounds the oil of consolation, the balm of heavenly grace."[2]

"You are now invested with the power of ordaining others to the holy office to which you have been yourself set apart. This power ever has been, and ever will be, one of the most important that can be committed to a minister of Christ. But there are periods in which it is especially important. Such a period is that in which we live. *The harvest truly is great, but the laborers are few.* The call for more laborers was never so loud or so urgent as at the present hour. Under these circumstances, there is danger of so far yielding to public and private importunity, as to thrust forth unqualified laborers into the harvest. Let your personal exertions and your official acts be steadily directed against this error. For an error it *is*, to imagine that we really serve the Church of Christ, under *any* circumstances, by giving her unqualified ministers. *Lay hands suddenly on no man; neither be thou partaker of other men's sins: keep thyself pure.*"[3]

[1] Pp. 28, 29. [2] Pp. 32, 33. [3] Pp. 34, 35.

25

In a note to this last extract, the author says, "*Presbyterians* seldom or never ordain a minister *by the laying on of the hands of the Presbytery*, without charging their newly admitted brother, among other things, to be cautious how, *as a member of Presbytery*, he exercises, in his turn, the ordaining power with which he is invested. They generally repeat, as is done above, the very words of the Apostle addressed to *Timothy*." It may not be wholly superfluous, to remind our modern presbyters of this habit of their fathers.

Mr. Spring, when called to the pastoral charge of the Brick Church, was a Hopkinsian, of a moderate school. In a late publication he makes the following statement in regard to Dr. Miller.

"—— My trial sermon was a frank avowal of my sentiments, and a bold and unequivocal statement of the views I THEN entertained upon the subject of human ability. It was this that embarrassed the Presbytery; and but for the strenuous efforts of the late Dr. Miller, who told the Presbytery that if they condemned *Mr. Spring* for those views, they must condemn *him*, so far as I could learn, they would have refused to ordain me."[1]

What exactly Dr. Miller meant by this remark, it may not be easy to determine; but he certainly did not mean, that he adopted the Hopkinsian view of human ability, which he never did adopt. To the distinction between natural and moral ability, as maintained by Dr. Twisse, and subsequent Calvinistic divines, or even as insisted upon by President Edwards, who made more of it than any of his predecessors,[2] he may have had no objection; the phraseology of this distinction he may have adopted, as conveniently expressing the obvious truth, that the possession of certain natural powers, as reason and conscience, was essential to responsibility; but he did not hold, with Dr. Emmons, that fallen men "can love God, repent of sin, believe in Christ, and perform every religious duty, as well as they can think, or speak, or walk;"[3] nor, with a writer in the Massachusetts Missionary Magazine, that "impenitent sinners are as really possessed of strength or capacity to love and serve God as saints:" that "their power or capacity to obey the divine commands is as great as to disobey them."[4]

---

[1] Reminiscences, 102, 103.

[2] See Dr. Alexander's article on "The Inability of Sinners," in the Biblical Repertory for 1831. 1 Princeton Theological Essays, 266.

[3] Sermons (1800), 246.   [4] 3 Vol., 415.

Dr. Spring has also said,

"The distinguished individuals to whom I was under the greatest obligations, so long as they remained members of the Presbytery, were the Rev. Dr. Miller and the Rev. Dr. Perrine, both of whom filled the office of Professor of Church History and Government in our theological seminaries, and died full of years and full of honours. Their uniform friendship, their kind and gentleman-like deportment toward me, their wise counsels, their active assistance in my arduous work, the interest they took in my usefulness, and the influence they exerted in my favour in seasons of solicitude, conflict and depression, demand from me this public and grateful acknowledgment."[1]

7. EXCHANGES WITH UNITARIANS.

The Unitarian controversy, although at that early day confined, on this side of the Atlantic, chiefly to New England, deeply interested men of evangelical sentiments all over the land. The appointment of Dr. Ware to the divinity chair of Harvard, in 1805, produced violent agitation, and awakened among the Orthodox a new spirit of resistance. Andover Seminary, as we have seen, was one of the more immediate results. The question of exchanging pulpits with clergymen of heretical opinions, easy of solution as it now seems, then greatly perplexed many good men, and was discussed most warmly in every part of New England where Unitarianism had raised its head. Mr. John Codman,[2] settled in the Second Church in Dorchester, in 1808, was one of the faithful few who resolutely set themselves against ministerial exchanges with those who preached "another gospel"; and the conflict which arose in that congregation, and threatened at first his removal, but resulted in his maintaining his ground, though not without a division of the parish, in 1812, was one of the most important parts of the great struggle. Dr. Miller entertained towards Mr. Codman an affectionate regard which lasted their lives long. On this subject of ministerial exchanges, he wrote to the latter, during his troubles, a long letter of encouragement, dated the 19th of November, 1810, which was published, afterwards, in the Pano-

---

[1] The Old and the New Church. By Dr. Spring. 1856. P. 12.
[2] D D., from 1822. See p. 277, Note.

plist, and also may be found in Dr. Allen's Memoir of Dr. Codman.[1] Two paragraphs will be sufficient here to exhibit the spirit of the whole.

"Exchanging with ministers of known or suspected heterodoxy appears to me inconsistent with fidelity to our Master in heaven. With the principles which we hold, we should not dare to preach to our people a *false Gospel.* We should consider ourselves, in this case, as falling under the awful denunciation of the Apostle, Gal. i. 9 : "If any man preach any other Gospel unto you than that ye have received, let him be accursed." But if we dare not preach another Gospel ourselves, can we be innocently accessory to this sin's being committed by others? And is not deliberately sending a man into our pulpits, whom we suspect and more than suspect of heresy, fundamental heresy, something very like being accessory to the propagation of that heresy? It is by no means a sufficient answer to this argument to say, that the persons thus sent to our pulpits may not openly preach their peculiar sentiments. Even if the *fact* were so, it by no means relieves the difficulty; because the very circumstance of our people's seeing us receive a heretic and practically bid him God-speed, will tend exceedingly to diminish their abhorrence of his heresy, and to make them suppose, either that we consider it to be a very small evil, or that we are very inconsistent if not dishonest men. But the *fact* is not commonly so. These men generally preach in such a way, that attentive hearers may readily perceive that they reject every fundamental article of evangelical truth. They are not only betrayed by their omissions, but also, at every turn, by their phraseology and by their theological language; so that, in fact, they seldom enter our pulpits without holding out to our people false grounds of hope. And is this a small evil? I must conclude that the minister, who views it in this light, has not well considered the subject.

"But solemn as this consideration is, there is another, which appears to me in every respect equally solemn. It is the tendency of the system of exchanging with heterodox ministers, to banish the peculiar doctrines of the Gospel from our own sermons and our own pulpits. I assume, as the basis of this argument, that preaching the peculiar doctrines of the Gospel in a plain, pointed and pungent manner, is the duty of every Christian minister; and that, without this, he cannot expect the divine blessing on his labors, or hope to see real religion flourishing among the people of his charge. I verily believe, that if an orthodox minister could, in conscience, leave out of his

[1] Pp. 100–107.

sermons all the peculiar and fundamental doctrines of the Gospel; if, without preaching any thing contrary to them, he were silent respecting the total depravity of our nature, regeneration, the divinity and atonement of Christ, etc., etc.; or if, to put the case in the most favorable light, he sometimes advanced those doctrines, but always did it in a *concealed, wrapped up* manner;—I verily believe, that by pursuing this course for twenty years, he would banish religion from his church, and prepare his people for becoming Arminians, Arians, Socinians, Deists, or any thing that the advocates of error might wish and endeavor to make them. If I wished to banish religion from my church in the most effectual manner, I certainly should not come forward openly and preach heresy. This would excite attention, inquiry and opposition. But I would endeavor to lull my people asleep by simply withholding the truth; and should expect to succeed, by this method, with the least trouble and in the shortest time possible. Now this negligent, spiritless, smooth kind of preaching is precisely that which frequent exchanges with the herterodox is calculated to produce. The most pious and faithful ‚minister living, when he goes to the pulpit of a heretical brother, is under the strongest temptation, if not absolutely to *keep back* truth which he supposes would be offensive, at least in a considerable degree to soften and polish it down, that it may be received with as little irritation as possible. Accordingly, he will be apt to take with him to such a place a discourse prepared upon this plan. If his exchanges be frequent, he will often prepare such discourses. If they become habitual, he will habitually preach such. The consequence is as evident, as it is dreadful. To expect that a man, who prepares *many* such sermons, will preach none of them to his own people, is an expectation not to be entertained. And to hope that the mind of that man, who preaches frequently in this strain, will suffer no diminution either of evangelical zeal or of ministerial faithfulness, is certainly an unreasonable hope. I think there can be no doubt, that the Apostle Paul, with all the ardor of his zeal for the truth, and with all the tenderness of his love to the souls of men, could not, without a miracle, have withstood the influence of such a habit; and that, if he had indulged in it for one or two years, he would have been found, at the end of that time, a less pointed, a less faithful, and a less successful preacher, than before."

The following extracts from letters of Dr. Miller's to Dr. Wm. B. Sprague, dated the 27th of June, and 31st of October, 1838, and relating also to the Unitarian defection and the decline of Orthodoxy, in Boston, afford a further illustration of the subject.

'There were two sources of the evil which you undertake cursorily to account for, which appear to me to deserve more particular consideration than you have given them. The one is the regular system of *exchanges of pulpits*, which, for a long time, pervaded the Boston churches. When I was first acquainted with that city, which is now nearly half a century ago, this system of exchanges was stated and uniform. No man was expected to be found in his own pulpit on Sabbath morning. And as there was known to be great diversity of creed among the ministers of the city, and as every sermon that a pastor wrote was expected to be preached in all the pulpits in town, as well as in his own, each got into the habit of writing on such *a general plan as would give offence to none.* Hence, those who believed the peculiar doctrines of the gospel, seldom brought them forward with any prominence or point; and those who did not, of course, whenever they came near such doctrines, wrapped up the discussion in general and inoffensive terms. The consequence was, that the most precious and peculiar doctrines of the gospel were seldom, from about 1756 or 1760, preached by anybody—i. e. after the decease of Drs. Sewall, Prince, Foxcroft, Webb, etc. Soon after that race of ministers passed away, the war came on; the order of society was deranged; general laxity increased; and it so happened that some of the most erroneous ministers were high Whigs, and greatly popular; and, of course, well adapted to secure a ready reception for their errors. Only let any set of pastors in the world forbear, for fifteen or twenty years, to preach the peculiar doctrines of the gospel, and the way will be prepared, at the end of that time, to receive any sentiments which artful and popular men may be disposed to recommend.

'Another source of the mischief was this:—In the early periods of the administration of our Puritan fathers, there was a close connection between the church and the state. All the conspicuous leaders in civil society were church-members. Nobody was thought of for any important civil station, but a professor of religion. As vital piety declined, while the leading men wished still to be professors of religion, without which they could scarcely expect the popular suffrage; they felt that they could not make a profession, excepting on some more lax and indulgent system than that which was taught by the Puritan fathers. Calvinism, its consequences, and its discipline were thought too strict, and a more indulgent system was sought in its place. The evil to which this led may easily be imagined.'

'The pernicious system of exchanges was broken up, if my impression is right, by Dr. Griffin, Dr. Codman, and Mr. Huntington of the Old South.'

This Old South Church of Boston, with which in Dr. Miller's mind were connected so many precious memories of his father and grandparents, was the only Congregational church, in that city, which was not carried away into Unitarianism; and it may be regarded therefore as the mother of all the churches of its own denomination which have since sprung up there, turning the tide so strongly in favor of orthodoxy. Dr. Miller has accounted for the defection of the rest: the *New England Puritan* gives as one reason for the Old South's steadfastness, that, in her early history, she not only adopted the Cambridge Platform, but required each of her pastors to subscribe it, as one of the conditions of his settlement; and received no one to membership who opposed anything in the Platform.[1] This fact is certainly deserving of serious consideration.

Dr. Miller's diary here presents the following renewal of his self dedication.

'This 22d day of November, A.D. 1810, I do solemnly and renewedly devote myself to the service of Christ. I have, heretofore, made many vows, and formed many resolutions; but, alas! how have I violated them, and departed from the best of masters! I desire, this day, to acknowledge my corruptions, deviations, and short-comings; to mourn over my sins; and to make new vows. Lord, I AM—I WILL BE thine—entirely thine. Accept of me! Enable me to live and act as becometh a child of thy grace: Help me, Oh, help me, to mortify every principle, and every disposition that is opposed to thy will, and to be entirely and forever devoted to thee! Enlighten, animate, guide, and preserve me! May the life that I live in the flesh be a life of faith on the Son of God!

'Sam'l Miller.'

As might have been expected, Dr. Griffin soon found his concurrent labors as professor at Andover, and stated preacher in the Park street Church, far too onerous, and the question simply was, which of these positions he should abandon. Dr. Miller wrote a letter of advice that coincided with Dr. Griffin's own final decision. The following is an extract from this letter, which was dated the 27th of December.

[1] The Presbyterian, 15th January, 1842, p. 11.

'The situation of Park street Church is truly critical and interesting! May the great head of Zion produce a result more favorable than your fears! After bestowing much serious and I trust, prayerful, attention on the subject, I am, on the whole, inclined to the opinion, that, if you can prevail on the Andover people to give you up, (which without flattering I suppose will be a very difficult thing,) it will be your duty to go to Boston. I have not time to detail my reasons for this opinion; but if, with my present views, I were in your place, I should suppose that Providence called me to put my life in my hand, and come into the middle of the hottest battle in Boston. I am firmly persuaded, as you appear to be, that you cannot be devoted efficiently to both objects. And I also think that a young man, unassisted, in Park street Church must sink. And, further, difficult as it is to obtain a professor for Andover, I believe it will be easier to find a candidate for that place, than a suitable one for the church. Looking all these difficulties full in the face, I do not see but that you must go to Boston. But the great Head of the Church will order every thing for the best.'

1811.

MISCELLANEOUS MATTERS.

---

1. HOPKINSIANISM.

DR. MILLEDOLER, not long before his death, gave, for this work, some reminiscences of his former friend and colleague. He says,

'My intercourse with Dr. Miller, after our more close ecclesiastical connexion in the city of New York, was confidential, affectionate, and long uninterrupted even by the transient shadow of a cloud. His countenance lighted up with intelligence and kindness, his gentlemanly manners, sound understanding, ability and taste as a writer, ardent piety, and fidelity in the performance of his sacred duties, endeared him to me not only, but to every one who could appreciate a character of this description. His praise was in all the churches. Of his published works I shall say nothing: they speak for themselves, and do honour to both the head and heart of their reverend author.

'Sometime about the autumn of 1811, commenced in New York what has been called the Hopkinsian controversy, which resulted in the separation of the Presbyterian Church into Old and New School. Without entering here into the nature or merits of this controversy, (though I have preserved some historical fragments of the germs of it in New York,) I will only say, that the new doctrines were opposed, on the ground of their breaking the peace of the Church, and the manifest wrong of subscribing and promising to support doctrines of the Presbyterian Church, which were neither believed nor sustained by the subscribers. It was also urged, that persons entering our churches, and subscribing our formulas, had no right to introduce a different system, and should either connect themselves with some other ecclesiastical body, or organize an establishment of their own. This, however, was not exactly what was wanted. They wanted churches, and it was easier to take

them than to build them. This introduction of Hopkinsianism is the only subject, on which Dr. Miller and myself ever
differed.

'Dr. Miller, in the apprehension of the writer, had long considered the inroads of Hopkinsianism into our churches, rather
as the march of an irregular troop than the tramp of trained
tactitians; and Hopkinsianism itself rather as an ephemeral
thing, which, if let alone, would die of itself, than a cool and
matured plan to revolutionize the Presbyterian Church. Our
beloved friend lived long enough to see, that the predictions of
those who differed from him were not so imaginary as he had
supposed. In relation to Dr. Miller, the writer considers it to
be his duty to declare, that he never had any other feelings
towards him, than those of reverence and love.

'The whole amount of our difference was this—that he considered me as acting conscientiously in this case, yet as carried
away by the ardour of my feelings; and I considered him as
carried away, by his natural amiability and Christian charity,
beyond the bounds marked out for those who are set for the
defence of the Gospel.

'This temporary embarrassment, however, occurred in the
whirls of a stormy day, and produced no alienation of heart,
as I verily believe, on the part of either. I received from Dr.
Miller a most kind letter of condolence on the death of my
honoured father, as also at the decease of my venerable friend
Dr. Livingston. Besides the honour of being formerly associated with him in many public and benevolent institutions; I
was appointed, at a later day, to take part with him in the organization of the Theological Seminary at Princeton, and the
inauguration of Dr. Alexander; subsequently in laying the
corner stone of the new Presbyterian church in Rutgers street;
and 1 hope to be joined with him, ere long, in the higher and
nobler services of the Upper Sanctuary.'

' The ' Hopkinsian controversy,' to which Dr. Milledoler
refers, as commencing in New York, in 1811, was closely
connected with the Rev. Gardiner Spring's settlement in
the Brick Church. At him particularly, the Rev. Ezra
Stiles Ely, then "stated preacher to the Hospital and
Alms House in the city of New York," aimed his volume
entitled, "A Contrast between Calvinism and Hopkinsianism," which was published in 1811. For half a century
had this controversy been carried on in New England, and
it had before now shown itself in the Presbyterian Church;
but from about the date of Mr. Spring's settlement, it as-

sumed among Presbyterians fresh importance, and gradually, though not fully or distinctly, until after the advent of Taylorism, divided them into the New and Old school parties.

The New England Fathers were agreed in embracing and maintaining strictly the Augustinian system of theology, which all the Reformed Churches had adopted. The Confession of the Westminster Assembly, when promulgated, was received and cordially approved in New England, as exhibiting the doctrines constantly professed and taught by the Puritan settlers, and their immediate descendants. But before the middle of the next century, Arminian, Pelagian, Arian, Socinian, and Antinomian errors had begun alarmingly to prevail. To account for this, it might be enough to refer to that depravity and enmity of the human heart, which ever and everywhere naturally turn it against the truth. But doubtless the connexion of the Church with the civil government, and the laxity of discipline resulting from that and other causes, contributed largely to the doctrinal decadence in question.

No one opposed the errors mentioned more earnestly, nor contended with greater force or decision for the old Puritan theology, than President Edwards. Yet, as a melancholy evidence of human imperfection, and of the consequences of a great man's aberrations, it stands confessed, that a departure, which seemed comparatively trifling, from the generally received creed, and philosophical speculations of the results of which their author little dreamed, have furnished the occasion for a multitude of the advocates of dangerous error, with more or less plausibility, to claim the authority of Edwards for their theological vagaries. He adopted substantially from Stapfer, following Placæus, or deduced from his own theory of personal identity, the doctrine of mediate imputation; and he resolved all virtue into the love of being in general, or disinterested benevolence. He also distinguishes between natural and moral ability; but by this distinction obviously intended nothing inconsistent with the old theology.

On the foundation chiefly of the errors of President Edwards, and of a perversion of his views of human ability,

Dr. Hopkins[1] built whatever could be called in fairness, and distinctively, Hopkinsianism. He was a fanciful man, and much given to metaphysical speculation without much ability for it. He did not carry out all his opinions to their legitimate consequences, and remained comparatively orthodox. His disciple, Dr. Emmons,[2] with far greater metaphysical skill, and flinching from no conclusion to which his reasoning led, developed the system much more fully. Hopkinsianism culminated in his teachings, and has sometimes, indeed, as by him presented, borne the appropriate name of Emmonism.

With Hopkinsianism, shooting into Emmonism, it was a radical idea that virtue consists in the love of being in general, or in disinterested benevolence. Of course such virtue required willingness to be damned for the good of being in general ; and to be the author of man's sinful acts was no sin in God, because his authorship was disinterestedly benevolent ; though these acts in man, uninfluenced by the same virtue, were sinful. If God was the author of sin, it was attributable to no evil human disposition or taste—to no corrupt nature. The idea of such a disposition or nature was therefore discarded ; the existence of a moral habit or taste, whether good or bad, was declared impossible ; man's acts, both holy and sinful, were represented as individually, and successively, immediate divine creations ; and, of course, all sin was resolved into voluntary acts thus created. The *originating* sin of Adam, then, was alone properly termed *original* sin ; and his descendants are all, by birth, inherently like Adam was before the fall—just as free and pure as he, just as able to fulfil the divine commands ; but as God determined, for the good of being in general, to produce sinful volitions in our first parents, so he determined, and for the same reason, to produce sinful volitions in their natural descendants ; who therefore all infallibly sin ; and, because born under this "divine constitution," are said, and for this cause alone, to be born in sin, and to be totally depraved. Imputation of sin, with these theologians, was, consequently, neither immediate, (with the old Calvinists,) nor mediate, (as with Placæus,) but was merely God's treating men as under a

[1] See 1 Sprague's Annals, 428.   [2] Id., 693.

"divine constitution" to make them all sinners, if Adam sinned. With the proper headship of Adam, the proper headship of Christ, and his vicarious atonement disappeared; so the atonement became, in this system, governmental and general. In fine, disinterested benevolence, including an unconditional submission to the will of God—a willingness to be damned for his glory—was taught to be the first holy exercise produced in regeneration; and, therefore, was prior, in the order of nature, to faith, and was produced immediately, without the instrumentality of truth, and without the illumination of the understanding.

This was a much more consistent scheme, and, perhaps, taken altogether, a less pernicious one in its immediate practical effects, than the "improved" and frequently re-hashed fragments of it which have since appeared as "New Theology." Its inculcation of the absolute sovereignty of God, though in a monstrous form, exerted a wholesome influence, which has been lost by various later schemes. These have been made up of some of the "soft parts" of Hopkinsianism, but without its skeleton, especially its backbone. The course of error has been always substantially the same. Commencing in what have been considered, at worst, harmless speculations, it has increased to the denial of most important truths. The sad results of admitting and tolerating it have been quite sufficiently exemplified in the short chapter which our country has contributed to the history of theological opinions. Never should we lose sight of the remote, any more than of the immediate, consequences of departing from the simplicity of the gospel faith.

Dr. Spring tells us, that Dr. Miller once remarked to him,

"I should hesitate to *lay hands* on Dr. Emmons; but, though I do not approve of all that Dr. Hopkins has written, I would ordain any man, otherwise qualified, who could honestly say, that he believed *every word* of Dr. Hopkins' system."[1]

The following letter from Dr. Hopkins finds just here, perhaps, a fitting connexion, although written ten years earlier :—

'Rev. Sir,   Newport, January 23, 1801.

'Yours of December 16th did not come to hand till the 12th instant. The most proper and satisfactory answer to your questions, perhaps, will be to refer you to my publications, the first of which was near half a century ago. You may see in

[1] 2 Reminiscences, 6.

them what doctrines I hold, and be able to judge wherein and how far I differ from those Calvinistic divines, who have written before me. I believe that most of the doctrines I have published are to be found in the writings of former divines; viz., Calvin, Van Mastricht, Saurin, Preston, Manton, Owen, Goodwin, Bates, Charnock, Baxter, the Assembly of Divines at Westminster, Ridgley, Willard, Shepard, Hooker, Edwards and many others. Most of these did not, indeed, fully explain some of these doctrines, which are asserted or implied in their writings. And they are, in some instances, inconsistent with themselves, by advancing contrary doctrines.

'If I am in any measure an original, in any thing I have written, it is in asserting, that the unregenerate, under the greatest mental light and convictions of conscience, and in all their external reformations and doings, are more criminal and guilty, than they were in a state of ignorance and security; and really do no duty: all their actions are sin. This is necessarily implied in the doctrine of *total depravity*, which all Calvinists hold.—That all true holiness consists in disinterested benevolence, and those affections which are implied in it. That all self-love, which is not implied in disinterested benevolence, is sinful, and that in which all sin essentially and radically consists.—That the original threatening, "Thou shalt surely die," does not mean, or imply, a separation between body and soul; but the destruction and misery of both in union in hell forever, which is, in Scripture, called the second death, which all finally impenitent sinners will suffer.

'But it is really no great matter who first advanced a doctrine. If it be agreeable to Scripture, it ought to be received: if not, let it be rejected.

'No scheme of doctrines has got the name of *Hopkintonian* by my consent, or the invention or desire of any of my friends. This was the invention of the late Rev. William Hart of Say Brook, a reputed Arminian, who published some remarks, about thirty years ago, on what Mr. Edwards, Dr. Bellamy and I had written; to which I made a short reply, and the controversy was, perhaps, too personal. He was irritated, it seems, and wrote a pamphlet, in which he mentioned a number of doctrines as mine, and endeavored to set them in a bad light; and, by way of reproach, to fasten an odium on me and them, he gave them the name of *Hopkintonian doctrines*. This epithet has been since used both by friends and enemies. The latter have, in many instances, used the term, as carrying an odium with it, while they do not know what are the doctrines implied in it.

'I am your friend and servant,

'Rev. Samuel Miller. S. Hopkins.'

In 1796 Dr. Hopkins said, "About forty years ago there were but few, perhaps not more than four or five, who espoused the sentiments, which have since been called *Edwardean*, and *new divinity*, and since, after some improvement was made upon them, *Hopkintonian* and *Hopkinsian* sentiments. But these sentiments have so spread since that time among ministers, especially those who have since come on the stage, that there are now more than one hundred in the ministry who espouse the same sentiments in the United States of America. And the number appears to be fast increasing, and these sentiments appear to be coming more and more into credit, and are better understood, and the odium which was cast on them and those who preached them, is greatly subsided."[1]

While Hopkinsianism, properly so called, was working out its own issues, New England Theology was taking another, though affiliated form in the speculations of Jonathan Edwards, the younger—Dr. Edwards. He discarded the two monstrosities of divine efficiency in producing sin, and the necessity of willingness to be damned for the good of being in general; which, indeed, had but a very limited currency; yet he maintained that entire resignation, or submission to God as a moral governor, was the first act in conversion—an idea now almost forgotten, though amazingly important in the view of a certain class of revivalists, not very long ago, when New Theology and New Measures were in their glory. Besides his father's views of imputation and the nature of holiness, he adopted the doctrine of a general and governmental atonement, and regarded love and repentance as the first exercises of a regenerate soul.

Dr. Dwight, in whose election to the presidency of Yale College Hopkinsianism, or, more properly, the Edwardean Theology, was regarded as having won a signal triumph, stood really on middle ground between President and Dr. Edwards, approaching nearer in his views to the former than to the latter. As to the doctrines of imputation and the atonement, with some connected points, he accepted Edwardean views: otherwise he was an Old Calvinist.

Not only were the more distinctive tenets of Dr. Hopkins and Dr. Emmons denominated Hopkinsianism, but under this name also passed currently all the aberrations of that New England Theology, which still claimed to be Calvinistic. We have seen that Dr. Griffin was called a

[1] Life of Dr. Hopkins, 102, 103.

Hopkinsian; yet he approached nearer than Dr. Dwight, and nearer perhaps as life advanced, to old Calvinism; and wrote with earnestness against the "New Divinity." His chief divergence was in favor of the doctrine of an unlimited atonement with its consequences, and even this doctrine he endeavored to bring into some sort of accord with the common Reformed creed. Dr. Miller certainly did not regard with as much alarm as some others, the introduction of this so called moderate Hopkinsianism into the Presbyterian Church, and constantly by voice and vote contended for its toleration. He is said to have suggested to Mr. Ely that he should write the "Contrast"; but not to have liked it when it was written. The result was, that he himself, about the year 1811, fell under the imputation of Hopkinsianism, and seems, at length, to have been at some pains to deny, as most consistently he might, that there was the least affinity between this exotic and his own Presbyterian creed.

In a letter of the 10th of December, 1811, Mrs. Miller wrote to a friend,

'I have had a conversation with Mr. Davis this afternoon: Mr. Miller was engaged in his study and could not see him; and he chose rather to talk to me than go away immediately. He was full of *disinterested benevolence*, and ready to attack everybody who was not of his way of thinking. He had heard of something which Dr. Romeyn had said against it, and seemed as if he could not rest without arguing the point with him. I found that he was likewise ready to advocate the doctrine of God's being the author of sin; but there I felt inclined to contend with him, and insisted that he had crossed the narrow path of orthodoxy.'

2. CORRESPONDENCE.

Earlier in the same year—on the 25th of March—Dr. Miller wrote to Dr. Griffin,

'I have, this morning, received your welcome letter of the 20th instant; and, though surrounded and pressed by engagements, I must take time to say, that the rumor of my having had a *fit* is wholly unfounded. I desire to feel thankful, that my health, during the past winter, has been, as it continues to be, better than usual. I cannot imagine what has given rise to the report. May God enable me to improve my numerous mercies, and to labor for him with growing diligence, while my day lasts!

'I will just add, that, if you can not only be installed by the Presbytery, but also get the Park street Church organized on the Presbyterian model, it appears to me a great, great deal will be gained.'

Dr. Miller, in writing to Dr. Adam Clarke, the commentator, had ventured to criticise some of his observations upon Calvin and Calvinism. Dr. Clarke replied as follows :—

'Rev'd and very dear Sir,   London, April 4, 1811.
    'When I say that I feel myself exceedingly obliged by your kind letter, I speak a language in which compliment has no share. That my work on Genesis should have afforded you any pleasure is to me a matter of high gratification; and that anything in the general preface should have given such a mind as yours a moment's pain is to me a subject of sincere regret. I have only to say that I have most sincerely studied so to write, as to give no cause of offence to any genuine Christian. What I wrote concerning Mr. Calvin and a few others, I weighed very maturely; and I really thought that, when it was considered, that, as is well known, I do not believe the doctrine of the *Decrees*, what I wrote on the works of men who were strongly opposed to the doctrine of General Redemption by our most blessed Lord, would be regarded as, at least, tolerably candid. In that article on Mr. Calvin, I deplored the evils that had been introduced among religious people by polemic writers on both sides; and I laid these evils equally at the door of each party. However, as my great design was to profit all if possible, and to give no cause of complaint to any who were embarked in the same work with myself, I cancelled the whole of that preface, and wrote another, considerably improved and enlarged, and have completely remodelled those articles at which some of my Calvinistic brethren had taken offence. If it pleased you at all before, I am sure it will be much more acceptable to you now; and I flatter myself that it does not contain one sentence that will give you any kind of pain. I rejoice, my dear Sir, in having this opportunity of shewing my unfeigned esteem for you; and had I your judgment now and then to consult, on my frequently occurring difficulties, I should esteem it a high privilege. Had I apprehended all the difficulties I have met with, since I began this work, it is absolutely certain, I never should have sent one sheet of it to the press. Now that I have gone so far, I feel myself obliged to go yet farther. I want more wisdom, more judgment, more learning, and, above all, more of the unction of God in my own soul. Help me, my dear Sir, by your

prayers to the Father of Mercies, that I may ever discern the truth as it is in Jesus, preach it, write it, and live according to it alone.   *   *'

In the year 1811, Dr. Miller had some correspondence with the Ex-president, John Adams. Two letters from the latter have been preserved, a few extracts from which will sufficiently exhibit the purport of the whole.

'Sir,   Quincy, April 12, 1811.

'Some gentlemen in this town have lately caused to be printed a sermon of Mr. Hancock, the father of the late President of Congress and Governor of Massachusetts; which, although I heard it delivered from the pulpit, and was familiar with it afterwards in print, in my childhood, I had not seen for I know not how great a number of years.

'Knowing your taste for antiquities, and believing it contains information concerning your own blood, I hope I am not committing an indiscretion in transmitting a copy of it to you; not for any uncommon merit in the composition, though considering the time, it is not in that respect by any means to be despised.

'* * Samuel Bass[1] married a daughter of John Alden, one of the adventurers in the first ship, who landed, in 1620, on that rock in Plymouth, which is now esteemed by many more than a lump of diamond of the same weight would be.

'The lady who bore the name of Hannah[2] Bass, whom you found among the memorials of your ancestors, I presume was a daughter of Samuel Bass, * * or possibly a grand-daughter. If you have no objection, I should be obliged to you for the year, in which that lady married your ancestor.

'I am, Sir, with great esteem, your humble
                'servant,   John Adams.'

On the same sheet he writes, next day, giving some facts which he had collected respecting John Alden and his descendants chiefly; adding,

'You, I presume, are among the most precious fruits of that marriage. That you may live as long, and be as useful in proportion, as either of your ancestors, Alden or Bass, is the wish of your humble
                'Servant,   John Adams.
'Reverend Dr. Miller.'

'Reverend and dear Sir,   Quincy, May 11, 1811.

'Your kind letter of the sixth of this month is this day received with great pleasure. I thank you for the facts

[1] John, son of Samuel Bass. See p. 14.
[2] *Mary* it should have been. See p. 13.

relative to your ancestors, and shall be obliged to you for any others you may be pleased to communicate to me. I may possibly furnish you hereafter with some information concerning your uncle, Joseph Miller; but this is mere conjecture at present. * *

'Your politeness inquires, whether I do not bear some relation to the family of Bass, and what that relation is. My grand-father, Joseph Adams, married Hannah Bass; but whether a daughter or grand-daughter of Deacon Samuel Bass * * I am not able at present to determine.[1] * * The records of marriages, births, baptisms and deaths, which ought to have been kept with precision, and which have been kept in this town and church with tolerable regularity, I presume might be searched with success, to determine most of these facts and dates; but I have given myself very little concern upon these subjects. Indeed, I have observed, that it is not till extreme old age, that people commonly begin to think much about their original and their ancestors. Then it often happens, when it is too late, and when all are dead who could give authentic information, men and women become intemperately anxious and inquisitive about such subjects.

'I wish to know, Sir, whether Dr. Miller, of New York, the physician, who is so much associated in medical investigations with Dr. Mitchill, is your brother.

'It is not without pleasure, nor without pride, that I am able to trace any connection of consanguinity between two gentlemen who have done so much honour to the Religion, Literature and Science of America, and your affectionate friend,

'John Adams.'

To Dr. Green, about the Theological Seminary, Dr. Miller wrote,

'Rev'd and dear Sir,   New York, April 22, 1811.

'Your letter of the 13th instant came to hand six or seven days ago, and was perused by me, as you may well suppose, with deep interest. If Governor Bloomfield's plan could be realized, it would be a grand and even prodigious thing. But, I confess, my fears greatly predominate over my hopes. The trustees will, I apprehend, never consent to commit a sort of suicide; especially as, on the new plan, a number of them would, undoubtedly, be thrown out of all place and influence in the business. Brother Romeyn will rejoice with us, more than can well be expressed, if the contemplated plan can be

---

[1] A grand-daughter. John Bass (p. 14) was Mr. Adams's great-grandfather, and the great-great-grand-father of Dr. Miller. They were therefore third cousins.

executed. But of this more when we meet in May. He and I are appointed, and expect to be at the Assembly.

'The principal object of this letter is to consult you respecting the present state of our subscriptions. We commenced them early in the winter, and were going on with vigor; but were urged to suspend our labors for a short time, on account of the extreme pressure of mercantile embarrassment; and were told that in April and May the times would no doubt be much more favorable, and much larger sums be obtained. We have, within a few days, commenced again, but with poor prospects, owing to the pressure under which several merchants of our denomination find themselves, from whom $500 or $1000 apiece were expected. The question which I wish to ask is, what, under present circumstances, we had better do. We have already procured subscriptions to the amount of between three and four thousand dollars. If we prosecute the matter with zeal for three weeks to come, I think we can bring to the assembly subscriptions (on paper) to the amount of $8,000 or $10,000; whereas, if we wait for a more propitious period, if such should ever arrive, I think we might calculate, with confidence, on raising in this city $20,000, by subscription, without difficulty.'

The plan of Governor Bloomfield, referred to in the foregoing letter, evidently was, to establish the projected Theological Seminary at Princeton, under the college charter, as a department co-ordinate with that of the arts. This plan certainly was proposed, and, for a time, was regarded with great favor, and sanguine expectations, by the friends of the new undertaking. But difficulties, which all saw from the first yet some imagined might be overcome, proved, doubtless, to be insuperable. The college board of Trustees, a close corporation, filling its own vacancies, must have had the whole legal control of both departments, with all the funds; and the interests of the Presbyterian Church, and its General Assembly, in the theological school, could have been secured only by "management" in the choice of trustees, "understandings" between the parties, and compacts of doubtful obligation in law; affording, upon the whole, a very precarious ground of confidence in the continued orthodoxy, or right direction in any respect, of the new department.

3. Memoirs of Dr. Rodgers.

In 1803, Dr. Rodgers, then in his 77th year, had begun to limit himself to one sermon upon the Sabbath; and even this labor he found, of course, more and more oppressive, until, in September, 1809, he preached for the last time. Towards the close of 1810, he became wholly unable to leave the house. From the period, therefore, of the separation of the collegiate churches, Dr. Miller was, virtually, sole pastor of the one in Wall street. Of Dr. Rodger's death he gives the following account:—

"Toward three o'clock, in the afternoon * *, he became in a small degree restless, and manifested symptoms of approaching dissolution. His colleague was immediately sent for, and in a few minutes entered the room. He found him unable to speak; but had the pleasure of perceiving that he knew him; and by signs, as well as by his countenance, that he enjoyed his wonted hope and consolation, and that he wished him to pray with him. A short prayer was accordingly offered up; and the venerable servant of Jesus Christ, without again recovering his speech, was, about four o'clock, P. M., on the 7th day of May, 1811, in the 84th year of his age, and in the 63d year of his ministry, quietly released from his mortal tabernacle, and translated to his eternal rest.

" * * The funeral was attended on Thursday, the 9th of May. Scarcely ever was there seen in *New York* so large a concourse of real mourners. The corpse was taken in the *Brick* church, where an impressive funeral oration was delivered by *Dr. Milledoler.*"[1]

On the following Tuesday, Dr. Miller preached a sermon in commemoration of his venerable colleague. This was afterwards published[2] as an appendix to his Memoirs of Dr. Rodgers, a work commenced, doubtless, soon after the death of the latter, and appearing early in 1813.[3] The Memoirs are dedicated "To the Ministers of the Presbyterian Church in the United States," in his address to whom the author says,

"The character and ministry of the venerable Man, with whose memoirs you are here presented, were dear to you all,

<hr>

[1] Memoirs of Dr. Rodgers, 287, 288.

[2] "A Sermon, preached in the City of New York, May 12th, 1811, occasioned by the death of the Rev. John Rodgers, D.D., late Senior Pastor of the Wall-street and Brick Churches, New York. By Samuel Miller, D.D., Surviving Pastor of the Church in Wall-street."—2 Kings ii. 12.

[3] "Memoirs of the Rev. John Rodgers, D.D., late Pastor of the Wall street and Brick Churches, in the City of New York. By Samuel Miller, D.D., Surviving Pastor of the Church in Wall-street. New-York: 1813."—8vo. Pp. 432.

In 1840, the Presbyterian Board of Publication issued an abridgement of this work, by its author, omitting altogether the Funeral Sermon and Appendix, which occupy about seventy-five pages of the original volume.

Most of you knew him personally; and all of you revered him as one of the Fathers of the American Church. Knowing this, I had no doubt that you would be gratified with seeing some account of his long, laborious and useful life: and knowing also, that no one could so naturally be expected to give this account as his surviving colleague, who served with him, as a son in the Gospel, for more than seventeen years, I did not hesitate to make the attempt.

"In the progress of the undertaking, I have greatly exceeded the limits originally prescribed to myself. What was at first intended to be a pamphlet of moderate size, has insensibly grown into a volume."[1]

On an after page he says,

"The distance between the residence of Doctor Rodgers, and that of the writer's Father, both in the State of Delaware, was about twenty-six miles. And, though they belonged to different Presbyteries, and differed in opinion on some points of ecclesiastical order, they were united in affectionate friendship, and had much official intercourse, especially on sacramental occasions."[2]

In regard to his own personal relations to his aged colleague, Dr. Miller gave repeated and grateful testimony. In a contribution to Dr. Sprague's Annals he remarked,

"My acquaintance with Dr. Rodgers began in 1792, when he was more than sixty years of age, and when I was a youthful and inexperienced candidate for the ministry. He recognized in me the son of an old clerical friend, and from that hour until the day of his death treated me with a fidelity and kindness truly paternal. And when, next year, I became his colleague, he uniformly continued to exercise toward me that parental indulgence and guardianship, which became his inherited friendship, as well as his Christian and ecclesiastical character."[3]

As late as the 30th of November, 1847, Dr. Miller wrote,

'I owe to the memory of my venerable colleague, the Rev'd Dr. Rodgers, a record of my deep sense of obligation to him, for the manner in which he treated me, from the hour of my settlement in New York until his latest breath. He was my father's affectionate friend; and, from my first introduction to him, he acted the part of a father and faithful friend to his friend's son. He took me by the hand; and did everything in

[1] Pp. 3, 4.   [2] P. 387, note.   [1] 3 Vol., 162.

his power to promote my reputation and welfare:—he counselled me; corrected my mistakes; defended me when misrepresented; appeared to take delight in every manifestation of public favour which he perceived to be extended to me; was ready to assist me in preaching, when he saw that I needed such assistance; and, in short, was prompt to say and do every thing that the most faithful and paternal friendship could dictate. Never did he, for one moment, deviate from that course of decisive and affectionate regard which he professed to pursue, and in which he seemed to take delight.

'On the other hand, I served with him as an affectionate son with a kind and tender father. No alienation, jealousy, or uncomfortable feeling ever arose between us. To the latest hour of his life, I labored with him as Timothy with "Paul the aged," and felt myself at once honored and rewarded by my union with him. I owe a large debt to the memory of that venerated man.'

About his Memoirs of Dr. Rodgers, we find Dr. Miller writing to Dr. Green, on the 2d of March, 1812,

'Apropos,—when I stood pledged to write the life of Dr. Nisbet, you promised me a long communication respecting that gentleman, in order to gratify my ambition to have it a sort of joint work. That being dropped, I have the same desire with respect to Dr. Rodgers's life. I have a real and ardent wish to receive a communication from you, which may stand as one of the chapters of the work, or any other way that you choose to direct; and which may be a monument of our acquaintance and friendship. I mentioned this to you last May; but you gave me no encouragement to expect anything of the kind. Are you still of the same mind? It would give me great pleasure to believe that you had come to a better way of thinking. If you can prepare two or three sheets, or as much more as you please, between this and the last of May, it will answer.'

In a letter, dated 'N. Brunswick, July 23, 1813,' Dr. Livingston, then Professor of Theology of the Reformed Dutch Church, in Queen's (now Rutger's) College, wrote,

'As to Dr. Rodgers's Life, you forbid me to say the only thing I can say upon the subject; but I must and will say, that I am surprised, pleased and edified with it. I have no remarks, nor would I wish to see any alterations or additions in a new edition. It is now good, very good. I see you have made use of my letter. Nothing will suffer in your hand: it is all right.'

Dr. Rush wrote as follows:—

'My dear Sir,   Philadelphia, April 13th, 1813.

　　　'I have more than *read*, I have *devoured*, your account of the life of our excellent friend, Dr. Rodgers. It is what the epicures call a *tit bit* in Biography. You have given an importance to the most minute incidents in his life by your reflections upon them. In doing so, you have happily imitated the manner of Tacitus. Mrs. Rush has been equally delighted with myself with your history of her much beloved friend. She says it has the variety and animation of a novel, with all the dignity and instruction of real history. I was particularly pleased with your having given so correct a view of the apostolic age of the Presbyterian Church in America. The names of the Tennents, Dickinson, Burr, the Blairs, Finley, Smith, Roan, Wilson and Allison, have been translated by your pen from their long repose in their graves to the skies, where they form a splendid constellation, which I hope will never cease to command the admiration and affection of their descendants in the same Church. I was pleased still further in observing, that you ascribe their preëminence in Scriptural knowledge and Scriptural preaching to their familiarity with the writings of Baxter, Charnock, Howe and other illustrious divines and saints, who adorned the seventeenth century. They formed the apostolic age of the Christian Church in Great Britain.

'I wish you had mentioned the names of Waddel, Kirkpatrick, Hunt, Caldwell and Strain among Dr. Finley's pupils in West Nottingham. They were excellent and useful ministers of the gospel. Mr. Strain was a great man. In eloquence, so far as it consists in sublime conceptions and expressions, he was not inferior to Mr. Whitefield. He was so truly a "burning and shining light," that he consumed himself. He died prematurely from the vehemence of his labors, particularly in the pulpit, in which, at times, unhappily, he rather *roared* than spoke. I will give you a specimen of the sublimity of his eloquence. In a sermon upon these words—"In him dwelleth all the fulness of the Godhead," delivered in Pine street church in our city, after mentioning most of the attributes of God, which dwelt in, and were exercised by the Son, he added, "Above all, the fulness of the LOVE of God dwells in him.— And here what shall I say?—Help me, Gabriel! Help me, Michael! Help me, Ithuriel! with your celestial eloquence, to do justice to the BOUNDLESS of the love of Son of God!" —Here, with his eyes elevated towards the ceiling of the church, he paused for half a minute. A solemn stillness instantly pervaded the audience.—Then, with a voice a little reduced and slow, he cried out, "See! they droop their wings, unable even to comprehend the mighty theme."

'There was great force in the word BOUNDLESS, used as a substantive, instead of an adjective.

'May we both be enabled to follow the examples of these great and good men, who are, now, through faith, inheriting the great and precious promises of the gospel!

　　　　　　　　'Adieu! from, my dear Sir,

　　　　　　　　　　'Yours truly and affectionately,

'The Rev'd Dr. Miller.　　　　　　　　Benj'n Rush.'

The following is part of a letter from the Rev'd George Burder, the well known author of "Village Sermons."

'Rev'd Sir,　　　　　　　London, June 15, 1814.

'I feel much indebted to you for the welcome present of your Life of that excellent man, Dr. Rodgers, which I have read with great pleasure, and from which I have ventured to make an extract for the Evangelical Magazine. You have contrived, Sir, to render your book truly useful, especially in America, by introducing subjects of general interest, and laboring to maintain the truth as it is in Jesus, which I understand is powerfully assailed, in your part of the world, by the Socinian adversaries.'

A late writer in the Presbyterian[1] speaks of this work as "that richly replenished store house, in which Dr. Miller has introduced, naturally and appropriately, nearly everything that was known, thirty years ago, of the history of our Church."

These Memoirs exhibited Episcopalians and Presbyterians repeatedly in conflict. As the latter were, before the Revolution, among the most determined resistants of ecclesiastical domination; so, since the Revolution, they have enjoyed the credit of being among the most active opponents of High Churchism. Those portions of the volume referring to the conflicts just mentioned, were, of course, noticed by Episcopal critics; but into the particulars and merits of their criticisms there is not room here to enter.

4.　THEOLOGICAL SEMINARY.

No place had as yet been fixed upon for the new seminary, but to the Assembly of 1811 the Trustees of the College of New Jersey, at Princeton, proposed the appointment of a committee to confer with one which they had already appointed on this subject. The Assembly's com-

---

[1] February 1, 1851.

27

mittee, of which Dr. Alexander was chairman, reported, three days afterward, recommending another committee of conference with the Trustees, with ample powers to frame a plan for uniting the college and the proposed seminary, and of course locating the latter at Princeton. A second committee, of which also Dr. Alexander was chairman, was accordingly chosen. Subsequently the plan of a theological school, from the pen of Dr. Green, of the committee appointed the previous year, was considered and, in substance, adopted. It appeared that some $14,000 or $15,000 had been subscribed for the seminary, including $8,000 or $9,000, the probable amount of the estate of Deacon William Falconer, who had lately died in Philadelphia, bequeathing all his property to this object. $3,000 had been subscribed in the city of New York. The Assembly made provision for a more vigorous prosecution of the business of collecting funds.

It is doubtful whether, at this time, there was really much wealth in the Presbyterian Church. At any rate, the efforts made to obtain, within its bounds, a proper endowment for the new seminary, proved abortive. The funds collected were all needed, and were not sufficient, to meet the immediate and most pressing demands of the institution. The times, moreover, on account of the difficulties with France and England, which, as to the latter power, soon culminated in the war of 1812, were unpropitious. Moved naturally enough by sanguine hopes, rather than rational conclusions, the thoughts of some of the gentlemen most deeply interested in the projected seminary, as they were busily beating about, under these circumstances, in every direction, turned towards New England, and several of its wealthy and distinguished patrons of religious learning. Dr. Green and Dr. Miller especially hoped for success, and made some effort, in that quarter; but they were disappointed. It was no wonder that none of these New England gentlemen were disposed to help build up the institution in Princeton, which they could not but regard, as, to some degree, however unintentionally, a rival of that at Andover. The nearer alike different denominations are, the oftener do the seeming interests of one clash with those of another.

In singular contrast with these negotiations for the establishment of the Theological Seminary by the side of the College, at Princeton, was a resolution of the college trustees, on the 19th of December, 1811, applying to the state legislature for permission to raise by lottery a sum not exceeding $25,000, on account of the impoverished state of the institution under their care. In this country revolutions in public sentiment are often peculiarly rapid; yet so complete and universal now is the condemnation of lotteries, and their classification with misdemeanors, that but for such a recent instance of their justification by good men, we should suppose they had been, for a much longer period, the resort of avowed gamblers only. We may, however, judge more leniently the trustees of the College of New Jersey, of more than half a century ago, when we remember how many devices, which are lotteries in fact, though not so called, are still employed among professing Christians, and in the name of humanity and religion, in connexion with church fairs and otherwise, to raise funds which a halting charity is backward to supply.

5.　TEMPERANCE.

Dr. Miller was a Commissioner to the four successive Assemblies from 1810 to 1813, inclusive, doubtless to give opportunity to his zeal on behalf of a theological institution. Before that of 1811, he preached a missionary sermon, for which the Assembly voted its thanks. The same year he was also appointed chairman of a large committee designed to devise measures, which, when sanctioned by the General Assembly, might have an influence in preventing some of the numerous and threatening mischiefs which were experienced throughout the country by the excessive and intemperate use of spirituous liquors; and this committee was authorized to correspond and act in concert with any persons who might be appointed, or associated, for a similar purpose, and were required to report to the next Assembly. Dr. Rush, of Philadelphia, had previously presented to the body one thousand copies of his pamphlet, entitled, "An Inquiry into the Effects of Ardent Spirits upon the Human Body and Mind," to be divided among the members for distribution in their congregations.

That donation, which the Assembly received with a resolution of thanks, had doubtless, in part, suggested a committee on this subject, which now, for the first time, engaged the attention of the highest judicatory of the Presbyterian Church; excepting that the old Synod had, in 1766, condemned the excessive use of intoxicating drinks at funerals. But a passage in the annual narrative of the state of religion, prepared for the Assembly from synodical and presbyterial reports, shows that from some portions of the Church itself had come up lamentations over intemperance. "We are ashamed," says the narrative, "but constrained to say, that we have heard of the sin of drunkenness prevailing—prevailing to a great degree—prevailing even among some of the visible members of the household of faith. What a reflection on the Christian character is this, that they who profess to be bought with a price, and thus redeemed from iniquity, should debase themselves by the gratification of appetite to a level with the beasts which perish."[1]

As the result of this reference of the subject, the Assembly of 1812 adopted a paper of some length, drawn up, probably, by Dr. Miller, chairman of the committee. It recommended to all the ministers of the Presbyterian Church that they should warn their hearers, both from the pulpit and otherwise, against the sin of intemperance, and all indulgences leading thereto; enjoined on church sessions faithful, though considerate, discipline, for the purification of the Church from this sin; advised the free circulation of tracts on the subject; and suggested the adoption of measures for reducing the number of taverns and liquor shops.[2]

6. Dr. Griffin's Installation.

After all, Dr. Miller was obliged to excuse himself from preaching the sermon at Dr. Griffin's installation. The following letter, dated the 8th of July, 1811, gives his reasons and expresses his regret.

'I had pleased myself with the thought, that your installation would take place under circumstances which would liberate me from my promise. But, to my regret, it has turned out

[1] Min. 467, 474, 483.   [2] Min. 511.

otherwise. Considering, however, the new and peculiar situation in which I am placed, I am compelled to request of you, as a particular favor, to release me from that promise. You know, my dear Brother, that there are few men living whom I both respect and love more than yourself; and that it would afford me very high gratification to have an opportunity of testifying this. But you shall yourself judge what I ought to do, after calmly reflecting on the following considerations:

'I have, within a few days, removed my family to a place of my brother's, at Bloomingdale, about seven miles from the city. The house which we occupy is in a wild and uncultivated place. I go to the city every day, and bring most of our family supplies with me in the chair, as I return from these daily visits. We have no servant who can possibly be trusted to take my place in this business; and the idea of leaving my wife and children alone, for three weeks, in this wild and solitary place, without supplies, or the means of obtaining them with comfort, in this warm weather, when they cannot be laid up, so afflicts my mind, and the mind of Mrs. M., whenever we think of it, that I shrink from an undertaking which would involve me in such a necessity.

'Nor is this all. My church is, at this time, in a very critical situation. The period of entering our new building has been constantly viewed as about four or five weeks ahead for near two months past. The time now talked of by our building committee is the last of July or the beginning of August. It is not certain that we shall be able to get in so soon; but our people find the edifice we now occupy so crowded and intolerable, especially in hot weather, that they are anxious to get into the new one at the earliest possible period. Under these circumstances, for me to engage in anything, which might delay this event for two or three weeks, would neither be agreeable to them, nor politic in me. In the midst of this ecclesiastical embarrassment, we have another. About two-thirds of the pews in our building are already disposed of to persons who had claims on seats in the old church. The rest are yet to be disposed of; and (as has always occurred in similar cases) there is no small difficulty about the matter. Many complaints arise. New and delicate cases present themselves and must be decided. The officers of the church consider my presence and agency as of some importance in the removal of these difficulties; and we are not likely to get through them entirely, until we enter the new building, and perhaps not for several weeks afterwards. But further—

'To my shame be it spoken, though I have had my dedication sermon for several months in view, yet so incessant has been my hurry and distraction, for six weeks past, that I have not written one line of that sermon, nor even chosen a text for it. Under these circumstances of unpreparedness and hurry; when I am obliged to spend the greater portion of every day in going to and from our country retreat; when I cannot have access to my library; and when, with every exertion, I can scarcely get time to make decent preparation for the Sabbath at home; how could I have the heart to engage, in the midst of a relaxing, warm season, in preparation for one of the most difficult, delicate, and arduous services that ever a minister performed?

'More than this, I was lately absent two Sabbaths at the General Assembly; and, though I took all possible pains to have my pulpit supplied during my absence, and had actually engaged two ministers for the purpose, yet it so happened, that they both failed; and the people, on each Sabbath assembled in church, and sat an hour looking on one another, until, despairing of the arrival of a preacher, they dispersed.

'Under these circumstances, for me to leave home for two Sabbaths at least, to the distress of my family, and to the endangering of the peace and comfort of my congregation; to travel two hundred and fifty miles, to perform a service which can be better done by a person on the spot—ought I to do it?

'My dear Brother, it gives me more pain than I can well express, to decline a service which I know you expected, and on which your heart has been in some degree placed. But let me appeal to your conscience and your feelings, whether under the circumstances which I have stated, I can possibly decide otherwise. Write me a line by the first mail, telling me that you are not angry; that you release me from my promise; and that my failure shall not impair your affection. I shall feel uneasy until I hear from you.'

After the installation, he wrote to Dr. Griffin,

'New-York, August 12, 1811.

'My very dear Brother,

'I embrace the earliest leisure moment, since receiving information of them, to congratulate you on the solemn and interesting transactions of the 31st ultimo. May God bless you, my beloved Friend, in your new charge, and go on to honor you, as he has so often done, as the instrument of saving good to many souls, and of rich benefits to his church at large! My heart was with you on that important day; and I wish it had been possible to be with you in body also.

'Your affairs in Massachusetts, my Brother, have been ordered differently, in some respects, from what we anticipated. I trust it will turn out to be eminently for the furtherance of the gospel. The great Head of the Church knows better, far better, than you or I, what he is about. Blessed be his holy name forever; and let the whole earth be filled with his glory!

'I cannot tell you how much I feel interested in the affairs of the Park street Church. God's dealings with them have been, heretofore, trying. I trust he is now preparing to manifest rich mercy towards them. Let me know everything concerning them that is interesting.

'We opened our new church yesterday morning. I was quite as anxious for the issue of the event as I ought to have been; and not a little agitated on the occasion. The church was immensely crowded. Dr. Romeyn attended and assisted. My sermon was from 2 Chronicles vi. 41—first clause. It will probably be printed. On the whole, the issue was favorable: much better than I feared. There appears to be, at present, only one family incurably disgusted and alienated about a pew. I hope all the rest will be quiet, if not satisfied. Considering the extreme difficulties which usually attend the delicate and invidious task of accommodating old occupants in new places of worship, I think we have done, and are doing, on the whole, remarkably well.

'Let me hear from you soon. Mrs. M. does not know of my writing, (she is at what Judge Benson calls "Tadmor in the wilderness,") or she would join in love to Mrs. G. and yourself with,

'dear Brother, yours affectionately,
'Sam'l Miller.'

Of the two following paragraphs, the former is from Mrs. Miller's diary, the latter from a letter of hers, dated the 22d of December, 1811, to a cousin, who had just made a profession of religion.

September 2, 1811. After my mind has been exercised with regard to my own spiritual state; after a season of trouble, when my soul has been anxiously inquiring, "Lord, am I thine?"—after having obtained that heartfelt satisfaction which those experience who are assured that they are amongst that happy number, who "have passed from death unto life," and that nothing—not even death—shall separate them from him who is the source of all their joy; with how much solicitude have I inquired, "O Lord, is my husband thine?—is he, too, of that happy number whose God is the Lord? Shew me some special evidence that he is thine: I ask it, if agreeable to thy will, in the name of him, through faith in whom thou has promised all blessings. Is he thine forever?" But no special evidence was granted, until during the last winter. This was one of the comforts which were given to support me in a time of trial.'

'I feel jealous over every professor, and especially every new one, because I was a professor myself between four and five years, before I had any spiritual knowledge of Christianity; and was prevented from settling down in a mere profession only by that God who had determined to make me effectually his.'

CHAPTER TWENTIETH.

AFFLICTIONS.

1812.

---

1. BURNING OF THE RICHMOND THEATRE.

EARLY in the year 1812, Dr. Miller published a sermon,[1] which was a fitting introduction to a year of unusual sorrow. The following extracts will explain the occasion of its delivery and publication.

"On the night of December 26, 1811, the theatre in the city of *Richmond, Virginia,* was unusually crowded; a new play having drawn together an audience of not less than six hundred persons. Towards the close of the performances, just before the commencement of the last act of the concluding pantomime, the scenery caught fire, from a lamp inadvertently raised to an improper position, and, in a few minutes, the whole building was wrapped in flames. The doors being very few, and the avenues leading to them exceedingly narrow, the scene which ensued was truly a scene of horror! It may be in some degree imagined, but can never be adequately described!—About *seventy-five* persons perished in the flames. Among these were the Governor of the State; the President of the Bank of *Virginia;* one of the most eminent Attornies belonging to the bar of the commonwealth; a number of other respectable Gentlemen; and about FIFTY FEMALES, a large portion of whom were among the Ladies of the greatest conspicuity and fashion in the city."[2]

"To the Young Gentlemen at whose request the 'following sermon was delivered, and is now published," Dr. Miller says,

[1] "A Sermon, delivered January 19, 1812, at the request of a number of Young Gentlemen of the City of New York, who had assembled to express their Condolence with the Inhabitants of Richmond, on the late Mournful Dispensation of Providence in that City. By Samuel Miller, D.D., Pastor of the First Presbyterian Church in the City of New York."—Lamentations ii. 1, 13.—8vo. Pp. 50.   [2] Pp. 50.

in a dedicatory address, "Your resolution to express your condolence with the mourning inhabitants of *Richmond*, did you
honour. Sympathy with the afflicted is ornamental to every
age, but especially to the Young. When, therefore, you requested me to address you on the occasion from the pulpit,
although a compliance with your request was not a little inconvenient, I did not dare to refuse. But when, after being apprized, that if anything was said by me in relation to the awful
Calamity in question, it must include a solemn protest against
Theatrical entertainments, you still unanimously persisted in
urging your application, my duty to comply with it appeared
no longer doubtful. It gives me pleasure to find that you so
far approve of what I thought myself bound to say on that
subject, as to wish it made still more public: for I will enjoy
the satisfaction of believing, that approbation of the truth had
much more agency in prompting your second request, than
civility to the preacher."[1]

The biographer of Dr. A. Alexander, after noticing a
sermon preached by the latter, upon the same mournful
occasion, in the Pine street Presbyterian Church, Philadelphia, of which he was pastor, and also given to the press,
remarks,

"It is worthy of note, as belonging to a parallel between
two long and blended lives, that the Reverend Dr. Miller, in
New York, preached and published a discourse, commemorative of the same afflictive event. It * * contains an able and
elaborate argument against theatrical amusements."[2]

2. DEATH OF EDWARD MILLINGTON MILLER.

Heavy affliction now fell, with repeated stroke, upon the
New York pastor's household. The first of these troubles
was the loss of a darling child, to whom the following
extract from Dr. Miller's journal relates. There were two
older daughters, but this was the eldest son.

'February 5, 1812. On the evening of this day, our dear
son, *Edward Millington*, departed this life, in the seventh year
of his age. * * He was sick about ten or twelve days. His
disease terminated in dropsy of the brain. Though he was so
young, we had a comfortable, nay, a delightful, hope in his
death. He expressed himself in language, which not only
shewed that he anticipated his departure; but led us confidently to believe, that, by the grace of God, he was prepared
for it.

[1] Pp. 3, 4.   [2] P. 312.

'Death has thus, for the first time, entered my family. O Lord, sanctify to all of us this dispensation. Prepare all of us, who yet survive, for our own departure. * * May we find mercy of the Lord in that day!'

To Dr. Griffin Dr. Miller said, on the 6th of March,

'Since I wrote to you, it has pleased God to take away our dear Edward. He died, about four weeks ago, of an inflammation of the brain. We have reason to be thankful, that we have had much consolation attending the melancholy providence. My dear Sarah has been supported in a most remarkable manner. "The Lord gave, and the Lord hath taken away: blessed be the name of the Lord!"'

To Dr. Green he wrote, on the 21st of the same month,

'Please to tell Mrs. Green, that Mrs. Miller unites with me in affectionate regards to her; that we have both of us been sick almost ever since the death of our dear son; but that our covenant God has not left us comfortless under this dispensation.'

3.   Death of Doctor Edward Miller.

In a little more than a month after his son's death, Dr. Miller met with one of the sorest bereavements of his life, in the decease of his last remaining brother, particularly endeared to him by constant and most intimate association, for more than fifteen years, in New York. If the estimate of this brother about to be given may seem to any reader extravagant, and, especially, too eulogistic from the pen of a near relative, the following considerations may perhaps furnish a partial apology. The description is taken, in a great measure, from eulogies pronounced upon him, after his decease, by fellow physicians and others, uninfluenced by relationship. Moreover, his name descended in the family with a precious unction, as the very synonym of brotherly devotion; and even the members of the household born subsequently to his death, were taught, by the frequent recurrence of those who had known him to his virtues, to admire his character and venerate his memory. The writer is only uttering what the warm love and gratitude of his parents often expressed in the family circle, and fixed in the hearts of all their children.

There can be no doubt, that the fifteen years in New York, of renewed and closest intercourse between the two brothers, had been of mutual advantage, chiefly, perhaps, in cherishing principles and habits which they had together formed in their Delaware home. Edward was more than nine years the older, and, of course, his advice, opinions, and example had, on that account, greater influence with his younger brother. This influence was not wholly beneficial. The literary and scientific pursuits, companions, and recreations quite appropriate to a physician, tempted, no doubt, the gospel minister too far from the high duties of his sacred profession. Doctor Edward Miller was, moreover, as before mentioned, a very warm and decided politician of the Republican, or Democratic, stamp. Into politics, indeed, he carried a preëminent delicacy of thought, taste, feeling, and habit, which effectually prevented his becoming, under any temptation, a brawler. But, however refined and elegant in his political associations and intercourse; however carefully abstaining from the asperities and foulness of common party conflict; however mere politicians might have profited by his liberal, dignified, unblemished example; that example was, for this very reason, only the more seductive to one, who, by the bent of his own mind, was already tempted to participate in party strife, though not often untastefully, yet far too much for a minister of the gospel. And, on the other hand, doubtless, the clerical brother, had he shewn more decisively, both at home and abroad, that he was determined not to know anything save Jesus Christ and him crucified, would have exerted upon the physician a much more effectual religious influence. There is no element of power in the gospel so mighty, as conclusive evidence in the lives and labors of its ministers, that they regard the salvation of souls as an affair of indeed infinite importance; and that their one, all-engrossing thought is, by all means to save some.

But, beyond doubt, as to many points, their mutual influence, and especially that of the older on the younger, must have been of the happiest kind. Samuel was a valetudinarian throughout his ministry in New York, and probably owed his life to fraternal care and watchfulness. In the strictest temperance as to all the enjoyments of the table, and an abhorrence of tobacco, as, in every form, odious, unhealthful, and a provocative to drink, he was confirmed by his brother's example, which was that of the most rigid delicacy and self-command. Perhaps Edward was hardly equal to Samuel in formal, impressive manner; but he was hardly a whit inferior to him in any other characteristic of either the inside, or the outside, of a gentleman and a scholar. In classical and general culture he was the superior; his style of composition was the more compact and accurate, indicating a better disciplined, if not a more acute, mind; he had the more retentive and exact memory; and he excelled in discernment, which his appropriate studies and medical practice naturally improved. He was enthusiastic in his profession; a most diligent inquirer after scientific truth; prompt to grasp, and skillful to improve, every new idea; an unusually agreeable and instructive lecturer; unselfish and ready to promote the schemes of others; ever willing to spend and be spent for the sake of science, of humanity, or of natural affection; winningly earnest in his pursuits and benefactions; very successful in his practice; of sound judgment and admirable discretion; the sympathizing friend as well as the physician; the light and joy of the sick room; attaching his associates most warmly to him; simple, courteous and unaffected, sincere and affable in social intercourse; modest, sensitive, neat in dress, refined and guarded in thought and expression. Among all his characteristics, self-negation and delicacy of feeling were ever prominent. Such an example could not have failed to exert on every one around him a most beneficial influence.

Yet all that has been said would convey but a faint idea of his character in the domestic circle. Without any family, he lived for that of his brother—although not an inmate of the same dwelling, yet, as if this family were his own, devoting himself, with remarkable affection, to its interests. The ties by which the two brothers were united were a singular evidence of the Christian influences under which they had been trained in their father's house. In that little Delaware home-garden, with none of the appliances of wealth, in the midst of a strife almost for the necessaries of existence, with no fortune except the covenant inheritance from a pious ancestry, the simple hearted, laborious pastor had found time to cultivate, and not without a measure of success, the rarest native and exotic virtues; which were now beautifying the homes of another generation, where ampler means gave but wider diffusion to whatever they possessed of attractive grace and delicate perfume.

Dr. Miller, in his diary, thus noticed his brother's death :—

'March 17, 1812. To-day, departed this life, my beloved and affectionate brother, EDWARD MILLER, M. D., Professor of the Practice of Physic in the University of the State of New York. He had been sick, for a fortnight, with a catarrhal fever; but was supposed to be decisively convalescent, when the fever suddenly assumed a typhoid shape, and closed his life in a few hours. The first impression I had of his danger was when I perceived a delirium coming on. But then it was too late to say a word to him concerning his eternal hope and prospects. I could only pray by his side; which I did a number of times.

'I am now the only surviving son of seven born to my parents. One sister and myself are all that remain of nine children. Solemn situation! When shall I be called to give an account of my stewardship? Lord God, thou knowest. Oh, prepare me for all thy will.'

Appended to this at a later date, is found an additional expression of grateful remembrance :—

'The brother whose death is noticed on the preceding page was one of the most affectionate and devoted brothers that ever man had. * * He devoted himself to my comfort with peculiar zeal and affection. And, after his decease, though he gave me no intimation of it before, I found that he had bequeathed to me his whole property, amounting to more than $10,000, and made me his sole executor,

Doctor Edward Miller had never made a profession of religion, yet there seemed to be good ground for believing that he had "hope in his death."

Doctor Miller had, in 1803, been appointed, by the Governor and Council of the State of New York, Resident Physician of New York City, according to an act of the legislature, designed to guard against malignant epidemics, especially the yellow fever. Excepting the interval of about a year, he had retained this office until his death. The fever in question he had made his particular study;

and had been noted for maintaining, in coincidence with Dr. Benjamin Rush's opinion, that it was of domestic origin,—not imported from abroad,—and was not contagious.   In 1807, Doctor Miller had been elected Professor of the Practice of Physic in the new College of Physicians and Surgeons; and in 1809, one of the physicians of the New York Hospital; in which institution he had soon been appointed Clinical Lecturer.   These appointments also he had held until his decease.

A few days after the death of his brother, Dr. Miller received from Dr. Benjamin Rush the following letters of most affectionate condolence :—

'My dear Friend,   Philadelphia, March 19th, 1812.

'Col. *M'Lane* communicated to me in a short note, yesterday morning, the distressing intelligence of the death of my much loved and invaluable friend.   It afflicted me in the most sensible manner.   He was very dear to me, not only from his uncommon worth, but also because he was my early and uniform friend.   In an intercourse of thirty years, I never saw anything in him that was not calculated to excite affection, esteem, and admiration.   During the confederacy of my brethren against me, in the memorable years in which the Yellow Fever prevailed in our city, he openly advocated my principles and practice; and by the weight of his name, and the learning and ingenuity of his publications, contributed very much to their establishment in our country,   Judge of my affection for him, and the value I placed upon his integrity and friendship, when I add, that, four or five years ago, in a private interview, in my own house, I committed my lectures and manuscripts to him, to be revised by him, and published or destroyed as he saw proper, after my death.   He received this communication with a good deal of emotion, and promised to fulfill my wishes, in case he should survive me.—But why do I complain of the loss I have sustained by his death?   Science, Literature, Humanity, the United States, have all been deprived of one of their strongest pillars, and most beautiful ornaments.   They will long, very long deplore his early and premature removal from the high and useful station he filled in life.   They now mingle their tears with yours and mine. When the late Reverend *William Tennent*, of *Freehold*, heard of the death of his friend, Doctor *Finley*, he cried out, " I feel as if I had lost my broad-side.   He was my brother.   I could have gone to prison and to death with him !"   I imagine we both feel disposed to adopt the same affectionate and pas-

sionate expressions, in revolving in our minds the uncommon
virtues and attainments of our departed Friend and Brother.
His death has rendered the republic of medicine a solitude to
me; for he filled a place in my bosom which no physician in
our country is able, or if able, willing, to occupy.

'But in thus venting our sorrows to each other, let us not
forget the dictates of the holy religion we profess. God never
created any creature comfort, not even the innocent delights of
friendship and fraternal affection, to rise in rebellion against
himself; and however severely we may feel the loss of them, it
is probably intended to teach us that they are not indispensably
necessary to our substantial and permanent happiness; and
that there is indeed "a Friend that sticketh closer than a
brother."

'I will endeavour to write something for the public eye on
this distressing occasion. But ah! my friend,

> " Grief unaffected suits but ill with art,
> And flowing periods with a bleeding heart."

'Since the death of my illustrious fellow-laborer in the science of Medicine, and the awful summons it has conveyed to
me from the grave, I feel my ardor in my professional pursuits
suddenly suspended, and am ready to say to the sources of all
my knowledge and pleasures, in the language of the Scotch
poet, a little varied,

> "Books, wander where ye like, I dun no care,
> I'll break my pen, and never study mare."

'Accept of my tenderest sympathy for the death of your
darling little boy. Ah! Dr. *Miller*, Dr. *Miller!* my son, my
friend, my brother!

'Reverend Doctor *Miller*.   Benjamin Rush.'

'My dear Friend,   Philadelphia, March 24th, 1812.
'I continue to sympathize with you in the loss of your
excellent brother, and my much beloved friend. He was very
dear to me. During an intercourse of thirty years, I never saw
anything in him that was not calculated to excite affection,
esteem and admiration. I have learned much from his letters,
conversation and publications; and I am indebted to him, not
only for the public and able support he gave my principles and
practice, at a time when they were opposed by most of the
physicians in Philadelphia, but for the ability and elegance
with which he improved and extended them. I have endeavored to relieve my feelings by publishing a short tribute of
respect to his memory, in one of our newspapers, which I here-
with send you.[1] I wish you would collect and publish in one

[1] Biog. Sketch of Doctor Edward Miller, 'xxiv.

volume all his original papers, which he has scattered through the Medical Repository, as well as his inaugural Dissertation. They will be a valuable addition to the Medical Science of our country.

'Adieu, my dear Friend, and be assured again and again of the sympathy of yours affectionately,

'Benj'n Rush.'

In a postscript Dr. Rush says,

'It will be gratifying to me to be placed upon record with him in the libraries of our country, and to appear before the public, and to those who are to come after us, as his friend.'

In a letter of May 9th, he adds,

'I long to see you. We will exchange our sorrows when we meet, and talk over the worth of our common brother. But let us not forget our duties to the living, in weeping at the grave of the dead. We have both many important duties yet to perform to our fellow creatures. Mine will be limited in their nature and short in their duration. Your destiny, I hope, is a much higher one. Your talents (one of which is your popular name) and your time of life, all mark you for a high station and extensive usefulness in our country.

'From, my dear Friend, yours with
'great sympathy and regard,

'The Rev'd Dr. Miller,   Benj'n Rush.'

'William Dunlap, Esquire, one of Dr. Edward Miller's earliest acquaintances and friends in New York, noticed his death most sympathetically in a periodical publication of which he was the conductor. The following is one puragraph of that notice:—

"Every class of men joined in sympathetic regret, and in mournful testimonials to his superior worth. The assemblage of citizens, who attended to pay the last tribute of love and respect to his mortal remains, was numerous beyond example, except in the instance of the funeral of General Hamilton, whose death not only excited an extraordinary sensation, from the loss of a great and distinguished military and political leader, but from the manner and cause of his dissolution. In the instance I am recording, the uncommon concourse, not only of spectators, but of mourners, was unexpected ; for the tribute of sorrow was paid to a man whose actions were not like Hamilton's, exposed to the gaze of millions, but were confined to the abodes of sickness, or the retreats of meditation. The expression of grief was strong and universal."[1]

[1] Biog. Sketch, ciii. civ.

Immediately after his brother Edward's death, Dr. Miller felt the propriety of publishing, in a compact form, the best of his writings, prefixing a sketch of his life. Dr. Rush, the warm friend of both, strongly advised, as we have seen, such a publication. It was not completed, however, before the lapse of a little more than two years, and until after Dr. Miller's removal to Princeton.[1] During the interval, Dr. Rush, who was to have furnished the preliminary sketch, died—the 19th of April, 1813. In reference to this matter, the editor of the volume remarks, ﹅

"The reader will perceive, * * that a sketch of the life and character of Doctor Miller was promised by one, "who touched nothing which he did not adorn." Had his invaluable life been spared, a memorial of his friend might have been expected, far more interesting than even fraternal affection has been able to form. But, alas! this purpose, as well as others of much greater importance, was broken off by death. The editor, under the circumstances·in which he was placed, felt constrained to undertake himself the melancholy task."[2]

It is a peculiarity of this volume, that different portions of it are dedicated, severally, by the editor, to different persons, particular friends of Dr. Edward Miller. The dedications are favorable specimens of Dr. Samuel Miller's style in such complimentary addresses. Take for example that to Dr. Warren.[3]

"To

"JOHN WARREN, M. D.,

"PROFESSOR OF ANATOMY IN THE UNIVERSITY OF

"CAMBRIDGE, MASSACHUSETTS.

"DEAR SIR,

"THE obligation of my Family to You is of long standing. More than thirty-six years ago, when my eldest Brother fell a sacrifice to exposures and hardships encountered in the service of his Country, he enjoyed all the tender assiduities of

---

[1] "The Medical Works of Edward Miller, M.D., late Professor of the Practice of Physic in the University of New York, and Resident Physician for the City of New York. Collected and Accompanied with a Biographical Sketch of the Author; By Samuel Miller, D.D., Professor of Ecclesiastical History and Church Government, in the Theological Seminary of the Presbyterian Church in the United States, at Princeton, New Jersey. New York; 1814.— Crown 8vo. Pp. cxi. and 392._

[2] Biog. Sketch, iv.

[3] Biog. Sketch and Works, 180.

your friendship; expired in your arms; and was honoured by You in his death.

"Be not surprised that the remembrance of such a fact, gratefully cherished, should suggest, in collecting the writings of a younger Brother, of the same Family and Profession, the propriety of inscribing some production of his pen to You. Had it been possible to consult him on the subject, his affectionate veneration for the name of WARREN would have more than sanctioned the choice which led to this public testimony of respect and gratitude.

"That You may long continue to adorn your Profession, to enlighten the students of the Healing Art, and to bless your Country; and, at the close of a life equally useful and happy, may be graciously received to that world, in which the glimmerings of human science shall be lost in the radiance of Unbounded Knowledge, and the feeble exertions of philanthropy give place to the unfettered activity of perfect and eternal benevolence, is the ardent prayer of,

"My dear Sir,
"Your grateful friend and servant,

"*Princeton, N. J.,*
Jan. 20, 1814.   THE EDITOR."

CHAPTER TWENTY-FIRST.

1812, 1813.

---

1. THE THEOLOGICAL SEMINARY AND DR. ALEXANDER.

MRS. MILLER, as well as her husband, was busying her-self to provide funds for the new theological seminary. We find the following from her brother, which shows that she had asked from him a contribution.

'My dear Sister,   Philadelphia, October 1, 1812.

'I received to-day your good letter of the 29th ult., for which I have to thank you. I am fully satisfied that in this, as in everything else, you feel anxious for what you believe will be for my happiness and peace. Having received a share of temporal blessings greatly beyond what I merited or could expect, I should show a very slight sense indeed of the grati-tude I owe for them, if I were reluctant, or slow to aid those institutions, which we hope and believe are acceptable to him who is the giver of all good, and calculated, with his aid, to do good to mankind. To the Theological Seminary I will give exactly what you shall say I ought. Be pleased to name the sum. My fees for the fortnight (computing from this day) shall be so appropriated; but I fear they will not amount to much. Be good enough also to say, how I shall send the money, and to whom.

'Brother Thomas returned last evening, but I have scarcely seen him yet. Remember me affectionately to Mr. Miller, and to your children.

'Very truly
'Your affectionate brother,
'John Sergeant.'

The projected Theological Seminary occupied a large part of the time of the General Assembly of 1812. After much discussion, and special prayer for direction, Princeton was fixed upon as the place of its establishment. An agreement made between the Assembly's committee and a committee of the Trustees of the College of New Jersey, was ratified. It left the Seminary independent, while ensuring to it some material advantages. A letter from Richard Stockton, Esquire, of Princeton, promised four acres of land for the purposes of the principal edifice and a campus in front and rear; to which two acres were subsequently added as a donation from Dr. Green. Rules were adopted for the choice of directors and professors. The first board of directors was chosen, and, subsequently, the first professor, Dr. Archibald Alexander. An unknown writer has given the following graphic account of the scene in the Assembly, when to the man of its first choice was thus proffered the great honor of having the most important institution of the Church, and the training of her most precious youth—her candidates for the ministry—committed so specially to his trust.

"In the year 1812, the General Assembly, then in session in the city of Philadelphia, resolved to go into the election of Professor. The Rev. Mr. Flinn,[1] of Charleston, South Carolina, was Moderator. It was unanimously resolved to spend some time in prayer previously to the election, and that not a single remark should be made by any member, with reference to any candidate, before or after the balloting. Silently and prayerfully these guardians of the Church began to prepare their votes. They felt the solemnity of the occasion, the importance of their trust. Not a word was spoken, not a whisper heard, as the teller passed around to collect the result. The votes were counted, the result declared, and the Rev. Dr. Alexander was pronounced elected. A venerable elder of the church of Philadelphia, of which Dr. Alexander was pastor, arose to speak. But his feelings choked utterance. How could he part with his beloved pastor? His tears flowed until he sat down in silence. The Rev. Dr. Miller arose and said that he hoped the brother elected would not decline, however reluctant he might feel to accept; that if *he* had been selected by the voice of the Church, however great the sacrifice, he would not dare refuse. Little did he dream that on the following year he should be called by the same voice to give up the attractions of the city, to devote his life to the labors of an instructor. The Rev. Mr. Flinn called on the Rev. Dr. Woodhull, of Monmouth, to follow in prayer. He declined. Two others

_____
[1] Andrew Flinn, D. D. See 4 Sprague's Annals, 275.

were called on, and they declined, remarking that it was the Moderator's duty. He then addressed the throne of grace in such a manner, with such a strain of elevated devotion, that the members of the Assembly all remarked that he seemed almost inspired; weeping and sobbing were heard throughout the house.

"Amid the tears and prayers of the Church, Dr. Alexander was elected to the office. Amid the prayers and tears of the Church, he was laid in the tomb. But three of the members of that Assembly, it is believed, are now living. *Instead of thy fathers shall be thy children.*"[1]

It appeared that subscriptions for the Seminary had been obtained, including those reported the previous year, to the amount of $23,219, of which only $5,813 had been actually paid. The result, perhaps, has proved, that the projectors and founders of the institution had more faith than money to go upon, when they ventured to carry their plan into effect. Dr. Miller was one of the first Board of Directors, as Dr. Alexander also was.

On the last Tuesday—the 30th—of June, the Board held, at Princeton, their first meeting, and adjourned to meet again on the 12th of August following, the day which they fixed for Dr. Alexander's inauguration, This ceremony was performed at the time appointed. Dr. Miller delivered the first discourse—a sermon upon the Duty of the Church to take measures for providing an Able and Faithful Ministry, which was subsequently published.[2] A large part of it will be found in "The Life of Archibald Alexander, D. D.," whose biographer introduces his quotation by saying,

"It was an able investigation of the question, what is to be understood by an able and faithful gospel minister, which was made to include piety, talents, learning and diligence; and of the means which the Church is bound to employ for providing such a ministry. As many years have elapsed since this venerable man uttered his weighty judgment, as the topics are still of great moment, and as the discussion evinces the views of

---

[1] From the Presbyterian.

[2] "The Duty of the Church to take measures for providing an Able and Faithful Ministry: a Sermon, delivered at Princeton, August 12, 1812, at the Inauguration of the Rev. Archibald Alexander, D. D., as Professor of Didactic and Polemic Theology, in the Theological Seminary of the Presbyterian Church. By Samuel Miller, D. D., Pastor of the church in Wall street, New York."—2 Timothy ii. 2.—8vo. Pp. 50.

those who began the work of theological seminaries, we shall indulge ourselves by inserting an extract of some length."[1]

Dr. Alexanner's Inaugural Discourse followed—"a learned argument in behalf of biblical study." Then Dr. Philip Milledoler delivered a charge to the Professor and Students of Divinity. The latter, all counted, were but *three*: the new professor's own sons, at this time, just out-numbered his students.

2. CALLS TO COLLEGES.

In 1811, the University of North Carolina had given to Dr. Miller the Degree of Doctor of Divinity, with which, as we have seen, he had been honored, seven years before, by two other institutions.[2] On the 18th of May, 1812, he received a communication informally offering him the succession to the Rev. Joseph Caldwell,[3] as president of that University. 'To this letter,' he says in a note upon it, 'I returned an answer respectfully but decisively in the negative, a few days after receiving it. On the 30th of the following July, he had notice of his appointment to the presidency of Hamilton College, an institution just founded with flattering prospects of success and usefulness. In reply, he wrote as follows :—

'Gentlemen,   New York, August 17, 1812.

'I had the honor to receive, a fortnight ago, your communication of July 23d, announcing to me my election to the presidency of Hamilton College.

'This unexpected and highly flattering testimony of respect and confidence I receive with much gratification; and shall always reckon among the most valuable distinctions of my life. I beg you to communicate to the Board, whom you represent, the grateful sensibility with which it has inspired me; and to accept for yourselves my best acknowledgments for the polite manner in which you have been pleased to announce my appointment.

'After bestowing on this subject all that serious and most respectful deliberation, which its importance and circumstances demanded, I am constrained to believe, that it is my duty to return a negative answer to your call: and, accordingly, such an answer I now beg leave, through you, to communicate to the Board.

[1] P. 333.
[2] See p. 178.
[3] D. D. from 1816.   See 4 Sprague's Annals, 173.

'I am by no means ignorant of the favorable prospects of Hamilton College; nor of the wealth, population and numerous attractions of the district of country in which it is seated. And the names of those gentlemen, who are entrusted with the government of the Institution, are to me a sufficient pledge of all that liberality and urbanity, which would render the situation of an office under them both happy and useful. But my delicate health; the ties by which I am bound to a large and most affectionate congregation; my domestic connexions and habits; together with some literary plans which render my continuing to reside in, or near, this city peculiarly convenient and desirable: all conspire to impress on my mind the deep and unwavering conviction, that I ought not, at present, to remove from New York; and especially to engage in an undertaking, which requires far more vigor both of body and of mind, than I can possibly consider myself as possessing.

'I would most willingly, Gentlemen, have complied with your request to make a visit to your part of our state, before forming such a decision as I have now communicated; were it not that a variety of circumstances render it impossible for me, at present, to leave home; and also that such a step might be supposed by some to indicate, that I was still deliberating on a subject, on which I wish my decision to be considered as complete and final.

'With earnest prayers that Hamilton College may speedily and long prosper; and that the views of the Board of Trustees may be more suitably and more successfully directed to some other candidate,

'I am, Gentlemen, with much personal respect,
'Your obliged and obedient servant,

'To Jonas Platt, Thomas R. ⎫
Gold, and Morris Miller, ⎬　　　　Samuel Miller.'
Esquires, Committee, etc. ⎭

3.   DR. GREEN AND THE COLLEGE OF NEW JERSEY.

Upon the resignation of the presidency of the College of New Jersey, by the distinguished Samuel Stanhope Smith, D.D., Ashbel Green, D.D., was unanimously elected his successor. Of this transaction the latter has given the following account:—

"On the 14th of August, 1812, I was unanimously elected by the Trustees of the College of New Jersey as President of the institution of which they were the guardians. Strange as it may appear, it is notwithstanding a fact, that eighteen hours

before this occurrence, I was not aware that such an event was
in the contemplation of any one.   My own mind was most decidedly opposed to it.   The facts of the case were the following.
At the first meeting of the Board of Directors of the Theological Seminary at Princeton, I had preached a sermon in which
I had laid down the doctrine that every minister of the gospel
was a *devoted man;* bound by the tenor of his vocation to serve
God in any place and in any manner to which divine providence should call him.   My special reference in this statement
was to Dr. Alexander, who at that time had not explicitly consented to assume the station which he has ever since most ac-
ceptably occupied.   The Board of Trustees of the College had
met at Princeton on the day before my election, and had chosen
a Vice-president of the institution, and had agreed to proceed
to the election of a President on the following morning.   Dr.
Miller, without my knowledge or suspicion, had gone to every
individual of the Board and persuaded them to give me a
unanimous vote, and to throw the responsibility of rejecting it
on myself.   He himself was the man that I had determined to
nominate as the President of the College.   Col. Ogden, who
sat next to me in the Board of Trustees, said to me while we
were preparing our votes for the Vice-president, "Suppose we
should give you a unanimous vote for this office, as a stepping-
stone to the one which we are to vote for in the morning."   I
immediately replied, "In that event, I would instantly and absolutely refuse both."   He replied, "We shall do what we think
right, and you will do the same."   After the Board of Trustees adjourned I spoke to Richard Stockton, and he told me
that "my friend Miller could tell me all about it."   I immediately went to Dr. Miller's quarters, and "he did tell me all
about it."   He informed me explicitly, that the Board would
give me a unanimous vote for the Presidentship of the College
on the coming day, and threw on me the responsibility of refusing the office.   I went to my lodgings much agitated.   My
wife was with me, and as soon as we had retired for the night,
I told her what had taken place, and added that my mind was
made up to refuse the appointment at once.   She cautioned me
against precipitancy, and said that she thought I ought to hold
it under consideration.   On my bed I made a new consecration
of myself, and resolved that I would abide by the doctrine of
my sermon to which I have referred, and then I was free from
agitation and slept comfortable till morning.   I rose early and
wrote a letter to the Trustees, of which I have a copy, telling
them that my appointment to the Presidentship of the College
was altogether unexpected, and that the indispensable condi-

29

tion of my holding it under consideration was, that my doing so should not be considered as any intimation that I would finally accept the appointment, otherwise they had my answer at once in the negative. This letter I gave to Dr. Miller, and he read it to the Board of Trustees in my presence. After this letter was read, I made a short address to the Board, thanking them for the confidence reposed in me, and then said that I should retire. The Board opposed this, and gave a unanimous vote in my presence."[1]

The prominent and active part which Dr. Miller took in the election of Dr. Green to the college presidency was, no doubt, due especially to the fact, that several leading and influential trustees had before conferred with him in regard to his accepting the office himself; assuring him that, if he would at all entertain such a proposition, the President's chair would be regularly offered to him at once. But, for the same reasons for which, chiefly, he had before refused similar overtures from other quarters, he now resolutely declined this proposal. He felt that neither his health was sufficient, nor his temperament fitted, for the peculiar duties and trials of a college president; and doubtless his judgment was right. To a more honorable post he could hardly have aspired; but his feeble, nervous body gave little promise of sustaining him, especially in that calm, prompt, firm, resolute discipline which the office would have required.

On behalf of the committee appointed by the trustees to confer with Dr. Green about his appointment, and as a personal friend, Dr. Miller had a good deal of correspondence with him at this juncture, some extracts from which may interest the reader. On the 18th of August, he wrote,

' I hope, my dear Sir, that your impressions in favor of accepting this appointment are daily becoming stronger; and cannot help cherishing the expectation, that your next letter will bring the most unequivocal encouragement in the case. When I recollect, how much depends, under God, upon the head of that college; how much he can do for or against the best interests of our church; and the extreme difficulty, not to say impossibility, of procuring a suitable president, if you decline accepting the office; I do not see how you can *dare to refuse*. But I forbear to enter more fully into the subject at present. We have, at different times, discussed it, in all its bearings, so

<hr>

[1] Lif of Dr. Green, 338, etc.

largely, that I know not whether I can suggest a single idea that is new. One thing, I think, may be confidently asserted; and that is, that you may expect from a majority of the Board of Trustees all that encouragement and support, which friendship and public spirit can dictate.

'Be pleased to communicate to me as soon as possible, what steps it will be proper for the committee to take, in prosecuting your call. If it be judged necessary, or even desirable, that we should go in a body to Philadelphia, to attend the Presbytery, we shall be ready, I doubt not, to go, whenever we shall be apprized of the time. I will, however, take the liberty of adding, that, as I have paid one visit to Philadelphia, and two others to Princeton, within three months; as I must be in Princeton again, if I live, the last week of September; and as I design, with the leave of Providence, to take a long journey for my health, toward the latter part of October and embracing the greater part of the month of November; if our going to Philadelphia can be dispensed with, *just as well as not,* consistently with due respect to you, and proper fidelity to our appointment, it will relieve me from a very inconvenient journey; especially now, when, in the midst of the printing of Dr. Rodgers's life, every absence of forty-eight hours incommodes both me and the printer. On this subject give me your whole mind without reserve.

'I hope you will not fail to tell Mrs. Green of the pleasantness of Princeton; of the healthfulness of the place; of the probability that her husband would continue to be at least ten years longer popular and useful there than in Philadelphia, etc., etc., etc. These things she ought to know; and I hope you will not conceal them from her. My wife is ardently engaged in favor of your going: scarcely an hour passes in which she does not suggest some measure for forcing you to go. I am fully persuaded she would make a much better trustee than several that I could name, who have seats at the Board. May the great Head of the Church direct and bless you! So prays

'Your affectionate friend and brother,

'Sam'l Miller.'

On the 27th of the same month, he said,

'* * I consider it as much that you do not positively say *No.*

'My wife and myself united with you in observing Tuesday last, as a day of special prayer. May the great Head of the Church give an answer of peace, and direct in this momentous concern!

'* * I have some reason to believe, that Hamilton College, in this state, which lately gave me a call to the presidency of that institution, will on receiving my negative answer, which I sent a fortnight ago, unanimously elect Dr. McLeod their president. If so, I have my doubts whether he will come to us. But, my dear Friend, I hope you will give yourself no uneasiness about this matter. If you accept the presidency, and Dr. McLeod declines, I hope the Trustees will, as one man, see the propriety of your having the principal voice in choosing your second in command, and will leave it pretty much with you to select. Although it would not do to use this language publicly, yet I have the most entire confidence, that a majority of the Board will feel thus and act accordingly.

'Being much hurried last week, and not having time to write several long letters; and feeling also, that, as I am personally acquainted with almost all your elders, it might seem invidious to write to one or two of them; I determined to address a letter to them collectively. I accordingly did so, and inclosed it to Mr. Ralston. Perhaps this was ill-judged, but I did it for the best. If I can do anything more in this way, please to direct me with as much freedom as if you were utterly uninterested in the business.'

With most unfeigned and very great pleasure, Dr. Miller hailed Dr. Green's acceptance of the presidency.

'I desire,' said he in writing to the latter on the 15th of September—'I desire, with all my heart, to bless God for the favorable accounts which your letter contains, with respect to the matter which has been the great subject of our correspondence for some weeks past. I have no longer any doubt that the whole affair has been of the Lord; and I hope and pray that his blessing may rest upon it. The same account substantially with that which your letter contains had reached this city, in various ways, before it came from yourself, and gladdened the hearts of the friends of religion and of the College more than I can express. Mr. Robert Smith, your worthy elder, visited us, with his lady, at Bloomingdale, and gave us distinctly to understand, not only that he believed you would, but that he thought you ought to accept of a station to which the providence of God appeared so unexpectedly and wonderfully to point. He talked like a judicious man and a Christian; and I further gathered from him, that, in the opinions and views which he expresssd, the session of your church was nearly, if not entirely, unanimous.'

The selection of a vice-president of the institution—one acceptable to Dr. Green and the Trustees, and well qualified for the professorial duties which would fall to his lot—presented no small difficulty. A few words which Dr. Miller adds respecting one candidate for this office shows that Hopkinsianism was still, perhaps increasingly, agitating the Presbyterian Church.

'With regard to Dr. —— I have also several objections. In the first place, I think his Hopkinsianism a solid, if not insuperable one; not as to a question of heresy, but as a matter of prudence, considering what has lately passed; and considering, too, that there is hardly any man in our Church who feels more sore and irritable on this point than ——, the great patron of the Vice-president and the largest contributor to the fund by which he is to be supported. But, at the same time, I should, on several accounts, much deprecate this question (Hopkinsianism) being made a subject of public discussion. Further, Dr. —— was not happy in ——: he is not happy in ——, and wishes to leave it. When I see things of this sort, I cannot help suspecting there is some material fault in the individual. Besides, I have learned from both —— and ——, that he is charged with a very inordinate money making disposition, which, it is said, leads him often to the meanest parsimony. If these things be so; and if the amiableness of his temper be also questionable, it will be better to think of some other person. * *

'After all, to say the truth, I think it would be much better policy, to take nobody, in the present case, from New England. I should prefer—much prefer—taking some respectable Western or Southern man. This would be, on various accounts, an important step toward making Princeton the great centre, which we desire to have it—and, more especially, since so much has been recently said about Hopkinsianism.'

The following plan for the inauguration of Dr. Green was adopted by the Board of Trustees :—

'I. That Dr. Woodhull introduce the exercises by prayer and singing.

'II. That, at the close of the Psalm, the presiding member of the board, in the name of the board, present to the President elect the key of the College, the key of the Library, and a copy of the printed laws, pronouncing him at the same time, in the Latin language, the President of the College, and invested with all the powers and privileges of that office.

'III. That immediately after this, Dr. Miller address the President in a short speech, also in the Latin language, to which he will be expected to reply in the same language.

'IV. The President then to deliver an inaugural oration in English.'

The following minute appears in proximity to the plan above given.

'After the adjournment of the board, and when President Smith had retired, Dr. Miller offered the following resolution which was unanimously agreed to, (viz.,)

'On motion, *Resolved*, that the members of the Board who are present will wait in a body on Dr. Smith for the purpose of expressing to him, in person, their tender sympathy on the infirm state of his health, their highly respectful and grateful sentiments towards him for his long and faithful services, and their fervent wishes for his welfare and happiness in retirement; and also to take an affectionate leave of him in his official character.

In communicating the plan of inauguration to Dr. Green, on the 2d of October—the day after its adoption—Dr Miller gives a little expansion to it, beginning with the third article, as follows :—

'3. Dr. Miller then to rise and address the President in a short speech, of the nature of a charge, in Latin; (N.B. This I am resolved to make *very* short;) to which the President will be expected to reply, in a few sentences, in the same language. This to be done on the stage.

'4. The President then to ascend the pulpit, and deliver an inaugural address in *English*, as *long* and as *good* as he pleases.

'5. Dr. Clark to conclude with prayer, singing and benediction.

'How do you like the plan? Dr. Smith disliked having any English, and called it *pie bald*. But a large majority of the Board thought differently. This is almost the exact plan pursued at the induction of Kirkland at Cambridge. His long speech was in English.

'I hope, with the leave of Providence, to see you in Princeton, about the 2d or 3d of next month, on my way to the southward for about eighteen or twenty days. It is my purpose to attend the inauguration on my way home again.'

On the 12th of October, Dr. Miller added,

'I wish you had sent me a copy of your reply to my charge. Let your son copy it for me. I have not yet written a line of mine; and I have no doubt yours would *help* me. Pray let me have it. I do not expect to begin mine for some days yet.'

The inauguration of Dr. Green was, for various reasons, delayed. The greater part of November Dr. Miller spent in travelling, doubtless for his health; and we find him writing on the 19th of that month from Baltimore, to inquire when the ceremony would take place. He records having preached, during this absence, in the city just named for Dr. Inglis,[1] in the Capitol at Washington, and in Wilmington for Dr. Read.[2] The destruction, by fire, of the church edifice, in which the inauguration exercises were to be held, and other causes, determined the Trustees, at length, to abandon the whole programme; and Dr. Green continued to wield the academical sceptre without being formally crowned. He tells us, that he turned his proposed Inaugural, partly, into a Baccalaureate discourse. The Latin addresses, which he and Dr. Miller were to have delivered, being wholly incapable of any such adaptation, sad to relate, were a total loss; unless Dr. Miller used his, as not improbably he did, eleven years[3] later, at the inauguration of President Carnahan.

4. CORRESPONDENCE.

The following letter from Dr. Miller to his niece, Ann Patten, afterwards Mrs. John Wales, of Wilmington, Delaware, contains some hints in regard to his method of preparation for the pulpit, as well as part of the history of a particular sermon—the same refered to by Dr Sprague in his reminiscences on a subsequent page. The 'Record of Preaching' shows that it was delivered on each of the three occasions just mentioned—in Baltimore on the 8th, Washington on the 15th, and Wilmington on the 22d—as also in New York on the 29th, of November, and elsewhere on several subsequent dates. Dr. Sprague probably heard it in the College Hall, at Princeton, on the 10th of August, 1817.

'My dear Niece, New York, January 23, 1813.

'I am ashamed to recollect, that it is now more than four weeks since I received your affectionate letter of December 22d. But when you learn that I have scarcely known the comfort of one day's health, since I saw you, owing to a succession of severe colds; and also, that, amidst all this tedious indisposition, I have been constantly hurried, in consequence of my studies and other professional concerns falling very much in arrears by my absence, in November, I hope you will pardon my long

---

[1] 4 Sprague's Annals, 278. [2] 3 Sprague's Annals, 301.
[3] Nonumque prematur in annum. *Horat. Epist. ad Pisones*, 388.

delay in writing this letter. I assure you, my dear Ann, I have fixed on twenty different times, in my own mind, to sit down and answer you; but have never found a leisure hour for the purpose, when my health admitted of writing, until the present.

'I need not say, it gave me great pleasure to find, that the sermon which I delivered in Wilmington, when last there, was agreeable to you and any of your young friends; and particularly that you wished for an opportunity of pondering more deeply and seriously on the doctrines and sentiments then uttered. I should most willingly send you a copy of that sermon, if I had one. But really the discourse, as you heard it, was never written. The *substance* of it I had committed to writing, in my *contracted short-hand* way; and I had delivered it on several occasions; but it would be altogether impossible for me to exhibit, now, on paper, what I uttered from the pulpit. To comply with your wish and that of your friends, I would sit down, and attempt to commit to writing, as nearly as my memory would enable me, what I delivered; but I must beg you to excuse me from the task on account of my health. My breast is so weak, and writing is such a burden to me, that I do not write a sermon out at full length more than once in two or three years.

'It gave me, my dear Niece, more pleasure than I can express, to read that part of your letter in which you speak of the impression which the death of your young acquaintance made upon you, and refer to the solemnity and importance of that event to every one of us. Yes, we must all soon die; and he alone who gave us life knows how soon. Remember, also, that nothing can enable a poor, sinful mortal to triumph in that hour, but *Christian hope*. The best wish I can form for you is, that, being made sensible of your guilt and pollution, by nature and practice, you may feel your need of that Saviour, who is the resurrection and the life, and receive him by faith as the Lord your Righteousness. Believe it, the more you examine your own heart, in the light of God's Word, the more clearly you will perceive your want of a better righteousness than your own; and the more you meditate on the Lord Jesus, the more you will perceive, that he is worthy of all your confidence and all your love.

'Do you know, my Dear, that the lines which you have quoted from the seventeenth Psalm by Watts, are the very lines which your Grandmother Miller had on her lips when she was dying? May you live as she lived, and die as she died!'

The following letter to Dr. Green, which shows unabated activity in planning and laboring, shows, too, that

Dr. Miller had not the slightest expectation of the call to Princeton which he received about two months afterward. His feelings, projects, and purposes all still bound him to New York.

 'My dear Sir,   New-York, March 17, 1813.

  'Dr. Romeyn, Dr. McLeod and myself have undertaken to be joint editors of a new religious periodical work—probably a monthly one. We hope some important advantages to the union of the Church in this city, and to the general advancement of religion, will result from its establishment.

 'Though our national rulers do not always provide funds to support their appropriations, yet, perhaps, it is always proper for clergymen to be more careful and provident. The object of this letter is to ascertain, whether you will allow us to rely on you and Dr. Alexander as stated contributors to the work. Can you not give us leave to depend upon each of you for eight octavo pages of matter once in two months; so as to furnish one original piece from Princeton for each number? If you cannot promise so much, can you not encourage us to hope for a communication from each once in each quarter of the year? Do not say, No! I scarcely need to add, that the pieces may be doctrinal, practical, critical, biographical, etc., as you please; and that any *fair* contrivance to eke out the number of pages will be admissible. In return for this, we will send each of you regularly a copy of the work, or two copies, if you please, and, over and above all, each of us make you a bow down to the very ground.

 'But, seriously, I hope, my dear Sir, that you and Dr. Alexander will consider this application as something more than a mere formality. I know not that we shall attempt to engage more than two or three correspondents besides yourselves; and unless four or five stated and able contributors, out of the city, can be counted upon, the work cannot proceed. I believe that important service may be rendered by such a work, well conducted, to the interests of religion in our country, especially in the present juncture of the Presbyterian Church. But, if it be not well conducted, and if there be not a fair prospect of its continuing for some time, it had better not be undertaken.

 'Will you have the goodness, as soon as convenient, to communicate this letter to Dr. Alexander, and to request him to consider it as addressed to himself? I have so much to do in the writing way, that I am tempted to seize with avidity all labor saving contrivances in my communications.

    'I remain, dear Sir,

                    'Yours respectfully and affectionately,

'Rev. Dr. Green.   Sam'l Miller.

'P. S. * *

'P. P. S. S. Our periodical work, which will perhaps be styled "The Scriptural Advocate," will probably not be commenced for four or five months.'

CHAPTER TWENTY-SECOND.

CALL TO THE THEOLOGICAL SEMINARY AT PRINCETON.

1813.

1. ELECTION TO THE SECOND PROFESSORSHIP.

DR. MILLER was a member of the General Assembly which convened in Philadelphia on Thursday, the 20th of May, 1813. On the 26th, it was resolved to choose an additional professor in the Theological Seminary; and, immediately, according to a rule formed upon the precedent in Dr. Alexander's case, special prayer was offered imploring direction in the choice, which was declared an order of the day for the 28th. On the 27th, as if foreshadowing the subsequent appointment of a professor of Ecclesiastical History, it was

"*Resolved,* That all the papers relative to the history of the Presbyterian Church in the United States, in the hands of Dr. Green and Mr. Hazard, be by them deposited with Dr. Miller, and that he be appointed and directed to continue and complete said history; and that the arrangement in regard to the copyright of this history, which right has heretofore been assured to Dr. Green and Mr. Hazard, be settled between them and Dr. Miller, as shall be mutually satisfactory to the parties severally."[1]

This resolution was passed at the instance of Dr. Ashbel Green and Ebenezer Hazard, Esquire, who had been appointed historians of the Presbyterian Church by the Assembly of 1804; had made considerable progress in writing the work contemplated, and in gathering materials; but, finding their own further attention to it impracticable, now requested that it might be transferred to Dr. Miller

[1] Min. 1813, 535.

for completion. Although the latter accepted the appointment, he seems to have been able to accomplish little or nothing in the fulfillment of its duties. By the Assembly of 1819,[1] Dr. Green was associated with him " in writing the history of the Presbyterian Church;" but, in 1825,[2] both requested to be released from their appointment. This request was " received with unfeigned regret;" but as, " under the circumstances, both reasonable and proper," was granted. The materials already obtained by Dr. Green, and his unfinished work gratuitously offered, were then deposited with a committee appointed to preserve them, and make further collections. In fine, by the Assembly of 1853,[3] all the manuscript materials of this kind, previously collected under their authority, were transferred to the custody of the Presbyterian Historical Society.

On the day appointed for the choice of a second professor for the Theological Seminary, it was first,

" *Resolved*, That the Professor to be chosen this morning, be the Professor of Ecclesiastical History and Church Government, and that his salary be eighteen hundred dollars per annum, and the use of a house."[4]

Afterwards the election was made by ballot, and resulted in the choice of Dr. Miller, who had been nominated by Dr. Green, at the request of the Board of Directors.[5] The Rev. Drs. James Hall and Ashbel Green were appointed a committee to wait upon him and inform him of his appointment.

2. DOUBTS AND FEARS.—ACCEPTANCE.

Although Dr. Miller had expressed himself, as we have seen, so strongly, in regard to the duty of Dr. Alexander to bow to the voice of the Church; and although, doubtless, his own unbiased conviction would have led him at once to yield; it is evident that serious difficulties in the way of his acceptance of the professorship rose before his mind; and that his decision to accept it, though a.ways, in his own thoughts and those of his friends, most likely, was not immediately reached. The following letter, written to Dr. Green three days after his election, and before he left Philadelphia, is, perhaps, the best record extant of his views at this time.

[1] Minutes, 718.   [2] Id., 254, 258.   [3] Id., 453.
[4] Minutes, 536.   [5] Life of Dr. Green, 348.

'Rev'd and dear Sir,   Philadelphia, May 31, 1813.
        'Upon mature reflection, I think the letter which I requested you to address to my session, on the late choice of the General Assembly, had better be written and transmitted to them with all convenient speed.

'I take the liberty of communicating this opinion, not because I have made up my mind, nor because I view a removal to Princeton at all more favorably than when I saw you ; but because it is my wish, as soon as possible after my arrival in New York, to know the temper and feelings of my people there; and I cannot conceive of a better introduction of the subject to them than through your communication.

'Please to address your letter to Dr. Rodgers, as your particular friend, to be communicated.

' If my heart does not deceive me, I desire to know simply the *will of God* on this interesting subject. As to considerations of personal comfort, they are so nearly balanced in making out the account current, that I could not lay much stress on them, even if it were proper to assign them a more important place than they ought to fill.

'Pray for me, my dear Sir, that it may please the Head of the Church to give me a single eye to his glory in forming my decision, and that the path of duty may be rendered plain. I am in a great conflict, and do not expect to be in any measure relieved from it until I return to New York. If your letter to Dr. Rodgers could reach his hands as early as by Thursday's mail, I should be glad.
                'I am, dear Sir,
                        'Most respectfully and affectionately yours,
'Dr. Green.   Sam'l Miller.'

Again he wrote,

' My dear Sir,   Bloomingdale, June 14, 1813.
        'Your kind letter of June 9th reached me on Friday last, just as I was engaged in removing my family to this place. We are now, through divine goodness, comfortably fixed here; and I seize upon the earliest moment of leisure to address you in answer.

'Your letter was duly received by Dr. Rodgers, and promptly communicated to his brethren of the session. It softened them and almost convinced them that I ought to go; insomuch, that if it had depended on the session, and a vote had then been taken, I believe they would not have dared to resist my leaving them for the new station. But, in the course of ten days, they have relapsed into nearly their original frame of mind on the subject; and how it would be if a vote were now to be taken, I cannot with confidence say.

'I did not know, until now, how much I loved my people nor had I the least idea that they would be so unwilling to part with me. One point, however, I believe is well secured. Though my people will not generally consent to my going; yet they will not be angry with me, or accuse me of improper motives, if I do go. Even those of them who suppose that in deciding to go, I shall decide unwisely, and very differently from what they can approve, yet fully believe that I shall decide conscientiously. I have not heard of one severe, or unkind suggestion from any person. For this I feel that I have much reason to feel thankful, and I hope it will, in any event, lighten my burden.

'I have not yet made any official communication to my Session or people. The former, with the leave of Providence, will have a meeting on Thursday next, when I calculate to have a free and full conversation with them. My decision is not yet definitely formed, yet I am strongly inclined to the opinion that I shall ultimately decide in favour of accepting the appointment. So much I shall probably tell the Session on Thursday: whether I shall go further, at that time, will depend, humanly speaking, on circumstances.

'If my decision should, as it probably will, be to remove to Princeton, it is not very likely that I shall be able to get away from New York till September or October. On this, however, as well as on every other point, I must leave things in uncertainty for the present. As soon as I gain any of the requisite materials for forming a definite plan on this point, I intend to write to Mr. Bayard about a house. Until then I should consider it premature to say anything on that subject.

'In the course of my last interview with Mr. Bayard, he suggested something about a probability that Mrs. Brown's house might be for sale, or to rent, in the course of two or three months. If there be any prospect of this, I should be glad to know it. With the best respects to Mrs. Green, in which Mrs. Miller joins,

'I am, dear Sir,
'affectionately yours,
'Sam'l Miller.'

Still again he wrote to Dr. Green,

'My dear Sir,   New-York, June 26, 1813.

'Mr. Bayard will probably have told you, that I have communicated to my session, that I deem it my duty to accept the appointment of the General Assembly. What course things are likely to take in the congregation, I cannot yet judge.

'Some near friends of Mr. ——, (the young man who so impiously cut the Bible in your college hall,) in this city, have applied to me with great importunity and tenderness, soliciting his readmission into college.   They are respectable people; and I hear from them that he is deeply penitent ; that he is ready to make any acknowledgment or reparation for his crime ; that he speaks, especially, in the most respectful and affectionate terms of Mr. Clark, whose name was so shamefully mentioned on the card ; and that they have the deepest persuasion, and are ready to pledge themselves, that he will manifest by his future conduct the sincerity of his repentance, and his determination not to abuse the favor bestowed upon him.

'As I never saw the young man to know him, I can say nothing from my personal knowledge.   But if the number and respectability of friends, and the deepest affliction and most solemn pledges on their part, can indicate anything favorable, there is much reason to augur well in his case.

'Whether the faculty would deem themselves at liberty to restore this youth without a vote of the trustees, I know not. But if they do, I will say, as a trustee, that they will not be blamed by me.

'I have been deeply affected by the importunity and tears of his friends, and should be glad to be able to say anything favorable to them.

'I am, dear Sir, yours affectionately,
'Sam'l Miller.

The student, referred to in the preceding letter, had been dismissed for cutting out portions from consecutive leaves in the large Bible lying upon the desk, in the College Hall, for use in public worship, so as to form a cavity, in which he had deposited a pack of cards.   This impious offence was among the events which led to the formation of the Nassau Hall Bible Society, and seems to have been overruled for much good.

3.   FAREWELL TO NEW YORK.

The following letter, announcing his acceptance of the Professorship at Princeton, was addressed

'To the joint meeting of the officers of the Church in Wall street, to be held this day.

New York, June 24, 1813.

'My dear Brethren,

'An event has occurred, of an interesting nature to you, and of the deepest importance to me.   A late appointment by the General Assembly of our Church—an appointment which I never sought, but made every justifiable exertion to avoid—has laid me under the solemn necessity of deciding, whether it is my duty to remain your pastor, or to leave my present charge for another station in the Church.

'After the most careful and serious view which I have been able to take of the path of duty in this case:—after maturely deliberating, on the one hand, on the peculiar and highly interesting state of our church, and the endearing ties, which, for twenty years, and more especially for the last four years, have bound me to you as a minister; and after weighing, on the other hand, my obligations to the church at large ; the importance and prospects of the Seminary to which I am called ; and the unanimity and decision with which my brethren in the ministry have pronounced, that I ought not to reject this call:— I have deemed it proper to intimate to the session, that it appears to me my duty to accept the appointment in question, and of course, to apply to the Presbytery, in due time, to dismiss me from my pastoral charge.

'The considerations, my dear Brethren, by which I have been chiefly influenced in forming this decision, are the two following:—a firm persuasion that my *usefulness* will be likely to be greatly extended by the contemplated change; and an equally deep and unwavering impression, that my *health* and *strength* are not equal to the *multiplied labours*, and the *constant exertion*, both in and out of the pulpit, which I believe to be indispensable, in the present state of the city, to the prosperity and growth of our church. Supposing these impressions really and strongly existed on my mind, (and I know that you believe me incapable of feigning them,) you will not wonder that I have come to the conclusion, that the Providence of God calls me to the new station, to which I have been so unexpectedly appointed.

'The theological seminary in which I propose to accept this office, is, indeed, at present, in its infancy. But my brethren in the ministry were of the opinion, that a second professor was indispensable in order to place the institution, in any tolerable degree, on a footing with others, of a similar kind, in our country ; and that no time was to be lost, in making exertions and sacrifices for the purpose of raising it to something like the station which it ought to occupy. And I can only add, that, after a most intimate acquaintance with all its affairs and prospects, from the beginning, if I had not been firmly of the opinion, that, with good management, and under the divine blessing, it will be likely, in a short time, greatly to increase, and to become extensively useful to the Church of Christ, I should never have thought of consenting to be one of its officers, and devoting the remainder of my life to its interests.

'In deciding, that it is my duty to retire from my present situation, I have had painful conflicts. If my attachment to the congregation which I serve were not strong and ardent, I should be among the most ungrateful and unfeeling of men. Their kindness, their indulgence, and their multiplied favors, have laid me under obligations which I can never cease to acknowledge. My long and happy connection with them renders the thought of severing the ties which bind us peculiarly painful. And I can truly say, that there is no pastoral charge in the United States, for which I should be willing to exchange that in which Providence has placed me. But verily believing, that, under the divine blessing, I can be more useful to the Church of Christ, as a professor in the new seminary, than in any pastoral charge whatever, you will, of course, so far as you give me credit for candour in this belief, fully justify my decision. God is my witness, Brethren, that worldly emoluments and worldly honors have not influenced me in this decision. You perfectly well know, from the circumstances of the case, that considerations of this nature *cannot possibly* have entered into my motives. I *may* be mistaken in my estimate of duty on the occasion; but, unless every feeling of my heart deceives me, the estimate is honestly made.

'I need not inform you, Brethren, for you already know, that within the last three years, the office of president, in three colleges, has been, at different times, placed fairly within my reach. But, as you also know, all these offers (though at least *one* of them was much more tempting, in a *worldly view*, than that which I now propose to accept) were firmly rejected by me, under a deliberate conviction, that I was more *useful* and more *happy* as your minister, than I was likely to be in either of those stations. I trust that facts of this kind will be considered as affording satisfactory proof, that I am sincerely attached to the people of my charge; that I have felt myself happy in my connexion with them; that their kindness to me has not been either forgotten or lightly esteemed; and that, in finally determining to leave them, if Providence permit, I am not actuated by *worldly* or *sinister* motives.

'My decision on this subject has been formed and announced the more speedily, because it appeared to me that further *suspense* would be injurious to the congregation. And if, in forming this decision, I have sought the advice and counsel of the officers of the church less than the importance of the question, both to them and to me, as well as our mutual friendship, might seem to demand; I beg you to be assured, that it has not been owing to any want of respect or affection; but to a deliberate conviction that their feelings would prevent them from being impartial judges; and that it had fallen to my lot, to have an extent and an intimacy of acquaintance with the importance, the prospects, and the general interests of the seminary, to which I am called, which none of my brethren among the officers of our church could possibly have.

'If, however, after all, you should still be disposed to think, that I ought to have *consulted* and *advised* more extensively with my friends, before deciding, I hope you will cover, what may be considered as my mistake, on this subject, with the mantle of charity, and not suffer it to interfere with that mutual affection and friendship, which it is my earnest desire may attend our parting, and continue through life.

'With respec tto the *time*, the *circumstances*, and the *manner*, of my withdrawing from you, both duty and affection dictate, that I should be governed, as far as possible, by your wishes, and your views of the interest of the congregation. If I reach Princeton by the latter end *of October*, or the beginning of November, it will, I presume, answer every purpose; and I should fondly hope, that, by that time, or before, you may not only have engaged, but also have actually brought into your service, another pastor. If you think that my stay, until that period, will promote your edification, it will give me great pleasure, with the leave of providence, to order my plans accordingly. If, on the contrary, you should be of the opinion, that my departure, at an earlier day, would be more advisable, tell me so with the most fraternal freedom; and, instead of being offended, I shall feel myself honoured by your frankness and confidence.

'I will only add, my dear Brethren, that, as long as I continue your pastor, it will not only be my *duty*, as well as my *pleasure*, to serve you as heretofore; but also, that, in the present exigency of your affairs, it will gratify me more than I can express, to be able to promote, in any way, the temporal or spiritual interests of our beloved church. Command my services, for this purpose, in any way that you think proper, without reserve; for as long as I have a memory to recollect, or a heart to feel, I shall cherish toward *you* as individuals, and toward the congregation which you represent, the most cordial affection, and a sense of deep and lasting obligation.

'With fervent prayers that you may be speedily and harmoniously directed to some able and faithful minister, whose labours in the Lord shall be eminently blessed to the promotion of your best interests,   'I am, my dear Brethren,

'Your obliged friend and affectionate pastor,

'Samuel Miller.'

This letter evidently shows, that Dr. Miller was acutely sensitive to the danger of being accused of worldly motives, or a want of affection to his people in New York; and it clearly discloses how painful to him, on these and other accounts, was the separation. No doubt his troubles with Dr. McKnight, the kindness he had experienced in that case, and the short time which had since elapsed, and during which he had been sole pastor of the church, added to the reluctance with which he permitted the pastoral tie to be sundered.

On the 23d of July, Dr. Livingston wrote to him from New Brunswick, 'I am glad that you are to be my neighbor: I could not be so, nor would I say so, if I did not esteem and love you.'

Dr. Miller's pastoral relation to the Wall street Church was dissolved by Presbytery on the 3d of September, the church offering no resistance—simply saying, ' While they deeply lament the proposed separation of their pastor from them, they do not think proper to make any opposition to the measure.'

The following extracts from Dr. Miller's diary carry forward the history of this critical juncture in his affairs :—

'September 22, 1813. Having had the call from the General Assembly to the professorship in Princeton put into my hands a few days ago; and having declared my acceptance of it, and received from the Presbytery the dissolution of my pastoral relation, and a dismission to the Presbytery of New Brunswick, in the bounds of which the Seminary is placed, I am preparing on the 29th instant to repair to Princeton, for the purpose of being inaugurated in my new office. This expectation brings the *solemnity* and *responsibility* of my engagement powerfully to mind, and calls upon me to-day to lay it seriously to heart, and to ponder well what is before me.

' I must, in candor, say, that when I think of the intellectual, literary and spiritual attainments and qualifications, which the office to which I am appointed demands, my heart sinks within me. I am constrained here to record my honest conviction, that I have not the appropriate qualifications for it, and that if I, in any tolerable degree, succeed, it will be rather owing to the charitable indulgence of the directors and pupils of the institution, and, above all, to the shielding and sustaining power of my covenant God, than to my own preparation for the work. I have not the talents; I have not the varied furniture; especially I have not the mature spiritual wisdom and experience, which appear to me indispensable. The choice to this office, I am well aware, would never have fallen on me, if there had not been a lamentable scarcity, in our Church, of ministers who have in any measure turned their particular attention to the studies appropriate to this office. May the Lord sustain me, and prevent my utterly sinking under the burden laid upon me! And may my beloved brethren, who have, by their suffrages, brought me into this situation, so follow me with their prayers, and their charitable allowance for all my failures, as to form a veil perpetually to cover my defects, and hide them from public view! O thou, who hast protected, sustained, and counselled me to this hour, be my protector, my support, and my counsellor still. Whatever may be my defects or my corruptions, thou canst glorify thyself in me and by me.'

4. INAUGURATION AS PROFESSOR.

'Princeton, September 29, 1813. I was this day solemnly inaugurated as *Professor of Ecclesiastical History and Church Government* in the Theological Seminary of the Presbyterian Church in this place. To this office I was elected by the General Assembly of the Presbyterian Church in Philadelphia, in the month of May last. I thought I had then, and at different periods since, some impression of the deep importance and awful weight of this undertaking. But to-day I could not help *trembling* under a sense of its unspeakable solemnity! Yes, this is an office which an *Owen*, or an *Edwards* would undoubtedly undertake with trembling. How, then, ought *I* to feel, with all my want of the requisite qualifications! God of all grace!— Thou with whom is the residue of the Spirit—I cast myself on thy care! I implore light, and guidance, and strength from thee! Oh that my deficiencies may not be permitted to disgrace me, and, above all, to disgrace the *precious cause* in which I profess and hope that I am engaged! Oh that I may have grace given me to be wise and faithful, and thus to be made a blessing to the youth whom I may be called to instruct.'

As providential circumstances prevented Dr. Miller's removal to Princeton for more than two months, it is proper here to notice the ceremony of his inauguration, mentioned in the extract just given from his diary.

The original plan of the Seminary, still in full force, provides as follows :—

"Every person elected to a professorship in this Seminary, shall, on being inaugurated, solemnly subscribe the Confession of Faith, Catechisms, and Form of Government of the Presbyterian Church, agreeably to the following formula; viz.—'In the presence of God and of the Directors of this Seminary, I do solemnly, and *ex animo* adopt, receive, and subscribe the Confession of Faith, and Catechisms of the Presbyterian Church in the United States of America, as the confession of my faith; or as a summary and just exhibition of that system of doctrine and religious belief which is contained in Holy Scripture, and therein revealed by God to man for his salvation; and I do solemnly, *ex animo* profess to receive the Form of Government of said Church, as agreeable to the inspired oracles. And I do solemnly promise and engage, not to inculcate, teach, or insinuate any thing which shall appear to me to contradict or contravene, either directly or impliedly, any thing taught in the said Confession of Faith or Catechisms; nor to oppose any of the fundamental principles of Presbyterian Church Government, while I shall continue a Professor in this Seminary.'"[1]

From the lay members of the Presbyterian Church is properly required belief in only the *fundamental* doctrines of Christianity, or simply what is regarded as essential to salvation; from ministers and ruling elders, the reception and adoption of the Confession of Faith, "as containing the *system* of doctrine taught in the Holy Scriptures," and the approval of the Form of Government and Discipline; from theological professors, in addition to what is required of them as ministers, that they should *teach* nothing in the least inconsistent with the Confession or Catechisms, or opposed to the essential principles of Presbyterian government. This gradation of requirement is obviously agreeable to the gradation of function, responsibility, and influence for which it provides. The special stringency of the subscription demanded from theological professors has been, however, often decried, particularly, of course, by those who have deviated more or less from the Presbyterian system of doctrine; unless indeed they were of that class who can freely sign any creed, and in the chemistry of thought easily assimilate it to their own views and feelings.

After the sermon preached upon the occasion, the professor elect is called upon to profess publicly, in the form just quoted, his adherence to the standards of the Presbyterian Church; after which, in a book containing the

[1] Plan of the Seminary, III, 3. See Dr. Miller's Brief History, 15; Baird's Digest, (1856), 415.

formula, with the subscriptions of previous professors thereto, he actually subscribes his name. Such was the practice when Dr. Miller was inaugurated; such it has always been.

Dr. Miller's inauguration discourse was a brief Sketch of the Characters and Opinions of some of the more conspicuous WITNESSES FOR THE TRUTH during the DARK AGES. From this sketch, he deduced the general observations, that all these Witnesses were zealous Trinitarians; that most of them, especially of the more distinguished, were Calvinists, Presbyterians and Pædobaptists; and that they were universally friends of sound learning; closing with the practical thoughts, (1) that their history gave powerful evidence of the reality of vital religion, and (2) striking proof that the doctrines of grace were the genuine doctrines of God's Word; (3) that it presented important examples for our imitation, and (4) beacons for our warning; (5) that it suggested, as very important, that men substantially united in zeal for the truth should know and love one another; and (6) taught us never to despair of the Church, or even allow ourselves to be discouraged, in even her most troublous and perilous times. 'Paul,' said he, 'is no more! Claudius is no more! Wickliffe, Luther, Calvin, are all gone! But the kingdom of Christ did not die with them! It still lives; and it will live forever!' This discourse was not published—for reasons disclosed by the following letter:—

'Gentlemen,   Princeton, September 30, 1813.
        'I feel deeply sensible of the honor done me by the request which you have been so good as to sign, and which has just been put into my hands. I took for granted that the Board of Directors had designedly omitted to request a copy of my inaugural discourse for the press; And I sincerely thought they had acted judiciously in taking this course.

'On mature deliberation, I think it is my duty to decline complying with your affectionate and polite request. The discourse was written amidst much hurry and distraction. You are sensible that it involves some matter which is as delicate as it is important, and which, in print, would require to be fortified with numerous references and some long quotations. For all this I really have not the requisite time at my command. I have so deep an impression of the overwhelming labor before me, that it appears not advisable to undertake any service which will create unnecessary work for even a single day.

     'I am Gentlemen, with
         'grateful and affectionate regard,
           'Your obedient servant,
'To the Rev'd Dr. Green   Sam'l Miller.
  'Mr. Richards
  'Mr. Hillyer, etc., etc.'

The following journal entries explain the delay of Dr. Miller's removal to Princeton :—

'October 31, 1813.   This day (my birth-day), in the adorable providence of God, finds me on a bed of sickness—extremely weak, but able to sit up, and manifestly convalescent.   I have been very ill ; but, blessed be God, never deprived of my reason, and favored with excellent medical attendance, and what is of still more importance, in some respects, with the excellent nursing, and care, and pious sympathy, and counsel of *the best of wives*.   The Lord make me thankful for this privilege; and grant that, if I should be restored to my wonted health, my life—my all—may be consecrated unreservedly to his glory! Oh for grace to improve this solemn dispensation of his providence !'

'December 3, 1813.   Immediately after my return from Princeton, whither I went to attend my inauguration as professor, I was seized with a violent inflammatory fever, which degenerated into typhus, confining me to my bed for nearly three weeks, and to my room for nearly three more.   My disease was considered, at one time, as threatening a fatal issue; but the Lord had mercy on me, and raised me up again, I hope with the purpose of employing me for his glory.   "Bless the Lord, O my soul! and all that is within me bless his holy name!   Bless the Lord O my soul! who healeth all thy diseases; who crowneth thee with loving kindness and tender mercy!" '

It was probably of this illness that Mrs. Miller used to relate, that unexpectedly she had found her husband's fever gone, a profuse perspiration breaking out upon him, and he apparently sinking fast into hopeless prostration ; and that, doubtless, his life had been saved by a little wine which, tremblingly, yet under a seeming conscious inspiration, she had at once administered.

CHAPTER TWENTY-THIRD.

NEW YORK LIFE.

1793–1813.

---

1. MATTERS ECCLESIASTICAL.

BEFORE we follow Dr. Miller to Princeton, it may be well to pause, and take a retrospect of his ministry of twenty years, just closing in New York, and a survey of his intellectual and professional proportions. He was now just on the dividing line between the two great periods of his public life—his pastorate and his professorship. The change from the one to the other was very critical; but the result, to him at least, was in many respects most advantageous and happy.

Of his real success as a pastor, we can form little idea. For about four years and a half only, had he now been alone in charge of the Wall street church: Dr. Rodgers indeed had remained his colleague nearly half of this time, but was so feeble from the first, and so soon laid entirely aside, that Dr. Miller may properly be regarded as sole pastor from the date of the separation of the united churches. He admitted to membership, in 1810, seventeen by profession, four by certificate; in 1811, the same number in the former way, six in the latter; in 1812, twenty-one by profession, and nine by certificate; and during the portion of 1813 that his pastorate continued, the numbers were twenty and four respectively. Upon examination, therefore, in less than four years, seventy-five had united with the Wall street church. Perhaps few pastors have been more abundantly blessed.

The difference between this day and that, as to the number of infant baptisms, is very striking. In 1810, 1811, and 1812, Dr. Miller reported, in the aggregate, one hundred and twenty-seven infants baptized. During these years, his adult membership ranged from one hundred and ninety to two hundred and nineteen. The infant baptisms, therefore, annually, averaged rather more than twenty-two per centum of the membership. And this, compared with the previous history of the New York churches, was evidently a diminished per centage. But what a contrast have we here to present numbers. To the Assembly of 1865, the Presbytery of New York, with six thousand four hundred and thirty-two reported members, returned but four hundred and eighty-two infant baptisms—the latter not seven and a half per centum of the former. The contrast, however, becomes much more wonderful, when we observe, that, of these baptisms, three hundred and twelve were returned by one German church, with seven hundred and ten members. Now, *first*, leaving this church out of the account, we have remaining but one hundred and seventy baptisms for a membership of five thousand seven hundred and twenty-two—not three per cent. Then, *again*, why should Germans have so many more infants to be baptized than Americans? Or, is it only that the former still pay great regard to this divine ordinance, while the latter treat it almost with contempt?

Church membership was not required of parents for the baptism of their children : a profession of religion included, or supposed to be included, in this ordinance itself was treated as a sufficient parental qualification—a practice which Dr. Rodgers had adopted, and his colleagues continued. It is adverted to repeatedly in other parts of this work. Dr. Spring has said,

" Among the embarrassments of my early ministry, was the practice of my predecessors on the subject of *infant baptism* Dr. Rodgers, Dr. McKnight, and Dr. Miller had been in the habit of baptizing *all the children* of the congregation, without regard to the Christian character and profession of either of the parents. I felt constrained to adopt a different course, and to baptize only those children, one of whose parents was a professed Christian. I felt bound to this course by the obvious principles of the Abrahamic covenant, the example of the apostles, and the spirit of the gospel."[1]

In 1810, three members of the Wall street church, one

[1] 1 Reminiscences, 124, 125.

31

a colored woman, joined the Baptists, two of them without asking for a dismission. The latter were called to account, and one, acknowledging the irregularity, requested a regular certificate; but the other, the colored woman, Margaret Cuffee, while she could give no reason but an " incontrollable impulse to become a member of the Baptist Church," could not see her error. Her case was decided as follows:—

'Although this session recognize the rights of conscience, and claim no power to control its dictates; and although, in pursuance of this principle, they do not consider themselves as at liberty to interpose any bar in the way of Margaret Cuffee's peaceably retiring from the communion of our church; yet they consider her conduct in this case as highly irregular and censurable; and against this conduct, as well as against what they deem an important error on the subject of baptism, they consider it as their duty to bear a decided testimony of disapprobation.'

The others received letters of dismission, in the usual form, with this addition in one case, and something like it in the other:—

'At the same time the session cannot forbear to express their regret, that Mr. Hendlin has adopted an error on the subject of baptism, which they view as highly unfriendly to the interests of the Christian church; and of which they deem it their duty to declare their disapprobation.'

Toward the close of life, Dr. Miller wrote to a young minister,

'When I was a pastor, forty years ago, I had no Bible-class— no Sabbath-school. But I met and catechised the children of my charge every week. In this work I was helped by one or more of the elders, sometimes by my wife, sometimes by both. We really do good to our helpers, as well as the children, by engaging them in this service."[1]

Each Wednesday afternoon the Catechism was thus recited.

The Lord's Supper was administered four times a year in each congregation.

The method of selecting elders and deacons, in the New York churches, during Dr. Miller's pastorate, seems to

[1] To the Rev. Ansley D. White, the 9th October, 1843.

have been this:—The Session nominated such persons as they considered best fitted for these offices; on three successive Sabbaths their names were announced from the pulpit; and, no objection being made, they were then set apart. They appear to have been ordained each to serve a particular congregation, although there were but one session, and one bench of deacons, recognized ecclesiastically.

Collections were taken up regularly for the poor, and the amount raised was divided among the deacons and pastors, the latter being regarded, apparently, as having the diaconate, as well as the eldership, included in their higher office. Thus, at the close of the year 1793, we find about one hundred and twenty pounds—say three hundred dollars—distributed—a hundred pounds to four deacons, and twenty to the three pastors. At the close of 1797, two hundred and forty-four pounds were divided. Every year there was a joint meeting of the Session and deacons for an open and exact settlement of accounts. Both ministers and elders were required to give formal excuses for absence from the meetings of session in which the former presided in turn.

2. THE STIPEND.

Mr. Miller's salary, when he was married, appears to have been five hundred pounds, equal to twelve hundred and fifty dollars. Very soon, if not at once, he began to pay over the whole, as received, to his wife, making her sole treasurer. In fact, for many years, all his receipts, of whatever kind, were thus disposed of, until, becoming possessed of a little property, he reserved, at length, to himself the revenue therefrom. Just when Mrs. Miller was installed as family cashier, we know not; but here is an account book of hers, commencing the 26th of March, 1802,—say five months after marriage,—and showing that this pledge of confidence had then been fully given to her. Perhaps the arrangement commenced at the latter date— after a short probation, more honorable to her than a precipitate investiture; for she sums up one year, at its close, in this memorandum:—Received from March 26th, 1802, until March 26th, 1803, $2112. The account is kept until the first of January, 1803, in pounds, shillings and pence,

New York currency, though interspersed with memoranda in dollars and cents. Afterwards the latter denominations lead the columns. The pastor's living was supplemented largely from outside of his appointed stipend. This was by presents and various perquisites. The first entry in this account-book before us is a 'Donation from the church of £100,' to which, in June following, £50 were added. Wedding and baptism fees—the former the larger and more numerous, and 'linen' and 'gloves' make up the most of the other items, until some of Dr. Miller's books begin to bring in small sums—never much. His 'Record of Marriages' from the commencement of his ministry in New York, has the fees noted on the margin, from January 1800 to January 1817. The highest are three of one hundred dollars each. Then there is a fee of seventy, and several of fifty, forty, thirty—down to *nothing* in a few cases. The whole number of marriages, during his New York pastorate of twenty years, was six hundred and forty-six. Baptism fees were not infrequent—given probably, for the most part, when the ordinance was administered to infants in private; a mode which accorded better with the theory of administration already adverted to, than with the requirement of church membership on the part of one parent at least. Nothing seems ever to have been paid, in money, for funeral services; but it was the universal custom, with those at least who could afford it, to present the officiating clergymen with white linen scarfs and black gloves. Not only was an abundant supply of these articles, for family use, thus furnished; but, as may well be imagined, they both accumulated sometimes so rapidly, that they had to be disposed of out of the family. From December 1802, the salary was fifteen hundred, and from June 1805, eighteen hundred, dollars.

3. In the Pulpit.

The Presbyterian clergymen of New York, with those of several other denominations, generally, if not uniformly, before Dr. Miller's settlement in that city, and during his pastorate, wore, in their public ministrations, clerical *bands*, and *black silk gowns*, the latter an academical rather than clerical dress. In the year 1844, the Rev. Horatio Southgate, missionary of the Protestant Episcopal Church, and,

subsequently, missionary bishop, at Constantinople, published a pamphlet, charging the Congregational missionaries of
the American Board to the Armenians of Turkey, or some
of them, with unwillingness to be known in their true character, with wearing black gowns, and with attempting,
thus and otherwise to pass themselves off as Episcopal
clergymen! In regard to this charge, Dr. Miller wrote,

'Who does not know that all classes of Presbyterians, Independents, and Congregationalists, in every part of the world,
in the sixteenth and seventeenth centuries, were in the constant
habit of wearing some kind of ecclesiastical robe, or black gown,
in all their public ministrations? Is Bishop Southgate ignorant,
that Calvin, Beza, and all their associates and contemporaries,
in Geneva, France, Holland and Germany, habitually appeared
in this professional dress? Is he ignorant that John Knox in
Scotland, and that Owen, Baxter, Charnock, Howe, Bates and
the great mass of their contemporary ministers in England, dissenting from the English Established Church, in the seventeenth
century, always preached in these clerical vestments? Let
him look into any biographical record of Dr. Watts, Dr. Dod-
dridge, or other dissenting ministers in Great Britain, in the
seventeenth and eighteenth centuries, and he will scarcely fail
to find them, in any likenesses' given, 'exhibited as wearing
some sort of clerical habit.

'Nor is this all. Who does not know that, fifty years ago,
every Presbyterian minister, in New York, Philadelphia and
Baltimore, invariably appeared in the pulpit in a black gown;
and that the same was the case with the Congregational ministers of Boston, Portsmouth and other populous places in New
England? Nor was this practice confined to great cities. * *
The Rev. Dr. McWhorter, of Newark, the Rev. Dr. Woodhull,
of Freehold, and a number of others who might be mentioned,
* * seldom, or never, entered the pulpit without the clerical
dress. All this is just as notorious as any fact in the history
of the Church; and are we now to be told that putting on such
a dress is an evidence that he who does it is aping the Episcopal
character?'

Dr. Sprague has remarked,

"* * Dr. Miller early took rank with the best preachers
of his day. His sermons were generally written, but in the
earlier periods of his ministry, as I have heard him say, were
almost always committed to memory,—as the prejudice against
reading in New York was so great, that it was at the peril at

least of one's reputation as a preacher that he ventured to lay
his manuscript before him. At a later period, however, especially after he went to Princeton, he generally read his discourses, but he read with so much ease and freedom, that, but
for the turning over of the leaves, one would scarcely have been
aware that he was reading at all. His voice was not strong,
nor yet particularly musical, but it was pleasant notwithstanding; and so perfectly distinct was his enunciation that he
could be heard without effort at the extremity of the largest
church. His attitudes in the pulpit were extremely dignified,
though perhaps somewhat precise; and his gesture, which was
never otherwise than appropriate, was yet not very abundant.
His utterance was deliberate,—possibly too much so to suit the
mass of hearers; but it was marked by an evident sincerity
and solemnity which were well fitted to make an impression.
He would occasionally deliver a sentence with an air of majesty,
and a degree of unction that would make it quite irresistible.
I remember, for instance, to have heard him relate in a New
Year's sermon on the text "How old art thou?" the well known
anecdote of the Roman Emperor, exclaiming at the close of a
day which had gone to waste, "Oh, I have lost a day!" and it
seemed scarcely possible that the exclamation should have been
uttered in a way to secure to it a higher effect. Still he could
not be considered an impassioned preacher; and his manner
was characterized rather by quiet dignity, and occasionally by
genuine pathos, than by any remarkable versatility or vigour.
But his discourses were decidedly superior to his manner of
delivering them. He never shot at random: he always had a
distinct object in view, and he went deliberately and skilfully
to work to accomplish it. There was the same symmetry about
his sermons that there was about his character—everything
was in its right place. If you did not expect to be thrilled by
such overwhelming passages as you might sometimes hear from
Mason or Chalmers, you knew that you would never be shocked
by anything of doubtful propriety. You expected that everything in the service would be fitting and reverent, and every
way up to the dignity of the pulpit; and you were never disappointed. No man was farther than Dr. Miller from that miserable affectation that throws together dry and doubtful speculations,—at best the refuse of philosophy, and then calls the heap
of chaos that is thus produced a Gospel sermon. While his
preaching was not common-place in any worse sense than the
Bible is so, he had no ambition for originality that led him to
stray beyond the Bible for the material of his discourses; and
while he was satisfied with what he found there, his object

seemed to be to work it up in a manner which should best subserve the great objects of his ministry."[1]

Of Dr. Miller's ministry in New York, Dr. Sprague has
said, elsewhere,

"His early and only settlement as a pastor was in the First
Presbyterian Church in the city of New York; which, probably,
at that time, embraced more wealth, talent and influence than
any other church in our connexion. In addition to this, it was
the general resort of strangers; and while Congress held its
sessions in that city, most of the members were accustomed to
attend it. The minister of such a congregation must of course
preside at a great fountain of public influence; many of his
stated hearers are among the men who give character to a city
and a country; and every sermon that he preaches, falls upon
the ear, and tells upon the destiny of some, whom he will never
meet till he meets them in the judgment.

"* * [Dr. Miller] contributed too not a little to elevate
the character of the American pulpit; and if there were others
who had a wider popularity and more control of the passions
of the multitude, there were few whose pulpit productions had
in them so much of weighty and well digested material, or
would so well abide the test of an intelligent criticism."[2]

Says a late writer,

"The position [of Dr. Miller in New York City] was one of
high distinction, and of peculiar responsibility, as it brought
him into immediate contact and comparison with many of the
most gifted and brilliant preachers of the times, who then filled
the pulpits of the city. But the young pastor was found fully
equal to all the demands of the situation—not only sustaining
himself amid his experienced and gifted compeers of the city,
but developing resources, and building up a solid ministerial
character, which soon sent his name through the whole church,
honored alike as a pastor, a preacher, and an author. He had
gifts and qualifications which from the first rendered his
preaching exceedingly popular with the church going people
of New York, although they were accustomed to hear Dr.
Mason, Dr. Linn, Dr. Livingston, and other great lights."[3]

A writer in the New York Observer,[4] in giving an account of his "First Sabbath in New York," says,

---

[1] 3 Annals, 603, 604.

[2] Discourse Commemorative of Dr. Miller, 23, 24, 26.

[3] From a forthcoming work entitled, "GREAT PREACHERS AND PASTORS,"
by the Rev'd L. J. Halsey, D. D., Professor in the Theological Seminary of
the North West. See the *North Western Presbyterian* of the 22d of August, 1868.

[4] 18th March, 1852.

"At three o'clock in the afternoon I went to the Wall street church, knowing that I was just in time to hear Dr. Miller; for, if my memory serves me, this was but a few weeks before his translation to Princeton. He walked into the pulpit with great deliberation and dignity, wearing the gown and bands, which I had never before seen on any Presbyterian, or, with one exception, orthodox congregational, minister. His fine person, and intelligent and benignant face, justified at once the very favorable account, which I had always heard of him in New England. His prayer, both in manner and matter, seemed exceedingly devout, and his tones I thought remarkably adapted to supplication. His sermon was on the character of Absalom; and as I have heard it since, and at a much later day, I may speak of it with confidence. It was one of the most beautiful biographical discourses to which I have ever listened. It deserves to be published, as well as many others of Dr. Miller's sermons, which, in some respects, are, in my opinion, unsurpassed as models of that kind of writing. I must not follow Dr. Miller from that "first Sabbath;" for if I were to allow myself to extend my remarks concerning him at all, I cannot say how far my affectionate veneration for him would carry me."

The late Dr. David Magie, of Elizabeth, upon his dying couch, said to the writer, 'When I first saw Dr. Miller, he was a very beautiful man: probably he looked much younger than he really was;' adding, 'He was always a very acceptable preacher to good people—those who delighted in the very marrow of the gospel. I remember hearing him preach once before he left New York, upon 'Meetness for the Kingdom.' I was not particularly impressed, not as yet being interested in such things; but an uncle of mine, a very good man, fed upon that sermon for a long time. He never went to Princeton, but he must call upon Dr. Miller, if it were but for a few moments.'

Dr. Gardiner Spring, when asked for reminiscences of Dr. Miller in the pulpit, replied, in substance, 'I did not often hear him preach, as I was commonly preaching myself at the same time. Upon first hearing him, I was struck with his removing the Bible from the desk to the cushion behind his back, and preaching without anything before him. I regarded him as a very accomplished preacher: that word —"accomplished"—best expresses my idea.'

After Dr. Miller's decease,—the 24th of May, 1850,—

Grant Thorburn, Esquire, wrote to one of the surviving family,

'When thy father was a boy, upholding the arms of the venerable Dr. Rodgers, I was clerk, chorister, or psalm-singer, or what you may call it, to Dr. Mason: in short, he was the shepherd, and I the watch-dog, for twenty years. He read the twenty-third Psalm, old Scotch version: I doled it out to the good old Scotch Copper-heads, line upon line, murdering the metre here, destroying the sense there—no matter: to them it was instruction. Great as Dr. Mason was, here was a soft spot,—* * he stickled for old psalms and old tunes. I petitioned the session to give out two, instead of one, line, and to introduce some new tunes. The Doctor was my only opponent: (our discussion was cool and friendly:) he spoke about innovation, about deviating from the simplicity of gospel worship, etc. Says I, "Doctor, I'm thinking you will be in a strange fix, when you get to heaven: there they sing a *new* song all day; and, as "they rest not," they sing another all night." The sobersided old Scotchmen smiled ; the Doctor followed suit ; I gained my point. I think, as a pulpit orator, the world has not seen his equal since Paul, the Apostle, preached at Rome. Mason (by the by, your father and he were close friends) was a preacher, not a reader of the gospel. Fifty-six years ago, (Episcopal churches excepted,) there was not a reader of the gospel in New York. Have our students less brains? Are there fewer schools for the prophets? Are books scarcer and the prices higher? The reverse is the fact. The Court, the Senate, and the Devil's church (theatre) advance; but the paper preaching has driven eloquence from the pulpit: it is tolerated nowhere except in the Church of Christ. A reader can never be an orator.'

Dr. Miller, when he left New York, was at the acme of his reputation as a preacher. From the date of his removal to Princeton, he gradually, if not at once, abandoned the more laborious method of memoriter preaching, for the easier one of reading his sermons. Moreover, lecturing to students of theology became his grand business as a public speaker; and that tended to confirm him in reading, and also in a plainer style of delivery. He might have resisted the influence of habit in this respect; but perhaps the importance of doing so did not occur to him ; at any rate, his preaching, thereafter, fell off in popularity. Each manner of public address, reading, speaking memoriter, and speaking extempore, has had its splendid examples and its earnest advocates. The truth seems to be, that any one of these methods may be made highly effective; that some persons may adopt one, and some another of them, with greatest effect; that they may be, and often have been, mingled with the happiest result; that practice in one is by no means essentially antagonistic to success in another; but that, without special native gifts, superior excellence in public speaking, whatever method is preferred, can be attained only by laborious and persistent self-training. Slackened diligence in such training, at any period of life, must be followed by a corresponding decline in the power of making a popular impression; a power without which the highest mere human wisdom, and the most splendidly rhetorical compositions fall nerveless upon the ear.

It was especially in prayer, if in any part of his public ministrations, that Dr. Miller excelled; and it is evident that his gift, whatever it may have been, for this religious exercise, had been assiduously cultivated. Here is a manuscript volume, containing about a quire of foolscap, nearly filled with short addresses delivered on sacramental and other occasions, and with prayers, all closely written—the latter forming the larger part of the collection. These belonged to the earlier portion of his ministry, bearing the dates of 1795 and 1796. Most of the prayers are of a special kind; some of them, for example, relating to the visitations of yellow fever, and some of them being intended for use before the Legislature.

On the subject of memoriter prayer and preaching, Dr. Miller has observed,

"I have said, that I would by no means advise any one to be in the habit of committing written prayers to memory, and reciting them servilely in the pulpit. There is something in the practice of uttering any thing in public from memory that is apt to beget in the speaker, in spite of every effort to the contrary, a formal, reciting tone. This principle seldom fails to be exemplified very strikingly in *memoriter* preachers. In the course of a long life, and with some range of opportunity for observation on this subject, I have never heard more than one, or, at most, two memoriter preachers who entirely avoided the reciting tone. The same principle applies, in some measure, to prayers recited from memory.   I do not believe that it is, ordinarily, possible wholly to divest them of the character and tone of recitation.   It is one of the rarest things in the world to hear any one read a prayer, or any other composition, in the perfectly simple natural intonation which is, of course, employed in extemporaneous, feeling, animated utterance."[1]

Of Dr. Nevins, the popular pastor of the First Presbyterian Church of Baltimore, who died in 1835, Dr. Miller said,

"He was a *memoriter* preacher; and, on the whole, the most natural and impressive memoriter preacher I ever heard.   He seemed to commit to memory with great ease, and to call forth and deliver what he had deposited in his memory, without the least hesitation or embarrassment.   Most of the memoriter preachers that I have heard, had a formal, reciting manner. In him scarcely any thing of this kind appeared.   His intonations and his whole manner were entirely natural.   He might easily have been mistaken for an extemporaneous speaker, had not the richness, the connexion, and the mature judgment and taste which his discourses seldom failed to display, evinced careful preparation."[2]

The writer has heard Dr. Miller say, that when he was accustomed to preaching memoriter, two or three readings of a discourse of his own, especially just after writing it, were quite sufficient to fasten it upon his mind.   No power improves more sensibly and rapidly, by use, than memory; but that is not the whole secret of the facility which memoriter speakers for the most part acquire.   Sooner or later, they discover, that when they commit to memory the ideas of a discourse, in their proper order and logical connexion— a much easier task than committing the words—the words, however, in which they have once thought out and expressed those ideas, cling to them, and recur with them.

4.   MISCELLANEOUS TOPICS.

Mrs. Miller, referring, long afterward, to the condition of things in New York, at the time of her marriage, and subsequently, speaks of 'a comparatively pure state of the Church, when the name and influence of a few such venera-

[1] Thoughts on Public Prayer, 298, 299.
[2] Dr. Plumer's Biog. Notice of Dr. Nevins, 74, 75.

ble and holy men as the Rev. Dr. John Rodgers, had thrown a restraint on the vices of the world around them, as well as on the constantly recurring disorders of the Church, so that the very vagrants of the street felt their presence.'

'The appearance,' she adds, 'of these servants of God, in any part of the city, seemed to make "iniquity hide its head," and was often the means of dispersing an idle, youthful group, in which profanity and disorder were beginning their destructive career. Through their influence, in a great measure, the Sabbath was, at least externally, a holy day, on which the public ways exhibited no crowd or bustle, but what was of necessity occasioned by a church-going people. Every pastor of a flock of Jesus Christ seemed to feel it his privilege as well as his duty, to feed the lambs of his flock himself, and did not commit them to the ever varying, heterogeneous instruction of others. The Scriptures and the Catechism it was his own business to inculcate; and the same afternoon, in each week, had been for many years, in several of the churches of the city, of various denominations, the season for this instruction.'

Among Mrs. Miller's papers, is found a prayer, dated 'Sabbath, 30th July, 1809,' which shows that she was endeavoring, to uphold, as she could, her husband's hands in his ministry. Its spirit may be seen in the following extract:—

'O Lord, we would look up to thy throne for a blessing, previously to entering into thine holy sanctuary. The preparation of the heart is from thee. * * O Lord, I, thine handmaid, would plead for the husband whom thou has given me. Thou hast called him to minister before thee in holy things: how awfully responsible is his calling! Without thine aid, what will become of him? But if thou wilt work with him, how efficacious may be his ministry! O Father, grant thine aid and thy blessing. * * May he have many seals to his ministry, and may he shine as a star in thy kingdom forever and ever.'

Before Dr. Miller removed to Princeton, he had begun to take a very active and prominent part in the higher judicatories of the Church—the Synod and General Assembly. We find him frequently appointed upon important committees, often as chairman. Thus, as also by his repeated publications, he was becoming well known; and his appointment to the professorship at Princeton was but an additional evidence of his established and growing influence in the Church to which he belonged.

In New York, Dr. Miller left behind him many warmly attached and devoted friends, from whom he received, afterward, frequent tokens of regard, and towards whom the respect and affection which he had earnestly cherished, during the happy years of his pastorate, continued unchanged to the last. Among these, while to name here many of them would be very grateful to those who entered most intimately and fully into Dr. Miller's feelings, only James Anderson, Esquire, and his son, Abel T. Anderson, Esquire, both deceased, will be mentioned. They managed all his pecuniary business in New York, commencing with the collection of dues to Doctor Edward Miller's estate, up to 1842—all but thirty years, without fee or reward—resisting, indeed, all his efforts to remunerate their services, and hardly permitting any acknowledgment of them. A letter from the former, dated the 27th of November, 1815, says, 'If you are satisfied with the way I conduct your business here, that is compensation sufficient for me. I desire no more.' Again, he says, of certain debtors to Doctor Edward Miller's estate, They 'speak in the highest terms of that amiable temper and disposition your late brother was so highly favored with.'

It may be mentioned, in this connexion, that in some cases in which Dr. Miller could force no remuneration upon persons who had rendered him material services, he manifested his sense, at least, of obligation, by making them honorary members of this or that board or society, in the evangelical work of which he, perhaps, knew them to be interested, or was desirous of interesting them.

32

INDEX TO VOL. I.

ABEEL, Rev. Dr., 199, 230, 234, 237.
Ability, Human, 290, 299, 300.
Accounts, Testamentary, 77.
Adams, Pres. John, 111. Letters of, 306.
Adams, Joseph, 307.
Address to Gov. Dickinson from Lewes Presbytery, 20, n.
Adopting Act, 23.
Afflictions, 321—331.
Alden, John, 13, 14, 306.
" Ruth, 14.
Alexander, Dr. A., 140, 141, 195, 196, 291, n. 314, 345. Elected Professor, 333. Inaugurated, 334. Sermon on burning of Richmond Theatre, 322.
Alison, Rev. Dr. F., 32.
Ancestors, Dr. M's, 13.
" Mrs. M's, 145—148.
Anderson, Abel T., 373.
" Christiana, 257.
" James, 373. Letter of, 373.
Andover, 229—234, 237—239.
Anniversaries, Observance of, 169, 170.
Arbitrators, 271.
Armstrong, James, Letter to, 248.
Associate Reformed Church, 196.
Atwater, Rev. Pres., 276.

Bainbridge, Dr., 147.
Balfour, Rev. Dr. R., 137.
Baptism, 360, 361. Fees, 364.
Baptismal Regeneration, 217.
Baptists, 362.
Bartlett, Wm., 239.
Bass, Bishop Edw., 22.
" Hannah, 306, 307.
" John, 306, n., 307, n.
" Joseph, 13.
" Samuel, 13, 14, 15, 306, 307.
" families, 63.
Beasley, Rev. Fred., 216.
Bethlehem school, 167.
Bible, Desecration of, 350, 351.
" Society, Nassau Hall, 351.

Bible Society, New York, 276.
Birth of Dr. Miller, 28.
" " Mrs. Miller, 148.
Black, Rev. Robert, 137.
Bloomfield's plan, Gov., 307, 308.
Bloomingdale, 286.
Boarding-schools, 167.
Boston, 229—234. Invitation to Park street Church, 277.
Bowden, Rev. Dr., 224, 226, 227, 279.
'Boy-minister,' 87—112, 89.
Brainerd, David and John, 146.
" Jerusha, 146.
" Martha, 146.
Brick Church, 82.
Broes, Dr. Broerius, 108.
Brown, Charles Brockden, 114—120.
" Moses, 239.
" Rev. Dr. Wm. L., 137.
Burder, Rev. George, Letter of, 313.
Burr, Col., 183.
Byles, D. D., Rev. Mather, 17.

Call to Dover, 62—66. To New York, 62—66. To Market street Church, 120, 121. To Dickinson College, 244—250. To University of North Carolina, 335. To Hamilton College, 335, 336. To Theological Seminary, 347—359.
Caldwell, Rev. Dr., 335.
Calvinism, 305.
Candidate, Dr. M. a, 61.
Candidates, Hearing of, 64.
Card Playing, 155—159.
Carey, Rev. Dr. Wm., 137.
Carlisle, Winter in, 57—60.
Carnahan, Rev. Dr., 343.
Catechising, 362.
Cedar street Church, 235, 267, 269.
Chaplaincy, 276.
Charge to Pastor, by Dr. M., 288.
Chilton, Mary, 14.
Christian's Magazine, 217.
Clarke, Rev. Dr. Adam, 137, 178. Letter of, 305.

Clergy of N. Y. City, 81.
" Politics and the, 134—136.
Clinton, DeWitt, 109, 110.
Codman, Rev. Dr. John, 277, 295.
 Letter to, 291.
College and Academy of Philadelphia,
 201, 202.
College Life, 42.
College of New Jersey, 201, 202, 228.
College Student, The, 34.
Collegiate relation, Dissolution of, 265
 —272. Evils of, 265, 266.
Colonizing, Church, 235.
Columbia College, 80, 81, 228.
Commencement of University of Penn-
 sylvania, 41.
Companion for Altar, 211—213.
Companion for Festivals, etc., 211—
 213.
Concert in Prayer, Monthly, 106.
 Quarterly, 106.
Confession of Faith, Exceptions to,
 55, 56.
Connecticut, Journeying in, 107. Del-
 egate to Gen. Assoc. of, 107.
Contrast, Dr. Ely's, 298, 304.
Convention of United States, Consti-
 tutional, 31.
Correspondence, Foreign, 108, 110, 137.
Cowper, 184.

Davidson, Rev. Dr., 244.
Deacons, Choice of, 362, 363.
Declaration of Independence, 28.
Delaware, 13. Attachment to, 71.
 Health of, 74. Life, 71. Ministry
 in, 56, 57, 61, 62, 65. Pilgrimage
 to, 71, 76. Visits to, 76.
Democratic party, 111, 112.
Diary, Dr. Miller's, 170, 171. Birth-
 day, 50, 96, 100, 101, 108, 127, 359.
 Ordination-day, 88, 96, 98, 101, 102,
 107, 112, 118, 119, 127. Wedding-
 day, 169. Miscellaneous, 33, 35, 43,
 45, 46, 51—55, 65, 66, 87, 103, 131—
 133, 168, 171, 193, 235, 295, 322, 326,
 355, 356, 359.
Diary, Mrs. M's, 319.
Dickinson College, Call to, 244—250.
Dickinson Sergeant, Abigail, 146.
Dickinson, John, 20, 69, 70. Letter
 to, 144. Letters of, 21, 22, 177.
Dickinson, Rev. Jonathan, 146.
Diplomas, 78, 79.
Directors of Seminary, Letter to, 358.
Disinterested benevolence, 300, 304.
Dismission to Baptists, Certif. of, 362.
Dismission to Presbytery of N. Y., 66.
Dissolution of collegiate relation, 265
 —272.

Dissolution of pastoral relation, 355.
Doctorate of Divinity, 178, 179, 335.
Dover, 72.
Duck Creek Cross Roads, 16, 17, 76.
Dunlap, Wm., 115. Tribute to Dr.
 Edw. Miller, 329.
Dwight, Rev. Dr., 230, 237, 274, 303.

Ebeling, Prof. Christ. Dan., 110.
Eckley, Rev. Dr., 237.
Education of Children, 78.
Edwardean Theology, 303.
Edwards, President, 291, 299, 300.
 " Dr., 139, 140.
Elders, Ruling, Choice of, 362, 363.
Elders, Ruling, Ordination of, 273, 274.
Election of First Professor, 333, 334.
 Of Second, 348.
Ely's Contrast, Rev. Ezra S., 298, 304.
Emmons, Rev. Dr., 238, 300, 301.
Episcopacy, 190—194. Claims of, 207.
Episcopal churches loaned, 82, 288.
Episcopal controversy, 206—210, 227,
 278—280, 313.
Erskine, Rev. Dr. John, 137.
Ewing, Rev. Dr., 42, 143.

Fagg's Manor, 148.
Farewell to Delaware, 66, 69. To New
 York, 351—356.
Farm, Rev. John Miller's, 74—76.
Fast day, Presidential, 111.
Federalists, 111, 112.
Fees and Perquisites, 364.
First Presb. Church, N. Y., 81, 82.
Fisher, Judge, 70. John, 74.
Flinn, Rev. Dr., 333.
Fox-hunting, 75.
Franklin, Benj., 31.
French Revolution, 94—96.
Friendly Club, 110, 111.
Friends in New York, 373.
Fuller, Rev. Dr. A., 137.
Funeral Perquisites, 364.

Gambling, 155—159.
Gemmil, Rev. Mr., Letters to, 130, 131.
General Assembly, (1789,) 39; (1801,)
 139—142; (1805,) 195; (1806,) 200,
 201, 205; (1809,) 280; (1810,) 284;
 (1811,) 313—316; (1812,) 316, 332—
 335; (1813,) 347, 348.
Graduation, Dr. M's, 41.
Grammar School in New York, 199.
Grave Yard, 72, 73, 76, 77.
Gray, Rev. Ellis, 17.
Green, Rev. Dr. A., 38, 39, 44, 45, 195,
 314, 333, 347, 348. Election to
 presidency of College, 336—343.
 Letter of, 63. Letters to, 44, 96,

101, 104, 105, 120, 121, 184, 185, 191,
192, 194, 228, 240, 243, 276, 278, 280,
283, 286, 307, 311, 323, 338—342,
345, 349, 350.
Griffin, Rev. Dr. E. D., 199, 200, 204, 229
—231, 237, 270, 283, 295, 303, 304.
His Installation, 316—319. Letters
to, 182—184. 190, 191, 193, 194, 97,
198, 200, 203, 228, 229, 232, 237, 238,
275, 277, 284, 295, 304, 316, 318, 323.

Hall, Rev. Dr. James, 348.
Halsey, D. D., Rev. L. J., Extract
from, 367.
Halsey, Rev. Dr. L., 55.
Hamilton, Alex., 31, 183.
    " Rev. Mr., 137.
Hamilton College, Call to, 335.
Hancock's Century Sermon, 306.
Hans, Old, 143.
Harris, 18.
Harvard College, 238, 291.
Haweis, Rev. Dr. Thos., 137.
Hazard, Ebenezer, 347. Letter of, 222.
Health of Delaware, 74.
Henshaw, Benjamin, 22.
    " Joseph, 22.
    " Families, 63.
Herzog, Rev. Dr. J. W., 137.
High Churchism, 206—210, 211—216,
313.
Historical Society, N. Y., 276.
History of N. Y., 108, 109.
    "   " Presb. Church, 347, 348.
Hobart, D. D., Bishop John Henry,
211—213, 216—218, 224, 227.
Home Theology, 43, 51.
Honorary members, constituted by Dr.
M., 373.
Hopkins, Rev. Dr. S., 300. Letter
from, 301.
Hopkinsian Controversy, 297, 298.
Hopkinsianism, 191, 290, 297—304.
Moderate, 303, 304.
Horse-race, 74, 75.
How, Rev. Dr. Thomas Y., 216, 218,
224—227.
Hudson, Henry—Discourse upon, 276.
Huntington, Rev. Mr., 237, 295.

Imputation, 299.
Inaugural Discourse, Dr. Green's, 343.
    "   "   " M's, 358.
Inauguration of Dr. Alexander, 334.
    "   " Dr. Green, (pro-
posed,) 341, 342.
Inauguration of Dr. M., 356—359.
Independent Church in Philadelphia,
184, 185.

Inglis, Rev. Dr., 313.
Inquiry into Effects of Ardent Spirits,
Dr. Rush's, 315.
Invisible Church, 213—216.
Italian gentleman, 115.

Jail Yard, Dover, 73.
Jamieson, Rev. Dr. John, 137.
Jay, Hon. John, Correspondence with,
123—127.
Jefferson, Thomas, 129, 131—134.
President, 235—237. Letter from,
236.
Johns, Rev. E., Letter from, 221.
Johnson, J., 180, 181.
Jones's Creek, 74.
Judicatories, Activity in, 372.

Kemp, Bishop, 224.
Kent, Chancellor James, 89. Letter
from, 221.
Kleest, Sister, 167.
Killen, Chancellor Wm., 17.
Kirkpatrick, Chief Justice, 204, 205.

Last Years of Pastorate, 332—346.
Latta, Rev. Francis A., 75, 97.
Laying on of hands on Ruling Elders,
273, 274.
Legislature of N. Y., Act of to facili-
tate Dr. M's searches, 109. Memo-
rial to, 111.
Letters of—
    Adams, John, 306.
    Anderson James, 373.
    Brown, C. B., 115—117.
    Burder, Rev. George, 313.
    Clarke, Rev. Dr. Adam, 305.
    Clinton, DeWitt, 110.
    Dickinson, John, 21, 177.
    Fisher, John, 74.
    Green, Rev. Dr. A., 63.
    Hazard, Ebenezer, 222.
    Hopkins, Rev. Dr. S., 301.
    Jay, John, 123.
    Jefferson, Thos., 236.
    Johns, Rev. E., 221.
    Johnson, J., 180, 181.
    Kent, James, 221.
    Linn, Rev. Dr. Wm., 219.
    Livingston, Brockholst, 219.
        "   Rev. Dr. J. H., 311, 355.
    McLane, Col. S., 56.
    Miller, Dr. Edward, 181.
        " James, 97.
        " Rev. John, 34—38, 40, 45—47,
        49, 50.
    Miller, Dr. John, 29.
        " Mrs. Margaret, 35, 37.

Miller, Dr. Samuel, (See under Armstrong, Codman, Dickinson, Directors of Seminary, Gemmil, Green, Griffin, Jay, Morse, Nisbet, Nott, Patten, Rodney, Romeyn, Rush, Sergeant, Sprague, Suicide, Verplanck, Wales, Wall street Church.)
Miller, Mrs. Sarah, 204, 234, 304, 320.
Murray, Lindley, 179.
Rush, Dr. Benjamin, 244, 245, 247, 311, 312. 327—329.
Sergeant, J., 332.
Speece, Rev. Dr. C., 223.
Suicide, (Intended.) 187.
Thorburn, Grant, 368.
Webster, Noah, 220.
Wilson, Rev. Dr. M., 25, 96.
Letters on—
    Christian Ministry, 216—227.
    hristian Ministry, Continuation of, 278.
Lewes, Minutes of Presbytery of, 18, 19, 23, 25, 53, 56, 62, 65, 74.
Licensure of Dr. M., 54—56.
Licentiate, 61.
Life, N. Y., 360—372.
Linn, Rev. John Blair, 121.
Linn, Rev. Dr. W., 129, 216. Letter of, 219.
Livingston, Brockholst, Letter of, 219.
    " Rev. Dr. J. H., 61. Letters of, 311, 355.
Log College, 201.
Lottery for College of N. J., 315.
Loockerman, Elizabeth, 114.
    " Mrs. Mary, 54, 75, 98. Death, 139.
Loockerman, Vincent, 30, 36, 54, 75. Death, 139.
Lord's Supper, Administration of 362,
Lovell, John, 16.

McCulloch, Rev. R., 137.
McDowel, Rev. Dr. Benj., 137.
McDowell, Rev. A., 32.
    " Dr. John, 257, 258.
McKnight, Rev. Dr. J., 82, 267—272.
McLane, Mrs. Elizabeth, 54.
    " Col. Sam'l, 30, 66, 141.
McLeod, Rev. Dr., 199, 345.
McWhorter, Rev. Dr., 231.
Magazine, Projected, 96, 119, 191, 345.
Magie, Rev. Dr. D., 368.
Manners, Dr. M's, 68, 69.
Manumission Society, N. Y., 91.
Market street Church, Call to, 120, 121.

Marriage of Mrs. Mary Loockerman, 98. Elizabeth Miller, 30. Rev. John, 18. Joseph Miller, 114. Mary Miller, 30. Samuel Miller, 139—144.
Marriage fees, 364.
Mason, Rev. Dr. J. M., 129, 199, 217.
Masonry, 98, 99.
Matters, Ecclesiastical, 360—363.
Memoriter preaching, 369, 371.
Memoirs, Mrs. Miller's, 148—167, 251, 264.
Memoirs of Dr. Rodgers, 308—313.
Mercer, Gen., 147.
Milledoler, Rev. Dr., 198, 267, 288, 335. Reminiscences, 89, 297.
Miller, Benj., 18, 28, 72.
    " Dr. Edward, 18, 32, 41, 54, 73, 74, 102, 103, 167, 171, 172, 175, 176, 178, 286, 303, 307. Letter of, 181. Death of, 323—331. Influence of, on brother, 323, 324. Character of, 325, 326. Biographical Sketch and Works of, 330, 331.
Miller, Edward Millington, 200. Death of, 322.
Miller, Elizabeth, 18, 30.
    " James, 18, 54, 96. Letter of, 97. Death of, 98.
Miller, John, the Grandfather, 13—15.
    " Rev. John, the Father, 16—25. Letters of, (See Letters.) Death of, 53, 54.
Miller, John, the Uncle, 15.
    " Dr. John, 18, 29, 30, 73, 75.
    " Joseph, the Uncle, 15, 307.
    "   "   (1) 18, 28, 72.
    "   "   (2) 18, 32, 33, 54. Death of, 114.
Miller, Mrs. Margaret, 26, 27. Letters of, 35—37. Death of, 45—48.
Miller, Mary, 30, 73, 98, 139.
    " Dr. Sam'l, Passim.
    " Mrs. Sarah, 145—167. Memoirs, 148—167, 251—264. Letters of, 204, 205, 234, 304, 320.
Millington, Allumby, 18.
    " Elizabeth, 18.
    " Margaret, 18.
Milton, Extracts from, 160.
Ministry in N. Y., Dr. M's, 88, 89.
Missions, 104—106.
Missionary Society, N. Y., 104—106.
Mitchill, Dr. S. L., 109, 116.
Moderators of Synod and Gen. Assembly, 23.
Moncrief, Sir H., 137.
Morgan abducted, 99.
Morris, Dr., 74.
Morse, Rev. Dr. J., 64, 65, 229—232,

237. Letters to, 61, 65, 108, 109, 119, 120, 193, 231, 274.
Mullins, Priscilla, 14.
Murray, Lindley, 179, 180.

Nevins, Rev. Dr. Wm., 371.
Newark, (Del.) Academy, 201.
 " (N. J.) settled, 145.
New Castle, Presbyteries of, 23.
New England Orthodoxy, 299. Tour in, 62, 63, 107.
New London Academy, 201.
New Side, 201.
New Theology, 301.
New York Bible Society, 276. City, 80—82. Churches, 81, 82. Clergy, 81—86, 88, 89. Historical society, 276. Life, 128, 360—372. Missionary Society, 104—106. Observer, Extracts from, 367, 368. Old Synod of, 22. And Philadelphia, Old Synod of, 23. Visits to, 61, 62.
Nineteenth Century, Opening years of, 183.
Nisbet, D. D., Rev. Charles, 57—60, 95. Lectures of, 185, 186.
Nisbet, Alexander, Letters to, 186, 197, 204.
Norris, John, 239.
Nott, Rev. Dr., 261. Letters to, 183, 193, 199, 203.
Nutman Sergeant, Hannah, 146.

Ogden, Col , 337.
Old Papers, 76—79.
Old Side, 201.
Old South Church, 15, 295.
Old State Road, 72, 74.
Ordination, Certificate of, 16. Of Samuel Miller, 87, 88. Of Ruling Elders, 273, 274.

Panoplist, 231, 274, 291.
Park street Church, Boston, 230, 295, 296.
Pastoral relation dissolved, 272, 355.
Pastorate in N. Y., Success of, 360.
Patten, Major John, 73, 76. Death of, 139.
Patten, Mrs. Mary, 76, 98. Death of, 139.
Patten, Miss Ann, Letter to, 343.
Paulding, James K., Letter of, 222.
Pearson, Mr., 230.
Pemberton, Rev. Dr., 15.
Perrine, Rev. Dr., 291.
Philadelphia, 31.
Phillips Academy, 239.
Phillips, 63.

Phillips, Mrs., 239.
Philological Society of Manchester, 178.
Pilgrimage, 71—76.
Pillory, 73.
Pinckney, Charles C., 131.
Plan of Union, 139, 140, 141. Another, 141—143.
Politics, 122—136. And the Clergy, 134—136. Party, 111, 112, 123—127, 129.
Poor, Collection for, 363.
Popery, 214.
Prayer, Public, 370. Precomposed, 370.
Prayer, Mrs. Miller's, 372. Union in, 106, 339.
Preaching, Dr. M's, 70, 100. Memoriter, 369, 370.
Preparation for College, 33, 34.
Presbyterial control, 56.
Presbyterian Church in United States, 81. Wealth of, 314.
Presbyterians, Opponents of High Churchism, 207.
Priestley, Dr., 154, 263.
Prince, Rev. Thos., 17.
Princeton Pulpit, 240.
 " Location of Seminary, 313—315.
Profession of Religion, Dr. M's, 33. Mrs. M's, 171.
Professor of Eccles. Hist. and Church Government chosen, 348.
Provoost, Bishop, 210, 216.
Psalms, Rouse's, 22.
Publications, Dr. M's. Fourth of July Sermon, 90, 91. Masonic sermon, 98. Fourth of July Sermon, 100. Manumission oration, 91, 92—94. Fast day Sermon, 111, 112. Thanksgiving sermon, 117. Sermon on Washington, 122, 123. Missionary Sermon, 168. Retrospect of Eighteenth Century, 173—181. Sermons on Suicide, 186—190. Letters on Christian Ministry, 216—227: Continuation, 278—280. Panoplist, Articles in, 231, 274. Sermon: Duty and Ornament of Female Sex, 239. Discourse on Henry Hudson, 276. Ordination charge, 288. Sermon on Ruling Elders, 274. Pastoral letter, 285. Dr. Rodgers's Funeral Sermon, 309. Sermon on Richmond Theatre, 321, 322. Inauguration Sermon, 334. Memoirs of Dr. Rodgers, 309. Biog. sketch of Dr. Edw. Miller, 330, 331.
Pulpit, Dr. M. in, 364, 371.
 " Politics in, 112, 121.

REFORMATION, Cardinal doctrine of, 215, 216.
Reminiscences, Dr. Spring's, 291.
" Dr. Milledoler's, 297.
Renshaw, Rich., Letter to, 48, 49.
Republican party, 111, 112.
Residences in N. Y., 113, 200.
Retrospect of Eighteenth Century, 173—181.
Review of Griffin's Sermon, 231. Of Dwight's Sermon, 274.
Revolution perils, 147. Preaching, 19, 20.
Richmond Theatre, burning of, 321, 322.
Ridgely, Dr. Charles, 32, 73.
" Wilhelmina, 73, 74.
Rittenhouse, David, 141.
Rodgers, Rev. Dr. John, 39, 61, 81—86, 88, 107, 210, 251, 256, 266, 268, 287, 310, 311, 372. Death and Funeral of, 309. Memoirs of, 303—313.
Romanism, 214.
Romeyn, Rev. Dr.. 229, 230, 231, 235, 267, 275, 277, 281, 287, 288, 307, 319, 345. Letter to, 235.
Ruling Elders, Ordination of, 273, 274.
Rush, Dr. Benj., Inquiry into Effects of Ardent Spirits, 315. Letters of, (See Letters.) Letter to, 245. Death of, 330.
Rutgers, Col. H., 107.
Rutgers street Church, 107, 198.
Ryland, Rev. Dr. John, 137.

Salary, in N. Y., 363, 364.
St. George's, 148.
Sansom, Philip, 137.
Schiller, Fred., 137.
Schism of 1741, 22.
Scott, Rev. Dr. Thos., 137.
Sergeant Fox, Elizabeth, 146.
" Mrs. Elizabeth, 141.
" Rev. John, 145.
" John, Letter of, 332.
" Jonathan, (1) 145.
" " (2) "
" " (3) " •
" " (4) "
" Jonathan D., 145—148, 151—153, 167.
Sergeant, Sarah, 115. Letters to, 142, 143.
Sergeant, Thomas, 111, 142, 148.
Sermon before Assembly, 205. (See Publications.)
Session, Church, 88.
Sewall, D. D., Rev. Joseph, 16, 17, 21.

Shirnding, Baron Von, 137.
Sides, Old and New, 22.
Slavery, 27, 90, 91—94. Convention for abolition of, 183.
Slaves, 77.
Smith, Dr. E. H., 115.
" Rev. Dr. S. Stanhope, 202, 236.
Smyrna, 16.
Society for Propagating Gospel, 104.
Southgate, Bishop, 365.
Speece, Rev. Dr. C., 269, 270. Letter of, 223.
Spencer, Rev. Dr. Elihu, 146—148.
" Jared, 146.
" Joseph, Gen., 146.
" Margaret, 146, 151.
" Mary, (Selden,) 146.
" Samuel, 146.
Sprague, Rev Dr. Wm. B., Extracts, 88, 92, 179, 365, 367. Letters to, 293, 294.
Spring, Rev. Dr. Gardiner, 288. Extracts, 290, 291, 301, 361, 368.
Spring, Rev. Dr. Sam'l, 229, 238.
Standards, Westminster, 23. Revised, 23.
Stilling, J. H. J., 137.
Stipend, 363, 364.
Stockton, Richard, 146, 333, 337.
Strain, Rev. Mr., 312.
Subscription of Confession, 357.
Success in Pastorate, 360.
Suicide, Sermons on, 186, 190. Letter of Intended, 187, 188. Letter to, 188.
Summer resorts, 286.
Swimming, 172.
Synod of New York, Old, 22. Of N. Y. and New Jersey, Concert, 106. Of N. Y. and Philadelphia, Old, 23. Of Philadelphia, Old, 22.

Tadmor in Wilderness, 319.
Tammany Society, 90.
Taylorism, 299.
Temperance, 315, 316.
Tennent, Sr., Rev. Wm., 201.
" Rev. Wm., 143.
Theological Education, 192—196, 200—203.
Theological Seminary, Andover, 229—234, 237—239.
Theological Seminary of Associate Reformed Church, 196.
Theological Seminary of Presbyterian Church, 195, 196, 233, 240—244, 280—287, 308, 313—315, 332—335. Report on, 281. Location at Princeton, 313, 315. Plan of, 314.

Thorburn, Grant, Letter of, 369.
Tin Head Court, 76, 98.
Travel from N. Y. to Albany, 203.
Treat. Rev. Joseph, 81.
Troubles from dissolution of Collegiate relation, 268, 269.
Trustee of Columbia College, 228. Of College of New Jersey, 228.
Twisse, Dr., 291.

VALETUDINARIANISM, 100—102, 103, 172, 197, 198, 200, 203, 204, 359.
Verplanck, Gulian C., Letter to, 69, 70.
Vestments, Clerical, 364, 365.

WALES, Mrs. John, 343.
Wall street Church, 81, 82. New, 287, 288, 319. Letter to Officers of, 351.
Ware, Dr., 238, 291.
Waring, Dr. Richard, 97.
Warren, Dr. John, 30, n., 330.
Washington, Gen. George, 31. Death of, 122. Religious character of, 123.
Webb, Rev. John, 16, 17.
Webster, Noah, Letter of, 220.

Westminster standards, 23.
Whipping Post, 73.
White, Bishop, 216.
Whitefield, Rev. George, 81.
Wilberforce's Practical View, 252, 255.
Wilberforce, William, 137.
Wilson, Rev. Dr. James P., 121.
   "   "   " Matthew, 24, 25, 38.
   Letters of, 25, 96.
Witherspoon, Dr., 147.
Woodhull, Rev. Dr. J., 257.
Woods, Rev. Dr. L., 229, 234, 239.
Woman's Rights, 239, 240.
Worthington, Hugh, 137.
Wright, Rev. Mr., 210.
Writing, Dr. M's manner of, 218, 219.

UNITARIANS, Exchanges with, 291—295.
University of North Carolina, Call to, 335.

YELLOW Fever, 101, 113—121, 143, 171, 172. Not contagious, 113.

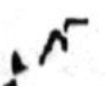

www.ingramcontent.com/pod-product-compliance
Lightning Source LLC
Chambersburg PA
CBHW021537110726
47902CB00004B/914

* 9 7 8 3 3 3 7 1 6 8 5 5 1 *